DEEP SLEEP

STEVEN KONKOLY

D0010927

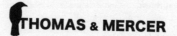

THOMAS & MERCER

Text copyright © 2022 by Steven Konkoly

Published by Thomas & Mercer, Seattle

www.apub.com

Amazon, the Amazon logo, and Thomas & Mercer are trademarks of Amazon.com, Inc., or its affiliates.

ISBN-13: 9781542029896
ISBN-10: 1542029899

Cover design by Anna Laytham

Printed in the United States of America

DEEP SLEEP

ALSO BY STEVEN KONKOLY

RYAN DECKER SERIES

The Rescue
The Raid
The Mountain
Skystorm

THE FRACTURED STATE SERIES

Fractured State
Rogue State

THE PERSEID COLLAPSE SERIES

The Jakarta Pandemic
The Perseid Collapse
Event Horizon
Point of Crisis
Dispatches

THE BLACK FLAGGED SERIES

Alpha
Redux
Apex
Vektor
Omega

THE ZULU VIRUS CHRONICLES

Hot Zone
Kill Box
Fire Storm

To Kosia, Matthew, and Sophia—
the heart and soul of my writing

PROLOGUE

Maya Klein picked up the pace as she passed another tight pack of shirtless university-age boys on the beachside promenade. Men, really. Short-haired, lean, and muscular—carrying beach towels instead of Tavor combat rifles for the first time in months. Recent basic training graduates on leave. A prominent fixture on the beaches just north of Haifa, near her family's home.

She'd been fascinated by them for as long as she could remember, especially the fierce-looking young women, who projected invincibility and pride as they roamed the promenade. She'd followed them around as a child, watching in awe as they rebuffed one group of men after another before staking their claim at a beachside café or stretch of sand and defending it from those persistent invaders.

Maya would join their ranks soon enough. She would ship off in a few weeks for a base in the Negev Desert to start *tironut*, the Israeli Defense Forces' basic training course. Four months from now, as a newly minted IDF combat soldier on leave, she'd walk this same promenade with her squad mates before reporting for duty with the Bardelas Battalion stationed along the Egypt-Israeli border.

Her daily runs along the promenade and through the sand were part of her preparation to meet the challenges of basic training. When she finished the hour-long run, she'd cool off in the Mediterranean before heading home and executing a forty-five-minute calisthenics routine. After lunch, she might head to the gym to lift some weights.

She was determined to show up in the best shape of any of the recruits, including the men.

She had nearly reached the end of the beachside promenade, where she would slog the rest of the way through the ankle-deep sand just above the high-tide line, when the city's air-raid sirens began to wail. Like everyone on the promenade and beach, her first instinct was to stop and scan the hazy blue sky to the northwest, above the midrise apartment buildings that dominated the horizon. Toward Lebanon, where most of the rockets originated. After a few seconds of staring at the sky, everyone sought hard cover, which was less than plentiful on the beach.

Maya hopped the staggered and mostly uneven rock wall that lined the Mediterranean side of the promenade and lay flat against the hot sand behind the one-and-a-half-foot-high barrier. As long as she kept her head down, the rock should protect against any shrapnel—unless the incoming rocket landed in the thin strip of beach directly behind her. Or it struck the promenade in front of her. Nothing she could do about that, but the odds were slim in either of those cases. In fact, the odds were slim that any of the rockets would hit a populated area.

Israel's Iron Dome air-defense missile system consistently intercepted close to ninety percent of the rockets fired at populated areas in Israel. The few that had gotten through had fortunately caused minimal damage or casualties. Most people still took the sirens seriously, but the overall drop in anxiety was palpable. Taking cover if you got caught out in the open was treated more like a temporary inconvenience than a matter of life or death.

She'd lived the first half of her life in fear of Hezbollah and Hamas rocket attacks. The deployment of an Iron Dome battery on the outskirts of Haifa in 2013 had been life changing for everyone. She peeked over the rock, surprised to see the sky filled with white contrails. Far more than she'd ever seen before. Thirty to forty already in a slow arc, high above the horizon, and more joining them every second—rising skyward from the launchers west of the city. A few moments later, the outgoing barrage ended. Based on the number of contrails, Maya guessed that the battery had fired all its missiles at the incoming threat. An unprecedented event, which didn't bode well for the city of Haifa and its surrounding suburbs.

She lowered her head and thought about her parents and sister several blocks away. They'd all be in her room right now, waiting for the sirens to stop wailing. Maya's bedroom had been designed as the apartment's safe room, featuring reinforced walls and a blast-proof window. Her family would be safe from shrapnel or nearby blast effects, but a direct hit to the building would likely kill or injure all of them. *Slim odds,* she told herself.

When the usual cacophony of distant, sharp aerial detonations didn't materialize, she started to worry. Something wasn't right. The interceptors would have reached their targets, and the sound of the explosions destroying the enemy rockets would have traveled back to the beach by now. She lifted her head a few inches above the rock to check the sky, catching a distant glimpse of an explosion toward the harbor. Something had gone very wrong with the Iron Dome system. There was no other explanation.

The beach shuddered, a searing flash and earsplitting crunch hitting Maya almost instantly. She pressed her body flat against the sand next to the rock wall, as fragments of glass and steel ripped overhead, peppering the sand behind her and splashing the water. She stayed put after the last concussive boom washed over the promenade, remembering the primary purpose for the deployment of an Iron Dome battery to Haifa: to protect the critical oil refineries and prevent a devastating secondary explosion that could vaporize much of the city.

After a few excruciating minutes listening to the screams and cries up and down the promenade, she got up to help with the wounded. Maya didn't get very far before coming across a young female soldier tying a tourniquet. Maya knelt next to the unresponsive man's chest and checked his breathing. She didn't need to confirm a heartbeat. A thick stream of bright-red blood pumped rhythmically from the mangled stump just below his knee.

"He's not breathing," said Maya, immediately beginning chest compressions.

"Keep that up," said the soldier. "I need to find a pen to twist this tighter. I'll be right back."

She kept up the rapid compressions long after the soldier returned to tighten the tourniquet—long after it had become obvious that the man had passed away. The soldier checked his vitals one last time before shaking her head.

"We did everything we could," said the soldier. "Let's lend a hand closer to the explosion."

Maya followed her into the dense black smoke washing over the promenade, catching a glimpse of a thick smoke column rising from the direction of her family's neighborhood. She stopped and backed up until the column appeared again.

"Over here!" said the soldier, barely visible on the promenade.

Maya hesitated before answering, her gaze fixed on the growing black pillar. "I think one of the rockets hit my street!" The soldier got up and quickly made her way to Maya, putting a hand on her shoulder when she arrived.

"You did good here. Go to your family," she said. "If you see a medical team on or near the promenade, send them this way!"

"I will," said Maya before taking off.

Maya followed a maze of tight smoke-congested streets out of the beach area to her neighborhood, the smoke intensifying as she approached the intersection just west of her family's apartment building, reducing visibility drastically. She stepped onto the sidewalk to avoid getting hit by a speeding emergency vehicle and reached the intersection corner a few moments later.

Hal Cohen, a close friend of the family, stepped out of the small market at the corner, blocking her path. He motioned for her to come inside.

"Maya. In here. It's too dangerous that way," he said. "A police car backed out of your street a minute ago and told everyone to stay clear until the firefighting teams arrive."

"I have to check on my family," said Maya.

"It's not safe," he said. "Fires and collapsing buildings everywhere. There's nothing you can do right now."

"I have to go," she said, pushing past him.

"You always have a home with us!" he said as she turned the corner.

Maya considered his words while blindly navigating the sidewalk. She could barely see more than ten feet in front of her at this point, her eyes stinging from the acrid smoke. Maya lifted her sweat-soaked shirt collar over her nose to ease her breathing, but the simple trick had little impact. She started coughing uncontrollably a half block from her family's apartment, which stood somewhere on the other side of a seemingly impenetrable wall of smoke.

Her lungs rebelling, she stumbled forward until a stiff breeze off the Mediterranean Sea momentarily drove the smoke inland, giving her a quick peek down the street. A tower of flames leaped skyward from the charred, skeletal ruins of her family's apartment building. Maya dropped to her knees on the sidewalk and screamed until the smoke once again engulfed her.

Maya tried to get up but was unable to rise to her feet—or even take a full breath. She reached for the car parked next to her and tried to pull herself up but found the task impossible. Her lungs were spent. She leaned against the car and gasped for air, realizing she'd made a costly error. A fatal error that would keep her from reporting for duty in a few weeks and avenging her family's murder.

She slumped a little farther, her sight dimming, until a familiar voice boomed nearby.

"I found her!" said Hal Cohen, his rotund figure appearing in front of her moments later.

Hands lifted her off the sidewalk and whisked her away from the darkness. An oxygen mask pressed against her face once the blue sky reappeared. Two paramedics crowded over her. She'd live to fight another day. And damn, would she fight.

PART I

PART 1

CHAPTER 1

Helen Gray gently shut her eyes before taking several deep, protracted breaths. The short meditation exercise was more symbolic than anything. A few pretend moments of calm wouldn't make a dent in her anxiety. The stakes were too high. Two decades of ruinous self-sacrifice had delivered her here. A single misstep tonight could render that painful journey meaningless.

She would have thrown away her career, destroyed her marriage, and—most painfully—alienated her children. For nothing. Helen had no choice but to see this through, even if redemption on any level remained entirely out of reach. At this point, she'd inflicted far too much misery on those she loved the most to fail or turn back. She opened her eyes, her hands still lightly trembling in her lap.

Helen turned the car off and placed the keyless ignition fob in one of the cup holders. The last thing she needed to worry about on her way out was finding the key to the car. Not that she expected to be flustered when she returned. Her plan to kidnap Donald Wilson was fairly straightforward, and she'd mentally rehearsed it, from start to finish, no fewer than a thousand times over the past year. She'd even created a list of possible obstacles, ranging from simple to elaborate—game-planning them until she was satisfied that she could handle just about anything and accomplish the mission.

Always the same plan, because Wilson's warm-weather-season routine hadn't changed since he'd taken up residence at the facility three years ago. The camera she had hidden along the western edge of the sprawling property had confirmed what she had suspected from a decade of off-and-on surveillance. Wilson had a fondness for an alcoholic beverage or three on the back patio at sunset.

In fact, as long as the skies were clear, he'd never missed a sunset here when the temperature equaled or exceeded sixty-seven degrees, and Helen's car told her it was seventy-five. Sunset was in ten minutes, so he'd be a few bourbons into the evening by the time she arrived. Barring any unforeseen complications, she should be back at the car with Wilson in less than a half hour.

She got out of the car and removed a canvas tote bag from the back seat. Helen had filled it with handmade snacks, fruit, and a small bouquet of flowers, the assortment designed to lend an air of normalcy to anyone who gave her a closer look. Nearly everyone who showed up to visit this place brought something to leave with their loved ones.

A side compartment sewed into the interior of the bag held three syringes marked with blue duct tape, each filled with enough ketamine to sedate and immobilize Wilson within a few minutes; two syringes marked with yellow tape, each filled with a 100-milligram ketamine "booster," just in case the 300 milligrams in the blue-taped doses didn't do the job; a short roll of beige-colored duct tape to keep Wilson from screaming; and a half dozen heavy-duty black zip-tie handcuffs to keep him tethered to his wheelchair. A watered-down agency abduction kit.

The walk to the entrance ate close to a minute of her time. She'd parked in the far reaches of the parking lot, near the southern end of the main building, for a strategic reason. Entering and traversing the facility unchallenged was surprisingly simple. She'd conducted four walk-throughs over the past year, carrying the same tote bag, and had never been questioned, either at the front desk or while walking the hallways. Getting out with Wilson was the hard part. She couldn't wheel him through the facility and past the front desk without drawing the wrong kind of attention. Especially when he appeared semiconscious. The sidewalk directly in front of the parking lot wound around the building, eventually connecting with the rear patio. She planned to use the walkway to discreetly remove him from the premises, away from the prying eyes of the staff.

When she reached the entrance, she paused in front of the automatic sliding doors to give them time to open, and quickly scanned the lobby. Helen recognized the woman at the desk from her last visit. Two gentlemen engaged in conversation sat in high-back chairs near the grand piano. As she started inside, a gray-haired woman in a motorized wheelchair turned the corner behind the reception desk and called out to the attendant. Perfect timing.

Helen made it through the lobby without drawing more than a casual glance from the two men. She navigated a short series of carpeted hallways to a sun-blasted space with floor-to-ceiling windows looking out onto the patio. A modest mahogany bar, with a severely limited selection of booze to match its three empty stools and moping bartender, stood against the wall on the opposite side of the cramped room. A faded HAPPY HOUR sign was taped to the wall next to the bar, completing the mortuary vibe. The bartender never looked up as she crossed the room and opened the patio door.

The patio was packed tonight. Four residents and a visitor—a middle-aged woman busy preparing a plate of cheese and crackers for her father. Or grandfather. Helen hoped to be long gone before she reached that golden age of ambiguity, and given the likely response to Wilson's kidnapping, she stood a good chance of skipping the nursing-home stage altogether. If they caught up to her before she could convince the agency to protect her, she'd end up in a gently heated barrel of lye. Turned into a DNA slurry over the course of several days and unceremoniously poured down a drain. Still sounded marginally better than melting into a bed here over the course of several years.

The other residents were spread out along the spacious patio, having parked themselves in chairs facing west. None of them were particularly well positioned to witness what was about to happen to one of their elderly compatriots.

Wilson sat at the far-left edge of the patio in his wheelchair, drink dangling precariously over the right armrest. She had to squint to see him, the deep-orange sun still glaringly bright as it touched the top of the distant trees. Helen reached into the tote bag and readied one of the blue syringes, keeping it hidden inside until she was directly behind him.

She lightly jabbed Wilson's upper-left shoulder with the syringe and injected its contents before sidestepping to the right. He muttered an obscenity and turned his head to examine the site of the injection, missing her entirely. She took the drink from his right hand and downed it in one gulp, tossing the plastic cup in his lap. Jack Daniel's from the bar, if she had to guess, and slightly watered down. Still hit the spot. He glanced at the cup, then her, an entirely bewildered look on his face. For a brief moment, she had second thoughts about the kidnapping. A senile Donald Wilson would be useless.

"What the hell?" he said, his eyes quickly shifting back to the cup.

"You spilled your drink," she said.

"I think something stung me," he said, touching his left shoulder.

Wilson appeared to have recovered from his initial confusion.

"I have a bottle in my bag," she said, reaching into the tote that hung from her shoulder. "Jack Daniel's. They told me my dad was out here. I thought you were him for a second. Care for a refill?"

"Sure," he said, lifting the cup a few inches.

She prepared an eight-inch strip of duct tape, gripping it by both ends.

"My dad drinks it straight. Sometimes right out of the bottle," she said. "I don't have any mixers."

"Your dad sounds like my kind of guy," said Wilson. "What's his name? Maybe I know him."

"Beautiful," she said, nodding toward the blood-orange orb sinking behind the trees.

"Sure is," he said, shifting his attention to the sunset.

She pressed the tape over his mouth and smoothed the edges firmly over both cheeks. Wilson's body tensed, his eyes going wide. Helen grabbed his left hand and yanked it across his body, slipping one loop of a zip-tie handcuff over it and cinching the loop tight around his wrist. She forced the other hand through the other loop and pulled it tight. Maybe it was the early effects of ketamine. Maybe it was shock. But Wilson barely protested as she secured the plastic cuffs to the right arm of the chair with a short length of cord.

Helen glanced over her shoulder and confirmed that everyone still appeared laser focused on the sunset—and not the man she'd just prepped for abduction right in front of them. Amazing how the human brain worked. She popped the brake on Wilson's wheelchair and turned it ninety degrees right, ready to maneuver him toward the walkway in the center of the patio. He stiffened, straightening his torso in an attempt to slide out of the chair. She reached around the back of the chair and grabbed his man parts through the fabric of his trousers.

"I'll rip these right off," she hissed in his ear. "Understand?"

No response, so she squeezed tighter. "Understand? Yes or no?"

He nodded, eyes shut tight—and she wheeled him off the patio. Several minutes later, they arrived at her car, nobody the wiser from what she could tell by scanning the parking lot and building windows. Helen positioned the wheelchair a few feet in front of the trunk, ready to tip him inside after injecting him with one of the yellow syringes. She had a long drive ahead of her, which included a lengthy surveillance-detection route, just in case someone had been assigned to watch over Wilson. She popped the trunk and turned to grab him, pausing at the unexpectedly wretched sight. His hands trembled, a confused and slightly unfocused look in his eyes. The drugs had probably started to kick in.

Helen stared at him for a few moments, not sure if she was savoring the moment or regretting it. Probably a bit of both. Finally standing in front of him, face-to-face, embodied a surreal experience. She'd spent the past twenty years contemplating nearly every aspect of the man's existence but had never met him before today—by design. She couldn't risk the possibility that he might recognize her. That he'd somehow been warned.

She knew him only through the lens of a surveillance camera, a pair of binoculars, or the comprehensive dossier she'd assembled, which meant she really didn't know him at all.

Donald Wilson. A man shrouded in mystery. She'd often wondered what his real name had been before. Not that it mattered. The name had been extinct for more than a half century, and probably meant nothing to him at this point. It certainly meant nothing to her beyond a curiosity. Helen was far more interested in his connection to the extensive conspiracy she'd uncovered.

CHAPTER 2

The cocktail was a lie. Water with a generous pour of olive juice to cloud the mixture, and two plump, blue cheese–stuffed olives held together by a stainless-steel cocktail pick. The bartender had even shaken it like a real martini, without him asking—seemingly all too familiar with the ruse. He took a long sip, casually scanning the crowded rooftop bar over the rim of his drink. The night's endgame loomed. Devin Gray tipped the glass back and emptied it.

"Any minute now."

He spoke loudly enough to be heard through the microphone, but softly enough to avoid drawing a glance from either of the politicos flanking him. Devin barely heard the team's acknowledgment over the ever-rising din of brash words and forced laughter. He resisted the impulse to fiddle with his earpiece. It may or may not help him, but it would most certainly give him away to a reasonably competent countersurveillance team.

Devin hadn't detected one, but his target gave no indication of being surveillance conscious. He'd been doing this long enough to read even the most subtle body language—and she wasn't concerned with anything but seducing her mark. Her mannerisms broadcast the kind of genuine calm and confidence that came only with trusted security in her line of work. She had backup close by.

He set the glass on the black polished-granite bar top and caught the bartender's attention, signaling for another. While waiting for his fourth drink of the night, Devin finished the seared salmon he'd ordered to nurture his cover—tasting nothing. He was singularly focused on the job at hand, his senses diverted accordingly.

A few minutes passed before his drink arrived, each second stretching into the next as he casually watched the scene come to its seemingly inevitable conclusion. The honey trap, a petite woman with straight jet-black hair, was a smooth, seasoned operator. Unhurried but moving things along just fast enough to seal the deal. She'd already managed to separate her mark from his three colleagues and isolate him at the bar, where they'd each downed two real manhattans. He'd watched the bartender closely. As their hushed conversation progressed, her hand spent more and more time petting his arm. Definitely a professional. Any second now.

He took a generous sip of the briny water, which would probably play havoc with his stomach later tonight, before taking out his wallet and removing nine twenty-dollar bills. The bartender took notice while hurrying past with two cocktails, and gave him a quick nod. Devin didn't have to time this perfectly. Just close enough to be in place for the next phase. The honey trap leaned in close and whispered something in her mark's ear, prompting him to rather hurriedly take out his wallet. She waved it off and produced cash from her purse, making sure the bartender saw the small wad of bills before she ushered the mark toward the exit.

"Honey trap is leaving with Mr. Chase," said Devin.

"Copy. Let us know if she has friends."

"Will do," said Devin before picking up his drink.

He needed to finish it in a timely but unsuspicious manner. Two minutes seemed right, and the countersurveillance dance continued. The bill arrived halfway through the drink, and he tucked the crisp twenties inside. The tidy sum well exceeded the total, but it wasn't his money, and the honey trap's employer was bound to make an inquiry or two later. The tip might work in Devin's favor. That and the fact that he'd insisted on paying regular price for the faux drinks. Fuzzy bartender memory and no hard proof he was part of the setup.

A minute and a half after Chase's departure, two men he hadn't given a second thought to until now made their way toward the exit, moving with a purpose. He didn't get a really good look at either of them, but it was enough. Devin reported the development as soon as they stepped out of the bar.

"Two men followed," he said. "One with blond hair wearing a navy-blue suit. The other dark hair with a dark-gray suit. Older guys. I'd say early fifties?"

"Copy. Give it another minute."

"One minute," said Devin.

With a little time to kill, Devin got up from his seat, drink in hand, and slid the bill toward the bartender before wading through the crowd behind him to reach the edge of the bar's open terrace. The East Wing of the White House dominated his view, its illuminated face impossible to miss a few blocks away. Beyond it, a thin, dark-blue strip stretched across the horizon—the last vestiges of what had been a perfect early-summer day in DC minutes from slipping away entirely.

To the south, the Washington Monument rose above the National Mall like a blazing beacon. Devin leaned out to get a better look. The view was definitely worth the upcharge. He'd love to bring his sister here the next time she flew out from LA. Dad too. Hopefully at the same time. It had been a while since they'd spent some time together. Things hadn't been the same since his mother's breakdown. Her final break from reality, and the family, had taken an awful toll on all of them. He didn't want to spoil the view thinking about it.

"Devin. Room four thirty-two. Take the western stairwell. Advise when in position."

"On the way," he said.

Now for the fun part. And by *fun* he meant *risky*. Possibly even *dangerous*.

CHAPTER 3

Devin waited for the green light to extract Chase. Barring any significant unseen complications, he'd have him back in the stairwell and on the way out of the hotel in under a minute. Keeping Chase safe until they reached the armored SUV standing by outside the hotel was his only objective. The firm's direct-action (DA) team would handle the rest. Specifically, room four thirty-four.

A member of the surveillance team had walked the floor a few minutes ago with a concealed radio frequency (RF) detector, identifying rooms four thirty-two and four thirty-four as RF hot spots—encrypted signals in frequency ranges typically associated with high-end video-surveillance equipment.

With the honey trap going down in four thirty-two, that put the shakedown team in the adjacent room. They assumed it to comprise the suits from the bar and at least two other heavies. This type of blackmail operation relied on shock and embarrassment. The more the merrier when they busted into the room and caught their victim in the act.

But nothing in that room was his concern. Either room, really. He just hoped the two men hadn't disappeared into a third room nearby, especially if it stood between four thirty-two and the stairwell. Nobody had actually seen them go into four thirty-four. Things could get ugly if the surveillance team's assumption proved to be incorrect. Devin carried an expandable steel baton, clipped to the inside of his jacket, that he could put to good use under most circumstances. Two against one in a constricted hallway, while trying to protect a client, wasn't one of those circumstances.

If that happened, he'd need help, which wouldn't be far away—assuming the DA team could handle room four thirty-four. A big assumption, given they had no idea whom they were up against. A corporate espionage team hired by a competitive company? A hostile-state effort? All they really knew was they were well funded and professional. A dangerous combination.

Devin had been somewhat surprised that DEVTEK hadn't gone to the FBI. The sophisticated cyberattack campaign waged against DEVTEK's research and development division was precisely the kind of case the FBI's Economic Espionage Section thrived on, especially given the company's sizable contracting footprint within the Department of Defense.

On the other hand, if DEVTEK strongly suspected a rival company, hiring a private counterespionage firm could turn out to be the more strategic play, especially if they could catch the other company red-handed. A little corporate leverage went a long way in the defense contracting industry.

His earpiece crackled.

"Devin. You're up. Proceed directly to the room," said the surveillance team leader. "Chase is flailing."

No surprise there. Brian Chase, a software engineer at DEVTEK, had very reluctantly agreed to serve as bait during a four-day business trip to the DC area. He was married with three young children, slightly overleveraged on his Bay Area mortgage, and active in his church. An ideal target for a honey trap, which was why MINERVA had picked him.

"I'm on the move," said Devin.

He bolted down the hallway, instantly slowing to a less suspicious pace when the door to four thirty-two suddenly swung inward. Chase backed out of the room, an elegant hand with bright-red nail polish yanking him halfway back inside. Devin kept walking, ready to play dumb if she leaned her head out and spotted him.

"I'm sorry!" said Chase, tugging fruitlessly at her grip. "I changed my mind! I can't do this!"

"Nobody will ever find out!" said the woman, only her arms visible to Devin.

She had him locked in place with a serious two-hand grip, which Devin found somewhat unusual. Devin removed the expandable baton from his suit coat and concealed it along the side of his leg.

"I don't care," said Chase, struggling to break her grasp. "Let go of me!"

The DA team rounded the corner at the opposite end of the hallway, six operatives rapidly headed in his direction. Their timing was solid. Everything was coming together as planned. Now he just needed to get Chase out of here safely, which appeared a little more complicated than he'd originally hoped.

"He's not cooperating," the woman stated abruptly. "We're gonna have to do this the hard way."

A lot more complicated. The honey trap had just turned into a kidnapping—or worse. Chase turned to Devin, a worried look on his face. His earpiece screeched.

"Get him out of there now!"

He flicked the baton open, the telescoping steel pieces snapping loudly into place. The woman poked her head through the doorway, glancing from Devin's face to the sixteen-inch steel baton in his hand. She turned her head in the other direction, spotting the team that had started to stack up on the door leading to room four thirty-four.

"It's a setup!" she said before taking a solid strike to the forehead from Devin's baton.

She released her grip on Brian's arm and dropped to her knees, eyes wide and out of focus. He'd hit her with enough force to stun or possibly knock her unconscious. The end result was still inconclusive, which represented a threat to the other team.

"Honey trap requires restraint," said Devin, pulling Chase away from the doorway.

"Is she out?"

"Negative," said Devin.

"Hit her until she's out. Then move Chase to safety. The DA team has its hands full."

He really didn't want to hit her in the head again. It wasn't as though he could dial in the desired amount of force, and the head could be tricky when hit repeatedly. But the situation had changed drastically enough to justify it. The DA team faced an alerted threat in room four thirty-four. The last thing they needed was a surprise coming at them from an unexpected direction.

"Copy," he said, raising the baton.

"What are you doing?" asked Chase, grabbing his arm.

He shrugged his arm loose and brought the baton down on the crown of her head with the same force he'd used for the first blow—switching her off like a light. She collapsed flat on her stomach, half of her on the hallway carpet, the other half on the polished marble foyer, just inside the room, jet-black wig a few inches askew to reveal strawberry-blonde hair.

Chase mumbled some kind of religious prayer.

"She'll be fine," said Devin, not exactly buying his own statement. "Stay right next to me. Like we rehearsed. Do exactly what I say."

Devin had just started moving him toward the stairwell when all hell broke loose behind them as the DA team vanished into room four thirty-four. Ferocious shouting, followed by the snap, crackle, pop of Tasers and stun batons. The shouting had morphed into panicked screaming by the time they reached the door to the stairs. He couldn't tell which side had the upper hand.

"I'm entering the stairwell with Chase," he said. "What's going on back in the room?"

"It's under control."

"It doesn't sound under control," said Devin, scanning the stairwell through the door's window.

"Just get Chase into the SUV. That's your only objective."

"Understood. Will advise when ready for pickup," said Devin before turning to Chase. "Just like we planned."

The moment the door closed behind them, the plan unraveled. Urgent footsteps echoed inside the stairwell, and the two hostile suits from the rooftop bar raced into sight on the flight of stairs below them. Devin hid the baton along the side of his leg as Chase moved behind him and started praying. The two men produced nasty-looking serrated blades and cautiously advanced up the stairs.

"Contact. Two armed hostiles. Fourth-floor stairwell. Sending Chase to your position," said Devin, motioning for Chase to take off.

"Copy. Sending backup your way."

"You know where to go, right?" he said to Chase.

Chase nodded, his eyes glued to the two men steadily approaching.

"Then go," said Devin. "Now!"

Chase took off, and the men bolted up the stairs side by side, heading straight for Devin. He waited until the last possible moment before pretending to follow Chase up the stairs—instead squaring off at the foot of the stairs, just out of their sight, and raising the baton. As he'd hoped, the two men bunched up taking the corner, the first head to appear absorbing a full-force, diagonal blow to the temple from Devin's baton. The crack against his skull left no doubt that he was out of the fight.

The second attacker pushed his wilted colleague out of the way, then sliced wildly to create some space before quickly settling into a tight knife-fighting stance. Blade in close, pointed at Devin, off hand raised to block or deflect the baton. The guy knew what he was doing.

Devin considered scrambling up the stairs but just as quickly dismissed the idea.

Timed with the right baton strike, Devin might be able to disengage from the fight and get up the stairs unscathed, but the chances were just as likely that he wouldn't. He'd be giving up a controlled close-quarters engagement for a mad dash—that might or might not work.

The guy made the decision for him, thrusting with the knife and taking a small, noncommittal step forward—a basic feint designed to test Devin's discipline. He kept the baton raised and remained in place, eliciting a grimace from his attacker. The man had just accepted the basic reality of their predicament. This would end terribly for one of them, and there was no guarantee it wouldn't be him. The heavy fire door on the stairwell landing above slammed shut, signaling Chase's escape onto the fifth floor.

His opponent's eyes tracked the noise, briefly flickering between Devin and the stairs a few too many times. Done right, the man could carefully retreat up the stairs and keep Devin out of striking distance. When his eyes darted in the other direction, checking out the stairwell door, Devin saw an opportunity to tip the entire encounter in his favor. He shifted a few feet to the left, subtly eliminating the stairs as an option. The man smirked—before breaking for the door.

Devin made short work of him. The combination of slowing to open the door and being in a compromised fighting stance sealed his fate. Devin's first blow struck his knife arm at the wrist, knocking the blade clear across the stairwell. The second came straight at his face, exploding the man's nose and knocking his head against the door edge. A third connected squarely with his right collarbone, most likely cracking it based on the sound made on impact. He grabbed the guy by the back of the suit collar and yanked him away from the door before sweeping the side of the man's knee with a full-force blow. The leg crumpled, and Devin tossed him onto his unconscious colleague.

Staring at them for a few moments, he noted that they looked older than he had originally reported. More like late fifties, possibly early sixties. Both of them in better shape than their presumed ages suggested, but definitely older than he'd expected. Which explained why he'd been able to put them down so easily. His thirty-seven-year-old frame had twenty years less wear and tear.

"Both hostiles neutralized. One unconscious. One immobile," said Devin. "Where do you want me?"

"We really need to get Chase out of here now. He's unraveling. He'll draw too much attention if he leaves with the rest of us."

"I'll be right up," said Devin. "We'll take the eastern stairwell down."

"I'll reroute the backup team to clear it. You okay?"

"Not a scratch. They were pros, but not top tier," said Devin.

"The team we sent into room four thirty-four might not agree. They took a beating."

"Sounded like it," said Devin. "I'm on the way."

A few mercifully uneventful minutes later, a black armored Suburban carried him away from the hotel along with Brian Chase, his three colleagues from the rooftop bar, and a heavily armed security operative from the firm's special activities group. Unlike his slightly inebriated and oblivious dinner companions, Chase had been traumatized by the evening's unexpected turn of events. The shallow, irregular breathing. Fidgety hands. Trouble focusing, which caused him to squint. Devin knew the signs. He was dealing with all of them himself.

Tonight had been a first for him. In the twelve years he'd spent "ghosting" foreign intelligence officers and spies for the FBI's Special Surveillance Group, he had never carried a weapon. Never needed one, even while working operatives known to be dangerous. The fact that he'd cracked three skulls on his first full field operation with MINERVA didn't sit well. That and having to square off against professional killers.

Maybe he should have known better, since they'd spent so much time on his hand-to-hand combat and weapons training, but he truly hoped tonight's fiasco was an outlier—or his time at the firm would be short lived. Where he landed after MINERVA was anyone's guess. Devin wasn't exactly a sought-after commodity in the industry, even if his dismissal from the FBI hadn't been his fault. More of an unfortunate and irreversible technicality, compliments of his mother's mental disintegration.

Being the son of a psychotically paranoid former CIA officer came with a few drawbacks. Losing his security clearance, a requirement to remain employed at the FBI, had turned out to be one of them. Going radioactive was another. A lot of good people at the bureau cashed in serious favors just to get him through the door for an interview. Quitting MINERVA this soon after joining would ensure he never worked in the counterintelligence industry again.

The best he could hope for was a corporate investigative security position on the other side of the country or private investigative work. If it came down to the latter, he'd go back to school and reinvent himself. Get a PhD in military history and teach at Annapolis. Or a law degree to specialize in representing foreign state clients accused of espionage. Really stick it to the FBI and Department of Justice.

He stifled a laugh, drawing a funny look from Chase. Who was he kidding? He wasn't going anywhere.

CHAPTER 4

Harvey Rudd fumbled for his phone, knocking it off the nightstand onto the hardwood floor, where it clattered and quickly came to rest, casting a dim glow on his side of the room. He'd just drifted asleep when it started buzzing. At least that was how it felt. Then again, as a tragically light sleeper, that was how it always felt.

Rudd woke several times a night for no explicable reason. Sometimes bolting upright in a panic. Most of the time just slowly opening his eyes, half expecting someone to be standing over him. He shrugged it off as a job hazard. His wife had suggested therapy. She was in the same line of work and slept like a baby.

He stretched an arm out to reach the phone on the floor, barely tapping it with the tips of his fingers. There was no way he'd be able to grab it without falling on his face. And he really needed to answer the call, or at the very least check the number.

"Son of a bitch," he muttered, throwing the blankets off and sliding out of bed.

The call ended moments before Rudd could press "Accept."

"Figures," he said, taking a seat on the edge of the bed.

He scrolled through the call log, relieved to see an 800 number. They'd never used an 800 number before. Always a local area code, which was obviously some kind of redirect from wherever CONTROL called home. He assumed it was somewhere in the United States. They wouldn't risk leaving any kind of electronic trail overseas. Rudd was about to lie back down when the phone vibrated again. Another 800 number.

An online retailer must have sold his number to a telemarketing company. Unfortunately, ignoring the call wasn't an option. He hustled out of the bedroom and closed the door behind him, more out of courtesy than necessity. His wife could sleep through a home invasion.

"Hello?" said Rudd, expecting the usual several-second delay before the telemarketer connected to the call and somehow still managed to mispronounce his name.

Still, he had to be sure. Rudd stiffened when a female voice immediately replied.

"Stand by to copy access code."

Damn. CONTROL had a job for him. Something that couldn't wait for the morning. Rudd took off down the hallway for the kitchen, the one place in the house where he knew for certain that he could find paper and some kind of writing instrument. He flipped the switch in the hallway, bathing the kitchen in the harsh fluorescent light they never got around to changing. A quick dig through the junk drawer next to the sink yielded a pen and Post-it pad.

"Ready to copy."

The voice recited the same twenty-digit alphanumeric code twice, and the call disconnected. Rudd took the Post-it into the dining room, where he'd plugged in his laptop before heading to bed. He sat at the table and logged in to the computer, waiting what felt like an eternity for the system to boot up.

He didn't like the timing of this call at all. CONTROL hadn't contacted him with a job in close to seven months. Long enough that he'd begun to wonder if they'd retired him and forgotten to pass along the news. At fifty-six, he wasn't exactly a first-string operative anymore. A fact apparently not lost on his handlers.

Work had slowed to a trickle over the past several years. Mostly stakeout surveillance or some light breaking and entering to acquire information stored on electronic devices. Not that he was complaining. He'd spearheaded a hit-and-run on a US Army major in the parking lot of a strip club near Fort Campbell, but that hadn't exactly been a complicated job. All the intelligence had been provided by CONTROL.

Rudd and his team had simply staked out the club for a week, until the major stumbled out a little drunker than usual one night and strayed a little too close to Route 41. Dead on impact with the pickup truck they had stolen a few states over. Rudd's wife, Jolene, had facilitated both those tragic circumstances, sidling up to the major in the club an hour earlier and plying him with shots of bourbon. She'd even walked him right in front of the speeding truck. For the next few weeks, Jolene had looked her happy self again.

Back in the early days, after they'd settled in the Chattanooga area, Harvey and his wife had done jobs like that several times a year. "Wet work," as their trainers called it. Mostly lowbrow stuff like the Fort Campbell strip club hit-and-run. No fancy poisons. No sniper rifles. No explosives. Rudimentary "make it look like an accident or a suicide" kind of assignments, with a kidnap and blind delivery job every now and then.

They had traveled as far north as Chicago and as far east as Norfolk for more complicated personnel-intensive jobs, but the vast majority of their work over the past thirty years had gone down a couple of hundred miles from Chattanooga. Atlanta and Nashville, mainly. None of it had fit any easily detectable pattern, and neither of them had given it much thought. They weren't here to ponder their work. They enjoyed a very comfortable life—with a single condition: obey CONTROL. A simple arrangement that had suited both of them fine. One he had always suspected hadn't been a coincidence.

When the laptop finished booting, he launched Tor Browser and navigated to a site on the "dark web" created by their handlers exclusively to communicate with the Rudds. Tor Browser's nearly undefeatable anonymity tool, combined with the use of a deeply buried "dark" website, provided one of the most secure and untraceable ways to pass along detailed mission direction and intelligence. The days of bouncing for hours between dead drops or sweating a live meetup at some grimy countryside café had vanished overnight with Tor's rise. The irony wasn't lost on him that Tor had been created by the United States military to protect online intelligence community communications.

After entering the alphanumeric code on the Post-it, followed by his username, into a text box that appeared on the screen, a page containing a single link appeared: OPERATION SUMMARY. He clicked it and read the two-page document line by line—twice.

Rudd shook his head. He had a bad feeling about this one. CONTROL was essentially throwing two borderline-retired teams that hadn't worked together in several years at a fairly complex hostage-rescue mission. In other words, a mad scramble to keep a kidnapped VIP from disappearing. To make matters worse, the target was on the move—and CONTROL wanted the teams together and moving to intercept in under two hours. No small feat, considering that the team comprised eight operatives spread across four states.

At least he didn't have to coordinate their routes. The initial rally points had been selected for each team. He needed to be in Gadsden, Alabama, which gave him a little over thirty minutes to assemble the suggested gear and retrieve the van he kept at a nearby outdoor storage lot. He checked his watch and determined he needed to be driving out of the garage in less than fifteen minutes. Not a problem. The only question left was what to do about Jolene. CONTROL had not included her name on the roster, which meant exactly what it implied. For whatever reason, they didn't want her involved in the operation.

Rudd resolved to tell her right before he walked out of the house, to minimize the uncomfortable scene guaranteed to unfold. Being sidelined wouldn't sit well with her, especially since they were unlikely to see a high-stakes mission like this again. Ever. But CONTROL had their reasons—and the Rudds had never failed to obey CONTROL.

On second thought, he decided the better approach would be to leave a note on the kitchen table and slip away without waking her. He'd rather face Jolene's wrath in the morning than CONTROL's. The latter didn't accept apologies. Not that Jolene was the forgiving type.

CHAPTER 5

Helen Gray jolted awake, hands locked in a death grip on the steering wheel. Her car was still on the two-lane road, slightly over the center line—traveling twelve miles per hour faster than the last time she remembered checking. She eased the sedan back into the right-hand lane and slowed to match the speed limit. The last thing she needed right now was to draw the wrong kind of attention.

A staccato series of thumps against the back seat, coming from the trunk, reinforced that sentiment. Getting pulled over would radically complicate an already thorny situation. She'd face an unthinkable question, requiring an immediate answer: Was the life of a police officer worth sacrificing to prevent a national catastrophe?

Helen didn't want to think about it. She'd already crossed at least one line that she couldn't take back. And that was just the beginning if the man stuffed in her trunk didn't feel like talking. She was willing to go to extreme measures to extract the information he possessed. The duffel bag in the footwell behind her seat contained everything she needed to encourage him to talk.

She was already looking at five to ten years for the kidnapping—maybe less if her theory proved correct. The contents of the duffel bag represented double that sentence, depending on how far she took the interrogation. But if she was right, the sacrifice would be worth it.

If she was wrong? She'd most likely spend the rest of her life in prison. But she wasn't wrong. She couldn't be. Something insidious had taken root in America nearly fifty years ago and had somehow gone unnoticed. Still, she couldn't shake the distant but ghastly suspicion that she had wasted the past two decades chasing a delusion.

Helen caught herself staring beyond the headlights, lost in thought and close to falling asleep again. She rolled down her window, the sudden blast of humid air chasing away the drowsiness. A very temporary fix, given that she had been awake for most of the past twenty-four hours. Only a coffee refill would get her through the final few hours of the trip, the twisty rural roads demanding her full attention. A few more substantial thuds from the trunk suggested she would have to stop soon—to administer another dose of sedatives. She couldn't pull into a gas station with her passenger creating this kind of racket.

The pounding against the back seat intensified. A quick look at the navigation app running on her phone showed a town coming up less than a mile away. If it turned out to be the sleepy little place she suspected, Helen would find a spot on the northern outskirts to pull over and give Mr. Wilson another shot of night-night juice. He'd be out cold by the time she reached the Road Star Travel Center at Interstate 40, where she could refresh her coffee and use the restroom.

A few orange-tinted streetlights appeared between the trees in the distance, followed by a blinking yellow light. The town turned out to be a handful of darkened businesses crowding Route 13, barely outnumbering the churches. Helen slowed when she reached the flashing stoplight, more out of habit than a concern for safety. The area looked so dead, she could probably park in the middle of the intersection for the next hour without having to move.

Moments after she passed through the intersection, an oversize pickup truck pulled onto the road ahead of her and effectively blocked both lanes, forcing Helen to slam on the brakes to avoid a collision. The moment her car skidded to a tire-screeching halt, mere feet from the side of the pickup, she shifted into reverse and floored the accelerator.

At once the rear collision alarm sounded and a van loomed large in the backup camera display.

She hit the brakes. The camera showed two figures already out of the van, rushing toward her. How the hell had they managed to track her? She'd been so careful. There was no time to think about that right now. Helen calmly put the car in park, released her seat belt, and removed a compact Sig Sauer pistol from the purse lying flat on the passenger seat. She pushed her door open and leaned out of the car, snapping off four center-mass shots at the closest ski-masked attacker.

The man dropped to his knees and pitched forward, his head catching the corner of the rear bumper. He immediately crumpled to the pavement, lying motionless in the red glow of the car's taillights as she slipped out of the car and searched for the second attacker. She found the assailant retreating fast, her bullets shattering glass and puncturing metal until he disappeared behind the van's hood.

A door slammed shut behind her, prompting Helen to spin and reflex fire at a masked figure illuminated by her car's headlights. The man grabbed his neck and screamed an obscenity before scrambling out of her line of fire. She emptied the pistol's few remaining rounds into the pickup's tinted windows, hoping for the best, before digging a spare pistol magazine out of her coat pocket. Everything went still after she slammed the magazine home and released the pistol slide. Too still. Nothing but humming engines and a faint ringing in her ears.

Were they holding their fire to avoid accidentally hitting Wilson? Doubtful. A moderately skilled shooter from either vehicle could hit her without endangering him. With that thought in mind, she slid back into the car and shut the door, making sure to stay low enough in the seat to see forward while presenting the smallest possible target.

To keep an eye on both threat directions at once, she engaged the parking brake and shifted into reverse, activating the backup camera and alert system while keeping the car in place. If they moved on her from the direction of the van, she'd receive an audible warning. Next,

Helen locked all the doors. She spent the next several moments listening and observing. Still nothing. Even Wilson had gone silent.

"Now what?" she muttered.

They had her boxed in, and she didn't see much hope in trying to ram her way past either vehicle. Her sedan didn't stand much of a chance of sufficiently budging either the oversize pickup truck or van out of the way without inflicting catastrophic damage to her own car. A thorough scan of her surroundings suggested that they'd put some thought into the location of this roadblock.

A short row of redbrick buildings immediately adjacent to the road prevented her from driving right, and a metal guardrail to the left blocked her from taking her car through an empty bank parking lot. Helen concluded that the only way out of this was on foot. And the odds were stacked solidly against her. She guessed she was up against at least six aggressors, maybe more. Impossible odds if they were armed, which she had to assume.

She might have a chance if they were more interested in reacquiring Wilson than killing or capturing her. Then again, how far could she really get before they secured Wilson and turned all their attention back toward her? Probably not very far, but it beat waiting for the inevitable. Helen removed the last spare pistol magazine from her purse and stuffed it in her coat pocket. Hopefully she wouldn't need it.

Helen took her phone off the dashboard mount and considered dialing 911—just as quickly dismissing the idea. The call was more likely to get a sheriff's deputy killed than save her life. Instead, she opened a nameless app in one of the folders on the phone and entered a ten-digit password. The app displayed two options: a green "Activate Fail-safe" button and a red "Cancel" button.

She hated to drag Devin into this, but the future of the United States depended on it. Any and all doubt about her two-decades-long obsession had been erased over the past few minutes. She hit the green button and pocketed the phone. If Helen somehow got out of this alive, she could let him know to ignore the series of messages he would begin to receive in ten days. She'd set the delay long enough for things to settle down around her son. The kidnapping alone would put him under plenty of scrutiny. Whatever happened after she bolted from the car would only compound the attention he'd receive.

While she had the phone out, Helen swiped through the few photographs she hadn't deleted, pausing on a family picture taken fifteen years ago, at Devin's graduation from the University of Maryland. It was one of the last pictures they'd taken together in which everyone still looked happy. Helen had still been with the CIA at that point—two very messy years away from being escorted from her office in the George Bush Center for Intelligence. Not that the years before that had been smooth sailing at Langley, or at home. She stared at the picture until her eyes teared up. She wished she could apologize to Kari for the hell she'd put her through. Apologize to all of them for everything.

"Time to get this over with," she said, pocketing the phone.

Helen was out of the car and halfway across the street before the panicked shouting started. A hiss passed inches from her head as she vaulted the metal guardrail, almost instantly followed by a sharp pain in her upper left buttock. She landed on both feet at the edge of the parking lot and pivoted, rapidly firing several times at each vehicle. Satisfied that she'd momentarily pinned her attackers in place, she ran her hand along her left rear side to assess the damage.

Instead of a bloody bullet wound, her hand came across a tranquilizer dart. She yanked it out and held it in front of her face, noting that the clear plastic medicine chamber was empty, its contents circulating through her bloodstream. This changed everything. They needed her alive. They needed to interrogate her—which she couldn't allow. Helen had hit the end of her road, but she had no intention of giving them any satisfaction. At all.

She reloaded the pistol, pocketing the partially expended magazine, and rose high enough to steady it against the top of the guardrail. Her mind cleared of distractions, and unencumbered by any consequences, she methodically emptied the pistol into the sedan's trunk area. Fifteen bullets. With any luck, a few of them hit Wilson, killing him outright or severely complicating her adversaries' situation. She'd settle for either at this point.

A second dart hit her just above the right collarbone, penetrating deep. She ducked behind the guardrail and pulled it free, the dart's drug chamber already empty. Helen wouldn't have much time before the tranquilizer incapacitated her. She took a seat on the crumbly asphalt, her back pressed against the guardrail. After taking a few deep breaths, she swapped her pistol's empty magazine for the half-empty one in her pocket.

CHAPTER 6

Harvey Rudd studied what little he could see of Gray through the magnified scope attached to his compressed-air dart gun. She remained mostly concealed, seated behind the guardrail; a red-and-blue bank sign across the parking lot cast just enough light for him to tell that she was working on something. Probably reloading the pistol she'd very unexpectedly handled like a seasoned operative. Dave Bender lay dead on the street, having paid a dear price for that misjudgment. Rudd had no intention of making the same mistake. The handheld radio attached to his belt crackled.

"We need to move this along," said Logan Walsh, the other team leader.

Rudd expected her to go limp at any moment. His last shot had definitely connected, and he strongly suspected that at least one of the darts fired by Walsh had struck home. A single tranquilizer dart should be enough to immobilize her within a few minutes. Two would knock her flat in half that time. He removed the radio and responded.

"Looks like she's reloading. I think we should give this another minute. Possibly two. Just to make sure she's out," said Rudd, checking his watch. "Sounded like she just worked you guys over pretty hard. The last thing we need is another body to deal with."

"We didn't take any fire," said Walsh.

"She just emptied an entire magazine," said Rudd. "Fifteen rounds. I counted them."

"Not at us," said Walsh.

"Then who the hell was she—" started Rudd, a grim thought interrupting. "Can you see the driver's side of Gray's sedan?"

"Not without getting shot," said Walsh.

Rudd had the same problem. To view the car, he would have to cross the back of the van, exposing himself to Gray's proven shooting skills. Unfortunately, he needed to know, sooner than later, whether his suspicion was correct. If he was right, they had no choice but to speed things up, as Walsh had suggested. Rudd leaned the dart rifle against the side of the van and handed his radio to the man crouched next to him.

"Be right back."

He rushed to the opposite side of the rear bumper and took a quick look around the corner of the van, confirming his suspicions. At least a dozen holes peppered the side of Gray's car—all concentrated on the trunk area.

"So much for an easy night," he muttered.

Gunfire erupted before he turned to leave. Rudd dropped flat against the cold asphalt and drew a small semiautomatic pistol from a concealed ankle holster. He turned on his side and took a two-handed grip on the pistol, keeping it pointed at Gray's position. He'd heard two quick shots, neither aimed at him from what he could tell. No yelling from any of his people, so she'd either missed her target or instantly flipped someone's lights off with a headshot.

He kept his pistol aimed in Gray's direction, praying that she'd pass out. CONTROL had been explicit about taking her alive; however, Rudd had no intention of letting her shoot him to meet that mission requirement. He'd fire first and hope she survived. If she didn't, he'd undoubtedly take her place in the interrogation room, struggling to answer some difficult questions. He'd be lucky to leave that room alive, but at least he'd have a chance. The possibility of him staring down the barrel of Gray's pistol at this range and surviving was nearly nonexistent.

Gray slowly rose off the ground, relying heavily on the guardrail to keep her steady. Just a few more seconds, and she'd topple over. He was sure of it. Incredibly, she managed to stand completely upright, her pistol still pointed straight down at the ground next to her. Rudd removed all the slack on his pistol trigger and shifted his aim slightly off-center to the left, hoping to wing her if she tried to shoot him. The small movement drew her attention.

They locked eyes for a moment, a grin spreading across her face, before her pistol hand moved. Despite his readiness, they fired at roughly the same time. Gray instantly crumpled in place. He must have jerked the trigger and unintentionally put his bullet straight through her head. Rudd had no idea what happened to her bullet. He hadn't heard it strike or ricochet off anything near him.

Logan Walsh dashed around the front of the pickup truck, headed toward him. He stopped next to Gray's sedan, his attention focused on the evenly spaced pattern of bullet holes.

"Check on Wilson!" said Rudd. "Then get Dave loaded up in the van. We'll take care of Gray."

"Got it," said Walsh before signaling his team.

Leo Ward stepped into the open, next to the van, holding a flashlight. "Can't believe she just blew her brains out."

"What are you talking about?" asked Rudd.

Ward gave him a puzzled look. "She shot herself."

"Nice try. I shot her."

"I saw her put the gun to her head and pull the trigger. Happened in a flash," said Ward. "I don't think you hit her."

"I'm pretty sure I hit her," said Rudd, holstering his pistol before picking himself up off the pavement.

Ward shrugged. "Only one way to find out."

They jogged over to the guardrail, where Gray lay facedown on the parking lot asphalt, a pool of blood rapidly expanding under her head. Ward's flashlight revealed a small hole in her right temple, surrounded by powder burns. He didn't see any other bullet wounds or blood. She'd killed herself, which actually worsened the situation. Gray had chosen to take her own life instead of submitting to an interrogation. She'd very intentionally chosen to deprive CONTROL of the information she possessed.

He glanced over his shoulder at Gray's car. Walsh had already popped the trunk, examining its contents with a flashlight. He glanced at Rudd and shook his head.

"Wilson's gone," said Walsh. "Took two to the top of the head."

"This is a mess," said Ward.

"Not entirely," said Rudd.

The original plan remained intact, despite her desperate, last-minute antics. Rudd had failed to accomplish the primary objective: capture Helen Gray alive. But he'd succeeded at the secondary objective: recover Donald Wilson. CONTROL hadn't specified dead or alive, which meant it didn't matter. One out of two had to count for something.

"Throw Dave in the trunk with Wilson! Don't forget to dig the tracking device out of Wilson's left calf," said Rudd. "Then clean up the shell casings."

Walsh gave him a thumbs-up before summoning the rest of his team. One of his men remained next to the pickup truck, pressing a bloodied bandage against his face.

"What about her?" asked Ward, nodding at Gray.

"Same thing. I'll start picking up the shell casings. Grab Nate to help you move Gray."

"Be right back," said Ward, handing him the radio and flashlight before taking off.

Rudd picked up the pistol next to Gray's hand and ejected the magazine. Still a few rounds left. He reinserted the magazine and stuffed the pistol into his waistband. A quick scan of the asphalt around Gray's body revealed about a dozen shiny brass shell casings and two empty darts. He'd have to search for the rest, which probably lay hidden in the grass in front of the guardrail. The cleanup didn't need to be perfect. With nothing more than a few reports of gunshots, local authorities wouldn't have much to pursue. And barring any unforeseen circumstances, this compact crime scene would be long vacated by the time the first law enforcement units arrived.

He knelt next to her and searched her pockets for a phone. If Gray had called 911 at any point since they had stopped her car, he'd have to assume that she'd provided the dispatcher with a description of their vehicles. That would demand additional changes to the route they'd take to reach the drop-off point given to him by CONTROL.

The bullet-riddled sedan and damage to the other vehicles already meant they had to use back roads. An all-points bulletin for the van and pickup truck would necessitate an immediate and discreet vehicle swap. In other words—grand theft auto. A difficult feat at four in the morning in rural Tennessee. Very likely impossible without adding to the operation's growing body count, which was the last thing he needed right now.

Failing to find anything in her jacket or pants, he rolled Gray onto her back to reveal the phone underneath one of her legs. Two bullet holes had penetrated the center of the screen, less than a half inch apart. Rudd picked up the phone and muttered a few obscenities as Ward and Nate Clark, the other operative assigned to his team, hopped the guardrail next to him.

"That isn't good," said Ward, nodding at the phone.

"No. It's not," said Rudd, backing up to make room for them. "Get her in the trunk and start looking at Google Maps satellite for some kind of semi-isolated rural property no closer than ten miles away, but no farther than a twenty-minute drive. We need to get off the road. Preferably a small farm with a few buildings. Definitely off the beaten path. We'll be spending some time there. I want to be on the move in under two minutes."

"I'll find us something," said Ward before grabbing Gray's ankles.

Clark took her wrists, and the two of them hauled her deadweight over the guardrail. While they struggled with Gray, Rudd went to work scouring the scene. By the time the two additional bodies had been stuffed in the trunk and Walsh's team had cleaned up the road, he'd collected twenty-five of the thirty-odd shell casings Gray had scattered near the guardrail. And two of the three immobilizer darts fired from their rifles.

Close enough. It just needed to satisfy a bored deputy creeping along and probing the darkness with a door-mounted spotlight. He pocketed the shells and made his way back to Gray's car. Walsh lay on his stomach, scanning the pavement underneath the vehicle with a flashlight. Rudd took a look around, satisfied with the scene.

"Looks good," said Rudd. "One of your guys will drive the car. If all goes well, we shouldn't be on the road for more than five or ten minutes."

Walsh rose to his feet. "Sounds like a plan. Do you want to space out the vehicles so we don't draw too much attention? I don't think these roads see more than three cars all night."

"Not a bad idea," said Rudd. "But not until we get clear of this little town."

"All right. We'll follow closely until—"

Walsh stopped midsentence, his attention drawn to something over Rudd's shoulder. Their radios squawked simultaneously.

"We've got company. Single set of headlights to the west, moving toward the intersection."

Rudd turned to face west, the distant lights flickering between the trees on the outskirts of town.

"Cop?" asked Walsh.

"I don't see how," said Rudd.

This little speck of a town didn't have a police force. It was part of a rural administration district that relied on the county for emergency services. Something he had taken into consideration when planning the ambush site.

"Looks like they're headed here in a hurry," said Walsh.

"It sure does," said Rudd.

"A cop kind of changes everything."

"It does and it doesn't," he said, fiddling with the fake FBI credentials in his back pocket.

"How do you figure?"

"Same plan, but we'll have to put some serious distance between here and our next stop," said Rudd. "The whole county will be crawling with cops by sunup."

CHAPTER 7

Devin clasped the hot mug of coffee with both hands, straining to keep his eyes open. The individual interviews, which felt more like interrogations, had lasted most of the night, eventually yielding to a general debriefing, which dragged on far longer than he'd anticipated. He sensed it all coming to an end, but he couldn't be sure. He'd come to the same conclusion twice over the past few hours, only to get up and refresh his mug when it became clear he'd been wrong. At least the coffee was good. Nothing worse than sipping a nasty cup of joe for hours—against your will.

The debriefing location wasn't too shabby, either. A posh estate somewhere in Virginia, about an hour out of DC if he had to guess. He'd quit paying attention about halfway through their three-hour sur-veillance-detection route. Definitely a welcome change from the flu-orescent tube–soaked rooms in the basement of the J. Edgar Hoover Building.

He took a measured sip, hoping to take this mug past the finish line. Brendan Shea, Devin's immediate supervisor and tonight's oper-ation lead, sounded as though he was wrapping up the debrief. Again. When Shea stopped to check his tablet, presumably scrolling through the intelligence feed he'd referenced earlier, Devin sensed they were done. For real this time.

"All five of our friends from room four thirty-four arrived at the KLM ticket counter at Dulles," said Shea, eyes still focused on the tablet screen. "The counter opens in a few minutes."

"Are we following them?" asked Jason Hart, the operation's surveillance lead.

"As far as we can," said Shea. "You know how that goes."

"Have we ID'd any of them?" asked one of the DA operatives.

Shea shook his head. "Nothing yet. We're working our contacts at the FBI for some fingerprint help and running their mugs through all of the proprietary digital identification software. If they have a social media profile or got their picture taken for the local paper at some point during the digital era, we'll get something."

"Any guess what we were dealing with?" asked the same operative. "The crew in four thirty-four looked a little crusty to me. Definitely professionals, but maybe not the highest quality? It felt like kind of a bargain-basement team."

"Same with the stairwell," said Devin. "The woman in four thirty-two gave off more of an A-team vibe."

"We probably won't have any idea until we get an ID hit or pull something from one of their phones," said Shea. "We grabbed two sets of car keys, one from the room and the other from the stairwell, but it'll be a little while before we can risk sending anyone into some of the nearby parking garages to snoop around. My guess is the five at the airport will be long gone by then."

DEVTEK wasn't dealing with a domestic adversary. Devin had guessed as much when the woman had instantly switched from honey-trap to kidnap mode. The two thugs in the stairwell had sealed the deal. A competitive company with similar resources would have hired a firm on par with MINERVA.

A truly professional crew, playing the long game for their client, would have let Chase break off the honey trap. Nothing lost. Nothing gained. On top of that, they would have stood down the moment they detected the inbound direct-action team, promptly deescalating the situation. Companies spied on other companies all the time. It was pretty much expected. They wouldn't have resisted. They would have taken pictures and video of the team breaking into the room, threatening to press charges—and MINERVA's DA team would have immediately walked away.

Instead, the thugs in four thirty-four, like the two goons in the stairwell, chose to fight. They showed little restraint, which suggested either an unsophisticated or arrogantly indifferent adversary. Given the complexity of the cyberattacks and effort put into the honey trap, it was hard to make the argument that they were unsophisticated. The fact that they were sitting in Dulles International Airport at five in the morning, waiting to hop on the next flight out of the United States, rang as a damning indictment.

"We should have taken Devin's lead and sent them all to the hospital," said Chris Murphy, the direct-action team leader. "Then we'd have all the time we need."

The entire team laughed, breathing life into the group slumped at the obnoxiously massive dining room table. Devin nodded stiffly, still unsure where his actions tonight landed on the spectrum of tolerability within the organization. He wouldn't be entirely shocked later if Brendan Shea pulled him aside to praise him for his quick thinking in the hotel, and just as quickly dismissed him from MINERVA, citing exposure issues or something equally nebulous. He'd single-handedly hospitalized three people within the span of a few minutes. All the yelling, zapping, and screaming in room four thirty-four had yielded nothing more serious than a few black eyes and a broken rib or two—on both sides.

"On a related note," said Shea, pausing to focus on the tablet. "And you're all going to love this. I've just been informed that everyone involved in the hotel side of the operation is on paid leave, effective immediately."

The room broke into a low-grade chorus of expletives.

"Don't get all worked up. This isn't a punishment," interrupted Shea.

"Kind of sounds like one," someone muttered, reigniting the grumbles.

"Given the proximity of our operation to the White House, you can bet your ass the Secret Service will investigate. Stuff like this makes them nervous. All we're asking is that you take a little impromptu vacation and get out of the Beltway. You don't want to be home when the Secret Service comes knocking with questions. And they will come knocking. They'll run every surveillance camera feed in the hotel and on the surrounding streets through their facial-recognition system—which will tag a good number of us. Let MINERVA's lawyers and executives deal with their questions. It's far less painful for everyone that way."

"How long do you think we'll need to stay away?" asked one of the surveillance techs.

"Two weeks. Plan on two weeks. You'll all get a one-time, tier-four performance bonus to help pay for the unexpected vacation," said Shea. "That comes straight from the top."

Devin turned to the DA operative seated next to him.

"Is that good?" whispered Devin.

"That's more than good," he said. "Ten percent of base pay, after taxes."

"Damn. They must really want us to leave town," said Devin.

Shea pointed at Devin. "Did everyone hear what Mr. Gray just said?"

When everyone quieted, he continued. "He very astutely said, 'They must really want us to leave town.' Any questions about what you'll be doing for the next two weeks?"

"Vacation. Far away," said Chris Murphy.

"Exactly. Starting today. Drop off your issued gear back in the office and head straight home to start packing. Preferably, you'll call the family on the way home, and they'll have a bag packed for you when you arrive," said Shea. "Anything else before we cut loose?"

Silence. Mercifully.

"All righty then. Let's load up and get back to the office. That should get you on the road and headed home before rush hour traffic gets crazy. Don't want to hold up any of your vacations," said Shea, to a round of grunts and groans. "Quit your bitching. It's a paid vacation."

Devin checked his watch on the way out: 5:35. Unless they were closer to DC than he'd guessed, that put him in heavy Beltway traffic on the ride from the office in Alexandria to his apartment in Hyattsville.

His estimate about the distance turned out to be pretty accurate. After a seventy-minute, light-traffic drive, and about a half hour inside the MINERVA headquarters building, he slumped into the leather driver's seat of his SUV and took a few moments to think about how he'd go about skipping town. His dad would not be keen on the idea of packing a suitcase and heading straight to the airport this morning, later today, or even tomorrow, for no other reason than he "required more notice than that." He could hear the words right now. His dad never rushed into things, or out of them.

He'd show up in a few days, which actually worked out better. Kari was a little more like herself when he wasn't around. A lot more. Mom's downward spiral had really done a number on her. Five years younger than Devin, she had been around for the worst of it, while he'd been away at college. He still felt guilty about that. He'd gone to school thirty minutes away, unaffected and mostly oblivious to their mother's unraveling. Kari had spent her high school years struggling with their mother's rapidly worsening psychosis and a just as swiftly dwindling collection of friends.

Falls Church, Virginia, was a small, densely packed community a few miles west of the National Mall, which put it just south of McClean, Virginia, home of the Central Intelligence Agency. Growing up, all Devin's friends' parents had either worked on Capitol Hill in high-visibility jobs or "for the government." Most of the kids had known to stop asking questions when you got the generic answer. Even the new kids caught on, because word got around—even when it wasn't supposed to. As it had with their mother.

Kari had pulled a Houdini after graduation and never looked back—more like she never *came* back. She had applied to schools on the West Coast and had gotten accepted to UCLA, spending nearly all her vacation time with friends and her summer quarters loading up on prerequisites. She had graduated in five years with a master of social welfare degree and had immediately been hired at a major nonprofit organization, where she'd worked nonstop for the past five years. She'd been home twice since leaving for college almost fifteen years ago. Dad had visited her at least once a year, usually with Devin. She wouldn't let Mom visit and had seen her only once during the two times she made it back east. Mom had seemed to understand, or she hadn't cared. It had gotten harder to tell over time, until he'd pretty much stopped seeing her, too. Devin didn't want to think about it anymore.

He opened the compact nylon satchel he'd thrown on the passenger seat and removed his phone. MINERVA required them to leave all personal items behind during operations, especially electronics devices. At the start of each operation, they were given a slim wallet preloaded with a basic identification card and enough cash to fulfill their mission, an encrypted and presumably untraceable smartphone, and any additional personal gear deemed necessary by the operation leader. They handed in their phones and wallets before departing for the mission staging area and retrieved them upon return.

Devin pressed the power button and set the phone on the seat before starting the SUV. He shifted into reverse and checked the backup camera. All clear. The last thing he needed, while his fortune somewhat shined at MINERVA, was to back over one of his colleagues. Shea would undoubtedly interpret that as the unceremonious end to his good luck streak.

The phone caught his eye before he let his foot off the brake. The home screen was filled with missed-call notifications and text messages.

He put the vehicle in park and grabbed the phone. Jesus. His dad had called and left voice mails seven times in the past two hours. He found text messages buried between the call notifications.

PLEASE CALL ME AS SOON AS YOU GET THIS. VERY IMPORTANT.

SERIOUSLY. NEED YOU TO CALL ME RIGHT AWAY.

DEVIN. CALL ME NOW!

DEVIN. I'M AT YOUR APARTMENT! WHERE ARE YOU!

JUST CALL ME. SOMETHING HAPPENED. I'M PARKED AT YOUR PLACE.

HEADING HOME. CALL ME OR COME BY ASAP!

IT'S ABOUT HELEN. PLEASE CALL.

Of course it was. It was always about her—though this sounded entirely different. His dad rarely overreacted to her antics, or anything for that matter. Devin had seen him frazzled once, maybe twice, since as far back as he could remember. And Mom had given him plenty of opportunities to lose his shit. He must have been one hell of an analyst at the CIA. A voice of reason in a troubled world, even as his own world fell apart. Respected enough that they kept him on for three years after dismissing Helen, which got him to thirty years of service and a full pension annuity.

He called his dad and braced for impact.

"Devin! I've been trying to get ahold of you for—"

"Dad. Dad. I was working all night. I just got my phone back," interrupted Devin.

"Okay. Okay. Jeez. I'm sorry," said Mason Gray. "I didn't even think of that. I just uh . . . I, uh. I don't know how to say this."

"Did Mom do something crazy?" asked Devin, regretting his choice of words.

His dad had made it abundantly clear over the years that he disapproved of the crude characterization. A part of him still cared for her very deeply, despite everything she had put him through.

"Sorry. I didn't mean to say that," said Devin.

"No. It's all right," said Mason. "Maybe she really was crazy. Maybe that's the only way to describe it."

Devin didn't like where this was going.

"Dad?" said Devin. "Is Mom okay?"

"No. She's not. She's dead," said Mason. "She killed herself—but that's not the worst of it."

"What?"

How could that not be the worst of it?

"Not on the phone. Can you come by the house?" asked his dad. "I'll make some breakfast. You must be hungry. What can I make you?"

"Dad. I'll be there in thirty to forty minutes," said Devin. "I'll grab bagel sandwiches on the way."

"Okay. I'll see you then."

He really didn't sound like himself at all.

"Dad?"

"Yeah?"

"How bad is the rest of it?"

"It doesn't make sense," said Mason. "They say she killed a Tennessee sheriff's deputy. Shot him right in the face."

"Jesus. Let's talk about this at home," said Devin, but his dad kept going.

"That was after she kidnapped a seventy-six-year-old man from an assisted living facility in Branson, Missouri," he said, with no hint of emotion.

"Dad. I'm on my way home," said Devin, shifting the SUV into reverse.

"I don't even know when or if they'll release her body. They wouldn't say much," said Mason.

"When did they call?"

"They didn't. A Falls Church officer came by the house a little after five. Tennessee police found an old registration in the glove box with my address. Everyone at the department here knew she had issues."

"All right, Dad. Just sit down. Do some of that meditation you do every day. And I'll be over before you know it. We'll figure this all out."

"I'll make us some scrambled eggs with cheese and toast," said his dad, as though he hadn't heard a word Devin had just said.

"Sounds delicious. Do you want me to stay on the line? Are you okay?" asked Devin.

"I can't talk on the phone and make scrambled eggs at the same time," he said. "I'll see you in a bit. Sorry I left all of those messages. Do me a favor and don't listen to them."

"I'll delete them," said Devin, taking a deep breath before continuing. "Did you call Kari?"

"No. I'll call her in a little bit," said his dad. "It was too early in LA."

"I'll call her with you. We can do it after breakfast or wait until later," said Devin. "There's no hurry."

A long pause ensued.

"She would never have killed a police officer," said Mason. "Something doesn't add up."

"I'll be right home, Dad," said Devin. "We can talk about it then."

"All right. I'll get breakfast ready," said Mason before disconnecting the call.

Devin stared at the phone for several moments, perplexed by his dad's statement about the police officer. None of what he had just learned about his mom's final hours added up. Not a single word of it. But his dad almost sounded as though he hadn't been surprised by the kidnapping. Or maybe he was reading too much into the conversation. Devin hadn't slept in over twenty-four hours, and his dad didn't sound like himself.

He filed the thought away for later and backed out of the parking space without checking the backup camera. His time at MINERVA would be short lived, no matter whom he ran down in the parking lot. He'd have to call Brendan Shea sooner than later and explain why he couldn't leave the greater DC area. When the circumstances surrounding his mother's death surfaced . . . they'd be forced to let him go. His mother was the gift that kept on giving.

PART II

PART 1

CHAPTER 8

Devin checked his watch. Two minutes later than the last time he'd looked. Ten minutes until the viewing ended. The hushed sound of feet brushing across carpet somewhere behind them turned his head. His sister didn't budge, her eyes locked on a point somewhere above their mother's closed coffin. Same expression for the last hour and fifty minutes. Indifferent. Dad pushed his glasses up the bridge of his nose and sighed, turning to Devin for any sign it may be a guest paying their last respects. He didn't have it in him to look for himself and be disappointed. They'd had one visitor, an old friend and almost girlfriend of Devin's, who'd sat behind them for ten minutes before heading out.

The funeral home director, a tall, long-faced elderly gentleman whom Devin remembered from every wake and funeral he'd attended here, going back decades, paused by the guest book located on a small table just inside the room and gave it a quick look. He glanced in Devin's direction and nodded almost imperceptibly before stepping out of the room.

Kari had been right. The whole thing should have been a quick graveside memorial service. Fifteen minutes at the cemetery—just the three of them and a minister. They hadn't expected anyone to show up, not after the grisly details of Helen's rampage made the news. But attendance hadn't been the point.

Their dad had insisted Helen get a full memorial, regardless of the circumstances. A wake, funeral service, and interment. At first Devin had resisted, firmly in his sister's camp, but he eventually relented. Mom deserved to be recognized for her entire life's accomplishments, not the tragic consequences of the treacherous illness that had so unfairly twisted her mind. He still remembered the good times. They were pretty vague as an adult, but the picture books at the house had brought it all back. Honoring the Helen Gray they had all once known was the point.

She'd been a wonderful, loving mother for more than half of his life. She had traveled frequently for the CIA, but she had always been vibrant and entirely present for them when she was home. Then something had changed. In 2004, Devin had spent fall break at home, during his freshman year at Maryland, and things had been different. Mom had been unusually distant. Dad had tiptoed around her. Kari wouldn't talk to either of them.

Her situation had worsened every year after that, Mom managing to pull it together for big occasions, like his college graduation. Sometimes she'd go a few months seeming entirely better—but she wasn't. She'd fall even deeper into the hole that had swallowed her, vanishing for weeks or longer. After his parents had separated, she'd disappeared for months. There was no point to dwelling on this any longer. She was gone. It was time to let it go.

His dad cracked his knuckles and stood up. "I think that's it. I'm going to pay my last respects. I'll talk to the funeral director on the way out. We'll skip right to the graveside memorial and be done with it. Sorry to put you through this."

Kari took his hand and hugged him. "It was the right thing to do. Sorry for being a pain about it."

Something caught his dad's eye, and he craned his head above her shoulder to get a better view. Devin followed his gaze to the viewing room's entrance. An older man in a black suit, with an unkempt beard, stood in the doorway—appearing hesitant to enter. Minus the deep tan, he looked like a Hasidic Jew who had misplaced his hat. His dad patted Kari's back.

"Looks like we have a visitor," he said, letting go of Kari. "Karl?"

The man stepped inside and smiled somberly. "I didn't think you'd recognize me after all the years. And the beard."

"I might not have been able to pick you out of a crowd," said his dad, glancing around the room. "But as you can see."

They met halfway across the room and shook hands, while Devin and Kari stayed behind.

"Do you recognize him?" asked Devin.

"Not at all," said Kari. "Are you gonna see Marnie later?"

"What?"

"Marnie Young. The hot fighter pilot friend of yours that stopped in," said Kari. "The only other person that stopped by tonight? She gave you her number."

"I know who you're talking about," said Devin. "Now isn't the time."

"Well. Whenever it's time, you should look her up," said Kari.

"I'll take that under advisement," said Devin before nodding toward his dad. "Here they come."

Mason Gray accompanied the mystery visitor to the front of the room, stopping to introduce him.

"This is Karl Berg. He knew your mother from Langley," said Mason. "I don't think you've ever met?"

Berg shook his head. "No. But I've seen the two of you in pictures on her desk. Kind of watched you grow up. In a noncreepy way. Though I'm sure it sounded creepy."

"It didn't," said Devin, shaking his hand. "Thank you for coming."

"I had to come," said Berg. "She earned it."

Kari took his hand reluctantly, maintaining a neutral expression.

"Good instincts. I wouldn't trust me, either," said Berg. "Hey. If you don't mind, I'd like to take a few moments to pay my respects."

Their dad stepped out of the way and motioned toward the casket. "Sorry. Of course."

Karl Berg, who Devin assumed had worked in the same line of business as their mother at the CIA—Directorate of Operations, a.k.a. the Clandestine Service—spent a few quiet moments next to her coffin before returning.

"I'm genuinely sorry for your loss," said Berg, looking torn about something. "I know things haven't been easy."

None of them responded right away, presumably because they didn't know what to say to a near-complete stranger who had just summarized the past decade and a half of their experience with Helen Gray in one sentence.

"It's been a long haul, but it's all behind us now," said their dad, offering his hand to Berg. "Thank you for coming. Seriously. It means a lot to me, and as funny as this might sound, I know it would have meant a lot to Helen. If you don't mind, I need to speak with the funeral director about tomorrow. We're going to cancel the memorial service. I hope that doesn't inconvenience you."

They shook hands. "No. I just wanted to pass along my condolences and respect in person."

His dad looked as though he was about to cry. He nodded at Devin and Kari.

"I'll catch up with the two of you at Provinces. Have them pour me a Guinness?"

"Got it. See you in a few," said Kari, turning to Devin. "I'm going to freshen up. Meet you in the lobby."

"Kari. It was good to meet you," said Berg.

"Likewise," said Kari, barely feigning a smile.

Berg took a business card out of his suit coat pocket and handed it to Devin.

"Never know," said Berg. "And please accept my sincerest condolences."

Devin examined the card while Berg walked away. Just a name, email address, and phone number. No salutations, degrees, or career headings listed. Exactly what you'd expect from a former CIA intelligence operative. Kari broke the silence after he left the room.

"That was a little weird, huh? Barely says a word and leaves? Dad looked uncomfortable. Do you think there was something going on between this guy and Mom?"

"I didn't get that vibe," said Devin.

"You're a dude," said Kari. "And you didn't get the vibe from fighter pilot girl, either."

"Helicopter pilot," said Devin. "And there was no vibe."

"I think your vibe reader is broken."

"I think we can find something else to talk about in front of our mother's casket," said Devin.

She started to back up. "Whatever. See you in the lobby."

"Aren't you going to say goodbye or something?" he asked, glancing at the casket.

"I've already made my peace with Mom," she said.

"Lucky you," said Devin. "I'll be out in a few minutes."

"It's not going to happen in the next few minutes. Trust me," said Kari. "Took me a few hundred hours of therapy."

"I'll give it a shot, anyway," he said, fairly certain his sister was kidding herself—and that none of them would ever truly come to peace with what their mother had done to them.

CHAPTER 9

The significance of meeting in Harvey Rudd's basement wasn't lost on anyone—particularly Harvey Rudd. The thought of bringing another operative to his house, for any reason, had never crossed his mind. It didn't even enter into the realm of possibilities, because it was strictly forbidden by CONTROL. In fact, no contact between operatives outside of a CONTROL-assigned mission was permitted for any reason.

Digital briefing packets outlining each operative's responsibilities on a mission were sent individually, so there was rarely a need to gather in advance to discuss anything, even for more complex operations. They'd either drive to mission areas individually or consolidate into one vehicle at a park and ride a few hours away, as they'd done for the Gray ambush. And the Gray arrangement had been a rare one, entirely dictated by the fact that she was a time-critical, moving target.

CONTROL did everything possible to keep them apart. Long, boring drives loosened tongues, and the less they knew about each other the better, which was why he had a hard time coming to terms with the scene in front of him. The same crew he'd commanded a week ago, minus the two Helen Gray had shot, lounged quite comfortably on the leather sectional sofa in his basement "man cave." Jolene relaxed in his recliner, mostly to keep anyone else from sitting in it.

He'd discussed the situation with Jolene before everyone arrived. Either CONTROL planned on retiring and relocating them after this operation, or they intended to extract them. Given Jolene's involvement in a high-profile mission last week, the Helen Gray fiasco, and now this, they were certain that their usefulness here had come to an end. At the very least, they'd have to change states. Most likely regions. Definitely identities.

If any of the six operatives sitting in his basement were grabbed by the FBI, they could lead the authorities here, where it wouldn't be very difficult to piece together the rest of the puzzle. He'd be surprised if CONTROL kept them here. He just hoped they would be able to live off their retirement savings after they were recalled. A silly concern in the grand scheme of things, but a worry, nonetheless. One of a thousand worries that surfaced when they had been notified of the meeting—at their house.

He took a seat on a folding chair he'd brought into the basement from the garage and placed in front of the group.

"Everyone good with the drinks and snacks?" asked Rudd.

Nobody had touched the assortment of sodas, chips, and candies he'd set out on the coffee table in front of them. Probably thinking the same thing: *One of them had orders to eliminate everyone else.* Jolene reached out and grabbed a handful of potato chips.

"The chips aren't poisoned," she said. "Only the M&M's."

A few thin smiles, but nothing beyond that—and nobody made a move for the snacks.

"Fine," said Rudd. "I know this is highly irregular. How do you think we feel? They picked *our* fucking house. This is obviously the end for us here."

"Or the end of us," said Logan Walsh. "And you get to live happily ever after—right here in this lovely house."

"Come on. How the hell would that even work? We have six cars, three with out-of-state plates, parked in front of our house," said Rudd. "We never have people over. It's probably big news on Nextdoor right now. How are we supposed to move all of your cars without someone noticing?"

"What's Nextdoor?" asked Leo Ward.

"It's a neighborhood-based social media platform that none of us are supposed to use," said Walsh.

"We're not members," said Rudd. "We joined for a few minutes just to see how active our neighbors were on the site. Trust me, someone has noticed that we have guests for the first time ever. I'm pretty sure we were all supposed to create an account for that purpose, and then delete it."

"We are," said Walsh, glaring at Ward.

"What? I live out in the sticks," said Ward. "My nearest neighbor is a mile away."

"This wasn't some kind of trick to get us all in one place," said Rudd.

"No offense, but I'll still pass on the snacks," said Walsh, a slim grin on his face.

Rudd honestly couldn't tell if he was serious about the poisoning stuff or not.

"Can we get on with the business at hand?" said Nathan Clark, a regular member of Rudd's team. "CONTROL didn't send us here so Harvey and Jolene could take a crack at us. They'd send in professionals if they wanted us gone. Us and our families."

Everyone mumbled their agreement.

"So why are we here? The mission briefing looked detailed enough," said Clark.

"A few things have changed since you got on the road. We're now staying in five different hotels, instead of just the Marriott."

"Sounds like an upgraded countersurveillance threat related to our target," said Walsh. "Something that very recently developed."

"All we know is that they don't want us bunching up. Maybe they took a second look at the original mission packet and decided to play it extra safe," said Rudd. "Or this could also just be an upgraded threat level issued by the Department of Homeland Security for the entire DC area—entirely unrelated to Helen or Devin Gray—and CONTROL isn't taking any chances on us somehow getting swept up into it."

"The timing suggests otherwise," said Clark. "CONTROL doesn't take unnecessary chances. If they split us up at the last minute—something changed."

"It's a fair assumption," said Rudd. "Which is why I assume we're meeting here to go over the changes, instead of there."

"What are the other changes?" said Clark, checking his watch.

"You in a hurry?" said Walsh.

Clark didn't respond. He didn't have to. The permanent dour look on his face answered the question. He was all business, all the time.

"CONTROL is looking for a second location used by Helen Gray. Her apartment yielded nothing," said Rudd. "They think the son might lead us to it, if such a place even exists."

"Was that in our briefing?" asked Ward.

"No. That was sent to me less than an hour ago, presumably while you were all in transit."

"Do we have any idea what CONTROL is looking for at the location?" asked Walsh.

"Or what kind of a location?" said Clark. "A house, apartment, locker?"

"No. We're in the dark as usual," said Rudd.

"And this Karl Berg? Any theories on how he fits into all of this?" asked Walsh.

"Ex-CIA, like Helen Gray. Directorate of Operations. The two of them worked off and on together in the mid- to late nineties. But their paths didn't cross much at the CIA after that," said Rudd.

"Doesn't sound like much," said Ward.

"He was the only person from the CIA to show up at her wake," said Jolene. "That's something."

"Exactly," said Rudd. "And the information I received this morning classified Berg as high-damage potential."

"He's retired, right?" asked Walsh. "Not working for any private entities of interest?"

"As far as CONTROL knows, or is willing to tell us," said Rudd.

"Interesting. That classification bears a lot of weight," said Walsh. "Normally we'd be sent to get rid of someone in that category."

"Which must be why we're having this meeting," said Rudd. "The mission sounded straightforward enough until I received the update."

"No doubt timed to arrive while we were on the way," said Walsh. "What else did they send?"

"And why aren't they using people closer to the area? Operatives that know the area like the back of their hand?" said Rick Gentry, a Kentucky-based operative whom Rudd had worked with a half dozen times before. "Or are they? I really hope this isn't a double-up situation."

A double-up or duplicate team operation involved two separate teams pursuing the same goal—most often unaware of each other. It was a recipe for disaster, particularly for a complex surveillance operation like they had been assigned. Double the chance of detection. The duplicate team worked best for assassinations or thefts. Single, compressed events requiring a fail-safe.

He doubted CONTROL had put two teams on this, for that very reason—and another that he couldn't share. Jolene had surmised from her recent assignment that the pool of operatives working the Washington, DC, area had been decimated. She knew this because she had been woken by CONTROL about an hour and a half after Harvey had been dispatched to deal with Helen Gray, and sent to DC, where she had slipped onto one of the recovery floors at Howard University Hospital and injected two fiftysomething-year-old men with syringes that had been provided to her along with doctor's scrubs, a stethoscope, and a hospital staff identification card.

Both men had sustained head injuries, which suggested she was involved in more of a cleanup job than some kind of strategic assassination. The information about her mission had not been included in the current operation file, and they had no intention of sharing their theory with the team—for obvious reasons. He fought the urge to look at Jolene.

"They wouldn't double up a surveillance," said Walsh. "And it doesn't make a difference if they do. Orders are orders."

"Yeah," said Gentry. "Just thinking aloud."

"Should we all log in to our computers and read the update before we start to analyze the plan?" asked Walsh.

"I don't think it's necessary. Outside of what I told you about Berg's new status and the focus on finding a second location used by Helen Gray, the only other update relates to fixed surveillance locations. CONTROL has secured an apartment on the third floor of a complex across the street from Devin Gray's building, with a view of his balcony and bedroom window. From that apartment, we'll be able to give the trail cars enough notice to get into place and for the ground teams to move into position in case he opts for a walk or run."

"That's you, Sandy," said Walsh, nodding at the blonde woman across the coffee table from him.

She grabbed one of the diet sodas. "Running or walking?"

"Does anyone else look like they run regularly?" said Walsh, getting a laugh from everyone.

"I should get paid more for staying in shape," she said. "They have to be thinking about retiring us after this one. I mean, look at us. How did we get this old?"

"Back to the plan. The apartment will be occupied primarily by Sandy, with one of us joining her when Gray is home. We'll work out a rotation for that. Since Sandy will be our primary ground surveillance point around Gray's apartment complex, we have to assume he'll take notice of her. So Sandy will not rotate into the trail cars or any surveillance duty outside of the restaurants or coffee shops within walking distance or reasonable driving distance from the apartment," said Rudd.

"I hate being stuck in place," she said.

"Sorry. There's a trail system adjacent to his apartment, and he's a runner, according to initial surveillance. He'll use it, and we can't afford to ignore the possibility he might make contact with Berg or whoever on familiar ground," said Rudd.

"What if he drives to a different trail or park to run?" said Walsh. "Places like that make ideal handoff or dead-drop points."

"We can put her in a logical place for runners. We just have to be judicious about it," said Rudd. "We can't have her show up everywhere he runs in the city. Hopefully, he runs near his apartment most of the time. He'll get used to seeing her."

Sandy Jones had a skeptical look on her face, which Rudd suddenly realized was shared by everyone.

"What?"

"We can't cover him all the time," said Walsh. "At best, we're looking at what, fifty percent coverage?"

"Maybe less," said Gentry. "Someone could slip into his apartment during the day and leave something. We'd never know. If he runs a solid surveillance-detection route, we don't have enough assets to track him."

"If he runs a remotely competent SDR, we'll lose him, and don't even get me started on his apartment. No listening devices or cameras authorized?" said Ward. "This almost feels like pointless busywork."

"What are you talking about? We'll be using tracking devices," said Rudd. "CONTROL made it clear that aside from Sandy, they want us to keep our distance. He's a trained countersurveillance expert. Former FBI intelligence investigator. This guy spies on spies for a living."

"We all read that in the data packet," said Walsh. "But his SDR might involve the Metro, an Uber, a public bus, changing vehicles. If he's as good as his file suggests, we don't stand a chance of following him without making it really obvious."

"And he probably sweeps his vehicle for bugs," said Gentry. "I agree with Leo. CONTROL can't seriously think we'll be able to keep good enough track of him. I bet they're prepositioning us for a hit. They probably have an entirely different team—a specialist group—looking for Berg or other contacts of interest. If Berg or someone else shows up, they'll call us off our pointless surveillance and ready us for action. Why else would they change Berg's status?"

Rudd considered Rick's theory for a moment. It didn't actually sound that far-fetched, given the reality of their next-to-impossible assignment. Jolene had said as much before everyone had showed up, and he'd agreed. CONTROL was asking the B-team, more like the C-team, to do a job meant for the A-team. Looking at it from Rick's perspective made a lot of sense.

"We'd already be familiar with his daily routine. His favorite restaurants, coffee shops, shopping stops. His habits," said Rudd. "Taking him out would be a simple job for this over-the-hill crew."

"Why not just tell us all of that up front?" asked Sandy. "If it's even true."

"Probably because they see some value in our surveillance and want us focusing on one job at a time," said Rudd. "It won't be a perfect surveillance job—"

"Not even close," said Gentry.

"They know that. They *have* to know that," said Rudd. "By putting us on the job, no matter how futile it turns out to be, they gain more surveillance coverage than they had before—without eating into their limited pool of specialists. This job would be near impossible for even the best in the business, especially given Gray's background. I think they're parking us on Gray in case they decide to eliminate him. If we happen to stumble on a clue to the whereabouts of his mother's suspected hideaway or catch him meeting up with Karl Berg, all the better."

"We're just pulling stuff out of our asses right now," said Clark.

"This is brainstorming," said Rudd.

"This is pointless," said Clark. "We execute CONTROL's orders to the best of our ability. Just like we've always done. If they decide to kill him, we kill him. Until then, we watch him. That's it. I don't understand why we're yakking about this. We do what CONTROL tells us to do. Period. Any questions?"

"Okay then," said Walsh, rolling his eyes. "I guess that's it."

"Always a pleasure," added Sandy, nodding at Clark.

Rudd still didn't understand why they had been brought together like this. The one thing CONTROL had most definitely accomplished with this awkward, impromptu social gathering was to drive home the fact that he wouldn't miss any of them when this was over. Maybe that had been a part of their intention. If so—mission accomplished. He hoped to never see any of them again after this trip.

Rudd had the same thought again, ten minutes later, after he'd backed their loaded SUV out of the garage and stopped at the bottom of the driveway. He pressed the garage remote and took Jolene's hand, watching the bay door slowly close on the home they had shared for close to three decades. If his instinct about this upcoming mission proved correct, this would be the last time he looked at their house. Oddly, he wasn't sad. He felt more relieved than anything. A little excited, even.

"I'm ready to move on from this place," he said. "All of it, if that's what they intend."

She squeezed his hand. "Me too. Just promise me one thing."

"Anything."

"I get to kill Gray."

"Only if CONTROL orders it," said Rudd, kissing her cheek.

"Of course," she said. "I'm not a psychopath."

They both chuckled a little. That was one of the many things he loved about Jolene. Her sense of humor. Of course, she *was* a psychopath. They all were. How could they not be—and still do this cold-blooded work for all these years?

CHAPTER 10

Devin dropped his toothbrush in the stainless-steel cup next to the bathroom sink and looked at himself in the mirror. He looked like shit, to put it mildly. The past ten days had taken an unexpected physical toll on him. He'd expected the emotional wipeout, which he understood would knock him down a few notches physically. But this was something entirely different. He felt as he had when he'd woken up the morning after his first marathon. Every marathon, for that matter. Utterly spent and fatigued to the bone.

The sleeplessness had to be a big part of why he felt as though he could take a twenty-four-hour nap. It hadn't been the stare-at-the-ceiling-all-night variety. That would have been too easy. He'd drifted in and out all night, thinking he'd never fallen asleep, his brain racing to make sense of the facts one moment and wrapping itself around some vaguely connected reality the next. Nine straight nights of this, with no end in sight.

He'd dropped his sister at the airport a few hours ago and grabbed some takeout from a nearby Mexican restaurant, hoping to eat himself into a coma. Maybe just the act of sending Kari home would break up whatever dynamic his mind had established over the past several days. Same with taking a short hiatus from his dad. Devin had told Mason that he'd swing by over the weekend, lying to him about needing to put in some face time at work. He'd never brought up the fourteen-day forced vacation triggered by the hotel job. As far as his dad knew, he was on bereavement leave.

He just needed a few days away from Falls Church. A little space from ground zero to recalibrate. The dark circles under his eyes told him a big part of his recalibration would involve sleep—or trying. A burrito the size of his forearm and the cheese quesadilla sitting in his stomach wagered he'd be out as soon as he went horizontal. Devin wasn't so sure.

He turned the light off and shuffled out of the bathroom to his unmade bed. Hadn't some famous Navy SEAL said something about making your bed if you wanted to change the world? Looked like the world would have to wait a few days. He sat down on the edge of the mattress and let his house sandals fall to the carpet before grabbing his phone off the nightstand. More out of habit than anything else, he activated the home screen to see if he had any messages.

He'd been texting back and forth with Marnie Young over the past few days, throwing around the idea of grabbing a drink or coffee when everything with his mom settled down. She'd just recently left the Marine Corps after fifteen years and was temporarily living at home in Falls Church with her parents—until she landed a job in DC.

She was looking for something on Capitol Hill, which could spring-board her into politics or a policy position. Her backup plan was to join the fairly large pool of the recently departed or retired officers working senior positions in the civilian side of the Department of Defense—in or as close to the Beltway as possible. She didn't want to shut the door on Capitol Hill.

The screen showed one text message, from a number he didn't rec-ognize. Actually, it was three numbers and a dash, followed by two numbers. Spam or some kind of automatic message update from some-thing he'd mistakenly opted into previously. Nothing from Marnie. He was about to activate the Do Not Disturb feature and put the phone back on the nightstand when he caught a line of the text.

Respond with first movie you saw in the theaters and the first and last name of your first prom date. No spaces. Help me, Obi-Wan Kenobi. You're my only hope.

72

What the hell? The last line was something his mom had said a lot throughout his childhood. They'd watched *Star Wars* as a family at least a hundred times when he was little, and she'd teased him with that line whenever it was time to do chores or she'd needed him to do something.

Intrigued, he typed HomeAloneEricaCohen and pressed send, surprised by how easily the information from his past had come to him. Now what? The phone buzzed in his hand, startling him. The number calling read *Unknown*. Seriously? Telemarketing shenanigans had just graduated to the next level. Somehow, they had linked him to one of his mom's old sayings. Probably something she'd submitted as a challenge question online and was subsequently sold to some data-collection outfit.

But what if this was something else?

Devin accepted the call. Why not? He could always hang up if it was indeed a new telemarketer.

"Hello?" he said.

His mother's voice answered.

"Devin. If you're hearing this, something has gone seriously wrong. You've either already attended my funeral or I've been missing for several days. I triggered this messaging protocol ten days ago, in response to what I either perceived as an imminent, nonsurvivable threat against my life or an attempted kidnapping. Funeral or missing, I'm gone. These people don't leave witnesses."

A short pause ensued, followed by: "I need to verify your voice now. After the beep, please tell me the make and model of the car we bought you in high school and then say, 'I'm really not interested in a new car. Please take me off your list.'"

What the hell? "Honda Civic. I'm not interested in a new car. Please take me off your list."

The call disconnected. *No. No. No. Wait. Did he say something wrong? Shit.* He'd forgotten to say "*really* interested." Did he really just mess up? A text message appeared a moment later.

Use headphones and click this link. https://dfe740-22GW3.

Interesting. She thought someone might be listening. He got up from the bed and made his way to the kitchen island, where he kept his running headphones in one of the drawers. With the headphones ready, he poured a glass of water to make his trip to the kitchen appear more natural to an outside observer. If they had cameras in his house, it wouldn't matter. He'd have to sweep for surveillance devices later. On his way back to the bedroom, he clicked the link, which connected him to a voice message.

"Dial or say two at any time if you're under duress." A long pause ensued before his mother's voice continued. "Devin. Sorry to keep this abrupt. I need you to see what I've been working on for the past twenty years. I'm not trying to make up for what I put all of you through. I can never do that. Take a look and decide for yourself what should be done with it. To continue this message, input the numeric digits corresponding to the year we took you to see your first Orioles game."

He didn't have to think about it, which was probably why his mother had picked it as a security question. They'd taken him the same year their new stadium, Camden Yards, had opened. But the answer contained the number two, which would trigger the duress protocol. She would have thought of that, right? Of course. He tapped "1993," praying he'd hear her voice again. Mostly because he wanted to hear her voice again. He hadn't made a decision one way or the other about her proposal.

"Smart kid. Here's what I need you to do. First: Assume you're currently under professional surveillance. Trust me on that. If I was even remotely close with my theory, they'll be watching you closely. Second: Please keep your father and sister out of this. Entirely. Press two to continue."

He sat down on the bed and pressed one, guessing she wouldn't follow the same pattern.

"Sorry about that. Can't be too careful. Here's what I need you to do, and don't write any of this down. Tomorrow morning, at a normal hour for you, place your phone in your safe and run a three-hour SDR. Check your vehicle for trackers before leaving. Physically disable any systems like OnStar. Leave your E-ZPass behind. You must go dark to and from this destination. No credit cards or anything traceable. I know what you're thinking—Mom can't even let go of this shit after she's dead."

He stifled a laugh. Mom's sense of humor could be wicked, particularly when things were tough going. Dad had called it gallows humor. Devin had never really understood it until he'd started working for the Special Surveillance Group. The long, thankless days and nights on stakeout that yielded nothing. Exhaustively choreographed, hours-long street-surveillance gigs to track a target to an adult video store. They became the stand-up comedians of gallows humor.

"I hope that made you laugh a little. Here's where you're headed tomorrow. It's a win-win situation no matter what. Head to the first place we took you for hard-shell crabs. At the marina, look for a boat named after our first dog. You'll find a waterproof pouch in the bottom galley drawer. In addition to a file with the information I need you to examine, you'll find a one-hundred-dollar bill to pay for lunch. A hundred bucks buys a lot of fresh crabs—and a few ice-cold beers to wash them down. Press three to repeat that message or one to continue."

Devin tapped one.

"I love you, Kari, and your father so much, Devin. I can't tell you how sorry I am that I put the three of you through all of this. Be very careful, and don't trust anyone—except the one I send your way."

The call ended, and he stared at the phone for several seconds. *Did that really just happen?* His mom had somehow put together an automated phone and text-message-alert system in case someone tried to murder or kidnap her? This either took her craziness to the next level or—he didn't know. It had to be more of the madness. Right?

He lay down with the phone still in his hand and stared at the ceiling. May as well get used to the view. The prospect of a food-induced sleep had just been revoked. His heart raced at twice its resting rate, his feet and hands tingling. It would take him a few hours to come down from this adrenaline rush. Whether he could fall asleep after that was anyone's guess.

Devin looked at the initial text message again. *Help me, Obi-Wan Kenobi. You're my only hope.* Of all the things she could have picked to say, this hit him pretty hard. He could picture them stuffed into the corner of the sectional, snuggled up under a blanket watching *Star Wars.* Mom and Dad in the middle. Kari on one side. Devin on the other. He wiped the tears from his eyes. *What the hell happened at that intersection in Tennessee, Mom?*

Maybe the answer waited for him in Annapolis, on a boat named *Sadie.* There was only one way to find out. Worst-case scenario? The information turned out to be nothing. Devin enjoying a lazy afternoon cracking open perfectly seasoned hard-shell crabs and downing a few cold beers while overlooking the water. Best-case scenario? It all depended on what was in the file. Either way, he'd enjoy cold beers and steaming-hot crabs for lunch. Like his mom said: win-win.

CHAPTER 11

Harvey Rudd braced one hand against the dashboard, his eyes fixed on the phone screen held firmly in the other. As the SUV lurched to a stop, his torso pressed against the lap and shoulder belts.

"Take it easy," said Rudd. "We're not in a race."

"That was the shortest yellow light I've ever seen," said Jolene.

"Uh-huh."

"Don't *uh-huh* me," she said.

"Yep."

"That's even worse."

"Uh-huh," he said, getting a sharp elbow to the ribs under his raised arm.

"Dammit. That hurt," said Rudd.

"Then knock it off," she said. "Unless you'd like to do the driving."

"I wish."

The truth was that Jolene drove like this all the time—and she knew it better than he did. Her driving fell somewhere on the scale between extremely impatient and overly aggressive, trending toward the latter. Because of this, she rarely drove during operations. They'd both agreed on that. Unfortunately, he had no choice but to put her in the driver's seat today.

Jolene could use electronic devices just fine, but she couldn't troubleshoot them to save her life. Their communications-and-control gear wasn't overly complicated, but they couldn't afford a critical technology slipup on this mission. The job itself would prove difficult enough, and their performance over the next several days would likely determine their future living conditions.

"Looks like he's pulling into a strip mall up ahead, on the left side just after Hartwick Road," said Rudd. "The map is showing a Starbucks. This is the southeast edge of the University of Maryland's campus. Gray's alma mater."

"The perfect place to discreetly meet someone. Lots of open space and publicly accessible buildings on campus," said Jolene.

"Or a nearby running trail. I bet there are several close to campus."

He relayed the situation to the two other teams over the push-to-talk satellite radio handset, sending Clark, their lone wolf operative, to the College Park–University of Maryland Metro station a half mile to the east, and Walsh to cover the bus stop a few hundred feet north of the Starbucks on Baltimore Avenue. He had Leo with him, just in case Gray decided to take a bus ride. Harvey and his wife would circle back and watch the bus station several blocks south.

If Gray got back into his car and headed to campus for a run, there wasn't much they could do. Sandy was back at Gray's apartment complex, installing discreet cameras on each level of the parking garage so they could get a sense of where he was headed each time he left. They'd only had time to install two trackers on his vehicle overnight. If the university proved to be one of Gray's regular running spots, they'd bring Sandy in to keep an eye on him. Given the close proximity to his apartment, he could start her tomorrow if Gray returned. No need to spend more time establishing a longer pattern.

They always worked moving surveillance like this. Basic surveillance cameras at the target's residence or work to make bigger-picture assessments about his movement. For the actual surveillance work, they employed a minimum of three cars: a control car to coordinate the overall effort and rotate into the active surveillance as needed; a car with two operatives so they could immediately follow their target on foot until the other cars could find parking and join the effort; and a car with a lone operative. If they had additional personnel, they'd add more lone operatives. This stretched their surveillance capability while provoking the least suspicion. Most cars on the road at any given time had a single occupant.

If he had unlimited resources, he'd put a few male-female teams together. Couples—real or fake—were often overlooked entirely by countersurveillance teams when forced to analyze more complex, dynamic settings like a crowded park or packed highway. By necessity, countersurveillance efforts became a probabilities game in those scenarios. A basic risk-assessment calculation, with couples at the very bottom of the list, due to the real and perceived complexities of two people working together seamlessly without giving themselves away. *Real indeed,* he thought, squeezing Jolene's hand.

Less than a block past the stoplight, Jolene parked them in front of a 7-Eleven, parallel with Baltimore Avenue and pointed north, where they could spot Gray if he decided to use the bus stop south of the Starbucks. A pair of binoculars ensured that. The only matter still in question was who would get to ride the bus with Gray. Marital instinct told him he'd pulled the short straw. Thirty minutes later, Gray's car still hadn't moved from the strip mall parking lot.

"He's been there for a while," said Jolene.

A half hour wasn't unusual for a single person at a coffee shop. You sit and relax with your drink. Read a book. Scroll through your phone. The Starbucks was close to campus, so maybe he was checking out the ladies. All within the range of possibility, but the longer it went past thirty minutes, the more it piqued his suspicion.

"Couldn't hurt to drive past once," said Rudd. "Just to make sure."

Jolene shifted the SUV into drive and had them in the Starbucks parking lot a minute later, well exceeding the posted speed limit the entire time. He'd started to guide her toward the location of Gray's vehicle, which sat one row over, directly in front of Starbucks, when one of the trackers started moving. The second tracker remained in place, which was entirely possible. The GPS trackers were motion activated to conserve batteries and reported their position every fifteen seconds.

If the initial vehicle motion didn't activate them at the same time, a lag occurred. The lag actually worked in the surveillance team's favor if it was long enough. A seven-second lag gave them what appeared to be real-time coverage. A skilled countersurveillance expert like Gray couldn't use the fifteen-second "dark" period to disappear in a covered parking garage or other preplanned evasion route.

"Gray might be on the move," he said.

Rudd scanned the parking area in front of Starbucks, expecting to see a black SUV backing out or driving in the opposite direction. Instead, a silver sedan drove by on the other side of the double row, its movement matching one of the trackers. The other still hadn't moved.

"Shit," he muttered.

"What's wrong?" asked his wife.

"Stop behind that white SUV. I think he gave us the slip."

"How? The tracker is moving, right?" she said.

"One of the trackers is moving, and it just passed us," said Rudd.

He hopped out the moment she stopped and followed the tracker to a parked minivan. The tracking app put the transmitter inside the vehicle. Or under it. He lowered himself to the pavement and searched underneath, spotting the garage remote–size, black rectangular box lying in the middle of the parking space. He pressed his body into the gap between the asphalt and metal chassis, stretching his arm until his fingertips grazed the tracker. After a few more tries, one of them nearly dislocating his shoulder, he retrieved the tracker. He stood up a little too quickly, a sense of light-headedness and vertigo overtaking him.

"You okay?" asked Jolene.

He nodded, leaning against the car parked next to the minivan to keep his balance. An SUV pulled into the empty space on the opposite side of the van, which he surmised had moments before been occupied by the silver sedan. Gray had placed one tracker on the sedan and tossed the other under his own SUV before backing out—carefully so he didn't run it over. He could have put them both on the silver sedan and let the owner of the car lead them around for a while, but that diversion could have ended at an office just down the street.

Instead, he'd split the trackers, keeping one in place in an attempt to convince them he'd found only one. Ten minutes after the silver sedan took off, he could have slapped the other one on any car leaving the strip mall and sent them on a second pursuit. Rudd looked around, wondering if Gray was watching him.

He could have removed the trackers and parked his SUV around the block. For all Rudd knew, he could be sitting in the Starbucks right now, taking pictures of him. *Shit.* He should never have gotten out of the SUV. What had he been thinking? He hadn't, because he was fifty-six years old and getting rusty. While he stood there feeling like an idiot, a woman burst out of Starbucks—headed directly for him. She wore hospital scrubs and carried a purse in one hand and a large to-go cup in the other.

"Excuse me, sir?" she said, slowing as she approached.

"Yes?" he said, feeling stable enough to stand on his own.

"Are you all right? It looked like you took a knee. I work in the ER at Doctors Community Hospital," she said.

"No. I'm fine. Thank you," he said, holding up the tracker—partially concealed. "My garage door opener fell out of our car somehow. We'd parked here about an hour ago, so I figured I'd take a look. Bingo. Except I stood up a little too fast. Got a little woozy."

"Does that happen to you often?" she asked.

"No. Not really," he said.

"Honey. We have to get going!" yelled Jolene. "We're already late."

"Sorry. I have to go," he said. "The boss is calling."

The woman laughed. "Smart man. If that happens again, you should schedule a checkup with your doctor. Could be the start of something more serious. Or maybe nothing at all. Better safe than sorry."

"Absolutely. I appreciate the advice," he said. "Oh. I do have a crazy question if you don't mind. Not medical related."

"Sure," she said.

"How long have you been in this parking space?" asked Rudd.

The woman looked understandably perplexed by his out-of-left-field question, but answered anyway.

"I'd say almost twenty-five minutes," she said, looking at him a little less trustingly than before. "Are you sure you're okay?"

"I'm fine. Thank you," he said before hurrying back to the SUV.

As soon as he shut the car door, Jolene sped away.

"Slow down. We're in no hurry. He's either long gone or he's watching us from somewhere nearby," he said. "Either way, we're done until he resurfaces at his apartment, or CONTROL gets a hit on a credit card."

"He won't use a credit card," said Jolene. "Not this guy."

"Yeah. We may have underestimated him," said Rudd.

"I'm thinking it might be in CONTROL's best interest to take him out sooner than later," said Rudd, checking the time. "Our mobile surveillance lasted a grand total of forty-two minutes, at least twenty-five of them spent sitting in the car watching tracker signals that had already been spoofed. Two of them smiling for countersurveillance photos."

"There's nothing we could have done about that," said Jolene. "Protocol dictated that we check on the target."

"Exactly. And Gray clearly knows this game better than any of us," said Rudd. "If CONTROL considers this guy to be a serious threat, they'd be better off getting rid of him immediately. My gut tells me this guy could disappear without a trace if he wanted to—and still operate right in front of everyone's noses."

CHAPTER 12

Devin guided his SUV around a tight turn on the narrow tree-lined road, hints of water shimmering through the lush branches. He hadn't been out here in a number of years, but knew he was close. A few more ninety-degree twists and he'd catch a glimpse of the marina beyond one of the gravel drives lining the road. A sailboat mast or maybe the blue hull of a boat hauled out for repairs and now living on stands. That was where he should turn. On the unmarked road leading directly to the marina. But Devin decided to take a different approach.

He took the turns slowly, stopping a few times to let oncoming traffic squeeze by. After passing the marina's unmarked gravel entrance, the towering trees opened to reveal a stark blue sky—and a sizable parking lot that marked the end of the road. Cantler's Riverside Inn, a favorite with locals, sat on the far side of the jam-packed lot, nestled right up against Mill Creek. It was the last thing you might expect to find if you had been out for a casual drive through Maryland's back roads.

He cruised around the lot for several minutes until a young couple, holding hands and pecking each other's lips, jumped into an open-top BMW and left him a space. Devin parked the SUV and gave it some time. Ninety minutes, to be precise, sweating through his shirt behind a stand of trees near the entrance to the lot. He had to be absolutely certain that nobody had tracked him here.

Whoever had tagged his vehicle with the two trackers had known what they were doing. He would never have found the transmitters without the aid of an RF detector. The placement was skilled enough to leave him wondering if they had installed a fail-safe. Something that transmitted far less frequently and would likely be missed on a typical electronic sweep. He'd spent an hour and a half at a little speck of a town on the Maryland-Pennsylvania border, testing that theory. Waiting for anything that resembled a surveillance team to drive down Main Street. Nothing suspicious turned up, which didn't entirely surprise him.

The couple that showed outside of Starbucks had looked genuinely concerned about the tracker stunt. The guy almost looked scared. Devin had snapped a few hundred photos of the couple and their vehicle from the third floor of the parking garage on the other side of Baltimore Avenue. A digital camera with telephoto lens was part of his standard countersurveillance kit, among other things, like a handheld RF detector.

He couldn't help but notice that the couple was older. Take away maybe thirty pounds from the red-faced guy who went fishing under the minivan for the tracker, and he'd look no different than either of the guys Devin had faced in the hotel stairwell a week or so ago. He'd revisit that thought later, when he asked Brendan Shea to run the couple's Tennessee license plates. The connection between the Tennessee plates and his mother's death couldn't be a coincidence, but he sensed something else. He just couldn't put his finger on it.

With the hour and a half expired and no bad guys in sight, Devin returned to his SUV and retrieved a small nylon day pack to carry whatever he found on the boat. He took another long look around the lot before making his way to the weathered stockade fence that separated the parking lot from the marina. After slipping through a rickety gate held open by a faded orange traffic cone, he emerged on a stretch of grass intended for marina members. The gate he'd just used appeared to be a convenience that facilitated dinner and drinks after a day on the water.

He spotted a sailboat on stands closer to the water and decided to head in that direction. His assumption was that he'd find *Sadie* on land, unless his mother had taken up boating—a possibility, given how little he appeared to truly know about her. The sailboat turned out to be *Screamin' Mimi*, so he turned his attention to a tightly packed row of three boats tucked away in the farthest corner of the expansive gravel lot. Two sailboats, one without a mast, and a very neglected-looking powerboat with a flying bridge. They were parked bow out, so he couldn't read their names.

He got halfway across the lot before he was accosted. A stringy-haired man dressed in grease-stained khaki pants and an equally grubby white T-shirt emerged from the trees along the waterfront, directly in his path. His weather-beaten face made it impossible to guess his age, but Devin would go with somewhere between forty-five and seventy if he had to estimate. He stood with his hands on his hips as Devin approached, appraising him the whole way.

"Looking for someone?" he said, cordially enough.

"Actually, I'm looking for a boat," said Devin.

"Well. All the boats are over there," he said, canting his head toward the water.

"Thanks. I'm looking for my mother's boat, which I assumed was not in the water," said Devin. "The boat is named *Sadie*?"

"Is that a question or a fact?" said the man.

"The boat name is a fact. I'm asking if it's here," said Devin, starting to get a little annoyed.

"Can I see some identification?"

"Sure," he said, glad he hadn't left his wallet back in the car.

The man, who he assumed to be more than a dockhand at the marina, scrutinized his driver's license, glancing back and forth between the card and his face several times, like an East German border guard. He handed it back with a nod.

"Sorry about all that," he said. "Your mother gave me some specific instructions, and a fair sum to back them up. Her boat is the one without the mast. It's been at the marina awhile."

"When did she buy it?"

85

"Last year, toward the end of the summer," he said. "She's only been up on it twice."

"Do you remember the last time she came by?"

"Yep. Saw her about three weeks ago. She spent about ten minutes on the boat. Paid for the next three years of storage," he said. "I kinda got the feeling she didn't buy it for sailing."

"I just learned about the boat yesterday," said Devin. "She passed away a couple weeks ago."

"Oh. Damn. I'm very sorry to hear that. She seemed like a nice lady."

"Thank you," said Devin. "How do I get up on the boat? They seem so high when they're on those stands."

"I'll get you a ladder and meet you over there."

Paying for three additional years of storage didn't make a ton of sense, but her visiting the boat a few weeks ago appeared to be tied to whatever had happened ten days ago. The man returned a few minutes later with a tall wooden ladder that looked as though it had been constructed during the Revolutionary War. Devin glanced at it skeptically.

"I know. It looks like a relic, but I guarantee this'll be around longer than one of those aluminum contraptions," he said, placing it against the hull. "Just so you know, the boat needs a lot of work to make her seaworthy. Given what your mom paid me in advance for storage, I could get her in the water in time for you to enjoy the tail end of the season. If you're interested."

"I don't know the first thing about boats," said Devin.

"Plenty of folks around here that do," he said. "I have the slip space for her—included in the price."

"How much did my mom pay for storage?"

The guy laughed. "She paid for storage—and discretion. Let me know what you want to do with the boat. No rush. Storage is all paid up for a while. My name's Frank, by the way. I own this fine establishment."

"Thank you, Frank. For your continued discretion," said Devin. "And I'll keep your offer in mind. I never thought of myself as the boating type, but . . . I'll think about it."

"You ever been out on the water?" asked Frank. "On something other than a cruise ship or ferry?"

Devin shook his head. "Nope."

"Then you be sure to come back when you're not busy, and I'll get you out there," said Frank. "You'll know right away if you're the boating type or not—and god help you if you are."

"Why's that?" said Devin.

"Because you'll be mortgaging your house in a few years to buy a bigger boat!"

Devin laughed. He liked this guy. If the file hidden inside the boat turned out to be a bust, he might take him up on the offer. Why the hell not?

"I'll let you know."

"And I'll leave you to your business," said Frank, saluting him before walking away.

Devin wiped the sweat off his forehead and grabbed the ladder with both hands, immediately gaining a sense of what Frank had conveyed about it. The thing felt solid, as though it had been carved from a single piece of wood. Still, he tentatively stepped on the first rung, testing it with a few bounces before pushing up with his full body weight. It was a wooden ladder, after all.

At the top of the ladder, he grabbed the nearest stanchion poles and gave them a tug to make sure they were secure before using them as leverage to climb into the boat. He stood perfectly still in the cockpit, unsure how stable the boat would be with him on board. The metal stands pressed up against the hull looked like a rickety arrangement to hold up an object that easily weighed several thousand pounds.

Sensing no movement, he moved to the salon door and stopped. Nothing. He quickly stepped to the left and right. No movement at all. He could probably jump up and down and nothing would happen, but he had no intention of doing anything but move slowly and steadily through the boat. There was nothing normal or natural about a sailboat suspended in the air.

Devin found the salon door unlocked and slid it open. He was greeted by a stale, mildewy odor that he assumed to be normal for compact space that gets aired out a couple of times a year at most. The interior, a combination of deep-stained wood, light-blue cushions, and white vinyl flooring, was well lit from the sunlight pouring through the long, narrow windows on each side of the salon. The galley was directly below the door, a few steps down a short wooden ladder. Easy enough.

He lowered himself into the galley and opened the lowest of three drawers next to the sink, removing a hefty gray waterproof pouch that took up most of the space in the drawer. Devin sat gently on the edge of the starboard-side couch and unzipped the pouch, placing its contents on the cushion next to him.

A handwritten note signed by his mother. A key chain with three brass house keys. A very high-end touch screen satellite phone. A manila file folder with metal fasteners holding together several typed pages. A little lighter than he expected. Two rubber-banded bundles of cash. Twenties and hundreds. Easily ten thousand dollars, if he had to guess. Much more than he expected. He wasn't encouraged by the fact that the money piled up higher than the file.

He started with the note.

Devin, I have good news and bad news. The good news is that there's more than a hundred dollars in the pouch. You can walk away right now and take a really nice vacation, which might sound like an attractive option after you hear the bad news. Before I get to that, please deliver the mailer to your father. It's a copy of my will, life insurance policy, and assets. Along with my estate attorney's contact information.

What's the bad news? I'm dead. Sorry. I couldn't resist. Ye olde gallows humor. Had to get one last joke in. The bad news is that the file in your hands is just the 30,000-foot view. You've probably guessed that much by the size of the file. There's simply no way to adequately explain or represent what I've assembled over the past two decades. I apologize for misrepresenting the size of Sadie's treasure, but I couldn't take the chance that you might not take the SDR seriously—and lead them to the source. Go ahead. Roll your eyes. But read the file and consider taking one more step in this journey, assuming you took the SDR seriously. Please don't execute the next paragraph if you're not entirely sure they didn't follow you. Did they try?

The next step, if you choose: Power the satellite phone. I inserted a fully charged battery a few weeks ago. Find "Mom" in contacts and give me a call. I'll reveal the location of the Bat Cave. I actually have one, if you consider a dingy apartment in a sketchy neighborhood a proper secret lair. There's beer in the fridge and harder stuff if you need it . . . you might after you see what I've been working on. Help me, Obi-Wan Kenobi. You're my only hope.

Love you, Mom

"Love you, too," he said, his eyes watering.

PS: Ask Frank about my car. I highly suggest you swap vehicles.

PPS: Don't skip out on lunch at Cantler's. A friend of mine may join you. You can trust him.

So . . . now what? Continue the quest? An untraceable car would definitely make things a little easier, but he wasn't sure about meeting with anybody until he got a better handle on what his mother suspected she had uncovered. Then again, what did he have to lose? He could always walk away from whoever showed up.

"Why the hell not?" he muttered, stuffing the file and the pouch into his backpack.

On his way back to the Cantler's parking lot, he spotted Frank near the marina's boat ramp, where he'd just hauled what looked like a mini sailboat out of the water. Two middle school–age kids wearing orange life jackets helped him drag it onto a small trailer. Devin headed in their direction. When Frank saw him, he patted one of the kids on the shoulder and told them he'd finish securing the boat. They headed for the dock, where he assumed a much larger boat and eager-to-please parents awaited them.

"Now that looks more my speed," said Devin.

Frank laughed. "We'll have to start you with something a little bigger if you plan on fixing up your boat. How did it look?"

"You really think you could fix her up by the end of the summer?"

Frank's smile widened. "Definitely before Labor Day weekend, which gives you a good month on the water and plenty of time to learn how to sail—or find a girlfriend that knows."

"And those are easy to find?" said Devin. "The girlfriend. Not the sailing lessons."

"A lot easier when you have a boat," said Frank. "What do you say? Want me to fix her up?"

He wasn't paying for it, so he responded with his new motto.

"Why the hell not?"

"You won't regret it. She's a thirty-foot Catalina. A reliable cruising boat," said Frank. "Not that easy to find, either, so you could always sell her if it doesn't work out for you."

"Easy enough," said Devin. "There's one more thing. My mom said I should ask you about her car, but she didn't leave any keys, and I forgot to look on the boat."

"Your mom keeps an old Honda Accord up by the main road entrance. She's never used it as far as I know," said Frank. "She left me a key to start it up every month or so to keep the battery charged. I can run up to the house and grab the key."

"That would be great. Also, would you mind if I left my SUV in its place for a little while?"

"Not at all. All I ask is that you come and go during marina business hours. Seven in the morning to ten at night."

"Works for me," said Devin.

He returned to the packed parking lot and studied the cars before approaching the waterfront side of the restaurant. Devin was mostly looking for anyone hiding in their vehicles—the obvious giveaways on this sunny, hot day being rolled-down windows or running engines. By the time he reached the restaurant entrance, Devin felt confident that the parking lot was clear. A blast of air-conditioned air washed over him when he opened the door to the bar and main dining area, where a young woman greeted him from the adjacent hostess stand.

"How many in your party?"

"One," said Devin. "Possibly two?"

"It's about an hour wait for a table," she said. "Or you can try and squeeze into the bar."

He glanced toward the packed bar area, not thrilled with the idea of reading his mother's file seated shoulder to shoulder among a boisterous crowd. Nor did he relish the thought of cracking open a dozen freshly steamed crabs under cramped conditions. He studied the faces for a moment, neither seeing anyone he recognized nor receiving a knowing glance that might indicate his mother's friend was here. Devin could study the file outside while he waited for a table, then enjoy the leisurely meal his mother had promised. Maybe by then her friend would have arrived.

"I'll put my name down for a table," said Devin.

"Sure. What's the name?"

"Devin."

"You don't happen to be Devin Gray, do you?" she asked.

"That's me," he said.

"Perfect. I have a table waiting for you," she said. "Your friend's been here about an hour and a half. I seated him ten minutes ago."

He followed her into the bar area to a bank of three pub tables, tucked away next to the windows facing the parking lot. The tables hadn't been visible from the hostess stand. Karl Berg sat at the farthest table, shaking his head and smiling. Devin wasn't surprised to see Berg here.

"I'll send someone over with menus," she said.

"That would be great. Thank you," said Devin.

Berg offered a hand, which Devin reluctantly shook before removing his backpack and sitting down. The man looked exhausted, his eyes red and watery behind a pair of black-rimmed glasses.

"You look like you drove through the night to get here," said Devin.

"I did. I received the oddest message last night around nine thirty," said Berg. "Thirty minutes later, I was headed to Annapolis. I assume you received a similar message?"

"*Odd* doesn't even begin to describe having your dead mother send you on a treasure hunt," said Devin. "How did she convince you to drive all night to be here?"

"She told me—well, her voice told me—that if I showed up at Cantler's at one in the afternoon, *you* would explain everything," said Berg. "She didn't specify what everything meant."

Devin suddenly felt guarded about the file and the phone in his backpack. He'd never met Karl Berg before his mother's wake. For all he knew, Berg could be connected to the people who had tried to follow him this morning. But that would mean he'd somehow managed to track Devin to the marina, arrive unobserved, and preemptively grab a table in the hopes of Devin stopping for lunch. No. Berg was brought here by his mother for a reason.

"By everything, I think she meant her conspiracy theory," said Devin. "And its connection to her death."

"I'm all ears," said Berg.

"I don't know any more than I did when we last spoke," said Devin, testing the waters.

Berg pushed his glasses back and squinted. "Seriously? She just put us together in a crab shack to see what might happen? Helen had to have told you something."

"I think she intended for us to take a trip together," said Devin. "She apparently has a Bat Cave. A secret apartment or something. My guess is it contains whatever research she'd conducted over the years."

"And you know how to find it?" said Berg.

"I can access the location," said Devin, leaving out the part about the file for now.

"I don't know what to say, Devin. Your mom became obsessed with her idea," said Berg. "I guess it really doesn't surprise me to hear that she had acquired a safe house to work on this. She would have been paranoid about secrecy, convinced they were following her so they could finally erase the evidence and eliminate her."

"Who?"

"It doesn't matter," said Berg, dismissively. "It's all a fantasy. She probably conducted long SDRs prior to arriving at her secret lair, re-creating the most intense parts of the work she'd done for the agency—years ago. Let me guess: She led you on some kind of decode-the-next-step journey to find the apartment?"

"It doesn't matter how I ended up here," said Devin.

"She did, didn't she?"

"For good reason. I removed two GPS trackers from my car this morning before starting the first SDR."

"Interesting," said Berg, finally sounding genuinely intrigued.

"I also took pictures of the team that placed the trackers."

"You made the surveillance team that quickly?" asked Berg. "Were they wearing black trench coats and pointing telephoto cameras at you?"

"Funny. No. The tracker placement was professional, and they had good reason to break cover. I more or less forced their hand," said Devin. "I do this for a living, remember?"

"Yes. I remember," said Berg. "Could it have been the FBI, local police, or some other federal agency?"

"I don't think so. The trackers were high end, but still the kind of stuff you can buy off the shelf. Definitely not the kind of gear we used in the FBI."

"How did you locate the trackers?" asked Berg.

"Radio frequency detector," said Devin.

"How long did you spend on the tracker sweep?"

"Not long enough to detect something that transmits infrequently, but I eliminated that possibility later," said Devin. "Helen's decode-the-next-step journey included a vehicle swap, a high-end, untraceable satellite phone, and about ten thousand dollars in cash. She'd obviously put a lot of thought into how to get me here undetected, and she took a number of these steps as recently as three weeks ago."

"She must have gotten mixed up with some bad people while chasing down this thing," said Berg. "Maybe she pissed off the Russian mob? I could see her getting desperate enough to go after them for information. Possibly staking them out. Now that I think about it, this whole thing kind of makes sense. If she'd put herself on Solntsevskaya Bratva's radar by pissing them off, it wouldn't take much for them to pull the trigger on her. Sorry to be blunt."

Devin shook his head. His mother's death wasn't a Russian mob hit. The people following him this morning didn't fit that profile.

"How much did Helen tell you about her theory?" asked Devin.

"Hold on," said Berg, nodding in the direction of an approaching waitress.

They ordered beers and a dozen crabs each, Berg continuing when the waitress was out of earshot.

"Helen was pretty guarded about what she'd tell me. I got the impression through some of the things she'd said that she was trying to protect me from ruining my career," said Berg. "She gave me just enough to test the waters. Enough to keep the channel of communication open."

"What did my mother think she'd uncovered?" said Devin. "I won't repeat any of this. I promise."

Berg looked torn.

"You didn't hear this from me. Understood? This is all still classified, as far as I know."

"Understood," said Devin.

"An operation she'd conducted had revealed the names of five sleepers."

"Russians?"

"Apparently. Two couples and—Donald Wilson," said Berg.

"Jesus," said Devin.

"Here's the thing. Technically the agency only knew about the two couples. Helen had only shared Donald Wilson's name with me, and I've never repeated it at Langley."

"Why would she do that?" said Devin.

"The FBI and CIA investigated the couples thoroughly. They turned out to be retired and living on pensions. Dead ends. None of them even remotely linked by work or social circle to the government or companies that contracted with the government. They were classified as low to no risk to national security and put on a travel watch list. Don't get me wrong. They were 'illegals,' as far as we could tell. Cold War relics based on their ages. Sleepers in the truest sense of the word. But everyone agreed that hauling them in for interrogation or deportation would alert the Russians and possibly create some kind of ripple effect that would undermine ongoing espionage investigations. The FBI was working Operation Ghost Stories at the time. Did you ever work on that one?"

"I had just finished training and reported to the Special Surveillance Group when they made the arrests," said Devin.

"The FBI's decision to back off the identified sleepers made more sense in light of those arrests. They took down ten active spies with Operation Ghost Stories, some who were making dangerous inroads within the Beltway—instead of busting a few retired schoolteachers and steelworkers," said Berg. "Helen had guessed as much and withheld Wilson's name. She never said why, but she felt there was more to Wilson than the others. One name consumed her for two decades."

Devin opened his backpack and removed the file his mother had put together.

"My mother says this is an executive summary of her conspiracy," said Devin, placing it on the table.

Berg looked extremely uncomfortable in the file's presence. As though its contents might be radioactive.

"Have you looked at it?" asked Berg.

"No," said Devin, pushing it toward Berg. "You first. I want your opinion before I read it."

Berg took the file and opened it, just before two sweating bottles of ice-cold beer arrived. Less than a minute later, he closed it and pushed it back across the table—his face impassive.

"You didn't finish it," said Devin.

Berg took a long swig from his bottle before answering. "I've seen enough to warrant a visit to the Bat Cave."

"That's it?" said Devin. "What did it say?"

Berg shook his head. "You need to read it yourself. Then we need to take our lunch to go. We may not be safe here."

Devin opened the file and started reading. By the time he finished skimming his mother's summary, he wondered if he shouldn't go back and tell Frank to hold off on refurbishing the boat. If any of what his mother had written turned out to be true, he didn't foresee a lot of time in his immediate future for sailing lessons. For the first time ever, he actually hoped his mom had been crazy, because if she had been sane all along, the United States of America had one hell of a problem on its hands. The kind of problem that could dramatically and permanently alter the course of the nation's trajectory—in the wrong direction.

CHAPTER 13

Devin's mother hadn't been kidding when she'd written "sketchy neighborhood." After conducting an abbreviated surveillance-detection route, which took them over the Chesapeake Bay Bridge and up through the back roads of eastern Maryland, he'd approached Baltimore from the northeast along US Route 40. He knew they were in for a treat when they got off the Route 40 bypass at Federal Street. The area started out fine but got progressively worse as he navigated the mile and a half west to the provided address.

Boarded-up windows and doors. Knee-high weeds growing through the cracked sidewalks. Corner convenience stores with faded signs—no real indication whether they were open or closed for business. Men huddled on stubby concrete stoops, eyeing him warily as he drove. The words **No Shoot Zone** spray-painted on the sides of buildings or larger pieces of plyboard.

The number of abandoned buildings and commercial structures increased the farther west he drove, until he reached a one-block section that looked as though it had been scheduled for demolition. The block ended at a tall stone wall topped with cyclone fencing and barbed wire. A sturdy barrier designed to keep troublemakers out of the Green Mount Cemetery, which lay on the other side. He turned left on the street next to the wall and followed it south until he could bypass the cemetery.

Greenmount West, a neighborhood on the other side of the cemetery, looked like a different world than what he could only assume had been Greenmount East. Still sketchy as hell in his opinion, but not a quasi-demilitarized zone. If he had to guess, he'd say this part of town was in the throes of gentrification. A chic coffee shop and a massive, new-ish-looking four-story apartment complex gave it away, even if every street-level apartment window was covered with tasteful stainless-steel grating.

Devin drove north along the western cemetery wall, the three-story row house–style apartment buildings to his left looking either well maintained or upgraded. Gentrification defined. He passed a second modern apartment complex before taking a left onto East Lafayette Avenue, where his mother had kept a secret residence since 2010. Upon turning, he immediately spied several brightly colored, full-building-fa-cade street art mosaics. Devin presumed the neighborhood had looked significantly different twelve years ago. A lot more like the neighbor-hood due east of the cemetery.

He pulled up to the address and stopped to scan the street. East Lafayette Avenue was a one-way with cars tightly lining both sides. No boarded-up windows. Nobody milling around porches. About a quarter of the street-level windows were protected by some variation of steel burglar bars. A lot of new or restored three-story redbrick facades—his mother's building not included. She must have missed the restoration memo or decided to ignore it. His money was on the latter.

The bricks had been painted a light gray, which was chipped or faded in several spots. The look hovered between intentionally weath-ered or recently neglected. Three mailboxes, squeezed together ver-tically, adorned the wall to the left of the white door. A rust streak stretched several bricks below the lowest mailbox. Not the darkest of stains, but on its way to being an eyesore. His mom also didn't share the same gentrified optimism about crime. The street-level windows featured decorative, but very sturdy-looking, black wrought iron gates.

Devin drove halfway down the block before finding a parking space, barely managing to squeeze the older-model sedan between two oversize luxury SUVs. He wondered what one of these apartments was worth now. His mother had probably bought here because it was cheap, and nobody would think to look for her in this neighborhood. She was most likely sitting on a tidy profit at this point. Or someone was sitting on it. Hopefully his sister.

Kari shared a place with two other social workers from her office—the only way any of them could afford housing within semireasonable commuting distance to work. It was only fair. He got the boat. She got to sell the apartment. Devin was getting ahead of himself. For all he knew, all this was going to his father, the most logical destination.

Devin and Berg got out of the car, both of them taking a long look up and down the street.

"What do you think?" asked Berg.

"Looks clear," said Devin, and Berg nodded. Nothing.

Devin hadn't expected anything. Even if his pursuers had managed to track either him or Berg to the Cantler's parking lot, they most certainly didn't follow him here. He'd made sure of that with his trip through the countryside. The SDR had been solid, and the car was untraceable to Helen, as far as Devin could tell. He couldn't find the registration anywhere in the car and assumed she'd bought it in a private transaction, keeping it off the books.

The license plate renewal sticker reflected the current year, which led him to believe his mother had a junker in storage somewhere and kept its registration current for the express purpose of getting an updated renewal sticker. As long as he didn't give the police a reason to run these plates, they should be fine.

He removed a black nylon duffel bag, containing the countersurveillance kit and his mother's waterproof pouch, from the trunk and locked the car before heading to the apartment. Devin caught some movement through the ground-floor apartment windows as they approached the stoop. Berg must have noticed it, too.

"My name's Fred," said Berg. "For their safety and ours."

"Fred doesn't sound suspicious at all."

When he got to the door, he started trying the keys, while Berg watched the street for signs of trouble. The keys hadn't been marked, so he had no idea which one went to which door. The first one didn't fit. Neither did the second. The door opened before he tried the third, startling him enough that he dropped the key chain. An elderly Black woman with white hair appeared in the open doorway. She looked around eighty years old, but stood like she was in her early fifties.

"Oh my god. I didn't mean to scare you," she said.

Devin scooped up the keys. "Just caught me off guard, ma'am."

"You must be Helen's boy, Devin," she said, glancing between him and Berg.

"I am," said Devin, giving her a puzzled look. "This is Fred. A friend of the family."

"I'm Henrietta Silver. I live on the first floor with my son and daughter-in-law. My granddaughter lives on the second floor with my great-grandson, who's at Johns Hopkins on a full scholarship. Pre-med," she said.

"Must be a sharp young man," he said. "I didn't even bother applying to Hopkins. I considered myself lucky to get into Maryland."

"He is a very sharp young man," said Henrietta, smiling warmly. "You look just like your mother. Sound like her, too."

He swallowed hard and nodded, worried that his voice would crack if he answered. He wasn't able to hide the tears.

Henrietta's smile faded into a mournful, sympathetic look. "I assume something happened to your Helen?"

"She passed away about a week ago," said Devin. "Unexpectedly."

"I'm so sorry, honey," she said, giving him a hug and holding on to him. "She was a kind woman. A bit of a mystery, but warmhearted. I could tell. And she talked about you and Kari all the time. Helen loved the two of you. She never explained her situation or what she was doing here, but I got the feeling over the years that she'd want me to tell you that."

"Thank you. That means a lot to me," said Devin. "Things kind of got away from all of us."

"It happens," she said. "Sometimes there's nothing we can do about it. Trust me, I know."

"Are you headed out?" he asked.

"No. No. I saw you stop in your car and recognized you immediately. Got my old bones up to say hello," she said.

"I'm glad you did," said Devin. "It was a pleasure meeting you."

"Likewise," she said before moving out of his way.

They stepped inside, and Devin shut the door behind them, checking for a dead bolt or some way to make sure it was locked.

"It self-locks. You need to use the key every time when entering," she said. "But if you lock yourself out, just wave through the window. One of us is almost always in the living room."

"I will. Thank you," he said before heading for the staircase.

"Oh, uh . . . Devin?"

He stopped at the foot of the stairs. "Yes?"

"Will we, uh . . . see you around much?" she asked.

"I can't say," he said, which was the truth.

He had no idea what he'd find up there.

"Well. I hope we see you around," she said, opening her apartment door.

Devin nodded. "Okay. See you later."

"It was a pleasure meeting you," said Berg.

Henrietta smiled as she went back inside her apartment and gently closed the door.

Devin reached the third floor, with Berg following closely behind, and made his way to the only door in the hallway, which had no doorknob. Just a dead bolt. Henrietta and her family must have thought that was more than a little bit odd. He glanced around the hallway, unable to locate the camera he assumed was recording him. Security seemed a little light for something supposedly this important. Then again, looks could be deceiving.

It took him two tries to select the right key to turn what felt like a heavy-duty dead bolt. Without a doorknob, he wasn't entirely sure what to do next, other than push his way in—which turned out to be the right answer. When the heavy metal slab swung inward, he quickly entered and located the framed print of Van Gogh's *Starry Night* in the empty family room, tilting its left corner upward to reveal a basic alarm pad set into the wall.

His mother wasn't kidding about the tight timeline. The display read six seconds—and counting. He pressed the pound sign, followed by the four-digit code she had provided in the phone message he had accessed by speed-dialing "Mom" on the satellite phone. She'd briefly walked him through the entire apartment process in that message. With the alarm system deactivated and Berg inside, Devin shut the door and threw the dead bolt. The door was solid enough, but not what he had expected from a security standpoint.

A quick look around explained why. The space contained nothing but a small wooden table and two mismatched kitchen chairs. This meant one thing. Whatever lay behind the next door would be epic. The question was, In what way? Epically critical to national security as she claimed or epically fucking crazy—and there was only one way to find out.

"I'm guessing she didn't spend much time in this room," said Berg.

"Probably a safe bet," said Devin before wandering into the kitchen. "Take a look at this."

Berg followed him to a hallway off the kitchen, which turned out to be more of a vestibule. A sturdy-looking door stood at the end of the stunted corridor, featuring a dead bolt, a regular keyless doorknob, and a touch pad embedded in the wall next to the doorframe.

"That looks promising," said Berg.

Devin pulled the satellite phone from one of the duffel bag's outer pockets and checked the last number he'd dialed. Exhausted from ten sleepless nights, he didn't trust his memory at this point. He'd inputted the eight-digit code and pressed send so it would appear in his recent calls for easy retrieval.

Devin tapped the screen, activating the digital touch pad. He entered the code and pressed the green SUBMIT icon. A mechanical whirring in the wall behind the touch pad started a moment later, followed by a solid thunk closer to the door. Some kind of power-driven locking mechanism. No wonder she hadn't invested much in the front door. The screen read OPEN DEAD BOLT, so he took the next step toward the big reveal and dug the keys out of his pocket.

A full minute later—the door wide open—Devin remained in the doorway, still trying to process what he was seeing. Mostly, he was afraid to step inside and get sucked into whatever had so entirely consumed his mother. Helen Gray had renovated the place, spending her available funds on her obsession, instead of the public-facing neighborhood gentrification effort.

All the interior walls had been removed and replaced by a dispersed pattern of cylindrical metal supports, initially giving the space an open feel. The complete absence of windows closed it right back up. If he'd blacked out and woken up in this room, he'd guess it was a basement.

The left wall, extending about twenty-five feet from front to back, consisted of floor-to-ceiling bookshelves. From what he could tell, the shelves housed numbered binders. Several hundred if he had to guess. The rear wall, about twelve feet wide, featured a sizable wall-mounted flat-screen television. A recliner and an end table with a lamp sat in front of the television. A short length of string hung down from a square attic door directly above the recliner.

The only other pieces of furniture were a simple black writing desk and chair in the center of the space, facing right—toward the room's pièce de résistance. A floor-to-ceiling, front-to-back "conspiracy wall," complete with red strings going in every direction, photographs, headshots, maps, Post-it notes, and newspaper clippings.

The difference between this wall and every wall he'd seen at the FBI or in the movies was that Helen's wall was meticulously organized. She hadn't continually tacked items to the wall as they developed, building a shantytown of information. She'd obviously rebuilt this wall dozens, if not hundreds, of times.

"Are you going in?" said Berg.

"I don't know," whispered Devin.

The effort that had gone into this project was mind-boggling. The very least he could do was give this a chance. Still, he couldn't bring himself to enter the room.

"Do you mind if I take a look?"

Devin shook his head and made space for him to squeeze by. Berg walked the length of the conspiracy wall, pausing a few times to stare at the displayed information. When he'd reached the end, he turned and crossed the room, taking in the wall of binders.

"What are we looking at?" asked Devin.

"On the surface, it appears that your mother uncovered an extensive network of Russian sleeper agents," said Berg. "Far more extensive than anything we've ever suspected—assuming this isn't some kind of elaborate delusion sprinkled with magical conspiracy theory dust. It's going to take some time to sort this out and draw our own conclusions."

"Where do we even start?" asked Devin. "How do we begin to make sense of this?"

Berg walked over to the desk and examined a yellow legal pad that sat next to a closed laptop. Tight handwriting covered the top sheet.

"True to form, your mother left instructions," said Berg, tapping the notepad.

She'd apparently thought of everything, which meant she clearly had understood that she might not come back from whatever she had set out to accomplish by kidnapping Donald Wilson. In other words, Helen Gray had convinced herself that what she had discovered was worth dying for. He stepped inside the room—well aware that the wall could swallow him just the same.

CHAPTER 14

Harvey Rudd moved the curtain a few inches away from the wall and studied Gray's apartment through a night vision scope. Darkness. Same as the past several hours—confirmed by a continuous recording made by the tripod-mounted camera in the bedroom. He checked his watch: 3:34 a.m. It was pretty obvious that he wasn't coming back tonight. Either the discovery of the trackers had spooked him enough to keep him away for a little while or he'd met with someone, after tossing the trackers, who convinced him to go dark. Neither scenario boded well for the Rudds' retirement plans.

The next step was to contact CONTROL and let them know that Devin Gray had significantly deviated from the pattern. He'd already made them aware of the tracking device incident, which they'd thankfully dismissed as expected. An encouraging sign that Rudd and the team had been right about CONTROL having low expectations about the surveillance effort. It was time to take the gloves off.

His phone rang, its screen softly illuminating the darkened room, his face, and the ridiculously thin curtain next to him. If Gray was watching from somewhere, it would have drawn his attention. Maybe he really was getting too old for this shit. Turning off your phone or at least flipping it facedown at night on a stakeout was basic procedure. He swiped the phone off the coffee table in front of him and answered the call.

"Yes, my love?"

"Anything?" asked Jolene.

"No. I was about to send an update up the chain," said Rudd.

"Maybe give it a few more hours?" she said. "Even if he's up to no good, which is pretty much guaranteed, there's a good chance he'll show up in the morning to grab some personal items. We've seen that before."

"That's why I want to update CONTROL," said Rudd. "If he very unwisely shows up tomorrow, which is unlikely given the circumstances, it could very well be the last time anyone sees him. CONTROL might want us to pop him if we get the chance, and I don't feel like jumping through hoops at the last second. I'd like the green light now, if that's where this is headed. We can get set up and do it right in the parking lot—or inside his apartment."

"Don't tease me," she said. "I can picture it now."

"Well. Like I said, he'd be crazy to show up, unless he just got spooked and decided to stay away for a night or two. We don't have anyone watching his father's place, or his work. He could be crashed out in his office or on a couch in Falls Church."

"I doubt he's anywhere obvious," said Jolene.

"I agree. It's wishful thinking," said Rudd, taking another peek at Gray's dark apartment. "I'm going to put together a message. See what they say."

"All right. Let me know their response. I won't be able to sleep until I know," she said. "I hate loose ends."

"Hopefully CONTROL will let us tie this one up," he said. "Love you."

"Love you, too."

He ended the call and took his laptop to the dining room table, away from the sliding glass door and its virtually transparent curtain. After negotiating the security protocols to access the dark web website designed exclusively for communicating with CONTROL, he typed CHATBOX followed by his username in the single text field on the home page. His cell phone buzzed a moment later, a text appearing with a twenty-digit alphanumeric code, which he typed in the now-empty text field. A rudimentary chat box opened, and he typed a quick update.

Despite his eagerness to speed up what he thought to be the inevitable with Devin Gray, he never made any assumptions or recommendations when communicating directly with CONTROL. He reported the facts and answered with facts. The group running the show on the other end of this gave the orders based on Rudd's reporting and information available from dozens of other sources that he'd likely never be made aware of.

HR (Harvey Rudd): Subject hasn't returned.

Several seconds elapsed before a response appeared.

CL (CONTROL): Sending mission addendum by 7 AM your time. Synopsis follows. Discontinuing mobile surveillance of DG. Focusing on likely personal contacts in area. Priority remains discovering possible secondary HG location.

HR: Copy. Will adjust and execute.

The chat box disappeared, leaving him with the generic home page and text box. He shut the computer down and called his wife with the update. She answered before he heard the first ring.

"That was fast," she said.

"I think they had already decided," said Rudd. "Sounds like we'll be following the father and a few other people they picked out as possible personal contacts. And we're still looking for this supposed hideout."

"Sounds exciting," she said.

"A real barn burner," said Rudd. "Go to bed. We'll get the details in the morning and figure out what that means for us in terms of splitting everyone up."

"Did they say how many folks we'd be watching?"

"No. But they did say no more mobile surveillance of this guy, so it sounds like we'll still keep someone here to watch over the apartment," he said. "Let's hope it's no more than four, or you and I will have to go our separate ways for a while."

"This is turning into a real turkey of a job," she said.

"If by *turkey* you mean low key and low risk, I'm not complaining," said Rudd. "I don't need to go all *Mission: Impossible* on my last job to feel fulfilled. Sitting in a car and staring through a pair of binoculars sounds like a perfect send-off."

"I guess," she said, clearly disappointed.

"Keep your chin up," said Rudd. "They didn't take popping him off the table."

"Well. There's that. See you in a few hours."

"Love you."

"Love you, too," she said.

Rudd had meant what he'd said about not complaining. Something gave him the sense that this whole mission could escalate at the drop of a hat. Like the situation with Helen Gray. Dave Bender probably never knew what hit him. She'd lit him up before any of them could react.

Devin Gray didn't strike him as the instantly lethal type, but as the old saying goes, the apple doesn't fall far from the tree—and he'd like to stay as far away from that family tree as possible this close to retirement.

CHAPTER 15

Devin massaged his chin, his fingers pushing through the thick stubble. Morning had finally arrived, the first vestiges of light appearing through the gaps in the living room curtains visible from his seat at the desk. They'd been up all night studying "the wall," both of them feeling like they had barely scratched the surface. Helen's binders were extensive, representing hundreds of hours of reading and study. Working continuously from the moment they stepped up to the wall until now, they'd only pulled about a tenth of the folders from "the library," mostly skimming each folder's contents for the context necessary to track his mother's logic chain.

Devin had followed her story from start to finish, admittedly skimming the files instead of scrutinizing them, and it all made perfect sense.

Based on the service background file she'd left behind, she had worked as a specialized skills officer, serving in an on-demand capacity as an NOC (nonofficial cover) throughout Europe, Russia, and Russia's former satellite nations. She spoke fluent Russian and German, and had earned a master's degree in international relations at Boston University. The CIA apparently hadn't wanted to potentially burn her identity by formally sending her abroad under official cover at an embassy. She'd been productive over the years as an NOC, often traveling behind the Iron Curtain to support intelligence operations that required an outside touch.

Helen Gray's skill and success in this specialized role put her in Saint Petersburg during the spring of 2003. A fateful assignment that would end two decades later with the kidnapping and murder of Donald Wilson, the point-blank killing of an off-duty sheriff's deputy, and her own suicide.

Wilson's name had been the third name provided to her by Sergei Kozlov, the retired GRU general she had been sent to meet in Saint Petersburg, during the spring of 2003. Brian Kelley had been the first. A *"puzzling hors d'oeuvre"* meant to whet the CIA's appetite—his mom had a way with words. The FBI hadn't been able to find a trace of him or his wife, Kathleen, in the United States prior to 1974.

The Kelleys had materialized in northwest Indiana during the spring of that year, when Brian took a job at one of the sprawling steel mills in the region—a job he held until his retirement in the late nineties. Kathleen had split her time between substitute teaching and staying home with their two children.

If the Kelleys were sleeper agents, as Sergei Kozlov had implied, they hadn't done any obvious damage to United States national security from their blue-collar enclave in northwest Indiana. From what the FBI could initially determine, the family rarely traveled outside the state. The Kelleys appeared to have spent most of their leisure time and money on a no-frills pontoon boat they'd kept at a nearby marina on Lake Michigan.

Not exactly a social circle that implied a productive espionage career for the couple. That said, intelligence gathered from defectors during the Cold War heydays strongly suggested that some Soviet sleepers served purposes beyond espionage. Targeted sabotage and discreet assassination topping their list of potential assignments. Even more troubling, these "deep sleepers" typically remained completely inactive until called on to execute their grim tasks.

Possible confirmation of a long-dormant network of saboteurs and killers in the US scared the hell out of CIA leadership. Unfortunately, the results of a more thorough investigation into the Kelleys would take months. Time the CIA didn't feel they'd had with Kozlov. The agency had dispatched Helen to meet him again, with instructions to demand a more compelling sample of what he hoped to trade for an exceptionally comfortable and secure life in the United States.

Her recall of the meeting was uncanny. She'd apparently sensed something was wrong the moment Kozlov arrived at the Saint Petersburg Botanical Garden. He had appeared agitated and nervous upon arrival, glancing over his shoulder a number of times and snapping at the clerk while he'd purchased a ticket for a guided tour of the garden's greenhouses. A stark difference from the stoic, unreadable GRU general she'd met a few weeks earlier.

He'd seemed to settle down once the tour started, the two of them keeping their distance and pretending to care about exotic plants for the hour or so it took the agency support team to give their meeting the green light. Deep inside the sprawling, densely wooded grounds south of the greenhouse complex, the two of them had sat for several minutes in the shade of a towering oak tree, on a small wrought iron bench facing a lily pad–covered pond.

He'd given her the name and address of Denise Holman, suggesting they study the similarities between Holman and Kelley. When she'd pressed him to explain the connection, he'd just stared at the pond for an uncomfortably long period of time—ultimately rejecting her demand. Kozlov had said the CIA needed to identify the pattern and draw the right conclusion on their own.

No more than thirty minutes after Kozlov had given her the second name and walked away, he'd been crushed under a trolley bus on Bolshoy Prospekt, less than a quarter mile from the entrance to the gardens. Helen had been scooped off the street moments later by one of the CIA countersurveillance teams watching over her, and driven straight to Pulkovo Airport, where she had been rushed on board a waiting Gulfstream jet. Barely an hour and a half later, a small convoy of armored SUVs had driven her onto the US embassy compound in Stockholm.

Kozlov's words had haunted Helen. The pattern she'd ultimately deciphered was chilling, but it had taken her a number of years to figure it out.

The agency had kept her at the embassy for close to a week. The Langley team flew in the day of her arrival and dissected the time she had spent with Kozlov. Second by second. Word by word. Memory by memory. By day three, the team's questioning had started to feel more like an interrogation than a debriefing to her. By the time they had wrapped up, she'd wished the Saint Petersburg fiasco had never happened. From what she'd gathered, so had the rest of the CIA officers involved in the operation. Preliminary investigative reporting on the Holmans hadn't looked promising.

Denise Holman and her husband had fit the same profile as the Kelleys. Another possible sleeper team—collecting public pensions and living nowhere close to an obvious espionage target. Retired teachers who had spent the better part of the past three decades working, raising kids, and putting them through college, all while carving out a nice life for themselves in a middle-class suburb of Minneapolis. The once-frightening specter of a potentially devastating sleeper network on US soil was starting to look more and more like an unconnected collection of unused, retired agents.

It hadn't taken long for the skeptics at Langley to start suggesting Kozlov had played the agency. That the GRU general had tried to pass off retired or deactivated sleepers in exchange for a cushy retirement in the United States. Unlike many of his high-ranking GRU colleagues, Kozlov hadn't leveraged his position within the still-feared and influential intelligence agency to amass a personal fortune during the rush to privatize the Russian economy.

He'd kept plugging along in the role of the loyal general until his retirement, long after the new oligarch class had risen from the dust and stolen the last of the privatized shares from the people. From what the CIA could gather, Kozlov had little to show for his devoted service beyond a modest government pension, a two-bedroom apartment in a drab low-rise beyond the Third Ring Road, and a tiny, run-down dacha on the outskirts of Moscow. They'd speculated that bitterness and jealousy had pushed Kozlov into an inconsequential betrayal of his country.

Helen Gray hadn't entirely agreed with the agency's assessment of the retired general's motivations, but it hadn't made a difference what she thought. Kozlov had been a dead end, along with the names he had provided. Despite the puzzling Cold War enigma surrounding the Kelleys' and Holmans' seemingly unexciting three-decades-long stint in the United States, nobody had wanted to put any more serious time or resources into the matter—including Helen.

Until she'd discovered a folded index card in the front pocket of the bomber jacket she had worn to the botanical garden in Saint Petersburg, accompanied by a note.

Fairly sure I won't be around for a third meeting. Consider this a parting gift. Don't let them waste it. Donald Wilson. Springdale, AR. The glue that holds the others together. Sergei Kozlov.

Kozlov couldn't have put the card into her pocket. The two of them had never come within three feet of each other at any moment during that afternoon. He must have directed someone else to do it after she'd left the garden. A real street pro, because neither Helen nor the surveillance team watching her had detected it. Kozlov must have suspected that the GRU was onto him. There was no other way to explain the card and the note.

But had he triggered its delivery after leaving the garden, or had it been his plan to give it to her all along? Had he committed suicide to keep the revealed names a secret from the GRU, or had he been murdered? Questions that would never be answered. Answers that didn't really matter. The only meaningful question that remained to be asked was, What should she do with the third name?

The obvious answer was to hand it over to her superiors at the agency, but Kozlov had covertly given it to her for a reason—along with a warning. *Don't let them waste it.* She'd understood what he had meant, which was why she hadn't turned over the name immediately upon her return to Langley. The agency had effectively closed the Kozlov file. They'd either deep-six the name with the rest of the file or hand it off to the FBI with a nonurgent request for a background investigation, where it would meet a similar fate.

General Kozlov had given her the third name, knowing his time had run out. He had ultimately decided that passing her the note card had been more important than taking Donald Wilson's name to the grave. She'd looked into Wilson on her own, ultimately ending up in the same place as Kozlov. Dead by her own hand instead of revealing what she'd discovered: a widespread, multitiered sleeper network— unlike anything the FBI or CIA had ever caught wind of.

His mother had identified seventy additional sleeper couples that fit the same profile as the Kelleys, Holmans, and Wilsons. Materialized out of thin air in the early seventies. Regular jobs. Nothing that would require a background check beyond running a basic police report. More than half of them had made their grand entrance in college. One moment they didn't exist. The next—they were college freshmen.

Like the Kelleys and Holmans, none of them had appeared to have ever held a position that might pose an espionage threat to the country. Sabotage or assassination was a different story. The traditional assumption had always been that the Soviet Union would activate sleeper agents if the two countries went to war, to create chaos in the United States. But according to Helen's theory, it had never really been about the parents. It had always been about the children. That was what his mother had figured out, and why she had become so obsessed with unraveling the sleeper network.

Helen's wall listed three members of the House of Representatives. An assistant secretary of defense for acquisition and sustainment. A

115

principal deputy undersecretary of defense for policy. A one-star Air Force general working in the Pentagon. A one-star Navy admiral serving as commander, US Forces, Japan. Several other high-ranking officers spread throughout the four branches. Two FBI special agents in charge. A few other high-ranking FBI agents. State Department personnel, including our Ukrainian ambassador. And at least two suspected CIA officers working at Langley, both of them in counterintelligence.

Karl Berg visibly reeled when they came across those two names. The Soviets had successfully launched an extensive second-generation network of sleepers who could breeze through the most rigorous security clearance investigations. The parents checked out. They checked out.

The only flaw in Helen's conspiracy theory was that she had absolutely no proof that the identified individuals were indeed Russian sleeper agents.

Devin's stomach growled, mercifully distracting him from the grim thought. He'd been running on Red Bull all night. There was no point in continuing this without eating. He could barely concentrate at this point. He searched online for a nearby breakfast spot, finding something within fairly easy walking distance. He got up from the desk, the sound of the chair scraping the floor and jolting Berg awake. The retired CIA officer lifted his head off the kitchen table, which they'd dragged into the room last night, and yawned.

He still didn't know what to think of Berg, but his mother had trusted him implicitly, according to a note he'd found on the first page of Helen's executive summary file.

"How long was I out?" asked Berg.

"Maybe an hour," said Devin. "I was thinking we could use some breakfast—and a lot of coffee. There's a bagel and breakfast sandwich shop about a fifteen-minute walk from here. The food ranges from moderately healthy fare to a guaranteed heart attack."

"Heart attack food sounds about right," said Berg. "I just need to use the bathroom."

"Watch your head," said Devin.

The bathroom had clearly been an afterthought. About the size of a modest walk-in closet, it featured a toilet, wall-mounted sink that you had to lean your head away from when sitting on the toilet, and the smallest shower stall Devin had ever seen.

When Berg emerged from the bathroom, he pointed a thumb over his shoulder.

"We're down to a single roll of toilet paper," said Berg. "Unless she has a hidden stash somewhere."

Devin shook his head. "I already looked. I'll make a run for some basics later."

"We're not moving in, so don't go overboard," said Berg. "Speaking of which, where do you think she slept?"

Devin shrugged. "I think she slept in the recliner. I found a few blankets folded on the floor under the TV."

"Clothes?"

"French wardrobe in the armoire in the living room," said Devin.

"What does that mean?"

"About ten pieces she could mix and match to go from casual to dressy. A few pairs of shoes. It's a minimalist trick."

"Jesus," said Berg, shaking his head. "But she had another apartment?"

"The FBI said it didn't look like she'd spent any significant time there over the past two months," said Devin. "They were light on the details."

"So they're looking for this apartment, too."

"That's what I assumed," said Devin.

"And there's no way the apartment can be traced back to your mother?" said Berg, looking slightly concerned.

"The building was purchased by a Nevada LLC, which Helen formed anonymously. One of the benefits of a Nevada corporation filing. I got a look at how she set it up when I reviewed the documents transferring the title deed to Henrietta Silver."

"That was very generous of her," said Berg. "What are your plans for Ms. Silver while we camp out here?"

"The effective date of the title transfer is forty-five days after her recorded death, so that gives us thirty-four days to work out of this apartment. I'm going to put Henrietta and her family in an Airbnb within the city, but far enough away from here," said Devin. "I'm hoping that will be enough time for us."

"It should be," said Berg. "How do you plan to pay for the Airbnb?"

"I'll give them ten thousand in gift cards and five thousand in cash. That should be enough for them to arrange a nice Airbnb or two and pay for incidentals for up to a month."

Helen had fifty thousand dollars in five-hundred-dollar Visa gift cards locked away in her safe, along with what looked like fifty thousand in cash. And that wasn't all.

"That'll be more than enough," said Berg. "Make sure they understand the stakes."

"I think they do," said Devin.

"Not good enough," said Berg. "Make sure they do."

"I will. I'll make it clear when I drop everything off with Henrietta later," said Devin.

The five-foot-tall-by-three-foot-wide safe, which had been built into the wall and hidden behind the bookshelf to the left of the hallway door, also contained a small arsenal, and an assortment of expensive, hard-to-acquire items when you wanted to remain off the grid.

A few semiautomatic pistols. A decked-out, short-barrel AR-15 that he suspected hadn't been properly licensed. One of those new Scorpion EVO nine-millimeter carbines. Plenty of ammunition. Two sets of body armor and night vision gear. A nice array of person-to-person communications equipment, along with dozens of burner phones and a few more touch screen satellite phones. GPS tracking devices. Knives. Flash-bang grenades. Ketamine vials. Syringes. The usual stuff you'd find in your mom's hidden safe.

"Sounds good. Let's get out of here for a few hours," said Berg.

CHAPTER 16

Harvey Rudd drove down the shaded, tree-congested street, keeping a closer eye on his phone than the road. He had no choice but to rely on the digital map to tell him when he'd reached the target house. There was no way to read the addresses without driving five miles per hour and gawking at the houses, which wasn't an option in this neighborhood. CONTROL had warned him that a significant percentage of the Falls Church population either worked for or had retired from the government. Many of them from the very agencies his own country had fought against for several decades.

And even if he drove slowly, the address numbers weren't always clear from the street. Bushes and trees often blocked the view, or the numbers were located in the oddest places. Not right next to the door as you'd expect. By the time he'd finally spotted a number on one of the houses, it was gone—leaving him unable to read the digits. On top of that, some of the houses were too far from the street for the naked eye. He'd need binoculars or some kind of scope to read the numbers. The FBI would probably intercept him before he got out of the neighborhood if he started studying houses with binoculars.

Rudd needed to be particularly careful during this quick reconnaissance. He'd even swapped cars with Rick Gentry on the off chance that Devin Gray had warned Marnie Young to watch out for a gray SUV—or that he'd surreptitiously installed a camera to watch the street. They couldn't be too cautious with this guy. CONTROL clearly didn't have much to work with if they were putting most of their surveillance eggs in this basket.

When the phone's map indicated he was about to pass the Youngs' address, he glanced to the right and took in the scene. Marnie Young's childhood home was an unassuming redbrick Cape Cod–style house with a stepped, brick walkway leading up the gentle slope of their well-kept front lawn from the foot of a well-worn asphalt driveway. A black four-door Jeep Wrangler with a United States Marine Corps spare tire cover and a gold naval aviator bumper sticker sat on the driveway about midway between the street and the garage. Easy peasy.

Credit card data put her in one of two area coffee shops almost every day for a few hours, and now they knew what to look for. According to CONTROL, Marnie Young, a combat-decorated Marine Corps helicopter pilot, had recently left active duty to pursue a civilian career, presumably in the DC area. She'd been one of only two people to attend Helen Gray's wake here in Falls Church—Karl Berg had been the other—which put her at the top of the likely Devin Gray contacts list. CONTROL assumed they had some kind of ongoing connection.

They'd slap a few trackers on her Jeep and hope for the best. Same with the car belonging to Devin's father, who lived in a very similar Falls Church neighborhood. *Hope for the best* pretty much described the overall surveillance strategy at this point, since it was in no way feasible for his team to physically stake out either of the houses.

Harvey and his wife, whom he'd just dropped at a nearby Enterprise Rent-A-Car office to acquire a new surveillance vehicle, would work with Rick Gentry to follow Marnie Young. They'd most likely take rooms at the Hampton Inn less than a half mile away and wait for her tracker to start moving. That way they wouldn't run the risk of unknowingly parking in front of an FBI agent's house and land them all in an interrogation room at the J. Edgar Hoover Building on the other side of the Potomac River.

Logan Walsh and Nathan Clark would take up residence in the Hilton Garden Inn a few miles north of here and follow the same procedure. Mason Gray lived a quarter of a mile from that hotel, on the other side of Falls Church. It was the best they could do with the limited resources and personnel available. The biggest flaw in the plan was the inability to watch either of these target locations. Devin Gray could drive right into Falls Church and hang out with Marnie or his dad at their houses, and there was nothing Rudd could do about it. It was a huge flaw, mitigated by the assumption that Devin Gray wouldn't risk visiting either location now that he knew he was the target of an active surveillance effort. He wouldn't know how thinly they were spread. In fact, he'd likely assume that the effort had been expanded since he'd so easily spoofed their first attempt to follow him.

Rudd felt so sure about this that he'd almost pushed back against CONTROL's insistence that he keep Sandy Jones and Leo Ward at the stakeout across the street from Devin's apartment. He was glad he hadn't, because after thinking about it for a while, Rudd realized he would have made a fool out of himself. The decision to keep Sandy and Ward in place was a hedged bet by CONTROL against the assumption that Devin Gray would stay away from any obvious surveillance traps.

What if the discovery of the trackers hadn't triggered some kind of deep conspiracy fears? What if he'd concluded that he was being ridiculous after a day or two of hiding from the deep state and returned to his apartment? Or that it had been the FBI that had tagged his vehicle? It wasn't unreasonable to assume that the FBI might want to track his movements for a while. His mother had recently kidnapped an elderly man for no apparent reason and shot a sheriff's deputy in cold blood.

Pinning the cop's murder on Helen Gray had been a stroke of genius, even if he hadn't been given a choice in the matter. The deputy had rolled up on them too damn quickly. He'd barely gotten to the intersection in time to keep the officer from spotting the van and the pickup truck, and possibly calling it in. Rudd's fake FBI credentials had gotten him to stop before he'd driven far enough into the intersection to see the other vehicles. He'd been especially thankful that Helen Gray had left a few rounds in her pistol's magazine.

If he'd been forced to use his own pistol, an astute forensics team might have cast some doubt on the initial conclusion drawn by the Tennessee State Police investigators, which might have prolonged or even deepened the FBI's involvement. Never a good thing when you were nearing retirement.

Rudd stayed just below the speed limit as he left the neighborhood, giving nobody a reason to look twice in his direction. When he reached Broad Street, he took a right and made his way toward the rental car office. Before they dispersed to stake out the coffee shops, he'd send his wife through with the rental car to make her own assessment.

She was at least twice as observant and would undoubtedly notice something important that he had missed. Like a sticker on the other side of the Jeep's bumper that read, **PROUD PARENTS OF A UNITED STATES MARINE**. Wouldn't that be embarrassing? Awkwardly, it wouldn't be the first time he'd glossed over something that had completely changed the game. He just hoped it was the last, and that CONTROL sent them home to Tennessee after this job to pack up for another part of the country or Moscow. He'd be fine either way—as long as he was still with Jolene. Or would she want to be called Ludmilla again? He was getting ahead of himself.

CHAPTER 17

Devin left Berg alone for a few hours while he headed out to grab some essentials at a nearby Walmart and dinner from a Thai restaurant about a mile north on Greenmount Avenue. Paper goods, a case of bottled water, two full-size air mattresses, two cheap sleeping bags, and an assortment of toiletries—mostly for himself. Berg had brought an overnight bag, an idea that hadn't crossed Devin's mind when he'd set off on Helen's treasure hunt yesterday morning.

Berg had already started arranging the take-out containers when he dropped the last of the Walmart bags inside the apartment. Devin shut and locked the door, breathing heavily from the back-to-back stair climbs. He wiped the thin film of sweat off his face on his shirtsleeve, suddenly remembering that he'd forgotten to buy a few changes of clothes. Tomorrow. He wouldn't have any trouble sleeping at this point, no matter how grimy he felt.

"Looks like enough food to last us several days," said Berg.

"I figured we'd be locked in here for a while," said Devin, heading for the refrigerator. "Drink?"

"A beer and a couple of those waters if you don't mind," said Berg. "I wasn't sure about drinking from the tap."

"I was more concerned about the grimy glasses in the cabinet," said Devin. "I bought some paper cups."

Berg laughed and shook his head. "Your mom has a hundred thousand dollars sitting in a five-thousand-dollar safe, and we're afraid to drink the water from her apartment. The world is a strange place, my friend."

Devin took a seat at the table without washing his hands. He was too tired for basic hygiene at this point. Berg set a can of Joint Resolution Hazy IPA in front of him and sat down across the table from him before cracking open his own beer. Devin followed suit and toasted Helen.

"So. After spending nearly a day in Helen's mind—what do you think now?" asked Devin.

"I think we have a nightmare on our hands. I kept searching and searching for that one piece of evidence or link that brought the whole wall down. A fatal flaw that I could point to and say, 'Dammit, Helen! This is where you went off the rails!' But I couldn't find it. On top of that, this is even worse than she thought."

With Berg's last comment, Devin finished the can and got up. "Can I grab you another?"

"May as well," said Berg. "This one will be gone soon."

Devin returned with the rest of the six-pack, placing it on the table before pulling a can free from the plastic binding.

"How does it get worse than a sleeper network penetrating nearly every level of government, the military, law enforcement, and industry?" asked Devin.

"Try tanking our economy, kneecapping our military, and eroding our allies' trust in us to the point of hostility," said Berg. "Israel almost broke off diplomatic relations with us over the Iron Dome failure. Antheon's stock dropped by half overnight, and now their SM-3 antiballistic missile program is under scrutiny. That puts several of our allies in an awkward position, since they rely on those missiles for protection from ballistic missile threats. Not to mention what they did to Boeing, Lockram Industries, and Ampere, if we're to assume that the Russian sleeper network penetrated those companies and sabotaged their flagship projects."

It all made sense to Devin. This wasn't just about espionage. The Russians had a much broader strategic goal in mind. They planned to use the network to reshape the geopolitical world in their favor, by flatlining US global influence.

"I think we have to assume those companies are compromised at the project management, engineering, and software levels. Helen's list is short on suspected sleepers within these companies, because the personnel information isn't publicly available. She could search through the government and the military, because much of those industries' personnel information *is* publicly available, especially higher up in the ranks. It's that key software developer or systems engineer working for Antheon on the telemetry components used by Iron Dome's Tamir missile that she'd never identify. That's the level she couldn't access, and that we need to identify. Because this isn't just about damaging the United States," said Devin.

"Exactly. This is about the resurrection of a superpower, but this time as a real superpower," said Berg. "Not as a drab, mismanaged zombie land with nuclear weapons."

"But the conspiracy was obviously conceived and implemented during the Cold War," said Devin. "Russia has come a long way since the collapse of the Soviet Union."

"Really? They export oil and weapons. Same as before. And when the price of oil craters, their economy tanks. The Russian economy has been stagnant since 2014, when oil prices dropped below one hundred dollars a barrel and never rose again above sixty dollars for any appreciable length of time. The Chinese have crushed them recently in the discount-arms trade market, with far less expensive, comparable weapons and technology—a lot of that based on research stolen from us. Russia's arms exports have flattened for the first time since 2001. Sabotaging our top defense industry exports kills two birds with one stone. It gives their arms industry room to grow and weakens the US economy, which weakens the dollar—resulting in higher oil prices. The US dollar and the price of oil are directly correlated."

"Russia gets richer and stronger while we get poorer and weaker," said Devin. "But they're still just exporting oil and weapons, and the difference between our two economies is massive. They can't possibly catch up."

"Nobody can catch up, except for maybe China," said Berg. "Putin and his cronies know that. This is more of a diversified reboot."

"I like that term. Even if I don't know what you mean by it," said Devin.

"I'm just riffing off what Helen started, framed by thirty-plus years of experience working the Soviet-Russian problem from a national intelligence perspective," said Berg. "The Russians have been playing a very long game, and it's about to pay off in ways we haven't anticipated."

"Beyond taking us down several notches and raising themselves a few?"

"Well beyond. Have you kept up with the situation in Hungary?" asked Berg.

"Assume I haven't kept up with anything outside of my immediate personal life and work."

"Fair enough. I spend far too much time analyzing this stuff. Like I said, old habits die hard," said Berg. "So. Orbán and Putin have been pretty cozy over the past two years, right? Especially since Orbán announced Russia's significant investment in Hungary's soon-to-be-launched electric car industry. Two state-of-the-art factories to open a year apart near Budapest, the first going live in two years. University programs in Russia and Hungary specifically tailored toward the industry. This is a big undertaking, almost entirely underwritten by Russia, leveraging Hungary's skilled and relatively inexpensive workforce. The target market is obviously Europe. Funny how Ampere's latest-generation battery was a flop. Random overheating issues."

"Ampere had a rough few years. First the SpaceV disaster, now this," said Devin, instantly understanding how they could be connected using Berg's logic. "The second cosmodrome in Kazakhstan."

"Bingo. Finished just in time to fill the void and meet the increased commercial space flight demand created by the SpaceV program," said Berg. "President Tokayev solidified power in Kazakhstan right around the time construction on the new cosmodrome began. The two countries have never been tighter since the fall of the Soviet Union. Think about the other messes connected to US technology and industry exports."

"Obviously the Iron Dome failure," said Devin. "The Russians will likely fill a lot of Antheon's missile-defense contracts outside of Europe. Then there's the never-ending F-35 debacle. Just when you think all of the kinks have been worked out—"

"A Russian sleeper agent inserts another bug," said Berg. "And the Russians' 'fifth generation' Sukhoi Su-57 fighter is selling like hotcakes around the world. Turkey just canceled its F-35 contract with Lockram Industries. Last year, India signed the largest single military aircraft order in United Aircraft Corporation's history."

"Speaking of the Russian Federation–owned United Aircraft Corporation, their MC-21-300 series sure took off—pardon the pun—in the wake of Boeing's 737 MAX's second string of flight system failures. Several near crashes that scrapped the aircraft. UAC's shiny new MC-21-300 manufacturing and repair plant in Minsk just happened to be ready to compete with Airbus for the abandoned Boeing contracts and 737 MAX replacements."

"They really did a number on us," said Berg. "And reclaimed some of their former satellite states. I think that's the ultimate goal here. To rebuild some of the former Eastern Bloc. Enough to better fortify themselves against what they truly see as NATO aggression—and make billions in the process. Putin and his oligarch buddies won't waste a good opportunity to make money."

"So it's not all about the money," said Devin.

"No. We don't have the time for me to distill what I learned over the course of three decades about the Russians, but I can tell you this: they called us the 'main adversary' for a reason. They no-shit believed we were out to get them and had always been out to get them—and that we drove every other country to do the same. And for a little while, that's exactly what we did. But this mindset didn't spring to life with the Cold War," said Berg. "The Russians had been invaded time and time again by European powers. Napoleon in 1812. Germany, Austria-Hungary, and the Ottoman Empire in World War I. Betrayed and invaded by Hitler's armies in 1941. One of Stalin's main objectives in the aftermath of World War II was to create a buffer from future European and Middle Eastern invaders, which he did by creating the Eastern Bloc. This need for geographical security is ingrained in their DNA."

"Right along with the need to add billions of dollars to the tens or hundreds of billions they've already bilked out of the system—converted to rubles, of course," said Devin.

"Especially if you're tanking the US dollar with your conspiracy," said Berg. "I think we're looking at the soft occupation of several former Eastern Bloc states. Hungary. Belarus. Kazakhstan. More will follow."

"We can't be the only ones seeing this pattern," said Devin.

"Probably not, but without the specific knowledge of a widespread sleeper network corrupting the shit out of our technology, why would anyone suspect this is a foreign state effort? This isn't like a normal cyberattack they can trace. This is an attack from within. A 'mistake' made by an employee who's held a security clearance for years. Who has no suspicious bank activity or sketchy contacts. The company investigates the hardware or software related to the accident and fires the employee—who could not care less. They're a Russian sleeper agent, after all. Story over. Rinse and repeat with a different company. As long as you don't get greedy and drop every plane, rocket, and satellite out of the sky at once, nobody will figure it out. My guess is that if we ever get to the bottom of this whole conspiracy, we'll find that every layer supports their long game. Slowly but surely expanding Russian influence in Eastern Europe."

"And weakening the US," said Devin.

"*By* weakening the US," said Berg. "They can't expand their influence without fracturing NATO, driving wedges between Western powers, and rendering the United States less relevant in Europe's eyes. This is a very long game. One they won't give up easily. Look what they did to your mother."

Berg's last sentence hit him hard. His mother had been right all along, and everyone had treated her as though she were insane. Devin included.

But she'd given them no reason to think otherwise! How the fuck were they supposed to guess she was fighting a one-person war against Russia? They weren't. For a good reason. Helen Gray had chosen to shield her family from this nightmare, by making the most difficult decision imaginable. By giving up her family for something she believed would save countless lives. From what he'd read in her library, she hadn't drawn the same end-game conclusion as Karl Berg.

Devin's mother had gone to her grave suspecting that hundreds of sleeper agents had penetrated American society, far more than the 109 born of the seventy-three suspicious couples she had identified. She had been well aware of her limitations. That she could only back trace public figures' family histories to determine if they fit the profile of sleepers dropped off in America during the seventies. That the sleepers working behind the scenes at big tech companies or in lower-level government positions would remain hidden from her.

He wished he could talk to her one more time, knowing everything he knew now. So he could thank her for protecting them and tell her she'd made the right decision. That he was proud to be her son, not embarrassed. Devin had never actually told his mother that he was embarrassed by her, but he didn't have to. He'd sent that message loud and clear by shutting her out of his life.

"Hey. Earth to Devin," said Berg, waving a hand in front of him. "Sorry I was so blunt. But I've seen what the Russians are capable of when they're trying to protect a secret. We have the fight of our lives ahead of us, with no room for error."

"Where do we even begin to start unraveling this?" asked Devin. "Kidnapping Wilson was my mom's Hail Mary pass, and I'm still not clear why she kidnapped him. Wilson wouldn't have kept a list of every sleeper. My guess is that nobody in the US ever had that list."

Berg started to open the containers that had sat untouched for the past several minutes.

"How far did you read into the Wilson file?" asked Berg.

"I skimmed it for now," said Devin.

"What about the Branson files?"

"I didn't look at those yet. They're connected to Wilson, so I figured I'd tackle them when I did the deep dive into his file."

"They're very connected. I dug into them while you were shopping," said Berg. "Helen needed something to break open the case. To give her something tangible she could take to the FBI, without being immediately escorted out of the lobby after a call to CIA—followed by her car blowing up the next time she started it."

"The exact same scenario I'd like to avoid," said Devin.

"Bingo. You and I are going to get along just fine," said Berg. "Anyway. Here's the big question that Helen had become convinced was the key to unraveling this conspiracy and led her to kidnap Donald Wilson. How do you successfully brainwash, train, and constantly assess the loyalty of a hundred kids, knowing that it would only take one of them to spill the beans and unravel the entire system you've spent decades cultivating? Would you trust it to the parents?"

Berg sat back and crossed his arms, waiting for an answer. Devin liked it better when Berg was in lecture mode. Less thinking.

"No. You couldn't count on the parents to objectively assess their own children's loyalty to the cause and report them up the sleeper network chain of command if they posed a risk, knowing it would sentence the child to death or kidnapping. Like you said, all it would take is one to break ranks and take the whole thing down. They'd need an organized method. Something intensive and possibly even fear inducing. A Branch Davidian–type cult setting for several years, at least, but it's not like they could create their own isolated community to support and raise the next generation of sleepers. That would be a big red flag on a security clearance or background investigation, and Helen's research didn't seem to identify any gaps in time fitting that pattern."

"Your mother had a theory that makes a lot of sense, given the number of children involved and something General Kozlov had written in the note he'd slipped into her pocket outing Donald Wilson. *The glue that holds the others together,*" said Berg. "She had become convinced that the sleeper families attended a summer-long camp every year, somewhere near Branson, and that Donald Wilson played an administrative role in that camp. Possibly the head administrator. He relocated to Springdale, Arkansas, from the Phoenix area in 1977, a few months after his family was killed in a car accident. Springdale is about ninety miles from the Branson area."

"I caught a snippet of that in at least two of the files. In the summary notes as *Confirmed Branson connection,*" said Devin.

"Right. While interviewing hometown neighbors of the sleepers—"

"Wait. My mom actually traveled the country interviewing their neighbors? I thought she did most of the research online. How did I miss that?"

"It was all in the Branson files. She interviewed anyone that could shed light on their lives. Neighbors. Teachers. Coaches. Local business owners. Longtime restaurant employees. Anyone that might have known them. She mostly posed as a security clearance investigator running background checks for the government or a reporter doing a story on the success of a sleeper. She discovered a pattern that clearly wasn't a coincidence. In nearly every case, she was able to find at least one person who remembered that the families spent most of the summer away. In some towns she found as many as a dozen. Most people didn't have much recollection of where they spent the time, but those who remembered referenced the Ozarks or Branson. One lady said Maine. A few others, Colorado. But the vast majority put all of these families in Branson, deep in the heart of the Ozarks, for at least two months of the summer. There's your isolated community. Part time, but I'm guessing they could have accomplished a lot in those two to three months."

"And if Wilson ran the show, he would be able to identify some of the sleepers she hadn't uncovered. In theory, at least. It's just human nature to assume that he's followed some of their careers over the years, if not many of them—to proudly watch the fruit of his labors pay off. Especially since he lost his children."

"Let's not get too Freudian," said Berg. "But yeah, your analysis tracks, and Helen clearly felt the same way. You know what's really sick? Beyond the whole concept of Camp Stalin in the Ozarks?"

Devin laughed. "Nothing can surprise me at this point."

"The seventy-three couples Helen identified had one hundred and forty-six children," said Berg.

"One hundred and nine," said Devin.

"Thirty-seven of them died in accidents between 1980 and 1989. Kids between the ages of six and seventeen. Most of them drownings on one of the four lakes along the Missouri-Arkansas border. Ozark country."

"That's actuarially impossible," said Devin, the implication of this statistic hitting him like a dirty family secret. "Holy shit. They killed those kids."

"Culled for security reasons," said Berg, raising an eyebrow. "Questionable loyalty. Maybe the kid defended Stalin a little too fiercely in history class. One too many slips about their family's summer-vacation itinerary. Could be anything."

"Liabilities to the program," said Devin, shaking his head in disbelief.

"Looks like the same thing happens to the parents. The original sleepers. Most of them seem to expire right around seventy years of age," said Berg. "Some even earlier. The fewer loose ends the better."

"The whole thing is monstrous on so many levels," said Devin.

"That unusually high number of drownings is what convinced Helen to travel the country and conduct interviews in the first place. She'd obviously spent a lot of time watching Wilson and waiting. My guess is the Iron Dome disaster got her thinking about all of the private sector sleepers she hadn't been able to identify, and the damage they could do," said Berg.

It made sense. Five hundred thirty-two killed in Haifa when the Tamir missiles that were launched to intercept the largest concentrated rocket attack fired from Lebanon in ten years mostly failed to hit their assigned targets. The Israelis acknowledged that luck alone prevented a direct hit to one of the refineries that could have resulted in a severely lethal chemical leak.

"It probably triggered the kidnapping," said Berg. "Grabbing Wilson was the only practical move left for your mother, and a pretty good one."

"And now that Wilson's dead?" asked Devin.

"We're forced to consider a less practical solution, but one that might work just the same. Your mother's plan, the Wilson gambit, as I like to call it, only needed to produce a single name to work. A sleeper at one of the companies that had recently imploded. She could run the background checks on the families and put together a dossier for the FBI, complete with her executive summary. They'd have no choice but to do their due diligence and check out the name.

"And when they did, they'd find that Mr. and Mrs. Sleeper—the parents of the software engineer investigated by their very own organization for their role in the failed Tamir missiles or by the National Transportation Safety Board for their quality-control work on the supposedly fixed 737 MAX flight-control system—had materialized out of thin air in the early 1970s. Just like the seventy-three other couples she'd passed along to them in her file.

"Now she's getting somewhere. If Helen could get more names out of Donald Wilson, even better. They wouldn't even have to be employees from one of the companies we discussed a little earlier. The Bureau would investigate the parents' background and discover that they arrived on the same spaceship that dropped the rest of the couples in various places around the country in the seventies. Case closed for Helen, but not for the FBI. Not by a long shot."

Devin couldn't help feeling skeptical of Berg's rosy scenario. "They probably would have shipped her off to Guantanamo Bay and thrown her in isolation for the rest of her life, after reaching some kind of agreement with the Russians to pretend the whole thing never happened. Everyone avoids the embarrassment."

"I wish I could say *that* would never happen, but I've seen both governments pretend something potentially more catastrophic didn't happen," said Berg. "Which is why we need to approach this differently. I'd like to locate the camp. My guess is that it has remained completely *off the grid* from inception to closing, which would serve to bolster the overall credibility of the conspiracy theory. You don't open a summer camp for a few hundred families and keep it hidden for no reason. Physical evidence of this secret camp—combined with the overall pattern that Helen discovered and the thirty-seven deaths occurring on the nearby lakes—might be enough to pique the FBI's interest. Should be enough. I know someone at the FBI who will hear me out, but I have to bring her something tangible."

"The camp or a name connected to one of these high-profile technology failures," said Devin.

"Right. But with Wilson gone, we've run out of options to acquire either. Specifically, options that don't get us sent to Leavenworth for life. I'm pretty sure the Department of Justice doesn't have a kidnapping-and-torture forgiveness program for people who hand over evidence of espionage crimes, regardless of the outcome. And just so we're clear, I am saying that the only way we'll find that summer camp or get a usable name is to kidnap and very likely torture one of the sleepers on her wall," said Berg.

"My mom was willing to go down that road," said Devin.

"Are you?" asked Berg.

Devin took a long sip of his beer instead of answering.

"We're going to need some help with this," said Berg. "This is way too big for the two of us."

"What kind of help?"

"The kind that advertises its services by word of mouth and is very picky about its clients," said Berg. "They also have a checkered past with Russia, so there's a chance they'll do this freelance."

"We have a hundred thousand dollars," said Devin.

Berg shook his head before biting into a fried egg roll.

"How much higher?"

"Out of our price range," said Berg. "Even with my discount."

"Discount?"

"I got them a lot of work back in the day. I also got them in a lot of trouble. We'll see if I came out ahead."

CHAPTER 18

Berg had an answer from his "picky" friends in the morning. *They'd do some poking around and get back to him.* Devin wasn't exactly encouraged by their cryptic answer, but Berg seemed to take it in stride. He wolfed down a cold plate of the leftover Thai food and went back to work in the vault with an espresso in one of the paper cups he'd bought at Walmart. Devin repeated the process with the Nespresso machine and joined him in front of the evidence wall with one of the better cups of espresso he'd tasted in a long time. Berg tapped the headshot photo of a dark-haired, blue-eyed man in his mid- to late thirties. His face had been circled with red marker and crossed out.

"Sean Walker. A rising star in the True America Party, when that was still a thing. A key adviser to President Alan Crane," said Berg.

"Shot himself in a drunken stupor while sitting in the hot tub attached to his pool," said Devin.

"Yeah. Yeah. I read all about it. Family conveniently gone for the weekend. Empty bottle of bourbon found next to the hot tub. A few more empties inside the house. Put a mystery pistol to his temple and pulled the trigger," said Berg. "Clean up on aisle five. Sleeper with no future blew his brains out."

"Makes sense," said Devin. "He would have represented a major liability after True America imploded. Crane resigned after the vice president was arrested for treason. Walker's boss, Raymond Burke, on the run—soon to be nabbed by the FBI. Walker was a dead man as soon as the VP went down."

"They didn't implode," said Berg. "They were exploded, but that's a story for another time. And the FBI didn't catch Raymond Burke. He was delivered to them bound and gagged in the trunk of a car."

"Story for another time?"

"Story for another life," said Berg. "So forget I even mentioned it."

"Got it," said Devin. "When will we hear from the crew you're in touch with?"

"They sounded interested," said Berg. "But like I said, they're a cautious bunch when it comes to jobs like this. I had to level with them about the severity of the situation. I forwarded a digital copy of Helen's executive summary."

"Jesus, Karl."

"Don't Jesus me," he said. "We need these people, and if they get the sense that we've misrepresented the situation at any point moving forward, they'll walk away."

"Are any of them between forty-three and fifty years old?" asked Devin. "With parents that stepped off a UFO in Fresno during the seventies?"

"If anyone on this team is a Russian sleeper, we may as well just book the next flight to Moscow, drive straight to Lubyanka, and turn ourselves in. Or fly to Tahiti with the money in your mother's safe. Tough call."

"Not that tough," said Devin. "Tahiti sounds pretty good right about now."

"You ain't kidding," said Berg. "I expect to hear from them by tonight. They work fast."

"Good. Because I don't see how we can move forward without their help," said Devin.

"I have a good feeling about them. This is their kind of cause. So fingers crossed," said Berg before turning away from the wall. "To expedite the process if they say yes, we'll need a place for them to set up shop. An Airbnb that can accommodate eight should work. No closer than ten minutes away. Preferably a decent area. Something we can occupy for at least a month. We should get that arranged no later than this afternoon."

"What if they say no?"

"Then we'll have a place with furniture, real beds, and showers to study the files and come up with another plan," said Berg. "Plus, we can't expect Henrietta and her family to keep clear of the building forever. I don't know how long this is going to take, or how long we'll need Helen's map and library, but at some point, we're going to have to cut the cord to this place, for their sake. It might not be a bad idea to find a place that will rent to us for six months."

"You're going to stay with this for six months?" said Devin.

"I'm here for as long as it takes to hit a home run or strike out. Whichever comes first," said Berg. "If it takes us six months to compile what we need to take this network down, looks like I'm eating crab cake sandwiches instead of Gulf shrimp—and rooting for the Orioles. That's true dedication."

"This all comes too easy for you," said Devin. "You don't look worried at all."

"This is all a practiced act I've mastered over three decades of uninterrupted fear and anxiety. Most of those spent looking over my shoulder. I don't see this ending well—for either of us, frankly—but I've thought the same thing before, more times than I can count. And I'm still here. They say I have nine lives."

"I want to feel reassured by that, but I'm afraid to ask how many lives you might have left," said Devin.

"It really doesn't matter. I don't plan on loaning you any. No offense," said Berg, patting him on the shoulder. "How are you planning on booking and paying for the Airbnb? We have to assume the sleeper network has access to the same kind of data tracing the FBI would use to track a suspect. We can't use credit cards, enter names into hotel systems—or anywhere, for that matter. We need to remain off the grid for as long as possible."

"I could create a fake account and use the five-hundred-dollar gift cards," said Devin. "But Airbnb could ask me to verify my identity, which would require me to take a picture of my ID and possibly a picture of myself to match to the ID. They're hit or miss with that, and I don't have a fake ID, anyway, so it's a moot point. I was thinking of maybe asking someone from my last job. I don't really know anyone at MINERVA well enough."

"I strongly suggest we leave the FBI out of this," said Berg. "Same with family and any friends you're in regular contact with. We don't know how long the Russians have been keeping an eye on you. We're looking for a friend that you haven't seen in a while that would do you a favor, or the kind of friend you see every five years and it's like nothing's changed. You're best friends again."

A name came to mind, but he shook his head just as quickly. Why would she do this for him? The better question was, Why would Devin expose her—even tangentially—in this potentially messy or even deadly conspiracy? Then again, she fit the profile Berg had described perfectly. They'd been best friends in high school, maybe a little more, though he'd never made a real move on her, and always regretted it. Whenever their paths had crossed after high school, which became rarer each year due to her Navy Reserve Officer Training Corps commitments, they'd picked up right where they'd ended last time, as though they'd just hung out the day before.

He hadn't seen Marnie Young for close to four years before she walked into his mother's wake, and despite the strained circumstances of the setting, the connection between them had felt the same. He'd furtively scanned her fingers for a ring, not that he hadn't done that before. She'd always had that effect on him, though it somehow felt different this time. Probably because she'd told him she planned on trying to find a job in the DC area. The prospect of being able to see her more than once or twice while she was on leave or in between duty assignments appealed to him.

After graduating from Northwestern University and receiving a commission in the United States Marine Corps, Marnie had spent the next fifteen years moving from one duty station to the next, much of that time spent deployed overseas, in both combat and noncombat zones, flying helicopters. Sikorsky CH-53E Super Stallions, to be precise. Devin knew all the details. He'd followed her career through letters and chats with her parents.

He knew that she'd been awarded the Bronze Star with "combat V" for dropping off reinforcements and evacuating wounded Marines during an operation in the Helmand Province of Afghanistan, "under blistering small-arms, machine-gun, and rocket-propelled grenade fire that had repulsed all previous landing attempts." She'd never said a word about it during any of her visits. Still hadn't. He'd found out during a quick stop by her house to return a book her dad had loaned him a while back. They'd very proudly showed him the citation but made him promise not to tell their daughter. That was Marnie Young in a nutshell. Amazing but unpretentious.

Devin had been thrilled to learn she'd be sticking around the area for a while, which made the decision to ask her for this favor painful. It was a lot to ask of her, given the full context of the situation, which he obviously couldn't reveal to her. If this whole thing publicly blew up on him in some spectacular way, her career aspirations in DC could be collateral damage.

Not to mention the possibility that the destruction might not be limited to just a tainted reputation. Real danger loomed over every move they made. If he asked her to do this, he'd have to level with her about the potential for disaster, however slim it might be. But was he really giving her a choice by coming clean with the hazard potential, or making it even harder for her to turn down a good friend in need? He'd help her if the roles were reversed, no matter what the stakes—and he knew she'd do the same. Just by asking, he wouldn't be giving her a choice. He'd be making it for her. But what choice did he have? The conspiracy his mother had uncovered was bigger than all of them. He'd just have to trust that the simple act of arranging an Airbnb wouldn't put her in danger.

"I know someone who fits the bill," said Devin. "I'll give her a call."

"Her? Ex-girlfriend?" asked Berg. "Probably not the best idea."

"No. A good friend from high school that I see every few years. A combat-decorated Marine helicopter pilot who recently left active duty," said Devin. "I didn't know she was back in town until she stopped by the funeral home."

"Is she looking to continue the adventure?" asked Berg. "We can pay a good salary in Visa gift cards."

Devin stifled a laugh. "No. I'm hesitant to even ask her to help. I don't want her getting dragged into this any further than making the Airbnb reservation and getting the keys. It's been four years since I've last seen her. Not counting my mother's wake."

"Did she stay long?"

"No," said Devin.

"Have you had any contact with her since the wake?"

"No. Just a few texts back and forth about grabbing coffee or a drink."

Berg appeared to be giving it some serious thought.

"She won't be on their radar," said Berg. "They probably started watching you the day after your mom's death, looking for any suspicious contact. If you haven't met with her, she's in the clear. You haven't met with her, have you? Now would be the time to fess up if you're keeping a secret."

"I haven't met with her," said Devin. "I wanted to, but—"

"Yeah. Yeah. I get the picture. You didn't want to look too desperate," said Berg.

"Well. I don't know if I'd go that far."

Berg raised an eyebrow, more or less shutting him up.

"Anyway. I highly doubt they're watching her if the two of you haven't met up," said Berg.

"I feel like we're taking a risk," said Devin. "And putting her in danger."

Berg didn't answer right away. He appeared deep in thought—a pose he had apparently perfected.

"We could have the crew run an electronic sweep on her vehicle and tail her for a little while," said Berg. "The more I think of it, the more I realize they'd be pretty pissed if I didn't suggest it to them. Due diligence and all."

"Can they get into position that quickly?" asked Devin.

Berg nodded. "They're probably watching this apartment as we speak. Like I said, they move fast. We'd most likely need to make her aware of the countersurveillance, so we could coordinate a point for them to start tailing her. They can assess the tracker situation on the go."

"They're that sophisticated?" asked Devin.

"They're the best," said Berg.

PART III

CHAPTER 19

Marnie Young set her phone on the coffee shop table and tried to act normal. She took a sip of her lukewarm coffee and scrolled through the last few pages of the United States Senate Employment Bulletin again, pretending to give the screen her attention. What the hell had Devin Gray gotten himself into? Actually, the better question was, What the hell had his mother gotten him into? Mrs. Gray had always been wonderful to Marnie, but something had shifted after they'd left for college in 2004.

Helen had been different when Marnie had visited Devin's house over Christmas of their freshman year. Cold and somewhat distant to Devin and the rest of the family, from what she could remember. She could see the embarrassment on Devin's face while they hung out in the family room, recounting "war stories" of their first semester in the dorms at their respective campuses, Helen politely nodding and staring off into nowhere—so unlike her previous self.

That was the last time she'd seen his mother. It had apparently gotten worse each year, and he'd never invited her over to the house again. On occasion, Devin had brought his dad along when they'd met up for lunch or coffee, but Helen had never come up in the conversation. Devin's dad had looked like a shell of the man she'd remembered. Still friendly and talkative, but on more of a surface level, as though he were pretending, which was probably closer to the truth than she'd realized at the time.

The details of Helen Gray's downfall still remained a mystery to Marnie. All she really knew was that Helen had done a number on Devin and the rest of his family. And it hadn't ended with her death. In fact, it sounded as though she'd passed on part of her toxic legacy to Devin, leaving him to clean up the mess. A big mess, judging by the precautions he was taking. Nothing about the conversation that had just transpired had been normal, except for one thing: Devin trusted her enough to reach out for help under desperate circumstances.

Things were still the same between them. As always, they could rely on each other for support, even though they were thousands of miles apart and she seemed to do most of the heavy lifting. She was just glad he still felt comfortable asking. Her decision to look for work post–Marine Corps had everything to do with her career aspirations, but she'd be lying if she didn't admit that a part of her excitement about landing in the Beltway after nearly two decades away had to do with Devin.

She navigated to another website dedicated to internships and paid staff positions on Capitol Hill and spent the next fifteen minutes clicking links and taking notes. Marnie got some real work done but was mostly killing time. Devin had said he needed an hour to move a countersurveillance team into place at the coffee shop. He'd text her when they were ready for her to roll.

From here she had been instructed to drive north on Broad Street to the Whole Foods just past Interstate 66 and to fill a handbasket with a logical assortment of items a thirty-seven-year-old single woman might buy—whatever that meant. Pay for the stuff and head home, where she could start looking for the Airbnb.

They didn't want her working on the Airbnb in the coffee shop for two reasons: One, it was "possible, but not probable" that someone could be watching her from inside the shop, snapping pictures of her laptop screen. Two, her internet connection to the coffee shop's Wi-Fi was vulnerable to snooping from someone inside or outside the shop. She hadn't connected to the internet using a VPN server, which is something she'd never thought to install and use before Devin explained its value a few minutes ago.

Supposedly, by the time she drove to Whole Foods, shopped for stuff she didn't need, and made her way home, the team sent to watch over her would be able to determine if a tracker had been placed on her Jeep or if anyone was shadowing her. If that turned out to be the case, Marnie was off the Airbnb job for obvious reasons. She'd started to suggest conducting a surveillance-detection run or whatever Devin had mentioned in their previous conversations about his work—but cut herself off.

Even though it didn't sound terribly complicated, particularly if he talked her through it, she figured it would probably feel the same as him suggesting he could land a helicopter with someone giving him directions. A little insulting. Above all, she didn't want to take the chance that she'd screw it up and put him at risk. If they grounded her from the Airbnb mission, she'd accept the decision and somehow try to go about her normal life, knowing that Devin was in enough trouble that he'd hired a countersurveillance team to do a job in which he specialized.

She'd almost finished her coffee when she received a text from Devin about a half hour later, green-lighting her departure for Whole Foods. She took her time as agreed, clicking a few more links before shutting her laptop and putting it in the leather satchel on the seat next to her, along with her phone. She chased the last bite of her cookie with the coffee and piled her napkins in the empty cup. It took nearly all her restraint not to look over her shoulder on the way out. Marnie stopped at the trash receptacle near the door and casually looked around the shop as she separated the recyclable items.

At least she hoped she looked casual. For the first time in her life, she felt as though she was second-guessing every decision, movement, or gesture she made, from how long to spend in front of the trash down to whether she was blinking naturally. Maybe this spy stuff wasn't as easy as it looked.

CHAPTER 20

Harvey Rudd snuggled next to Jolene on the leather couch, facing the front of the coffee shop, pretending to read through the *Washington Post*. Marnie Young had just walked out of the shop about five minutes ago, vanishing from view into the packed parking lot, where Rick Gentry would pick up her trail. Not that they needed to follow her too closely while she was in transit. They just needed to stay close enough to watch her wherever she stopped.

He'd attached three trackers to her vehicle. Two standard GPS transmitters and one long-haul tracker typically used in commercial fleet vehicles or tractor trailers. The long-haul trackers included an option to transmit less frequently to conserve battery power, in case the company didn't want to hardwire them to their vehicles or cargo trailers. Rudd added one of these to Young's Jeep in case Gray instructed her to buy an RF detector and sweep her vehicle.

He suspected that was how Gray had found the two they had installed on his SUV so quickly a few days ago. They had hidden them well enough that it would have taken him some time to get under the chassis and locate both devices. The long-haul device may have remained undetected, since it only transmitted twice an hour, instead of every fifteen to thirty seconds.

Even if the RF detector measured a quick spike in activity, without repetition, it would take forever to locate. In Marnie Young's case, she was more than likely to think it was a one-time blip in RF activity, likely originating from somewhere in her neighborhood. Off-the-shelf

RF detectors weren't exactly the most reliable or accurate devices. Then again, all this could be moot. There had been no indication to this point that Devin Gray had been in touch with Young.

CONTROL had indicated they had texted back and forth about possibly meeting up for drinks, which had put Young on their radar, but beyond that, nothing had materialized. Her routine looked solid, like it hadn't varied in a while. Gym by six, which was what one might expect from a fifteen-year veteran Marine. Back home for an hour. Coffee shop by nine. A few hours working on her laptop and phone, mostly job websites. A trip to Trader Joe's before heading home for lunch, presumably. She'd spent a few hours there during the middle of the day. Back out to a different coffee shop in the afternoon until 5:00 p.m. A run through the neighborhoods before dinnertime. Home for the rest of the night.

"You ready?" asked Jolene.

"I suppose so," said Rudd. "Feels like a dead end, though."

"We've only been watching her for one day," she said. "Who knows what she's been up to?"

"I guess," he said, putting the paper down and getting up.

They'd just stepped outside when he got a text from Gentry.

She's at the Whole Foods about a mile and a half north on Broadway. I'm heading in to keep an eye on her. It's pretty busy.

He showed Jolene the text, and she nodded. "Let's get in position for the handoff. We might want to pull Walsh off Gray's dad—just in case she heads somewhere else before heading home. I don't know how observant she is, but my guess is she'll recognize the two of us if we show up at her next stop. Rick is good at ghosting folks, but it's bad fieldcraft to use the same person twice in a row."

"Yep," he said, squeezing her hand. "Give Logan a ring and get him in position near the Whole Foods. Like you said, it's only been one day. We might use up everybody by the time she calls it quits for the morning."

"They need to send us another team," she said, grabbing the push-to-talk satellite phone from the center console. "Or at least free up Ward. It's a waste of resources to have him sitting on Gray's apartment with Sandy."

"I think he's there in case Gray shows up," said Rudd. "So CONTROL can exercise all of its options."

"Sandy is more than capable of taking out Gray by herself," said Jolene.

"I agree, but two exponentially increases the odds," said Rudd. "Then again, we could use some help with Young. I have a feeling she's the key to finding Gray."

A few minutes later, they followed Logan Walsh's inconspicuous Honda Accord into the Whole Foods parking lot. Walsh had pulled directly in front of them from the Hilton Garden Inn parking lot, which lay halfway between the coffee shop and the shopping center, on Broad Street.

"What the hell is he doing?" asked Rudd.

"It's my fault," said Jolene. "I guess I needed to explain to him that it might not be a great idea to stuff half of the team in the same place at the same time. Do you want me to send him back to the hotel?"

"No. He's a new face to Young," said Rudd. "We're the ones that should probably back off."

"It's not like we were going to park right next to her and sit there like idiots."

"I know. I know. Let him know we're going to circle the lot and head across the street," said Rudd. "We'll wait and see where she heads next. If she goes home, he's off the hook."

She contacted Walsh, while he turned them around in the parking lot and crossed Broad Street. They waited several minutes in front of the Trader Joe's until Young got back on the road, headed south. Once she passed downtown Falls Church, Rudd felt pretty confident, based on what Gentry had reported from Whole Foods, that she'd picked up lunch and was headed home. When she turned left off Broad Street onto Noland, he told Jolene to send him back to his hotel. Young's house was one street over. She was headed home.

"Young is a dead end," he muttered. "I can feel it."

"This whole job is a dead end," said Jolene, betraying a tone he hadn't heard from her previously.

"What do you mean?" he asked.

She glanced at him. "I mean all of this feels pointless. On purpose."

"Like we're being set up for a fall?" asked Rudd.

"A fall from what, though?" said Jolene. "They can't blame us for losing Gray. We'd need three to four times the number of people to adequately follow him, and even that wouldn't guarantee full coverage. We've both read all the books these former American spies publish. They all managed to meet with their contacts in Moscow after conducting crafty SDRs—even under full KGB or FSB surveillance! I don't know why they sent us here on this fool's errand, but there's a reason, and I suspect the story doesn't end well for us. They could have dragged in teams from the New York tristate area. Upstate New York and Pennsylvania. New England. But for some reason they dragged the Kentucky-Tennessee crew to DC instead. To work this alone."

"Maybe we're not alone," said Rudd.

"That would actually make the situation worse for us," she said. "They don't trust us to work with other teams?"

"I don't think there's another team working Gray," said Rudd. "We would have noticed."

"Probably," she said.

"I see this as more of a compartmentation issue around Helen Gray," said Rudd. "She was obviously important to CONTROL. Same with that Wilson guy. They wouldn't have scrambled two over-the-hill teams in the middle of the night to intercept them if they weren't critically important."

"Helen Gray must have really caught them off guard," said Jolene.

"Right. And things went completely sideways—through no fault of our own," said Rudd. "Now there's nothing left to do but chase down a few pointless leads and possibly tie up some loose ends, so why bring in a new team? Even if they didn't back brief the new crew, the whole Tennessee fiasco would pop up during the team's first Devin Gray Google search. They'd be sitting around wondering, Why didn't CONTROL tell us about Helen Gray and this Donald Wilson guy? Who are they? Et cetera. Et cetera."

"I guess," said Jolene. "It's just that all we've done for the past thirty years are grimy-ass jobs that didn't seem connected to anything important. Planting drugs, money, or kiddie porn on people. A few hit-and-runs on high school kids and military folks. Lots of blackmail pictures. This is all different, but not in the right way. The job they sent you on was important. No doubt about that. But it didn't work out. Same with the job I did a couple weeks ago in DC. That was the first time I actually felt like I'd done something important, until I finally put two and two together and figured out that I'd probably killed two of our own. That didn't feel too good then, and it doesn't feel good right now."

"We're fine," said Rudd. "I think they gave us this job because it's low key, and it keeps the Helen Gray connection compartmentalized. They're not expecting anything from us on this one. We just do what we're asked. Do it right. And that's it. Maybe we get to retire when this is over."

"Or maybe they wipe the Helen Gray slate clean while we're all in one place, busy doing nothing."

"Not much we can do about that, I suppose," said Rudd.

"I suppose not," said Jolene. "But promise me one thing, Harvey."

"Anything."

"If we see it coming, we don't go down without a fight," she said.

"They aren't going to get rid of us," said Rudd. "Not after thirty years. They'll put us on a—"

"Harvey. Promise me."

She leaned over and kissed his cheek, which did little to ease his anxiety. The thought of being tossed aside like garbage after thirty years both terrified and angered him. Mostly it angered him. They'd served Mother Russia faithfully, never hesitating or questioning orders. If the GRU decided to sweep them under the rug like dead insects at this point, there would be hell to pay.

"If they come for us, we go out fighting," said Rudd. "From now on we don't leave the hotel unarmed."

CHAPTER 21

Rich Farrington pulled the silver Suburban up to the Whole Foods entrance and waited for Scott Daly. The lanky operative, dressed in jeans and an untucked light-blue oxford shirt, emerged a few moments later and got into the passenger seat. He immediately tossed his phone between the seats to Anish Gupta, who sat in the second row rapidly typing on a laptop. He'd upload all the photos taken by Daly in the Whole Foods for future reference. Behind Gupta, the SUV's remaining space housed the surveillance and communications suite they'd custom configured for this vehicle.

Gupta had worked with a body shop crew they trusted to install and conceal all the antennae used by the gear. Satellite for their primary data link. Dedicated VHF and UHF for working with P25-encrypted communications. RF detection and pinging. Multiband antennae for frequency scanning and eavesdropping. Even to a trained eye, the over-size SUV looked no different than any of the other behemoths carting kids and families around the DC suburbs.

He drove out of the parking lot and turned south on Broad Street, heading in the same direction as the convoy of vehicles trailing Marnie Young's Jeep. First, a black Subaru Outback, which parked on the fringes of the lot and waited for Young to depart. The driver, a gray-haired guy with a giant head, made little effort to look as though he was doing anything but waiting. No sandwich on the dashboard or drink in his hand. Not pretending to talk on his phone or scroll through social media. He just sat there as though he were invisible.

Then the maroon Dodge Durango driven by the couple photographed by Devin Gray outside of a Starbucks in Hyattsville—who had at some point inserted themselves into the coffee shop with Marnie Young. They'd parked across the street in the Trader Joe's parking lot after inexplicably following the Outback almost bumper-to-bumper into the Whole Foods parking lot and taking a quick spin around.

Finally, the gray Nissan Pathfinder they'd identified outside of the coffee shop, driven by a dark-haired guy who also looked to be in his early fifties. He'd trailed Young's Jeep to Whole Foods and followed her inside, keeping his distance inside the store—under Daly's watchful eye. The man had forgotten to grab a handbasket or shopping cart on the way in and ended up following her around with a bag of tortilla chips in one hand and his phone in the other.

Farrington couldn't shake the impression that the crew assigned to follow Young might not be on the varsity Russian team. More like junior varsity second string. He definitely found that to be at odds with what Karl Berg had suggested they might be up against. It certainly didn't square with the greater conspiracy outlined in Helen Gray's executive summary. Or maybe it did.

In the grand scheme of things, assuming Devin Gray had told the truth about his relationship with her, Marnie Young would be classified as a low-potential contact. Third tier out of four at best. The Russians wouldn't park their best people on her, and they certainly wouldn't risk burning an embassy operative, which meant they had brought in a network of low-level "illegals" to work the edges. This would leave their top-tier people available to pounce on Gray or Berg at a moment's notice. Definitely something to keep in mind for tonight's mission. They'd have to clear the area quickly to avoid a run-in with the Russians' A-team.

"Any luck with the trackers?" asked Daly.

"No. They've had at least one watcher in each parking lot. It would have been too risky," said Farrington. "It doesn't really matter. We've

155

ID'd three of their vehicles. Two with Tennessee plates. One from Kentucky. I'm sensing a trend. I don't expect we'll have any trouble picking out the rest of them tonight."

"What about Young's Jeep?" asked Daly, glancing over his shoulder at Gupta.

"Bugged up like a motherfucker," said Gupta. "Three trackers in total. Two standard types transmitting every fifteen seconds. One dormant that I had to actively ping to get a response. My guess is it transmits less frequently."

"Yeah. They've upped their game a little. Gray managed to ditch this crew after detecting and removing two standard trackers," said Farrington.

"Did he check for the other type?" asked Daly.

"He ditched that car entirely and ran an SDR with a vehicle his mother had prestaged for him," said Farrington. "Prior to that, he also executed two ninety-minute washouts to determine if anyone had somehow tracked him."

A lengthy washout like that could theoretically entice a team tracking Devin by GPS signal into thinking he had stopped to meet with a contact. From a concealed location nearby, Devin could confirm he was under surveillance and ID a few more of his tails. It was a time-consuming process, but well worth the effort—and the mark of a true professional.

"Sounds like he knows what he's doing," said Daly.

"He better. He does this for a living," said Farrington. "Anish. Anything else I should pass along?"

"No. But I think I found something that could be very useful later," said Gupta.

Silence ensued, which he knew was intentional. Gupta could be intolerable on occasion. But you tolerated the best in the business, which was why Gupta had been an essential part of his crew for fifteen years. Fifteen very long years when he considered moments like these. After about a half minute, Gupta gave in—like always.

"Do you want to know what I found?" asked Gupta.

"Not unless I need to pass it along to Berg," said Farrington, giving him a dose of his own medicine.

A shorter silence this time.

"You're getting harder to crack as you age," said Gupta.

"And you're getting more and more predictable."

"More like a one-trick pony," said Daly.

"I could always revive my gangsta phase," said Gupta. "We'll be chillin' like villains for the rest of this op-er-ay-sheeun! Sippin' on gin and juice!"

"Okay. Okay," said Farrington. "You win. What did you find?"

"Push-to-talk satellite communications corresponding to the Dodge Durango at two points during their transit down Broad Street toward Whole Foods. Short but sustained radio frequency bursts around 1620 megahertz. A little frequency hopping between bursts, but well inside the Iridium satellite phone frequency range. I didn't detect a back-and-forth conversation during the first set of bursts. There was a long enough pause between each burst to indicate I didn't detect the responder's emission."

"In layman's terms, please?"

"The other satellite phone user was not in our line of sight yet, like the Durango's," said Gupta.

"Yet," stated Farrington.

"They joined in for the second set of bursts. Back-to-back radio frequency traffic in the same 1620 megahertz range," said Gupta. "Which corresponded with the Durango's little loop through the Whole Foods parking lot. My guess is they were talking to the Outback's driver. There was another back-and-forth a few minutes after all three of the cars departed south on Broad Street, probably coordinating surveillance after Young turned home."

"The Outback appeared out of nowhere," said Farrington. "Especially in the context of the radio frequency analysis. It pulled in front of the Durango at some point after the first call and before they reached Whole Foods. I just don't remember when."

"I can tell you," said Gupta. "I had our camera tracking the Durango the entire time. Give me a minute."

Part of the Suburban's retrofit had included the installation of two high-definition, 30X-zoom, controllable block cameras, one mounted to the ceiling next to the rearview mirror, flush with the windshield to prevent optical glare. The second was similarly mounted against the rear cargo hatch window. It didn't take Gupta long to locate the segment of video.

"Looks like the driver of the Outback is staying at the Hilton Garden Inn on Broad Street," said Gupta. "He pulled out right in front of the Durango. It's coming up on the left if you want to take a quick look for the other vehicles."

"Can't hurt to know where everyone is staying," said Farrington.

"It's a block past this next traffic light," said Gupta. "I'll run the license plate identification application in live-match mode and see if we pick up any other vehicles from the coffee shop or Whole Foods."

When activated, the application automatically recorded license plates captured by the Suburban's cameras, compiling them in a database by time and location filmed, state, and plate number, which they could analyze later. It also ran newly recorded plates through the entire database, looking for matches. The application would allow them to drive through hotel parking lots and identify a vehicle they might have missed while visually surveilling the morning's other areas of interest.

It also gave them the capability to detect a tail. While driving, they could capture the license plates in front and behind them for a predetermined amount of time. The heavier the traffic, the longer the camera needed to grab all the plates. It would zoom out as far as possible to accomplish this. Thirty minutes later, after executing a few soft evasion techniques—such as slowing down or running a repetitive street-grid pattern—they could reactivate the application with the live-match feature enabled, and identify every vehicle that had stuck with them.

"Scott. Why don't you climb in back so you don't get made, just in case they're having a meetup in the parking lot," said Farrington.

"Good thinking," said Daly before leaning his seat back as far as it would go and crawling over it.

Daly returned the seat to its upright position as Farrington turned into the Hilton Garden Inn parking lot. A long driveway passed underneath the hotel's covered entrance, paralleling the hotel until it opened into the parking lot situated behind the building. He spotted the black Outback immediately, its owner still seated behind the wheel. The man glanced through the driver's-side window as the Suburban passed but didn't seem to take interest. Thankfully, the lot was nearly full, the two spaces remaining clearly too tight for his oversize vehicle. He made an attempt to park in one of them, lining up a few times before driving away, to demonstrate to the Outback's driver that he'd tried.

"Was he watching me the whole time?" asked Farrington.

"No. He went back to looking at his phone as soon as you passed by," said Gupta. "Looked up once after that, but just for a moment."

"Thank god the lot was full," said Farrington. "I wasn't expecting it to be this small, with one way in or out."

"That's my fault," said Gupta. "It looked like it connected to the street behind it on Google Maps, or I would have said something."

"Any hits on any other vehicles?" asked Farrington. "I didn't see the Durango or Pathfinder."

"None. But I have two Kentucky plates. The rest are regional, with a few Floridas and an Illinois," said Gupta. "They're all in the system now, so if they come up again tonight, we'll have a heads-up."

"Might not be a bad idea to take a spin through any nearby hotel parking lots," said Daly.

"Actually, that's a stellar idea," said Farrington. "What are we looking at?"

"There's a Hampton Inn on the southern edge of Falls Church. Pretty close to Marnie Young's house," said Gupta. "We should definitely swing through there. I also see a few motor lodge–type places a little farther down Broad Street. And a Marriott TownePlace Suites a few streets over to the west. An Econo Lodge in East Falls Church."

"We may as well hit all of them," said Farrington. "It'll take Young some time to arrange the Airbnb. We can't really start any serious planning until we have that address—and the rest of the team, which should be in place before rush hour starts."

CHAPTER 22

Devin Gray paced the vault while Berg spoke with the man who held their fate in his hands. Berg mostly listened, responding here and there with a question or a brief answer—none of which gave Devin any indication one way or the other what the team had decided. This went on for another minute, until the call ended, and Berg stood with his hands on his hips, staring at the evidence wall. Not saying a word.

"Well," said Devin, approaching him.

Berg turned his head and nodded, a satisfied grin on his face. "They're in. No cost to us."

"No cost?"

"No major costs. We'll pay for their food, incidentals, and emergency purchases. Little stuff like that."

"That's really generous of them," said Devin. "They can spend everything in that safe as far as I'm concerned."

"They won't need it. The team was given access to a generously funded account for this job. I contacted someone with a vested interest in national security matters. A well-intentioned and thoroughly vetted benefactor."

"I feel like this isn't going to be a secret for very long at this rate," said Devin. "How much did you tell this benefactor?"

"Very big picture. No details. She trusts my judgment."

"Is there anyone else in on the secret that I should know about?"

"No. That's it," said Berg.

"What is the team's timeline?"

"Rich is flying in five operatives to help with the heavy lifting. They'll arrive at different times throughout the afternoon and early evening. The team should be assembled and ready to meet with us tonight. I know most of them on some level. We're in good hands."

"Sounds like he made up his mind a little earlier than this call," said Devin.

"I didn't want to get your hopes up," said Berg. "But he started moving the pieces into place last night. I knew the specter of a massive Russian sleeper conspiracy would pique his interest. He still wants to dig through all of this with the team to make sure we're not full of shit."

"That seems to be everyone's first reaction to learning about this," said Devin.

"It's a big pill to swallow," said Berg. "I only drove up here out of respect for your mother's wish to try and keep you from getting yourself killed. I'm not sure this is what she had in mind—but here we are."

"Thank you for doing this," said Devin, feeling choked up. "Though I get the feeling this is exactly what she had in mind."

"You're probably right," said Berg. "I had developed a bit of a reputation for working outside of the system toward her later years at the CIA. I wonder if that made a difference. When did she leave exactly?"

"Two thousand nine."

"Jesus. Yeah. That was one hell of a year. I had gone from director of the Special Operations Group within the Special Activities Division in early 2008 to sitting in an obscure cubicle with nothing of any consequence crossing my desk by the spring of 2009."

"Wow. That's one hell of a demotion," said Devin, feeling kind of awestruck to be in his presence.

He'd presumed that Karl Berg had been some kind of big deal at the CIA at one point, but to find out he'd run the black ops side of the house for the agency? No wonder his mother had asked Karl for this favor.

"What happened, if you don't mind my asking?"

"True America happened," said Berg. "Right around the time your mother was ousted, come to think of it. You know, she was still doing really good work for Langley at that point—pet sleeper project aside, which ironically turned out to be her best work. I wonder if her removal wasn't somehow related, given the fact that one of President Crane's top advisers was one of those sleepers. True America cleaned house in 2009. It wouldn't surprise me if whispers of her theory reached the wrong ears, and Sean Walker made sure she was swept up in the political purge."

"Why did they push you so far out of the fold?" asked Devin.

"True America had some serious skeletons in their closet, and I had one of the keys to that closet," said Berg. "Anyone with one of those keys was run off the road into a ditch and left there."

"Did you have anything to do with their downfall?"

"What do you know about that?" asked Berg, raising an eyebrow.

"I heard rumors at SSG that there was more to it than an election fraud scandal," said Devin. "Something related to the 2007 True America incident."

"Rumors," said Berg, shrugging.

He got the hint. Time to change the subject.

"I assume Marnie is clear to book the Airbnb?" asked Devin.

Berg looked as though the question had caught him off guard.

"Yes. They ran a passive radio frequency sweep of her vehicle and actively pinged for a possible long-haul device. Her Jeep is clean. They watched the coffee shop, followed her to Whole Foods, and one of the operatives ghosted her inside the store. Nothing. She can proceed with the booking. Let her know they need the address as soon as she has it. They'll likely get there ahead of her to watch for any suspicious activity while she's checking the place out with the owner and immediately afterward."

"They're extremely thorough," said Devin. "That's for sure."

"They're extremely paranoid and thorough. That's how they stay alive in this business," said Berg. "Which brings us to the most important condition of my continued participation and theirs."

Devin cocked his head a bit. He wasn't going to like what Berg had to say. That much was obvious from his tone and the fact that he'd waited this long to give an ultimatum he probably could have led with last night at dinner.

"What's the condition?"

"We do this my way," said Berg. "I don't say that because I'm a control freak. I say that because I've learned a thing or two about the Russians over the years. One of them being that they don't play by the rules or respect any conventions. You leave the rule books and the referee manuals behind when you're dealing with the Russians."

"Fine," said Devin.

"It's not that simple," said Berg. "Some of the time, my way will not resemble your way—at all. In fact, I can guarantee you we will reach a point, at least once or twice, where you find my way to be the antithesis of everything you thought you stood for. You'll be repulsed by it, but it will be the only way to effectively deal with the Russians."

"I think I understand," said Devin.

"You can't, yet," said Berg. "I just need you to trust me when your instincts are screaming otherwise. Once we reach a certain point in this little venture, we can't turn back without catastrophic results for everyone."

Devin didn't need to ask what that meant. It certainly didn't mean standing in the unemployment line with a black mark on your résumé. It meant ending up facedown in the Chesapeake Bay with your throat slashed or buried in a field somewhere off the beaten path with a bullet hole in your forehead. He asked the next logical question.

"When do we reach that point?"

"That's the tricky part, Devin, and it's never a clear path," said Berg. "It's why I need you to trust me enough to do this my way no matter what your gut is telling you."

"My mom trusted you—so I trust you," said Devin.

Berg nodded. "Then I better not let her down."

CHAPTER 23

Marnie Young left her parents' house a little after 6:15 to meet with the owner of the town house she had rented in the Canton District of Baltimore. The owner agreed to meet her at 8:00 p.m. to walk her through the place and give her the keys.

Devin said he'd arrive around nine with an "associate" to check the place out and pay her for the two weeks she'd fronted. Finding a thirty-day rental in the city for twelve occupants, in a good neighborhood, hadn't left her with any bargain-basement options—especially at the start of the summer. Four hundred and fifty a night, with a two-week deposit, had been the best she could manage, which didn't seem to faze him in the least.

The rest of his new associates would supposedly arrive later that night. She still had no idea what he meant by "associates," or what he was up to, but she was determined to find out. They had concluded that she wasn't under surveillance, which had been a huge relief. She'd packed an overnight bag and had every intention of sticking around until she could fully assess Devin's mental state and determine how she could help. He'd probably argue with her, but she didn't care. That was what friends did for each other, and unless her status as a friend had lapsed in his mind, which she highly doubted for a number of reasons, she wouldn't take no for an answer.

She also wanted to take a good look at these so-called associates, to make sure Devin was acting in his own best interest—or his own interest at all. She'd stuffed her pistol and a few spare magazines in the overnight bag, just in case. Devin simply didn't sound like himself. He'd looked shaken and dazed at his mother's funeral, which was to be expected, but something was really off with him right now. He sounded rushed and unfocused. Or maybe *unfocused* wasn't the right word. Scripted? There was no real way to tell over the phone, which was why she'd insisted on handing over the keys in person and sticking around for a while.

Marnie merged onto Interstate 495 several minutes later, coming to a complete stop just a few seconds later. Eight thirty p.m. might be a more realistic estimate. Traffic was heavier than she'd anticipated. If it didn't break up after the George Washington Memorial Parkway interchange, about five miles north of here, she'd call the town house owner and let her know that she was behind schedule. Hopefully that wouldn't be a problem and push things back until the morning. The last thing she wanted to do was add more stress to Devin's situation right now. He sounded as though he was at a breaking point.

CHAPTER 24

Harvey Rudd scraped the last of the marinara sauce out of the tiny bowl before shoving the final mozzarella stick into his mouth. They never gave you enough sauce for the whole basket. He licked his fingers clean, a Chattanooga barbecue-joint habit that Jolene loathed. She shook her head and looked away as he went from finger to finger. Long gone were the days when she would complain.

They'd gotten along like that for as long as he could remember. From the beginning, actually, which was why they'd eventually been put together as a team. He remembered the first time he'd laid eyes on her like it was yesterday. They had been flirting for a few months between classes during their first semester at Moscow State University, not quite dating, when Soviet Main Intelligence Directorate (GRU) agents abruptly plucked them out of school and sent them to an intensive American studies institute on the outskirts of Novosibirsk. GRU authorities told them the academy was a temporary extension of their studies at the School of International Relations, but both of them knew better.

The institute, which reminded him of a Komsomol academy he had attended a few summers ago for a young communist leadership camp, was run more like a military program than an academic extension. They lived in well-worn but solid barracks buildings, and participated in rigorous physical training twice a day, once in the early morning and again after classes ended in the late afternoon. The instructors had been conditioning them for something big. That much was obvious.

Despite the harsh, scarcely academic conditions, he had never considered leaving. On most weekends, the hundred or so students were bused in groups to downtown Novosibirsk for a few hours of leisure time, where they spent most of their university stipend on restaurant meals they could never afford back in Moscow. He'd spent most of that time with Ludmilla, a.k.a. Jolene, building the relationship that would lead to their marriage and get them posted together in the United States. She had gotten him through the darkest of days with little more than a smile, and the prospect of her companionship on the weekend.

Five years and three military bases later, the GRU smuggled Vadim Krukov and Ludmilla Alyev into the US with perfectly forged identities, a generously padded bank account that was refilled regularly, and a paid-off house in the Chattanooga suburbs, where they'd posed as Harvey and Jolene Rudd for nearly thirty years.

His phone chirped and buzzed at the same time. A quick look at the screen told him Marnie Young was on the move. *Crap.*

"Looks like we'll be needin' a to-go bag," he said, passing the phone to Jolene.

"I'll take care of it," said Jolene, waving down one of the servers. "You get the car."

"See you out front," he said, getting up.

On his way out, he stopped at the host stand and notified the young man managing the wait list that they had to leave immediately due to a family emergency—just to double up on Jolene's efforts to get them out of here quickly. He jogged through the parking lot to their SUV and put his phone in the holder attached to the dashboard. After backing out of the space, he took the satellite phone out of the glove box and gave Rick Gentry a call.

"I see it," said Gentry. "On my way out of the room. She just turned north on Broad Street, so maybe she's headed back to the coffee shop?"

"CONTROL indicated little to no evening activity since she moved back to DC," said Rudd, headed for the restaurant's entrance.

"She's thirty-seven, single, and has been living with her parents for a few weeks," said Gentry. "This night could go in any of a dozen directions."

"I hope they go in Devin Gray's direction," said Rudd.

"It doesn't sound like it if he hasn't answered her texts," said Gentry.

"He went dark on that phone," said Rudd.

"Same result," said Gentry. "Who knows. Maybe we'll get lucky. I'm in the lobby. I'll be on the road shortly."

Jolene barreled through the door several seconds after he'd stopped and put on the SUV's hazard lights. She carried a take-out bag and two large to-go drink cups as she hustled to the car. He leaned across the passenger seat and opened the door for her.

"I can't tell you how happy I am to see those bags!" he said. "And you, of course."

"Uh-huh," she said, handing him the cups. "I didn't want to have to fight you over the last granola bar in my purse."

He set the cups in the cup holders, and she dropped her purse into the footwell, keeping the take-out bag balanced on her knees while she buckled her seat belt.

"We'll deal with this later," she said, placing the bag on the rear passenger seat row.

"Hopefully sooner than later," he said, driving them to the exit onto Broad Street.

Young had passed the restaurant about a minute ago, still headed north. He squeezed into traffic and managed to cut the distance between them in half by the time they reached the Whole Foods from this morning. When she kept going, he started to suspect they were in for a long night. At the Capitol Beltway, any lingering doubt was removed. She took the on-ramp headed north, which was the last thing he'd expect anyone to do with rush hour still in progress. If Young were driving anywhere nearby, she would have been better off staying on local roads.

About an hour and a half later, Young exited the Beltway at the I-95 interchange that took them north toward Baltimore. Twenty-two miles in ninety-three minutes translated into Rudd being ready to eat the rib eye steak he'd ordered at the restaurant with his bare hands. A single hand. One would have to remain on the steering wheel. He was about to suggest that Jolene crack open their dinner when the satellite phone rang. "Rick," she said before answering the call.

"Hope you had dinner. Looks like we're headed to Baltimore," she said.

Rudd couldn't hear the other side of their conversation, but his wife hadn't rolled her eyes yet, which usually meant she agreed with whatever was being passed along. She lowered the phone.

"Rick is thinking we should get Logan and Nathan moving in this direction," she said. "In case this pans out. Possibly Sandy."

He was right. If Gray surfaced, CONTROL might order them to make an immediate move against him, capture or kill being the only two options. Killing Gray on the spot wouldn't require more than the three of them. Kidnapping was a different story. They should be able to make it work with three, but the more the merrier.

"Let's get them on the road," said Rudd. "But Sandy stays in place, on the outside chance that Gray shows his face at the apartment."

She passed that along to Gentry and called the rest of the team. When that was done, she reached between the seats, and for a brief moment he thought she might be going for their dinner. Instead, her hand reemerged with their laptop. She shook her head, smiling.

"I'll work on dinner in a minute," she said. "We need to contact CONTROL with an update and transfer primary communications to the encrypted chat app on one of our mobile phones. Things will move fast if Gray materializes."

"Agreed," said Rudd.

She retrieved the Iridium SatSleeve from the glove box and inserted her smartphone, enabling satellite call capability. A few minutes later, after accessing the dark web chat box through the laptop and explaining the situation to CONTROL, she opened an app on her phone and entered a long code provided in the chat session. Shortly after that, Jolene shut her laptop and returned it to the back seat.

"We're good," she said.

They'd now established a direct communications channel to CONTROL through the satellite-converted cell phone, which could get tricky. The specifically designed application replicated the dark web chat box but required them to enter a memorized "start word" every time they typed into the text field. The application randomly prompted them with a number between one and one hundred by displaying it at the top of the screen—each number corresponding to a unique password. They both knew these words by heart. Only one mistake was tolerated. Two incorrect attempts shut down everything, including their laptop's access. He had no idea what happened after that and didn't want to find out.

At 8:34 p.m., Harvey Rudd dropped his wife at the corner of Fait Avenue and South Glover Street in what looked like an upscale part of Baltimore, even though it was hard to tell with the flat redbrick facades. The map said they were in Canton, which was within walking distance of the northwest harbor, just to the east of Fells Point—a high-rent district. They'd have to be somewhat cautious here. People paying a premium for a one-bedroom loft with a view tended to keep an eye on the neighborhood. He wanted to keep his drive-bys to a minimum, if not eliminate them altogether. Young had parked her Jeep about halfway between Fait and Foster Avenues on South Glover Street.

They'd turned off Foster Avenue onto South Glover just in time to see her disappear into a town house on the east side of the street with another woman. Young carried a backpack that looked large enough to be an overnight bag. The other woman was dressed in a business suit. The Rudds drew no conclusions from the little they witnessed, which was why he dropped Jolene off to keep an eye on things while he looked for a parking space with a view of the town house.

The problem was that South Glover, like almost all the north-south streets in this neighborhood, was a one-way street. In this case directed south. It took him several passes to finally score a parking space, which was ill suited for any of their possible follow-on missions. Located south of the town house, on the other side of Fait Avenue, he'd have to throw the SUV into reverse and blindly cross Fait Avenue, a marginally busy two-way street, to reach the town house—if CONTROL gave them the order to hit the house.

As much as he'd like to be positioned upstreet from the target house, pointing him in the right direction, he didn't dare give up what might end up being the only parking opportunity on the street. From here, he'd guide the rest of the team into place on nearby streets, where they'd be in quick striking distance if Devin Gray made an appearance. Rick Gentry had found a space two blocks over, facing Foster Avenue. He could arrive in front of the target house within thirty seconds.

Jolene joined him moments after he backed into the space, insisting that they prepare for possible breaching orders. They moved a duffel bag packed with flash-bang grenades in case they suspected armed opposition inside; bolt cutters for simple but persistent chain locks; a handheld, solid-steel battering ram for bypassing dead bolts or standard doorknob locks; and a pistol-gripped, short-barreled shotgun loaded with breacher slugs in case the locks proved to be resistant to brute physical force. Along with the compact pistols hidden in concealed holsters along their waistbands, they were ready for pretty much anything.

"You hungry?" asked Rudd.

"Hold on," said Jolene, focusing a pair of binoculars on the town house.

She passed them to him a few moments later. "Take a look."

Marnie Young stood in the open doorway of the town house, nodding and laughing with the woman, who handed her a set of keys and a folder. The two of them shook hands after another minute or so of conversation, and the smartly dressed woman departed—walking to her car, which had been parked at the end of the street, on the corner of Foster Avenue. A near-perfect position for their purposes! He was about to suggest relocating to that spot when another vehicle slowed to turn onto the street as the other car departed, sliding into its place. It wasn't meant to be. He shifted the view back to Marnie Young, who glanced up and down the street before shutting the door behind her.

"She's up to something," said Rudd.

"Yep. Let's eat before this goes down," she said. "I give it fifteen minutes tops."

CHAPTER 25

Timothy Graves parked the rental sedan on the corner of South Glover Street and Foster Avenue and passed the keys between the seats to the woman lying on the back row under a blanket. She didn't say a word, which was fine by him. He wanted to get as far from here as possible. Just minutes ago, he'd driven out of a parking space down the road to make room for one of their targets before slowly circling the block to take the Airbnb owner's space—moving the final chess pieces into place.

If the couple in the Durango noticed that the cars were the same, a remote but existent possibility under the circumstances, trouble could escalate quicker than any of them had planned. And unchoreographed trouble was the last thing he was looking for tonight. Graves much preferred the kind the team could control, since they typically directed it away from him.

He wasn't a combat type. Far from it. And he was here only as a favor. He'd emerged from his mostly permanent retirement because Anish needed his help on a short-fused job, and Graves was within easy striking distance.

He'd settled into a nice living on the southern Outer Banks, near Emerald Isle, where he'd vacationed as a kid. Hauling himself to Jacksonville to get on a flight to Baltimore hadn't been any trouble at all.

"Good luck," he said.

"Yep," she said.

He got out and shut the door, the vehicle's locking system immediately chirping behind him. *A little early on the locks, Emily.* The average system took a little longer than that to arm itself. Hopefully, nobody would notice. He'd never worked with Emily Miralles before today. She'd joined Farrington's crew a year and a half ago, replacing Cassiopeia, a.k.a. Caz, who'd accepted a lucrative head security position for one of Capitol Hill's more influential senators. Miralles didn't say much, which, once again, suited him fine. The less he knew about any of these people the better, and the less they knew about him? Priceless.

It wasn't that he disliked any of them. He'd enjoyed his years working for Sanderson's program and subsequently with Farrington's spin-off operation. They'd taken on some giants in that time and come out on top, making the world a better place—he hoped. It was just that he could count on one hand the number of people who had been around from the beginning. Some of them had split and gone their own way, like him, but most of them had been killed on missions or assassinated in retribution for some of their more notorious jobs.

The fact that this job involved the Russians had almost kept him from showing up. The Russians had long memories, and Farrington had done a number on them in the past. More than once.

He walked a block east on Foster Avenue and crossed the street at South Lakewood, heading for the tricked-out silver Suburban Anish called home these days. Graves had to admit that his former partner in crime had made some aesthetic and functional improvements to the original concept of their undercover communications hub.

Back in the day, they'd just bolt a folding desk and some industrial metal bookshelves to the floor of a cargo van, relying on a combination of Velcro, zip ties, and bungee cords to keep everything in place. Gupta had even completely hidden the antennae array, which had always posed a detection risk to them in the past. The only issue with the new arrangement was interior space. He'd traded the expansiveness of the somewhat conspicuous Mercedes cargo van for the assured cover of the oversize SUV—ubiquitous in the suburbs and city these days.

The Suburban was parked in a row of diagonal spaces on the left side of the street, facing out for quick egress. The rear passenger door opened the moment he stepped off the curb, Richard "Rich" Farrington hopping down with a wide grin on his face. A rarity in Graves's experience.

"Timothy. Sorry I missed you earlier. I was putting the final magic touches on a few things," said Rich. "Good to see you. Sounds like life on the Outer Banks is treating you well."

"I can't complain too much," said Graves. "It wasn't the easiest adjustment to make after spending close to two decades in this line of business, but I'm making it work. Every day my shoulders relax about a quarter of a millimeter."

Rich laughed. "Well, I apologize for setting your shoulders back a few months, but I do appreciate you coming out of retirement temporarily. My guess is we're going to need all the help we can get on this one. Did Miralles bring you up to speed on the mechanics of the operation?"

"She did. Is this really the Russians?" asked Graves.

Rich nodded. "Long-dormant sleeper network. Second generation—if it checks out."

"Second generation? Holy shit," said Graves. "Wait. You haven't vetted this yet?"

"Tonight's operation has been vetted," said Rich. "But Karl Berg says it's connected to a much-bigger conspiracy. We'll all get a chance to scour the evidence and try to poke holes in the theory."

"This is Berg's theory? I thought he was retired."

"He is. Or was. Kind of like someone else I know," said Rich, patting him on the shoulder. "A former colleague of his at Langley apparently spent close to the past two decades investigating this theory. She was killed under suspicious circumstances about two weeks ago. Killed herself, but too many aspects of her case don't add up. She handed over the reins to her son, Devin Gray. He reached out to Berg at his mother's recommendation—and here we are."

"And Berg is convinced?" asked Graves.

"He sounds convinced," said Rich. "But he's open to criticism. Same with Devin Gray. They both want to be wrong about this."

"I knew I should have left my phone behind when I took the boat out this morning."

"What kind of boat?"

"Nothing too fancy," said Graves. "Just a fishing boat."

"Does it have a flying bridge?" asked Rich.

"It might."

"Sounds kind of fancy," said Rich. "Don't worry. We'll get you back to your yacht in one piece."

"I'll hold you to that," said Graves. "And take you fishing if you make good on it."

"Deal," said Rich, shaking his hand. "Keep your friend out of trouble. He hasn't matured since you left."

"I heard that," said Gupta.

"Be good, guys," said Rich before crossing the street and getting into the passenger seat of a black SUV that hadn't drawn Graves's attention until now.

In the fading light of the evening, he recognized Scott Daly, former Navy SEAL, behind the wheel of the SUV. Daly waved at him, and he nodded back. They were in good hands. Graves climbed inside and gave Gupta a high five before shutting the door.

"Thanks for answering the call of the wild, bro!" said Gupta. "The band is back together, baby!"

"Is it too late to go home?" asked Graves.

"You know you missed me," said Gupta.

"Not really," said Graves. "What are we looking at here? They shoved me behind the wheel of a car a few minutes after I showed up and parked me on Glover Street with the least talkative operative I've ever met."

"Miralles? Yeah. She's all business, and good at it, too," said Gupta. "All right. So here's what we've got for coverage. Two low-light-capable, high-def block cameras placed on the town house adjacent to the target house, giving us a good enough view up and down Glover Street. The trees kind of mess with the view at certain distances, but we have a good overall picture of the street. I have that on a split screen here. I'm running the feeds through motion-detection software, so it'll draw our attention to anything larger than a dog."

Gupta leaned forward and tapped the space bar on the laptop sitting on the Suburban's wide front-seat armrest, activating the screen. Graves saw what he meant about the trees. Not ideal but not bad. The motion-detection software would overcome that issue.

"We also have a basic fish-eye dome camera set up on the fence behind the town house, off the alley. One-hundred-and-eighty-degree coverage. Motion activated. It'll pop up as a window in the bottom-right corner of the screen if it's triggered, or you can click on the rightmost tab to open the feed at any time. We both have the same access on our laptops, in case we need to split our attention between the front and back of the town house. I anticipate doing that during the pickup."

Graves clicked the tab and liked what he saw. The concrete alley was well lit.

"Other than that, I have a multiband antenna on one of our vehicles on Glover Street, plus one on each adjacent street—attached as high up in the trees as we could manage. They have a very limited power supply. Our Russian friends have mainly used encrypted push-to-talk satellite communications. We should be able to map them out as they move into position."

He handed Graves one of the laptops on the seat between them and took the other for himself.

"There's no difference between either of these laptops, for redundancy reasons," he said, flipping the screen up. "I figured I'd analyze the frequencies and sensors, while you maintained the bigger picture and communicated with the teams?"

"Sounds like a plan. Same comms arrangement?" asked Graves.

Gupta reached behind the seat and retrieved a headphone set attached to a heavy-duty-looking coiled cord. He handed them over to Graves.

"Same. Same," said Gupta. "Right ear is the primary communications channel. We're using one channel. Left ear is whatever you want. I currently have it tuned to the local police frequency. You can change it through the computer interface. If for some reason we need to leave the vehicle, there's a handheld radio preset with the same frequencies and an earbud headset in the seat pocket directly in front of you."

Graves didn't like the sound of that at all, but it came with the job, along with a wide variety of other possible unpleasantries—like getting shot in the leg and walking with a slight limp for the rest of your life. Unfortunately, things like that didn't go away like tensed shoulders. He knew that from experience, which led to his next question.

"What's our security situation?"

"Rich and Scott will be across the street until the extraction," said Gupta. "Other than that, there's a loaded Sig Sauer compact pistol with two spare magazines in each door pocket."

"Wonderful," said Graves.

"Back into the frying pan, man," said Gupta. "Just like old times."

"It wasn't that long ago," said Graves, suddenly remembering just how much he didn't miss this.

CHAPTER 26

Devin Gray drove up and down the streets east of the town house for close to twenty minutes before a parking space opened on South Belmore Avenue. He spent the next few minutes trying to squeeze his car into the opening left by a Prius. The end result wasn't pretty—the back end of his car protruded about a foot into the street—but it would have to do. Berg's people were anxious to offload their gear and get started. From what he had gathered, most of them would remain at the town house overnight, while the team leaders joined Devin and Berg at Helen's apartment to examine the evidence.

Before they set off down the street, Berg grabbed his arm. "Are you sure there's no way to convince Marnie to leave the keys in the mailbox and get out of there? Right now. Her insistence on staying at the town house isn't sitting well with the crew. I don't want to give them any reason to back out of this."

"She's a good friend and a combat-decorated Marine. Completely trustworthy," said Devin. "All she wants to do is make sure I'm not being put up to something or being forced to do something against my will. I know how that sounds, given the fact that I came to you with this, but she's not going to let this go. She's doing what a good friend would do. The harder I try to get her to leave, the less likely she will. She made that clear. You heard the phone call."

"Yeah. Well, she's getting in the way," said Berg, sliding his satchel's strap over a shoulder.

"She won't stick around for long. She'll see everything's fine with me, and that'll be it."

Berg shook his head and started walking, almost mumbling to himself. They got to the corner of Foster Avenue, where Berg stopped. "I need you to remember what we discussed earlier today," he said. "About doing this my way."

"I remember," said Devin. "I simply can't force Marnie to leave without making her even more suspicious than she already is. She'll just hang around in her car all night. I know her."

"That would be even worse," said Berg, looking somewhat exasperated.

"What?" asked Devin, thinking he might have misspoken.

"Nothing. Let's go," he said.

They walked the two blocks to South Glover Avenue, Berg checking his phone every minute or so for texts and immediately assuring Devin that everything was on schedule. They didn't encounter much foot traffic on the way. A college-age student with a backpack bopping along to whatever music was pumping through his headphones. A thirtysomething-looking couple headed in the opposite direction, probably on their way to a cozy dinner in one of a number of Canton neighborhood restaurants. He'd pictured the streets here to be a little busier, due to the proximity to the waterfront, but it was still early by city standards. Just a little past ten.

South Glover was packed with cars, like every street in the area. He imagined having a dedicated garage or parking space behind your town house in the alley was important if you owned a place here. The parking situation around his mother's apartment was bad enough, but nothing like this. While they walked down the street, he scanned the vehicles without being obvious.

"Karl. Would it be fair to assume that your friends are already watching the town house?" asked Devin.

"It's possible," said Berg. "Why do you ask?"

"We either passed by two friends or two hostiles a few cars back," said Devin. "One close to the intersection. The second on the other side of the street. Both sedans. The car windows are cracked open for air, which means they've probably been there for a while. I also saw some movement in the back seat of one of the cars. Very subtle, but definitely movement."

"They've been here for a few hours," said Berg. "To make sure Marnie hadn't been followed."

"They need to work on their surveillance fieldcraft," said Devin.

"I'll pass that along," said Berg.

Devin watched the numbers on the front of the brick townhomes, stopping about two-thirds of the way to the next cross street, in front of a brightly lit redbrick stoop with a single black handrail, which pretty much looked like every other stoop in the neighborhood. He imagined this hadn't been exactly the best part of town a decade or so ago. Fully rehabilitated now, but not much you could do with the squat row house facades.

"Seven-twenty-seven," said Devin, raising his hand to knock on the door.

He'd be lying if he said he wasn't more nervous about seeing Marnie than Berg's mercenaries. A different kind of nervous. More like butterflies in the stomach.

"Hold up," said Berg, checking his phone.

"I have a third surveillance vehicle down the road, before the next intersection," said Devin. "Make sure that's ours."

"It is," said Berg, typing a response on the phone before looking up at Devin. "They're being extra cautious. Ready?"

Devin knocked on the door.

"Just remember. I need you to trust me. No matter what happens," said Berg. "When Marnie opens the door, we get inside fast. Okay?"

"Are you sure everything is all right?"

"Couldn't be better," said Berg.

Marnie opened the door a moment later, smiling warmly.

"I thought you might have stood me up," she said, glancing at her watch.

"Definitely not," said Devin. "We just ran a little behind—"

"Why don't we talk about this inside," said Berg, basically shoving him into the town house.

Marnie's smile evaporated as she backed out of the doorway, her lips pursing and eyes squinting.

"Devin. What the hell is going on?" she said, pulling him out of Berg's way. "Who is this asshole?"

Berg shut and locked the door.

"My name is Karl. I was a friend of Devin's mother at the CIA. Devin trusts me, and I need you to trust me. At least for a few minutes. Our lives depend on it."

"What is he talking about?" asked Marnie.

"Karl. I think you're being a little overdramatic," said Devin before turning to Marnie. "I don't know what his deal is right now."

"Whatever it is, I don't like it," she said.

"Yes. I'm an asshole. Agreed. Let's move to the back of the town house, please," said Berg. "It's safer."

Marnie didn't budge, shaking her head instead. "I'm not going anywhere."

"Please. We're about to have company at the front door. Russian houseguests with no manners. If we move now, we'll be long gone before they arrive."

"Devin?" she said, giving him a puzzled look.

"Karl. How does that make any—" started Devin.

Jesus. He'd used them as bait!

"You son of a bitch. You let them follow her here, didn't you?" said Devin. "This whole town house is nothing but a setup. I knew it didn't sound right."

183

"Yeah. And I'm half of the bait," said Berg, starting to walk away. "So please. Can we get the fuck out of here? We really don't have time for this. Our ride will be out back any second."

"Don't take another step," said Marnie, pointing a compact pistol at Berg. "We're going to make some time."

Berg's shoulders slumped and he exhaled deeply.

"Did you give her your gun?"

"No," said Devin.

The pistol he'd taken from his mother's safe had been a Smith & Wesson M&P9 Compact. She was holding some kind of modular Sig Sauer.

"Jesus. Please talk to her. Quickly," said Berg. "We're out of time."

"Marnie. I need you to trust me," said Devin. "If he says we need to go, we need to go. I'll explain everything at my mother's apartment."

"Your mother's apartment is still an active crime scene," said Marnie.

"My mother's other apartment," said Devin. "She wasn't crazy. She discovered a Russian sleeper network, and nobody believed her—but it's all true. She kept a second apartment with all of the evidence."

"Devin. I want to believe you, but I'm really having a hard time with this."

CHAPTER 27

Harvey Rudd nudged Jolene's arm. She'd been turned in her seat, staring through the binoculars for too long without saying anything.

"Knock it off," she said.

"What are you seeing?" asked Rudd.

"Let me see the pictures again," she said.

Rudd held the pictures of Karl Berg and Devin Gray in the subdued light cast by the open glove box. Jolene glanced down at the pictures for a few seconds before returning to the binoculars.

"It's Karl Berg and Devin Gray," said Jolene.

"How sure are you?"

"One hundred percent. They just entered the town house," said Jolene. "Call it in."

Rudd could barely believe their luck. Two of CONTROL's high-priority targets in one place. He'd been expecting only Gray, and even that had been a long shot. He opened the chat app on Jolene's phone and typed the code word corresponding with the number at the top of the screen, followed by a dash and then his message.

DANDELION-Berg and Gray just entered town house. 100% positive ID. Have 6 members of team standing by with breaching kit and weapons. Advise how to proceed.

The number at the top of the screen changed several seconds later, followed by a reply.

Is Young in town house?

UNICORN-Yes. Young, Berg and Gray.

Kill Young. Abduct Berg and Gray. If only feasible to abduct ONE, take Berg and kill Gray. Advise of results when complete. Will pass directions to safe house for delivery. Acknowledge receipt of this order.

The number changed again. They weren't taking any chances.

STARWARS-Order received.

Execute orders immediately. Authorization code CARWASH.

CARWASH was the code the other members of the team would receive via text. He'd have to recite the code to prove that he'd received authorization to deviate from their previous order to locate and follow Devin Gray and/or Karl Berg. It was a crude method that still left a lot of room for abuse. He could essentially tell the team anything he wanted, and they wouldn't have any way to verify the actual orders.

"Read this," said Rudd, handing the phone to his wife.

She gave it a quick look. "Call Logan. We need to move quick, while they're standing around making introductions. I assume Young has never met Berg before."

"Yep," said Rudd, grabbing his satellite phone and pressing the push-to-talk button. "Put me on speakerphone," he said to Logan, doing the same.

"You're on speakerphone," said Walsh. "We all just received text messages."

"CARWASH. CARWASH. Berg and Gray just entered the town house. CONTROL gave me the green light to hit the town house," said Rudd. "We're going to try and take both Berg and Gray, but if grabbing both of them starts to go sideways, we kill Gray and take Berg."

"What about Young?" asked Walsh.

"We kill her right away," said Rudd. "We don't need any Marine heroics."

"We're ready to roll," said Walsh.

"Get everyone set and move up to the corner," said Rudd. "You'll have to be my eyes when I back across Fait Avenue. I won't be able to see the cross traffic."

"I'm already on the move," said Walsh. "No traffic right now. I'll keep you posted."

"Let's do this," said Rudd, starting the Durango. "Breach kit is in the back seat."

"We're at the corner," said Walsh.

He glanced in the rearview mirror and saw Walsh's Pathfinder pull into place at the intersection.

"You ready?" he said.

Jolene had already drawn her compact stainless-steel revolver. "Quit talking and start driving."

Rudd maneuvered the Durango out of the tight space and lined up with the intersection using the backup camera screen on the center console. His phone chirped, followed by Walsh's voice.

"You're all clear."

He pressed the accelerator, starting slow and picking up speed. Eyes glued to the screen, he raced across Fait Avenue, immediately slowing when he'd crossed to the other side safely.

"Tell me when to stop," said Rudd.

187

He proceeded at a manageable speed until Jolene squeezed his knee. "A few more seconds."

Rudd counted to three and slowed to a crawl, turning his head to check the street addresses. Seven thirty-one. Seven twenty-nine. He tapped the brakes, bringing them to a stop directly in front of the target address.

"Jesus, Logan!" yelled Jolene, as Walsh's SUV screeched to a halt just inches from Rudd's front bumper.

So much for the element of surprise.

CHAPTER 28

Car tires screeched outside, turning all their heads.

"We have to go—right fucking now," said Berg, taking off for the back of the town house.

Devin put his hand on Marnie's wrist and lowered the gun. "I'll explain everything later. Right now, we need to do what Karl says."

Marnie fumed for a moment before bolting through the town house, with Devin in close pursuit. Once out the back door, he spotted a black SUV parked in the alley just beyond a low concrete wall. A man he'd never seen before whisper-yelled obscenities at them through the front passenger window as they raced across the brick patio toward a black wrought iron gate.

"Hurry the fuck up!" he hissed as they piled through the gate and into the back row of the SUV.

The vehicle took off the moment Devin jumped inside, the door still wide open. He reached out to pull it shut, a plastic garbage bin clipping the end of the door and slamming it against his hand. Devin pulled the door shut with his other hand, groaning in pain.

The man in the passenger seat glanced over his shoulder. "What was the damn holdup? Half the Red Army is in front of the town house."

"Just a little disagreement," said Berg. "It wasn't my best moment."

"No worries. We're still good to go," he said before fully turning in his seat. "Devin. Marnie. I'm Rich, the de facto team leader. And this is Scott. I apologize for this sudden stunt, but we needed to get a handle on who's been following both of you."

Scott turned left out of the alley at Fait Avenue and picked up speed.

"I thought my Jeep was clean," said Marnie. "And that nobody was following me."

"That's what I was told," said Devin. "I would never have put you in any danger."

Rich glanced down at the pistol in Marnie's lap. "My guess is she can take care of herself."

"You lied to me, Karl. For an entire day. How am I supposed to trust any of you?" asked Devin.

"Devin. There was no other way to pull this off. We needed all of the Russians in one place, which meant you and me showing up at the town house to offer an irresistible target," said Berg. "Ms. Young insisted on staying at the town house. I begged you to get her out of there."

"I wasn't going anywhere," said Marnie. "I needed to see for myself who was pulling the strings. Now I know."

Scott took a hard left on South Belnord Street, tires screeching.

"Take it easy," said Rich.

Scott slowed the vehicle down significantly.

"We'll explain everything later," said Rich. "Right now, I'm going to drop the two of you off at Devin's car, and you're going to run a short SDR to the northeast. Thirty minutes tops. Just get out of the city and into the suburbs. Work your magic in a nice, quiet neighborhood, then back to your mother's apartment. Stick north of the city on your return. The police will be all over this part of town."

"What's happening back at the town house?" asked Devin.

"Bad shit," said Rich.

"Point-of-no-return shit, to be precise," said Berg.

CHAPTER 29

Harvey Rudd had pulled the nylon duffel bag containing their breacher kit onto the sidewalk by the time the entire team had assembled in front of the door. They wasted no time rifling through its contents, removing the battering ram first. Leo Ward took possession of the forty-pound, two-handed chunk of metal, and headed for the town house stoop. Logan Walsh grabbed the shotgun, which they'd preloaded with twelve-gauge slug shots, and followed closely behind Ward. Rick Gentry stuffed a few of the flash-bang grenades into his cargo pant pockets, keeping one out for immediate use.

They stacked up on the door like a SWAT team: Ward with the battering ram first, lining it up with the door handle; Walsh racking the shotgun to chamber one of the lock-shattering slugs and positioning himself on the hinge side of the door—in case the battering ram didn't do the trick. Gentry stood at the bottom of the stoop, flash-bang grenade in hand, ready to toss it inside if they met with any immediate gunfire. Clark stacked up behind Walsh, ready to rush in and shoot Young. Everything was in place.

Rudd threw the duffel bag in the back seat of the Durango and drew a compact Glock from the concealed holster on his hip.

"Do it! Breach!" he said, heading straight for the town house stoop.

Ward retracted the battering ram, ready to smash it against the handle, when his head snapped sideways, a watermelon-size scarlet blotch exploding against the yellow door. Walsh's neck erupted a fraction of a second later, painting Ward's expressionless face deep red. Both of them crumpled to the stoop as bullets tore through the rest of the team.

Gentry pitched forward, striking the brick stairs with his head, the grenade rolling down the sidewalk—pin and safety lever still intact. Clark whirled to his right, snapping off two shots into the darkness, before a long burst of bullets thumped into his head and chest, knocking him backward like he'd been hit by a bus. He slammed into Jolene, who lost her balance and stumbled sideways until she tripped over her own feet.

Rudd launched forward and broke her fall with one arm, keeping her head from bouncing off the sidewalk. He kept his pistol hand extended, for no real reason other than to feel as though he were doing something to protect his wife. He hadn't seen a single muzzle flash, and the sidewalks were empty. Whoever had positioned these snipers had orchestrated this moment perfectly. They'd probably been behind everything that had gone down today. All leading to this stoop, and the annihilation of his team.

He managed to say "sorry" to Jolene before a bullet hit the crown of her head and switched her off forever. Rudd pressed the Glock's trigger repeatedly, aiming at nothing in particular, before he joined her.

CHAPTER 30

Jared Hoffman searched through the night vision scope attached to his suppressed rifle for any movement, finding the stoop and sidewalk completely still aside from the occasional postmortem twitch. He took his eye out of the scope and observed the entire street. Nothing. The three sweltering hours he'd spent hidden in the back seat of this car had come down to a five-second, very-one-sided gun battle. Well worth the price. He pressed the transmit button hidden inside his shirt collar.

"Melendez. You see any unfinished business?" he asked.

His earpiece crackled. "Negative. Six targets down. The couple and the four that arrived in the second SUV. Down hard."

He agreed with that assessment. Hoffman had fired nothing but head and neck shots, connecting with each burst.

"Graves. You got any funky chatter out there?" asked Hoffman.

"No. Satellite push-to-talk traffic went quiet right before the vehicles moved in," he said. "I'm monitoring the police frequencies closely. We heard the shots from here."

Hoffman was mad at himself for that. He should have plugged the husband first, especially when he didn't drop the pistol to catch her. Those five shots would guarantee a dozen or more 911 calls. The first two, fired by the other guy, might have kept people inside the townhomes guessing for a while before they finally decided to play it safe and call the police.

"Copy that," said Hoffman. "Miralles. It's all you. We'll keep you covered."

A car started on the other side of the street, down toward Foster Avenue. He caught a brief glimpse of Miralles's ski-masked face and a gloved middle finger when her vehicle raced by.

"I saw that," said Hoffman over the net.

"You were supposed to," she said.

Miralles squeezed her car past the two idling SUVs and parked in the middle of the street. She worked the scene fast, first emptying the loose contents inside each SUV into a heavy-duty black rectangular gym bag. She'd search under the seats. Inside the glove box. The seat pockets. Everywhere.

Next, she searched the bodies, emptying pockets and tossing everything but the weapons into the bag. When she'd finished with that, Miralles removed a digital camera from one of the outer pockets of the gym bag and took close-up pictures of the Russians' faces—what was left of them. A few dozen flashes later, she pocketed the camera and started on the fingerprints with a handheld scanning device. Thumbs and index fingers only.

"I'm getting a lot of police scanner traffic," said Graves.

"How long do we have?" asked Hoffman.

"Software just picked up a unit responding with 'one minute ETA.' Get out of there now," said Graves.

"Pack it up, Miralles," said Hoffman, pulling down his ski mask. "Melendez. Blaze a trail for us."

"I'm already Oscar Mike," said Miralles, headed for her car with the gym bag.

An SUV parked about five spaces beyond Miralles's sedan pulled into the street and stopped.

"Ready to roll," said Melendez. "I can hear sirens. No lights yet."

Hoffman could hear them, too. He climbed over the reclined driver's seat and slid into place behind the steering wheel, then straightened his seat before starting the car. The keys had been in the ignition the entire time. He'd left them there when he'd rolled the windows down all the way to keep from slow cooking himself to death. The last thing he needed was to be fumbling for keys at a critical moment—like his escape. A quick scan of his mirrors caught some faint red and blue flashes on the buildings at the intersection behind him.

"I have lights coming down Foster Avenue," said Hoffman. "Can't tell the direction. Get out of here. I'll catch up."

He yanked the wheel all the way to the left and pulled out of the parking space at full speed, somehow avoiding the vehicle parked in front of him. A once-in-a-lifetime stunt, he graciously accepted. Every second would count here. He sped down the street toward the Russians' SUVs, centering his car on the narrow gap between their vehicles and the cars parked along the right side of the road. He shot through the opening, once again emerging unscathed. Things were going entirely too smoothly for him so far. He'd probably broadside a police cruiser at the next intersection.

With that thought in mind, he slowed as he approached Fait Avenue, looking in both directions as he crept through the empty intersection. A few blocks west, two police cars turned onto Fait Avenue, headed in his direction. He floored the accelerator.

"I have two police cruisers coming up Fait Avenue from the west," said Hoffman. "Not sure if they saw me."

"I haven't picked up any pursuit calls," said Graves. "All town house units. Take the first left off Glover. We need to get you out of sight."

Up ahead, Melendez and Miralles turned off the road, their taillights racing left and vanishing. He hoped to get to that turn before the police cars reached the intersection behind him. Red and blue lights flashed in his mirrors, momentarily disappearing—then reappearing. They looked a lot farther away than he'd expected. Mirror tricks? Another glance in his rearview mirror left him believing they'd turned onto Glover Street beyond the Russian SUVs. He ripped off his ski mask and tossed it on the passenger seat.

"I think I have police units approaching the town house from Foster Avenue. Nothing off Fait Avenue yet," said Hoffman. "Almost at the turn."

"Confirming the units turning off Foster," said Graves. "Fait is still clear."

He glanced in the side mirror, confirming that the police units approaching from the west on Fait Avenue had not reached a point where they could see him. He had a few more seconds at most before they raced into sight. No time for stop signs. His four-door sedan skidded into the intersection ahead of him, tires screeching the entire time—as he cut directly in front of a minivan. The woman honked her horn, and kept it blaring as he drove away.

"I'm clear," said Hoffman. "But I nearly hit a minivan when I was turning off Glover. Fifty-fifty she calls nine-one-one, especially given all the police activity she's about to encounter. That and the fact that I'm still wearing a ski mask."

"You're kidding, right?" asked Melendez.

The masks were meant to prevent one of the neighbors from getting lucky with their smartphone camera. Same with the opaque license plate covers, which they'd have to remove sooner than later.

"Yeah. But I'm not kidding about the minivan. I think she's still laying on the horn," said Hoffman.

"This is Rich. Even if she calls nine-one-one, we'll be long gone before they piece any of this together. Good job, everyone. Let's run Hoffman, Miralles, and Melendez directly to Gray's apartment. The police will get makes and models from the neighbors, or the minivan lady. We don't need you reentering the city later tonight after a long SDR. The chances of getting pulled over are too high. The rest of us will—"

"Rich. This is Graves. Are we sure that was the only Russian team working the town house? A shitload of push-to-talk satellite traffic just lit up my screen. We're trying to pinpoint, but all I can give you is a general direction at the moment."

"Where?" asked Farrington.

"Somewhere east of our current location on Linwood Avenue. A few blocks away, I'd guess, based on signal strength."

"Where's Gray and Young?"

"Turning onto Eastern Avenue off Robinson Street," said Graves. "A few blocks east of here."

Hoffman hit the accelerator and blew through his second stop sign of the night. Definitely not his last.

CHAPTER 31

Devin Gray turned his mother's car onto Eastern Avenue, which ran parallel to the southern edge of Patterson Park for several city blocks. His plan was to take Eastern to Interstate 95 and drive north for a good twenty to thirty minutes, exiting in one of the city's suburbs, where he'd run a few countersurveillance drills through some of the quiet neighborhoods. Anyone following them would stick out immediately once he got off the interstate.

"How am I supposed to get my Jeep?" asked Marnie.

It was the first thing she'd said since they'd been dropped off at his car. To say that Marnie looked angry would be an understatement. Seething might be a more accurate description.

"I honestly don't know," said Devin. "I wasn't aware that the town house was a setup. I swear."

"I heard gunshots, Devin," said Marnie. "Gunshots. My name is on the Airbnb agreement."

"Tell them you ran out the back door when you heard the gunshots," said Devin, instantly realizing the many flaws in that plan.

"But I didn't call nine-one-one or hide in the alley until the police arrived," said Marnie. "I suppose if we turned around right now and you dropped me off a few blocks over, I could approach the nearest police station and ask a few questions. Maybe try to figure out if anyone reported you and Karl showing up minutes before the gunshots, so I don't totally get caught in a lie when I say that I ran away in fear. You know, get my alibi straightened out and all that."

"Marnie. You didn't do anything wrong," he said, now utterly convinced he'd be better off just shutting up.

"True. I could probably just lawyer up and tell the police that it's none of their business why I rented an Airbnb for twelve people in Baltimore for five hundred dollars a night and that same town house got attacked a few hours later. And that the two guys who showed up a few minutes before it got attacked was just a random coincidence. Spend some time trying to explain you and Karl. All while the Russians, or whoever is really after you, decides to up the ante and stop by my parents' place. Speaking of which, I need to call them."

Devin hadn't thought of her parents, or even his dad, for that matter—because he'd had no idea any of this would happen. He'd come to terms with the possibility that he might have to hide his dad and sister at some point but figured that was weeks away. Plus, Berg had said he could help with that, especially if Devin could convince his dad to fly out to Los Angeles. Apparently, Berg knew a crew out there that specialized in hiding people. But tonight's events had come as a complete surprise. He should do the same as Marnie and call his dad. Get him on a red-eye flight to Los Angeles. Same with Marnie's parents.

"You might not want to hear this, but Karl knows some people in LA that can disappear our parents for a while," said Devin. "I'm going to make my dad take that option. Karl said it would be an entirely comfortable experience. Not some desert bunker somewhere."

Devin's attention shifted from Marnie to a dark SUV speeding into the intersection. *Shit.* His satellite phone rang a moment later, the name KARL appearing on the screen.

"Sounds wonderful," said Marnie. "I'll let you explain to them. I'm sure they'll—"

Devin slammed on the brakes, the car skidding to a halt well short of the black SUV.

"What the hell, Devin!" said Marnie, bracing her arms against the dashboard.

199

He detected movement in his peripheral vision, his eyes shifting to the driver's-side mirror. A sedan parked itself diagonally across the two-lane street behind him, blocking most of it. He briefly considered turning left and driving into the park, but the doors flew open on both vehicles as a second SUV screeched into the intersection in front of him. If he turned the vehicle, he'd expose the sides of his car to gunfire.

"Russians. Get down!" said Devin, ducking below the dashboard and opening his car door. "Take out the guys behind us first. We'll use the car as cover until help arrives."

"How do we even know—" she started, the windshield instantly spider-cracking from several bullet holes.

"That's how!" said Devin, sliding out of the car and staying low. "Get behind the car!"

He drew the M&P9 from the concealed holster on his right hip and sighted in on the masked attacker who had just jumped down from the rear driver's-side seat. He fired as he moved toward the back of his car, pressing the trigger five times in rapid succession and knocking his target against the back of the sedan. He shifted the pistol's sights to the driver, who had dropped to both knees—arms by his side, pistol clattering to the street. The man's head snapped back before Devin pressed the trigger, Marnie finishing him off.

Bullets from the intersection snapped inches overhead and to his side as he emptied the rest of his magazine at the shooter who had crouched next to the sedan's rear bumper. The man pitched forward and caught his fall with both hands, his pistol still clutched in one of them. Devin ejected the spent pistol magazine and grabbed one of the spares concealed on his left hip, his brain doing the math. Time was not on his side.

His reload was quick and flawless, but the man had his gun up and pointed in his direction before he'd thumbed the slide release and chambered a round. Devin should have reserved a few bullets and assessed his first volley. He'd made a fatal error. Gunfire exploded in his ear, the heat from repeated muzzle blasts warming the side of his face. The shooter next to the car's bumper slammed against the street, his arms giving out beneath him as several bullets peppered his body. The business end of Marnie's Sig Sauer suddenly appeared in Devin's peripheral vision, its barrel smoking.

He released his pistol's slide and scooted behind the car, bullets fired from the intersection chasing him around the bumper. Devin searched the sedan for movement, finding none at the moment.

"Any left back here?" asked Devin.

"No. I took out the driver, front passenger, and the guy that was about to shoot you," said Marnie, reloading her pistol. "This is my last mag."

"I thought you were a helicopter pilot," he said.

"Marine first. Helicopter pilot second," she said.

A burst of automatic gunfire raked the sedan. Glass blasted across the top of the trunk and rained down on their heads, the car's metal chassis thumping from multiple bullet hits along its side. Devin risked a look around the corner of the car, drawing more automatic fire, a few bullets punching through the trunk near his head. He counted at least three attackers moving in on his side.

Marnie's gun barked twice before she was driven back by gunfire, sparks flying off the pavement next to her. She moved toward the center of the trunk moments before the taillight exploded, spraying her with plastic shards. Devin peeked around the taillight next to him with his pistol, firing at a man who had reached a point even with the hood of the car. His bullets caught the attacker high on the left side of his torso, spinning him to face the hood. Before Devin could drill the man again, a hail of bullets pushed him back-to-back against Marnie. They were out of room and nearly out of time. He saw only one way out of this now—for one of them.

"Get ready to make a run for the back of the sedan. Stay low and focus your shots on targets to the left side of this car. You should be screened from any gunfire on the other side. Empty your gun and pick up one of theirs," said Devin, nodding at the dead guy lying behind the SUV. "They probably have something that packs a bigger punch in the vehicle. I'll buy you some time."

"What does that mean?" she said, before popping up to squeeze off three quick shots.

A furious maelstrom of bullets answered her gunfire, a few skipping off the pavement underneath the car—miraculously missing their feet. The car dropped several inches, its tires flattened by the latest fusillade of supersonic projectiles.

"They're right up next to the car," she said. "We won't make it."

"I'll draw their fire down the left side," said Devin. "You empty your pistol at anyone you see. You'll make it."

"But you won't. We stick together," said Marnie, winking at him. "That's the plan."

A bullet creased his left shin, dropping his knee to the pavement. Marnie grabbed his shirt and kept him from falling forward. He raised his pistol over the trunk and fired a few blind shots, hoping to dissuade anyone creeping along the side of the car.

"I got you into this," he said. "I'll get you out. Get ready to run."

"I don't think either of us is getting out of this, but I'd rather go down trying," she said before extending her pistol around the shattered taillight next to her and blindly emptying her magazine.

Screams erupted from her side of the car, once again answered by more gunfire than they could hope to repel with one pistol remaining between them.

"Let's go," she said, taking off.

Devin grabbed her wrist and yanked her back, having heard the screech of tires somewhere nearby.

"What the hell are you doing?" she said.

The volume of gunfire passing over and next to them doubled instantly, muzzle flashes appearing from the corner of the nearest building at the intersection one street behind them. More tires screeched, this time clearly coming from the intersection ahead.

"Our backup arrived," said Devin.

He quick-peeked around the side of the car with his pistol, seeing two masked figures. Both of them fired their submachine guns over the hood at Berg's newly arrived associates. One of them noticed him and started to swing his weapon back in Devin's direction, but it was too late. Devin pressed the trigger twice, punching two holes in his face, before shifting aim and firing the remaining six bullets center mass—knocking the second shooter flat. A short burst of bullets fired from one of Berg's people stitched across the guy's torso just moments after he hit the street.

The mix of gunfire changed over the course of the next several seconds. More and more suppressed gunfire, which sounded more like hands clapping than regular gunfire—until everything went quiet. Devin started to get up.

"Stay down!" yelled a voice from the intersection. "We'll tell you when it's clear!"

Devin crouched beside Marnie and reloaded his pistol while a brief symphony of suppressed gunshots played out in the intersection against a background of police sirens.

"I can't believe this just happened," she said, a single suppressed shot punctuating her sentence. "That it's still happening. They're just walking around intersections popping people in the head, aren't they?"

"I can't see exactly what they're doing, but—"

"It was more of a rhetorical question," she said, a nearby shot startling both of them. "Of course they're executing people. How is any of this even possible—in the middle of fucking Baltimore? What did your mom stumble on?"

"You'll see soon enough," said Devin. "It's big."

"It must be," she said.

"Devin. Marnie. It's Rich. I'm standing directly in front of your car," he yelled. "We're clear, and we need to get out of here immediately."

"You okay?" asked Devin.

"I didn't get shot, if that's what you mean," said Marnie. "You?"

"I'm good," he said before slowly rising from a crouch to a standing position.

His shin burned from the bullet that had grazed him, but that was about it. He'd been extremely lucky. An inch back, and the bullet would have torn muscle and possibly fragmented bone. They were both lucky, when he thought about it. Several bullets had zipped under the car during the gun battle, any one of them with the potential to have altered the night's outcome.

Rich met them along the side of the car, next to three dead operatives. Suppressed assault rifle slung across a black-plate carrier vest, he pointed at a black SUV parked at the edge of the intersection.

"Get in the back with Karl," said Farrington. "We're out of here in fifteen seconds. Go!"

They took off for the SUV, Devin surveying the carnage as they ran. Rich and three of his associates quickly spread out among the vehicles, yanking the masks off several of the shooters and taking pictures. The moment Devin and Marnie reached the SUV, Rich spoke into his microphone and the crew bolted in their direction. Marnie opened the door and got inside, while Devin watched a precision machine in action.

Rich stopped next to Devin's car and took something that looked like a phone from one of the dead shooters' hands. After pocketing the device, he tossed two cylindrical devices in the car, one in the back seat and one in the front. He took off for the SUV as soon as the second device left his hand. Down the street, beyond the sedan that had boxed them in from behind, a massive billow of smoke exploded in the middle of the intersection, followed by a second, rapidly expanding cloud of smoke about twenty yards past the first.

Scott sprinted by him and continued past the two cars parked tightly behind the SUV. He pulled the pin on a smoke grenade and overhand threw it at least fifty feet down the street. On his way back, he prepped another grenade and tossed it about half as far as the one before. The distant grenade detonated, instantly obscuring the street with a pure white smoke. The second popped a few seconds later, thickening the smoke screen. They did the same at all points leading into the intersection, as the sound of sirens approached, and police lights started reflecting off the trees in the adjacent park.

A blinding flash lit the entire intersection, followed almost immediately by a hollow-sounding explosion. Devin turned in time to see the second incendiary grenade detonate in his mother's car, ejecting a shower of brightly burning pellets out of every window in a hissing fireworks-grade pyrotechnic display. The interior of the car burst into flames instantly. Rich raced up to the SUV and handed him a satellite phone, which he recognized as his own. One of the Russians must have taken it.

Devin slid inside and shut the door. The SUV lurched forward and pinned him against the seat. Visibility beyond the windshield dropped to zero as soon as they turned onto Eastern Avenue. They drove blind for several seconds before emerging from the smoke. The traffic light a block ahead was green. Flashing red and blue lights reflected off the intersection's buildings. Scott slowed the SUV as two police Ford Interceptor SUVs raced into view and turned in their direction.

Rich raised his rifle a few inches, adjusting his grip. Devin glanced at Marnie, who had apparently noticed the same thing. Berg leaned forward.

"Rich. We had an agreement," he said.

The rifle lowered. "Sorry. Just a little wired."

The Interceptors sped past them, and Devin turned to watch them through the cargo compartment windshield. The two police vehicles stopped at the edge of the expanding street-wide cloud and immediately backed up, their white reverse lights already hazy from the smoke. The two sedans carrying other members of Rich's team peeled left at the intersection they'd just crossed, headed north on South Ellwood Avenue. The Interceptors stopped backing up about halfway to the intersection, but none of the officers got out. A lone police car swerved into the intersection from the north, where Rich's associates had just turned, and parked next to the SUVs. It appeared that the police hadn't taken notice of them. Yet.

"Looks like we're clear for now," said Devin.

Rich glanced between the seats. "*Clear* is a relative term at the moment. This changes things."

"Changes everything," said Berg.

"Definitely changes our escape and evasion plan. I think we'll head to BWI and abandon these in long-term parking. Pick up some rentals in the terminal. I'll have Gupta make the arrangements through a business account," said Rich. "We have to assume all four of the vehicles involved with the town house have been made. This one and the three sedans."

"Scrap the airport rental car idea," said Devin. "They'll have people watching the rental agencies inside and outside of the terminal. That's what I would do. We need to find a twenty-four-hour parking garage just north of DC, near a Metro station. A number of the parking garages offer monthly parking, payable on the spot. Silver Spring has a few. Ride the Metro for a little while, then grab a taxi back to the general vicinity of my mother's apartment. Cash only. Nobody will find the vehicles."

"Devin's right. We can rendezvous with the Suburban along the way and transfer all of our weapons and gear," said Rich.

"We need to be careful with the Suburban," said Berg. "They must have had someone watching the front of the town house and possibly the back. The timing of this attack suggests they knew when to start looking for vehicles leaving the area."

"I'll tell Graves and Gupta to be careful and take their time. It's going to be a long night," said Rich.

"There's no way they could have known the town house address before we set up our surveillance," hissed Scott. "We should have detected them."

"Not if they started off assuming the whole thing was a setup," said Devin. "They would have kept their distance and used text messages to communicate. They probably had four teams out there like the one that hit us. Each team spread out to cover the most likely routes away from the town house in each direction."

"Who the hell are we dealing with?" asked Marnie. "That's a lot of personnel to throw at a problem on US soil. Russians or not."

"I have a sneaking suspicion we're dealing with two groups tonight. Pulled by the same strings," said Berg.

"When we run the photos taken of the group that boxed you in by the intersection, my money is on matching a few of the faces to Russian embassy or consulate employees from DC and New York City. The rest are probably nonofficial cover types. Tourists flown in for this job or Russian nationals that work or study in the US. That's the new thing. No need to build up an alias to run missions in the US. All you need is a nonimmigrant visa, which isn't hard to come by."

"This felt like more of an assassination team," said Devin. "And not a subtle one."

"Not a good one, either," said Rich. "Neither of you should have made it out of the car. You certainly shouldn't have been able to take out the entire team that pulled up behind you."

"We managed just fine," said Marnie. "For a while, at least."

"My friend has a point," said Berg. "They threw a junior varsity team at you. Probably all they could put together at the moment. They thought it would be enough, but you surprised them. Unlike Rich, I give credit where credit is due."

"Some consolation," said Marnie.

"So if they saw the two of us walk into the town house together, why didn't they try to take us both out?" said Devin. "What good am I dead, when someone else obviously knows about their secret plot?"

"They just wanted your phone," said Rich. "They could have hacked your location data and figured out where your mother's apartment is located. That's why one of them grabbed it in the middle of a gun battle."

"Makes sense," said Devin. "Then what about the other team?"

"I've been trying to put my finger on this," said Berg. "The team that has been following you—"

"And me," said Marnie.

"And you," said Berg, pausing as though he might say he was sorry. "That team looked and acted old school. I mean, all in their mid- to late fifties? They've been around for a while, probably doing low-level stuff to stay off the radar. SVR or GRU illegals planted right after the Soviet Union collapsed, probably in the early nineties—when our guard was down."

"Still *is* down," said Rich.

"Good point," said Berg.

"This is kind of odd," said Devin, remembering the crew he put in the hospital a couple of weeks ago. "I think I've run into this crew before."

"The group following you?" asked Berg.

"No. I worked a sting at MINERVA, the same night everything went down with my mom. It was a counter-honey-trap operation, except that everyone but the honey trap was in their fifties. I put three of them in the hospital that night; the rest flew out of Dulles the next morning. One of our surveillance teams followed them to the KLM ticket counter."

"That's very interesting," said Berg. "Did MINERVA identify any of them? I know they can be pretty thorough."

"I don't know. Everything blew up with my mother right after the operation," said Devin. "They were reaching out to law enforcement contacts to get some help with fingerprints. None of them carried ID. I can reach out to my boss to see if they found anything."

"We'll have to vet him first," said Berg.

"Yeah," said Devin. "He fits the profile."

Marnie ran her fingers through her shoulder-length hair, back and forth, before making two fists in her lap, hands shaking.

"You okay?" asked Devin, wondering if once again he should keep his mouth shut.

"I feel like you guys are talking in code," said Marnie. "On purpose."

"We're not," said Berg. "It's too much to explain without showing you. Trust me. This is complicated in an epically bad way."

"I can't wait," said Marnie.

"Neither can I," said Rich.

"You haven't seen it yet?" she asked.

"I got Helen's executive summary," said Rich. "What she prepared for Devin or whoever took over the fight for her. That was enough to get me out here. Seeing the first Russian team move in was enough to convince me this was real. The last attack? That sealed the deal."

"I don't suppose there's any way I could get my hands on that right now?" she said.

"I have a copy in the glove box," he said.

"You don't really have a copy in the glove box," said Berg.

"I do," said Rich. "I hate reading on my phone."

"Marnie. You don't have to get involved in this any further than I've involved you," said Devin. "We need to get your parents to a safe house or something until Karl can reach out to that group in LA that's good at hiding people. I'm really sorry about all of this."

Rich turned in his seat. "I've already taken the liberty of making those arrangements. I prepositioned two of my people in Falls Church in case something went wrong tonight. I figured this qualified, so I activated the plan. My team will escort them to a private terminal at Reagan National Airport, where they'll board a private jet and fly to Los Angeles. Same with your dad, Devin. Unless they refuse. Nobody is forcing anybody to do anything."

"I need to call them and let them know it's okay," said Marnie, pulling out her cell phone.

"One call and then we have to toss that phone," said Rich.

"We could drop her off at Reagan instead of BWI and grab a few rentals there," said Scott.

Marnie stopped dialing. "I am not going to LA."

"You don't have to stick around," said Devin. "Seriously. This will more than likely get way uglier."

"I can guarantee it," said Rich.

"You're not getting rid of me that easily," said Marnie. "I want to see exactly what your mother was up to. To see why the Russians would go this far to bury it."

"Careful what you wish for," said Berg. "If you gaze long enough into this abyss—"

"Russians try to kill you?" said Marnie.

"Sounds about right," said Rich, handing her the document that had started all this.

PART IV

CHAPTER 32

Yuri Pichugin nodded at the squat mercenary standing next to the mahogany door set into the thirty-foot-high white marble wall of the five-thousand-square-foot indoor arboretum, his favorite place to relax in his palace-size mansion on Lake Ladoga. Especially in the winter, when Saint Petersburg became quite dark and dreary. On five-degree, blustery overcast days, the exquisite tropical paradise provided a welcome refuge when he was in town. In fact, he so preferred this space to any other that he'd replicated a small section of his office overlooking the lake in one of the corners of the arboretum, adjacent to the main house.

The ex-GRU Spetsnaz soldier opened the door for his surprise guest. Unexpected in that he'd anticipated receiving a simple phone call confirming that the threat to FIREBIRD had been extinguished. Not a personal visit. General Kuznetzov's trip obviously heralded bad news. The kind that required a one hundred percent secure method of communication. A face-to-face discussion. The value of which could never be understated, or more importantly—intercepted.

Yuri stood up from his desk and walked over to greet him. A carafe of vodka and two shot glasses sat on a sprawling coffee table between two oversize blue velvet couches, along with a three-tiered silver stand loaded with finger sandwiches and toasted crostini. Two silver caviar servers flanked the sandwiches. Normally he wouldn't roll out anything but the vodka for Kuznetzov, but his visit coincided with lunch.

"Grigory! Please come!" said Pichugin, expending all the fake enthusiasm he could muster for the man.

He personally couldn't stand Kuznetzov, but their fates had been inexorably tied together for two decades. The man had been in the right place at the right time—at the right price. If Yuri had thought he could have run FIREBIRD after the last Directorate's purge without the general's help, he would have encased the rotund man in cement after taking over the program and dropped him in the Baltic Sea years ago. The man had proved instrumental during those early years, systematically migrating all control and evidence of the highly compartmentalized secret program out of the GRU's hands and into Pichugin's.

He'd be lying if he said he didn't think of disappearing Kuznetzov in the years immediately following the handover, but FIREBIRD had proved more difficult to manage than Pichugin had assumed—and the general had led him to believe. They needed the GRU's long-established and expiring network of illegals to pave the way for FIREBIRD's second generation. To remove any obstacles from their assigned paths.

Pichugin could have attempted to outsource this work, but the GRU operatives had proved their loyalty and effectiveness for decades. He didn't see any reason to risk the use of men and women whose sole allegiance rested in a bank deposit when he had an army of well-paid idealogues at his disposal.

Kuznetzov emerged indispensable. Even more so when Pichugin brought FIREBIRD and his revised plans for its use to Putin, a mutual confidant and partner in several enterprises at that point. Putin endorsed FIREBIRD's repurposing without hesitation, ensuring them access to whatever resources they required to make it succeed. Once Putin linked Kuznetzov's name and face so intimately to FIREBIRD's success—the general became untouchable.

"Yuri!" said the general, eyeballing the spread. "You shouldn't have gone to any trouble."

"I figured I might need to settle my stomach during our chat," said Pichugin. "This can't be good."

The door shut behind Kuznetzov, the security operative leaving them alone.

"Nothing we can't handle," he said, taking a seat opposite him across the table.

Pichugin poured two shots of vodka and handed one to the general.

"Za vstrechu," he said, and they downed a premier version of Russian Standard. "So. Tell me about this problem we can handle but requires you to fly out from Moscow."

"Devin Gray made some new friends over the past couple of days," said the general. "Some very deadly and resourceful friends. Do you remember the name Karl Berg?"

"Vaguely," he said. "CIA?"

"Ex-CIA," said Kuznetzov. "Pegged to General Terrence Sanderson's troublemakers."

"Now that's a name I'm more familiar with," said Pichugin. "Never crossed paths with his people, but the name has come up at the highest level before. I thought there was some kind of understanding in place."

"There is. But this would fall well outside of that back channel deal," said the general. "For obvious reasons."

"I suppose it would," said Pichugin.

"And Sanderson is supposedly retired these days. Richard Farrington reportedly took over what was left of Sanderson's black ops program. He has apparently rebuilt it to some degree."

"What happened?"

"The illegals sent to the town house to grab Berg and Gray were killed at the doorstep. All of them dead within seconds. The only survivor was the illegal left to watch Gray's apartment."

"I want her dead as soon as possible," said Pichugin.

"Already taken care of. She's melting in a barrel of lye as we speak," said the general. "The real problem is that the GRU team comprised

215

of consulate and NOC operatives was wiped out several blocks away, attempting to intercept Gray. There's going to be a little bit of a shit-storm at GRU headquarters. Frankly, I'm glad to be out of town right now."

"There's going to be a considerable shitstorm," said Pichugin. "I hope you have your story straight."

Kuznetzov shrugged. "The illegals team was expendable. I had used them as bait—just in case Gray was onto them. Apparently he was, probably with Berg's help. The other group's mission will pass scrutiny, because there will be no scrutiny. I gave it the 'from the top' label. I hope it won't be a problem."

"I'll make sure he's aware of that situation," said Pichugin, slyly referring to Putin. "I don't see a problem. But we can't use any more Russian Federation assets moving forward."

"Including the old illegals?" asked the general.

"For now. Especially in the DC area," he said. "I'll assemble a top-drawer mercenary crew and move them into position to strike when we locate Gray and Berg."

"Shall I leverage a few of our more well-placed FIREBIRD assets to help expedite the process of finding them? Gray and his new friends obviously know better than to use their credit cards or cell phones."

"Yes," said Pichugin. "Devin Gray's mother has obviously been working on this for some time. The fact that she uncovered Donald Wilson leaves more questions than answers. Like how many more did she discover?"

"I see three scenarios. None of them is good. Unfortunately, we'll never know which one has materialized, so we have to assume the worst. Best-case scenario is that Kozlov only passed one more name to the Gray woman: Donald Wilson. We know she received at least two names from General Kozlov," said Kuznetzov. "We deactivated both families six years ago after one of the FIREBIRD assets discovered that both families had been investigated by the FBI in 2003."

"Remember how close we came to shutting everything down after Kozlov?" asked Pichugin.

"How could I forget?" said the general. "I don't think I slept for the next two years, waiting for the whole thing to fall apart."

The general poured more vodka, which they tossed back immediately. Followed by another round.

"Back to the Wilson scenario. If Kozlov indeed passed his name, he would have done it for the express purpose of exposing SITE ZERO. Wilson oversaw the program for most of its years," said the general.

"But she never found it," said Pichugin.

"Exactly. She nosed around the lakes for several years, but never located it," said the general.

"Remind me again why we didn't kill her years ago?"

"Because she was kicked out of the CIA for obsessing over a possible Russian sleeper conspiracy. We were afraid that her untimely death might trigger a serious look into her theory," said the general. "And we never got any real indication that she'd uncovered any of the FIREBIRD families outside of the two names she had been given. She'd vanish for weeks at a time, but nobody reported anything unusual. Not even Wilson."

"I think we might have underestimated her," said Pichugin.

"On some level, yes. Which brings me to the worst-case scenario, which I don't believe is in play—but we have to consider," said the general. "Kozlov gave her the whole list."

"I don't think so," said Pichugin. "The CIA would have taken a list like that seriously. They would have investigated the families, like the other two, and determined they had a serious Russian sleeper agent problem on their hands. There's no indication that this occurred. Helen Gray was working alone when she kidnapped Wilson."

"Agreed. I think we need to assume that Helen Gray discovered Wilson on her own years ago, based on some publicly available connection to one of the two names Kozlov provided," said the general.

"And that she eventually figured out the greater pattern that the CIA overlooked—the kids. She could start a list of politicians or government types that fit the age group and work backward."

"No evidence of grandparents," said Pichugin.

"A dead giveaway. Not conclusive, but a start," said the general. "My guess is that she'd put together a list and wanted to run some names by Donald Wilson."

"The timing couldn't be worse. We're too close to the endgame to have this unravel on us," said Pichugin. "I want you to alert the entire FIREBIRD network. Basic surveillance and security precautions for now. We have to assume that other FIREBIRD assets have been identified by Devin Gray and his new friends."

"I'll instruct Gusev to send the alert when I get back to Moscow," said the general. "We'll also bring US National Security Agency and law enforcement support on board to locate Gray for your mercenary team."

Gusev ran one of the most tightly guarded secrets in Russia from a nameless, ultrasecure compound on a sprawling estate west of Moscow—known only as CONTROL to the agents it directed in the United States.

"Contact Gusev from my secure line, after we finish lunch," said Pichugin. "We need to get the ball rolling on this."

Everything was at stake if Gray and his new friends fully unraveled their secret.

CHAPTER 33

Marnie Young sat cross-legged in one of the far corners of Helen Gray's vault, sifting through the last of the Branson file papers. She'd been up most of the night absorbing as much of the information Helen had assembled as possible, in the order Karl Berg had recommended—which ended with the accordion file in front of her.

Rich sat next to her in the corner, his legs extended along the evidence wall. She handed him the packet she'd just finished, which he started reading without comment. Marnie had made her peace with Rich and Karl last night during their lengthy drive around Baltimore. *Cleared the air* might be a better description. She still intended to keep a close eye on the two of them, until they fully earned her trust. Marnie got the impression it wouldn't take long. They seemed just as vested in getting to the bottom of what Devin's mother had uncovered as Devin—and now Marnie.

After spending close to six hours digesting Helen Gray's documentation, there was no doubt in her mind that the conspiracy was real, and possibly worse than Devin's mother had believed. The double-layered attack on Devin last night demonstrated that the Russians were desperate to erase this evidence and anyone who had seen it. Now they were all targets. Something Berg said last night had stuck with her. She hadn't known what it meant at the time, but it made perfect sense now. They'd crossed the point of no return.

She skimmed the last few packets, having seen enough. Berg's overview last night painted a clear enough picture. They needed to find this suspected camp in the Ozarks, if it even still existed, to lend credibility to the entire conspiracy. This second generation of sleepers couldn't have been radicalized at home. She had no doubt that their home lives were strictly regulated to ensure that they remained loyal to Mother Russia, but Helen Gray was right. The Russians would need a way to test and reinforce this loyalty.

One break in allegiance could burn the entire conspiracy down, and it was clear from the research that thirty-seven children pressed into service to the Russian Federation from birth had been murdered to maintain the program's secrecy. The thought of it was spine-tingling. Parents had delivered their children to their executions, or at the very least looked the other way when the grim reaper came knocking.

She passed the rest of the packets to Rich.

"Seen enough?" he asked.

"Yep," she said.

He dropped them on the pile he'd built on his lap. "Me too. The whole thing is mind-boggling, but the Branson file is just sick. They ran a brainwashing camp right in the heartland of the country, complete with firing squads and everything. Unbelievable."

"I feel terrible for Devin's mother. And for Devin. They thought she was slowly going crazy for close to two decades," said Marnie.

"Sometimes a conspiracy, or any big idea, I suppose, is simply too big or hard to believe for its time."

"Or both," she said.

"Right," said Rich. "Conversely, if you don't give people enough, they can't even begin to see the bigger picture and take it seriously. The downfall of the United States—an economic, political, and military superpower—is a hard pill to swallow. From her notes, it appears that she started with the big picture, instantly alienating everyone she approached. That poisoned her later attempts to trickle information to her remaining allies, who started avoiding her entirely. She could never seem to strike the right balance, and maybe there wasn't a balance to be struck at the time. On top of that, the CIA had its hands full right around the time she'd started to strike gold with some of her investigative work. Full of Russians and domestic terrorists. Bad timing all around for Helen Gray."

"It was awful for her family," she said.

"How long have you known Devin?" said Rich. "Seems like a solid guy."

"We've been friends since middle school. Better friends in high school," she said. "We've kept in touch since then. Mostly off and on, but anytime our paths cross, we grab dinner or a drink. We've both been pretty busy since college."

"Just friends?" asked Rich.

"More or less," she said.

"I see," he said, slightly raising an eyebrow.

"What do you mean by 'I see'"?

"Nothing," said Rich, nodding toward the vault door. "Here comes Mr. More-or-Less right now with our breakfast."

"Funny," she said.

Devin and the operative named Jared walked through the doorway carrying brown oil-stained bags and two carryout cartons of Dunkin' coffee. The rest of Rich's team came to life as they started to move files to make room on the table that had been dragged into the vault from the kitchen.

As much as she wanted to use the term "motley crew" to describe Rich's team, they didn't fit that description. Everyone looked ragged after sleeping on the floor in the same clothes they'd worn yesterday, but this wasn't the kind of rogues' gallery you might connect to the words *mercenary* or *soldier of fortune*.

The two operatives who had escorted her parents and Devin's dad to the airport looked as though they'd just returned from a business conference, dressed in pressed khaki pants, oxford shirts, and windbreakers— to conceal their holstered pistols. Alex and Michael. Just two regular guys who could probably draw those pistols and drill every person in this room through the head in the span of a few seconds.

Then you had Scott, who she'd really only seen drive an SUV at this point and throw a smoke grenade farther than she'd ever seen someone throw a grenade before. Berg said he was an ex–Navy SEAL, which would have been her first guess. Tall with a muscular swimmer's build, totally contrasting with the rest of the team members, who looked like career ground-pounders. Muscular and stocky.

She assumed Rico and Jared were the team's designated snipers, based on the assignments they'd been given at the town house. Emily could be anything. A taut, unsmilingly serious woman of few words, with catlike reflexes, who looked just as at ease with a knife as a firearm. Earlier she'd balanced a daggerlike blade on her fingertip while studying the wall, flipping to the handle and then back again repeatedly. Of all the mercenaries in the room, Emily scared her the most.

The two surveillance gurus had expressed similar sentiments earlier. Graves and Gupta had nodded toward her on a few occasions, shaking their heads and rolling their eyes at something Emily had said. Those two intrigued her the most. Gupta might be in his early forties, but he acted like he was twenty-two, and stuck in a late-nineties rap video. Graves, who spent most of his time calming Gupta down, was clearly pushing fifty and walked with a limp. The two couldn't be more different, but between the occasional sibling-like bickering, they worked together seamlessly. All in all, she could see why Karl had placed so much faith in this crew.

Devin opened the bags and started tossing aluminum foil–wrapped breakfast burritos around the room. Everyone snatched them out of the air as though their lives depended on it. Devin hand delivered her burrito, along with Rich's.

"They're all the same. Chorizo and eggs, with cheese and a bunch of other stuff," said Devin.

"Sounds heavenly," said Marnie, thinking she sounded like an idiot.

"Two thousand calories of heaven," said Rich. "How's your leg?"

Devin lifted his pant leg to expose a napkin-size compress taped in place over the front of his shin. A few specks of red poked through the sterile white dressing.

"It's not bad at all. Normally this would take a few stitches, but it'll heal up fine," said Devin.

"Emily can stitch you up if you want. She's a former combat medic," said Rich. "Her kit includes a serious local anesthetic. You won't feel a thing."

Marnie nodded. "I'd take them up on the offer. God knows what we'll be up to over the next several days."

"We'll be up to no good. That's for certain," said Rich, getting up. "What kind of coffee do you have in the kitchen?"

"Nespresso machine. No idea about the coffee itself," said Devin. "Berg seemed happy."

"Berg knows his coffee. I think I'll grab one of those," said Rich. "Be right back."

Devin took Rich's place next to Marnie, unceremoniously tearing open one end of his breakfast burrito and taking a bite large enough to have possibly included some aluminum foil. He glanced at her and covered his mouth.

"Sorry," he mumbled.

"I'm right there with you," she said before hungrily attacking her own breakfast.

They'd finished half of their burritos before Devin broke the silence.

"What do you think's next?"

An odd question, she thought.

"The consensus seems to be that we need to find this summer camp in the Ozarks."

"Yeah. But how?" said Devin. "I'm a little worried about what I'm hearing."

Marnie hadn't heard any talk beyond locating the camp, but she'd given it some thought and probably came to the same conclusion reached by Rich and Karl. She wasn't sure how she felt about it, but what choice did they have? And as long as they could keep things under control, which they seemed more than capable of doing, nobody innocent would get hurt. At least that was what she kept telling herself.

"What are you hearing?" she asked.

He leaned over and whispered, "I'm hearing the words *kidnap* and *interrogation*."

"It's in their hands," said Marnie. "They know what they're doing."

Devin lowered his breakfast and considered her for a moment. "You're okay with that?"

"What are the other options?" she said. "From what I've read, your mother spent weeks down at the Missouri-Arkansas border, with nothing to show for it. Given the stakes here, I can't say I disagree with them."

Devin looked conflicted, but he nodded. "I know. I'm just worried about how far they'll go to secure the information. This group doesn't fuck around—at all."

"We'll have to be the voice of reason," she said. "Draw the line at innocent family members. Especially kids."

"I don't think we'll have to worry about Rich and his crew hurting kids," said Devin. "I don't see them as the types to go that far, and there may be no point trying to leverage the kids against the parents. This second generation of sleepers lived through a modern-day pogrom. Thirty-seven of their summer camp friends executed. Nearly a third of their numbers. I don't expect anything different from this generation of sleepers. They'll more than likely sacrifice their children before betraying the cause."

She squeezed his hand. "Promise me the children are off limits."

Devin took her hand firmly. "No kids. No innocent victims. That's the line. That's also the reason we can't let them sideline us."

"What do you mean?" she asked.

He let go of her hand. "Berg made it very clear that he didn't think I was, uh . . . up to the task—for lack of a better phrase. That's why he kept me in the dark about the town house ambush. He knew I would have freaked out and blown the whole operation."

"Why would you freak out?" she asked.

"Because of you," he said abruptly before pausing for an uncomfortable amount of time. "The thought of causing you or your parents any harm would have driven me to—look, it's not like you would have left the town house if I had asked you, right?"

"Right. I had no intention of leaving until I was satisfied that you were mentally sound and not under duress," she said before scanning the room. "From Karl and his associates."

"Which is why I would have done something rash to warn you off. Something that could have blown the whole operation. I would not have sat on my hands and let you get sucked into this. Or worse," said Devin. "He knew that."

"What's worse?"

"Worse is what almost happened at the intersection," said Devin. "Berg was smart not to say anything. My concern is that he's already warned everyone on the team about my reservations, and they won't level with us during the planning phase. Then they'll bench us at the last minute to keep us out of it altogether."

Marnie took his hand, for no other reason than she needed to hold someone's hand right now. At least that was what she told herself.

"There's nothing we can do about that, ultimately," she said. "But we can't stay silent. We need to make our position clear on this. Trust me, it'll make a difference."

She let go of his hand when Rich returned with one of the coffee mugs Devin had previously advised her not to use for sanitary reasons. He glanced in her direction and vaguely nodded, presumably acknowledging what he'd just seen transpire. She nodded back, still unsure what to make of the undeniably special connection she shared with Devin.

CHAPTER 34

They wolfed down their breakfast burritos in silence, Devin wanting to expand on his earlier sentiment about keeping her out of danger. Put a more personal spin on it. He'd already reviewed his words several times and decided it sounded a little too perfunctory, like an obligation. It was more than that for him, but this wasn't the time or the place to risk making her feel even more uncomfortable. The moment was awkward enough.

They had a job to do and couldn't afford any distractions moving forward. As last night had clearly demonstrated, the difference between life and death in Karl and Rich's world could be defined by fractions of a second. Devin had managed to respond quickly enough to salvage the initial situation, but he couldn't help thinking that if he'd been paying better attention, he could have bypassed the roadblock altogether by turning into the park.

Instead, his only real option had been to slam on the brakes to avoid a collision, which had forced them into a lopsided gun battle. If Rich's team hadn't arrived when they had, neither of them would be sitting here munching on breakfast. He finished the last few bites and started to put the Branson file back together. Rich was making the rounds, and it sounded as though they were about to kick off their first planning session as a group. Devin guessed the file would be a key part of any discussion regarding their next move.

"Need anything before we get started?" asked Devin before standing up.

"Coffee? Maybe one of those Nespressos?" she said, accepting a lift off the floor.

"Coming right up," he said.

Devin dropped the file off next to his mother's desk, which had been converted into Graves and Gupta's workstation. Their fingers had been clacking on three laptops all night, their screens mirrored on a fifty-inch curved screen that spanned the desk to make it easier to highlight their findings. On the floor next to the desk, they had set up a proxy server to filter all data traffic sent and received through the satellite dish they had mounted outside the kitchen window. Devin got the distinct impression that they'd done this hundreds of times in support of Rich's operations, in much tighter and less accommodating spaces.

When he returned with the coffees, everyone had gathered in a stretched semicircle behind the desk. A few sitting cross-legged, Graves and Gupta in chairs off to the side with laptops. The rest standing. Everyone nurturing a cup of coffee like it might be their last. He squeezed behind the group and stood on the edge, next to Marnie. She took the paper cup and gave it a try.

"Lives up to the hype," she said, giving him an approving look.

"My mom always loved her coffee," said Devin. "I feel like we're dishonoring her memory by serving that other stuff."

She nudged his arm with her elbow, as she'd done countless times before, but it now felt infinitely more distracting. He was going to get them killed if he didn't focus better.

Rich nodded at him. "Ready?" he asked.

"It's your show," said Devin before turning his head to acknowledge Karl Berg. "And Karl's."

"With all due respect," said Karl, who occupied the only other chair set off to the other side of the semicircle, "this is your mother's show. I wish she were here to be a part of this. For those of you who don't know—or only caught a whiff of the story—everything you see here is the work of a single person: Helen Gray. Devin's mother. Helen took her life under what can only be described as inexplicable circumstances, though I have a theory, for another time. She put this together after trying to warn authorities for years. She even warned me back in 2007, but as most of you know, I was a bit preoccupied with another conspiracy. I just wanted everyone to know that one woman, a true American patriot in every sense of the word, easily spent several thousand hours of her time, at great cost, to assemble this. A truly remarkable accomplishment."

Berg looked teary eyed, which made this difficult for Devin. He simply nodded at Berg, focusing all his remaining energy on not crying. This didn't strike him as an emotional crowd, and the last thing he wanted to do was give them the final nudge toward shelving him during the upcoming operation. Marnie squeezed his hand briefly as Rich raised his coffee mug.

"To Helen Gray. To your mother," he said.

Rich got down to business the moment the toast ended.

"Everyone has been briefed on the overall concept of operations moving forward. Find the Ozarks camp, if it exists. Still a big *if*. The camp should shed some more light on the size and scope of the sleeper network. If we can directly link it to these sleepers, jackpot. At the very least, finding the camp could put some federal eyes on the situation. If we can get that ball rolling, I'm fairly certain it will grow wings and fly. Backup to that is to target the seventy-three sleepers identified by Helen Gray and look for a crack in their armor. Someone willing to spill the beans. Given the program's history of sacrificing their young, I don't know if that will yield anything short of a tortured confession, if that. Not exactly what we want to package up and deliver to the FBI. G and G. What do you have for us?"

Graves nodded at Gupta, who tapped a few keys to bring up an array of faces on the widescreen monitor. Eight faces split into four pairs. Pictures taken at the intersection last night compared to what looked like candid surveillance photographs.

"To start, last night's festivities were undoubtedly sponsored by the Russian Federation. We cross-referenced all of the photos taken last night to our database and came up with four hits. Three with suspected ties to the DC consulate and one confirmed to be a consulate employee in New York City. This is going to cause a bit of an international-relations stink."

"I'm sure Putin will get over it," said Berg. "But this raises an important issue. Ms. Young will most definitely have to remain off the grid—the entire grid. I know we discussed this earlier, because Baltimore PD will be looking to question her as a possible witness to last night's festivities, but the Russians have a nasty habit of throwing names into the mix out of spite—and in hopes of getting the feds involved. They do this all over the world. The FBI will be keeping an eye out for Ms. Young by the afternoon at the latest. Same for myself and Devin. The entire team, essentially. It won't take them long to figure out who lent me a hand with this. We should also strongly consider taking precautions to thwart facial-recognition software."

A new set of faces emerged. He recognized one of the faces from the photos he'd taken in front of the Starbucks near the University of Maryland. Gupta nodded at him.

"I thought you might find this particularly interesting," said Gupta. "We did a deep dive through the bowels of the internet and found three deaths directly linked to patients transferred from the W Hotel to area hospitals on the night of your honey-trap sting. Two men, in their early to midfifties, succumbed to the angel of death the morning after they were stabilized. The angel of death being Jolene Rudd, who you photographed following you a few days ago and who we photographed dead in front of the town house. She was caught on security camera entering and exiting both of their rooms posing as a member of the Howard University Hospital."

"Busy lady," said Rich.

"Even more interesting? Her husband was photographed right next to her outside of the town house. Harvey Rudd. Both from Chattanooga, Tennessee," said Gupta.

"Driver's licenses collected at the town house put the whole group within easy driving distance around central Tennessee and Kentucky. One from northern Georgia," said Graves.

"Odd that they would be working this far away," said Rich.

Devin had a theory. "Not if they were involved with my mother's situation. The Russians would have wanted some continuity for compartmentalization reasons. Right? If they had something to do with intercepting my mother in Tennessee, it makes sense to use them again on a related operation."

"Very good point," said Berg.

"Who the fuck are these people? They look like people you'd trust to watch your house when you went on vacation," said Alex, one of the most nondescript people Devin had ever met, by design, no doubt.

"Based on their ages," said Berg, "I'd say they were planted here in the early nineties, right after the Soviet Union collapsed. Possibly for the express purpose of supporting the sleeper network Helen discovered. I think the connection to DEVTEK needs to be considered. What role does Brian Chase fill at the company? The Russians clearly wanted something from him."

"We weren't given those details," said Devin.

"DEVTEK is primarily an information security company," said Graves. "Deep ties to the Department of Defense and pretty much every government agency that requires secure mobile communications. Rumor has it that the CIA accepted their recent bid on a classified CIA request for proposal—which my research suggests is a groundbreaking, modular communications encryption system. A one-size-fits-all, easy-to-implement encryption solution for computers, office phones, mobile phones, radios. It would basically create an interoperable, secure communications platform usable across agencies and across the spectrum of assets within an agency or group. A CIA officer on the India-Pakistani border could contact an available air-support asset with their satellite phone and direct an airstrike on a high-value target of opportunity. Normally that would require a UHF radio with encryption compatible with the aircraft's system. A logistical nightmare. This would streamline everything. It's a game changer."

"That sounds like the kind of system the Russians would love to corrupt or steal," said Devin.

"Or both," added Marnie.

"If they were running a honey trap, sounds like they needed a way into the company," said Rich.

Berg shook his head. "I don't know. Why use a team on the verge of retirement for that? I know that springing a honey trap isn't complicated, but following through with the blackmail side of an operation is tricky. Especially if you're asking someone to commit a crime. Not something you'd put in Harvey and Jolene Rudd's hands. I think this was more of a one-and-done situation. My guess is they were trying to get him to quit the company, so someone could take his place. Whoever filled his shoes is most likely another one of these second-generation sleepers."

"So there's more of these things out there," said Emily Miralles.

Devin liked her use of the word *things* to describe the sleepers. Like manufactured goods.

"We have to assume there are more," said Berg. "In total, possibly twice the number Helen discovered. The rest of them hidden in tech companies like DEVTEK, where they can remain mostly anonymous— and do untold damage. That's why it's so important to get a look at this camp. If it exists. There's always the possibility that it doesn't. She spent a significant amount of time looking for it and came up empty handed."

"Locating the camp appears to be the tricky part," said Rich. "But Gray has been right about everything else up to now, so this is where we start. Graves?"

Graves started typing, and a list of names filled the left third of the screen. A map of the United States filled the remaining two-thirds—red dots appearing across the country. Devin guessed immediately that they were looking at a list of the 109 sleepers and a map corresponding to their locations. Frighteningly, but not surprisingly, a majority of them resided around Washington, DC. The rest were scattered across the country, corresponding with a major military base, state capital, or larger city.

"For obvious reasons, we'll remove anyone connected to law enforcement or the military from the list," said Graves.

About thirty names disappeared from the left side of the screen, their red dots vanishing with them.

"We went through the rest of the names and disqualified anyone with a sensitive or an on-call position in state or federal government, along with anyone at a high-enough level in that we might be running an outsize risk by grabbing them. Anyone protected for sure."

The list dropped to less than twenty names.

"That doesn't leave us a lot to work with," said Berg.

"Even less if we want to avoid five-day car rides," said Graves, clicking his mouse and eliminating everyone west of the Rockies.

Twelve names remained.

"We may as well focus on opportunities within easy or easier driving distance of the Ozarks," said Rich.

"That leaves us with Susan Belker. Secretary of state for Missouri," said Graves.

"Too high profile," said Rich.

"Harrison Jeffries. Deputy chief of staff to the attorney general in Illinois?" said Graves.

"That's a possibility."

"Or William Barber, the supervising deputy attorney general for the litigation division in Indiana?" said Graves.

"Let's look at Barber's profile," said Rich.

"These seem like low-profile jobs for Russian sleeper agents," said Scott.

"State-level secretary of state is a stepping-stone toward governor, which can launch a national political career," said Berg. "Deputy chief of staff to the AG puts you in a position to run for AG, and failing that, an appointment to the state supreme court or US district court. The sky's the limit from there. Politics. Higher courts. Same with a supervising deputy attorney general position. Governor. AG. Courts. Politics. These are solid roles."

Barber's face appeared on the screen.

"William Barber. Forty-four years of age. Married to Stacy Barber. Same age. She works as an IT specialist at Defenders in Indianapolis. That's an ADT subsidiary."

"As in the home security company?" asked Devin.

"Yes. ADT bought them out a few years ago," said Gupta. "That's actually good news. We have some regularly updated, custom hack kits for ADT systems. We can shut it down so it'll look like it's still working."

"That's a disturbing thought," said Marnie.

"Just a little," said Devin.

Graves continued. "They have two children, David and Melissa. Sixteen and fifteen years old, respectively. All-American family."

"That's how it's supposed to look," said Berg. "What do you think, Rich?"

"Can you bring up an image of their neighborhood?" asked Rich.

Gupta brought up a Google Earth satellite image of a wooded lot on a golf course. An expansive patio featuring a pool and hot tub. The level of detail they could glean about the property from this publicly available tool was disturbing.

"Nice and private. Easy access to the backyard from the golf course. We won't even have to drive up to the house, until we're ready to leave.

233

And it doesn't look like a gated community," said Rich. "Can you confirm that?"

The image shifted a few times, zooming in to street level on a few of the roads leading into the neighborhoods surrounding the golf course. No gates.

"I say we start with William Barber," said Rich.

"Looks about as good as it gets," said Berg. "Not too far of a drive from the Ozarks, if we manage to strike gold."

"Seven hours and thirty-seven minutes," said Gupta.

"Harrison Jeffries will be our backup plan," said Rich.

"Rich?" said Marnie. "Or Karl?"

Rich took a sip of his coffee before answering. "Yeah?"

"Why don't we just digitally package this entire room and send it to every media outlet in the country? Put it in their hands and let the chips fall where they may. Post it online if they won't take it seriously," said Marnie. "I'm not doubting this team's abilities, but we are talking about a long shot strategy here. Exposing the entire network, or at least what Helen uncovered, would effectively shut it down, right?"

Rich glanced at Berg, who addressed what Devin considered to be an excellent suggestion.

"It's tempting, but here's why I fear it won't work," said Berg. "One: The Russians will deny everything and feign outrage. Two: We have things like due process, courts, evidentiary standards, and a whole list of other safeguards designed to protect our own citizens, and everyone on Helen's list is entitled to them, particularly the second-generation sleepers who were born in the US. The names would be public, so the government couldn't pull any of their secret shenanigans. And all of the first generation is deceased, so they can't confess. Wilson was the last alleged sleeper, and Helen shot him to death after stuffing him in the back of her trunk. This is sounding crazier by the minute to the public and the ACLU—and the Department of Justice task force assembled to investigate this bombshell conspiracy theory."

"But it would draw an unhealthy amount of attention to the conspiracy—and the network," said Devin. "Stopping it."

"Maybe. Maybe not. The alleged sleepers would leave their jobs, because that's what a normal person assumed by colleagues to be a spy would do, so we would have accomplished that much. But then what? The most dangerous sleepers may be the ones your mother didn't find."

"This would make national headlines. Defense and technology companies would start to dig into their employees' backgrounds," said Marnie. "Especially employees that fit the profile."

"Would it make national headlines?" asked Berg. "Because of the lack of any verifiable evidence, even the *National Enquirer* would pass on the story. The libel danger would be very real. Anyone losing their job anywhere to the McCarthy-esque purge that followed would have a strong case against whichever media outlet ran the story. This would have to be published online, anonymously, and my guess is that a few billion dollars' worth of Russian-backed Bitcoin would quickly push the story into online obscurity. I'm not saying we won't end up taking this public at some point. But we need tangible evidence before we consider putting this out there, because we'll only get one shot at bringing this into the public sphere—and it'll need to be our best shot."

"Then we do it the hard way," said Marnie.

"In my experience," said Rich, "there is no other way."

"I knew he was going to say that," said Devin.

CHAPTER 35

The Jeep Wrangler crept along the rutted, gravel-dirt road, Felix Orlov rapidly alternating his attention between the map on his satellite phone screen and the seemingly impenetrable, untamed forest passing down the right side of their vehicle. He couldn't imagine trying to reach this place in the dead of winter. The 6.2-mile trip up Bear Creek Mountain Road on a clear June day had been sketchy enough.

He could see why this had been chosen as a cache point, even if it was a little extreme. Nobody was likely to stumble onto it. Since turning off the paved road that forked into this one, they hadn't seen a soul. Only a few closed gates clearly marked with **No Trespassing** signs. Isolated from prying eyes, but less than an hour from Interstate 80. Once on the interstate, they could be in any major city on the East Coast within six to seven hours or most Midwest cities within eight to nine hours.

That said, he didn't anticipate them staying here for long. This was more of an equipment run than anything.

They'd grab all the gear they might need and wait until night to shuttle it back to the two RVs parked at a campground closer to the interstate. None of the sites available at the campground had been entirely private. Transferring a dozen or so overstuffed nylon duffel bags from the Jeeps to the RVs was a sight he'd rather keep concealed from the public. From there, they'd wait for further instructions, possibly relocating to a more private site.

He hadn't been provided with their next destination, which either meant Pichugin was releasing the information in stages for security reasons or that they didn't have a location on the team's target. He got the impression from Pichugin's proxy that it was the latter.

"I see something," said Oleg, slowing the Jeep to a crawl.

He'd worked with Oleg for a number of years now, mostly in Europe and Asia, where Pichugin needed them the most. Like Felix, he spoke fluent English, with no hint of an accent, which had made him a shoo-in for this trip. Similarly, he was former Russian Federation Spetsnaz. Along with Valerie and Oksana, who drove the Jeep behind them, they made up the core direct-action element of his team.

Ksenia, their electronic surveillance specialist, and Lashev, a police-trained sniper, had remained behind with the RVs. Maybe not the best decision, given that they spoke only broken, heavily Russian-accented English, but he needed his best people on the cache mission—just in case the location had been compromised.

"We should be right on top of the entrance," said Felix, putting down the phone.

"Looks like a break in the trees . . . and a gate," said Oleg, pulling as far over to the left side of the road as possible to make room for the tight turn.

He cut the wheel sharply to the right and pointed them directly at a rickety wood gate partially overgrown with thin, new growth from the adjacent bushes. Felix hopped out of the Jeep and approached the gate, which turned out to be significantly more solid and secure than it appeared. The dilapidated-looking wood had been affixed to a thick steel barrier, which was latched to a metal post. The latch was secured in place by a fist-size, heavy-duty combination lock. He reached over the gate and lifted the lock so he could align the four numbers to match the code he'd received.

With the lock open, he pushed the gate inward, surprised that it moved almost effortlessly. He waved the Jeeps through and locked the gate behind them before getting back into his seat for the rest of the journey, which he had been told spanned about seven hundred yards on a hardened 4×4 trail. The trip from the gate to the cabin turned out to be smoother than the ride up Bear Creek Mountain Road. At several points along the gently twisting dirt road, he saw evidence of recently chainsawed trees, which had likely fallen during a recent storm and blocked the approach. The cache location was obviously well maintained.

The road opened into a football field–size, slightly overgrown clearing, a modest two-story log cabin with a green metal roof standing in its center. Solar panels lined the south side of the roof. A sizable metal shed sat about ten yards from the house. It looked large enough to house a pair of ATVs, possibly more. An exhaust vent poking through its sloped roofline suggested it might contain a generator.

"Pull up to the front porch," he said, rolling his window down and motioning for the other Jeep to do the same.

He got out and approached the long porch, stopping short of the stairs and putting his hands on his hips. The rest of the team gathered around him.

"Looks self-contained," said Valerie. "Kind of elaborate for some kind of Soviet-era weapons cache."

"It was probably just a concrete cellar at one point," said Felix. "More like an underground shelter than anything else."

"A Pichugin upgrade," said Oleg. "In the middle of Pennsylvania."

"Yeah. And his proxy said we had access to more of these around the country, if needed, along with an unlimited travel budget. Whatever he's up to here must be serious," said Felix. "We need to keep that in mind moving forward. I'd like to be around to spend the money he's paying us."

He stepped onto the porch and unlatched the weather-sealed faux mailbox next to the door, revealing a touch pad and biometric scanner. Referencing the message sent to him less than an hour ago on his satellite phone, he entered a ten-digit code and waited for instructions. The screen asked him to press his index finger on his right hand against the scanner, followed by the thumb of his left hand. A new instruction appeared on the screen.

"Oksana. I need your thumb immediately," he said.

The dark-haired operative smirked and flipped him the middle finger.

"The digital counter on the screen says you have seven seconds to press your right thumb against the scanner," said Felix. "Six. Five."

She scrambled up the porch and pressed her thumb against the glass, stopping the countdown at two seconds. A series of heavy-duty mechanical clicks came from the door, the screen now indicating they could proceed.

He patted her on the shoulder. "Thank you, Oksana. You can go back to making jokes now that we're not going to be vaporized in an explosion."

"Don't be an asshole," she said.

"That's my job," he said, grabbing the door handle and nudging the hefty door inward.

"Is it stuck?" she asked.

"No. It's heavy like a vault door," said Felix, reaching his hand inside. "And it must be five inches thick."

They pushed it open together, a motion-triggered bank of fluorescent lights above revealing exactly why the designers had installed a vault-level door. Racks of military-grade weapons lined three of the walls, suspended a few feet above drawers labeled with different bullet calibers. Pistols. Assault rifles. Light machine guns. Submachine guns. Sniper rifles. He stepped inside, noting that the windows had been for show only. Not a crack of light peeped in where the windows should be. The wall facing the porch was stacked with night vision goggles, binoculars, weapons scopes of all varieties, tactical radio rigs, helmets, and several types of body armor carriers. And this was just the outer room.

A keypad-guarded door sat in the middle of the interior wall, leading to the "heavy stuff," as Pichugin's proxy had stated. Stuff they were to "show restraint when selecting," whatever that meant.

"Welcome, Kmart shoppers," said Oksana.

While the team walked around, inspecting the weapons cache, Felix entered the code to open the second door, which proved to be equally as substantial as the first—for a good reason. After shoving it several inches inward, he caught a glimpse of a military-grade revolver-style grenade launcher inside. A few more inches took his breath away. Pichugin could start a small war with the weapons in this cabin. And there were more of these across the United States?

"If this room is Kmart," grunted Felix, pushing the door all the way open, "then this one is Harrods."

CHAPTER 36

Marnie took the motel stairs in a hurry, eager to return with a bag full of soft drinks she'd acquired from the vending machine room next to the lobby. She'd announced her intention to run out and grab a Mountain Dew a few minutes before their scheduled briefing, unintentionally inviting close to a dozen requests from the rest of the team. She'd gotten to the midpoint landing of the U-shaped stairs when she heard an argument above her. Karl Berg and Rich in a heated debate—about Devin. She slowly made her way up the rest of the stairs, taking in the whispered dispute as she approached the second-floor walkway.

"You have to trust me on this," said Berg. "Devin has a sixth sense when it comes to surveillance. The FBI's Special Surveillance Group is about as elite as it gets. He spent twelve years learning the tricks of the trade, then landed a position with MINERVA—against all odds. His mother poisoned that well, so to speak, and they still hired him, because he's that good at what he does. He's an asset to the team."

"I'm not disputing his surveillance or countersurveillance skills," said Rich. "But my team is pretty well versed in the same game, and we've been doing it for decades with our very lives on the line, which trumps Devin's experience, in my opinion."

"I don't agree," said Berg. "He's been one step ahead of everyone from day one. He busted the team following him from his apartment. He detected all three of the operatives you placed outside of the Airbnb town house. And he anticipated the ambush a few blocks away from the town house."

"Not soon enough," said Rich. "They survived because we rescued them."

Marnie stepped onto the walkway, immediately drawing their attention. "We survived because of Devin's quick thinking. He was able to assess threats from multiple directions and make a split-second decision about what to do next. The right decision. It bought us enough time for your team to respond."

"My concern is with the direct-action side of future operations," said Rich. "We don't always have the luxury of separating combat from the surveillance."

"Devin can hold his own in a gunfight," said Marnie. "I saw that firsthand."

"And I'm absolutely useless in any kind of fight," said Berg. "But nobody is trying to sideline me."

"That's because you've always understood your role," said Rich. "I'm worried about Devin getting in over his head if he starts swimming outside of his area of expertise."

"What about me?" said Marnie. "I'm just a former Marine helicopter pilot."

Rich shook his head. "The same goes for you. I can't have two non-operators in the middle of a covert raid. It puts my people at risk. You know how this works, Marnie. Imagine flying into a heavily contested landing zone while you're taking fire from multiple directions—"

"I don't need to imagine. I've been there," said Marnie. "And we didn't sideline new pilots. They flew the same missions as the rest of us."

"Sure. But in a dual-control helicopter, an experienced pilot could take over at any time," said Rich.

"How is this any different?" asked Berg. "In this case, the ratio of experienced operators to inexperienced is more like four to one."

"It's different," said Rich.

Berg shrugged. "Some circumstances and missions may be different, requiring the sole use of your veteran operators, but tonight's job doesn't meet that threshold."

"And when it does?" asked Rich, nodding at Marnie.

"Neither of us is suicidal, and we're well aware of our limitations," said Marnie. "I know I'm speaking for Devin when I say that he won't be sidelined without a damn good reason. Same for me."

"You go where Devin goes," said Rich.

"Exactly," said Marnie. "This is personal for him."

"That's a big part of what worries me—about both of you," said Rich. "Too many attachments. Karl, you can't tell me this doesn't worry you, too."

"It's a potential liability," said Berg. "I just don't think that liability outweighs the gain. Yet. It's something we need to keep a close eye on. I'm sure Marnie would agree—and be willing to help make sure we don't have an unexpected problem at a critical time."

"I can't control Devin," said Marnie.

"Can't or won't?" said Rich.

"A bit of both," said Marnie. "But I'll do what I can to make sure that neither of us overextends ourselves and jeopardizes any of the missions. That's the best I can offer at this point."

Rich barely changed his expression. "That works—for now."

CHAPTER 37

Devin sat on the floor between the two motel room beds and watched the widescreen monitor on top of the dresser. Marnie sat on the bed to his right, next to Karl Berg, her hands balled tightly on her thighs. Rich stood next to Karl, arms crossed and a focused look on his face. Emily sat on the foot of the other bed next to Scott, her feet tapping a nervous rhythm against the carpet next to Devin's leg.

The door to the room was cracked several inches, Jared visible outside, leaning forward on the second-floor walkway's railing. He kept watch over the parking lot and the antenna array attached to the railing next to him. The array was directed northeast, in the direction of the golf course community about two and a half miles away. Everyone looked half-asleep except for Rich. The man had a remarkably boundless amount of energy for someone who had to be in his late fifties.

He somehow hadn't skipped a beat after going without sleep for forty-eight hours, unless Devin had somehow missed him taking a catnap or two. Marnie hadn't seen him sleep, either, and the two of them had agreed that either Devin or she be awake at all times to make sure Karl Berg and Rich didn't alter the plan in some unacceptable or unthinkable way.

In fact, he had insisted on driving the entire overnight route from DC to Indianapolis, leaving Devin exhausted. While everyone else in the SUV had slipped into deep sleep, including Marnie, he spent most of the drive waking every few minutes in the back seat to check on Rich, who would occasionally glance over his shoulder and crack a joke about it. They were curious people, somehow reminding him of his former SSG colleagues in the FBI. Hardened by years of uncomfortable and stressful work—but wired for the job from the beginning.

He'd seen people come and go within the Special Surveillance Group. Some didn't last more than a month or two. Others quit after a few years. Plenty were sent away. Devin never had a moment of doubt about the job. He may not have been very good at it in the beginning, but he loved it, each field operation reinforcing his attachment to the work. A few years into the job, and he was running with the big dogs. Never looking back. He wondered if people like Rich and the members of his team had evolved the same way. Unconventional people drawn to unconventional work.

Gupta swiveled in his chair to face the team. He was seated in front of two open laptops, one of which would serve as his primary flight-control monitor. A rather expensive-looking remote flight-control transmitter lay on the desk in front of the laptop. Graves sat next to him on the chair they had dragged in from the adjoining room, his laptop screen featuring a satellite map of the target area, which looked as though it was linked to the overall flight system. A small aircraft icon sat in the middle of the map, blinking.

"The launch team is ready, and pretty anxious," said Gupta. "They gave up on launching from a road and are in a nearby church parking lot. This town is crawling with police. They've seen a half dozen cruisers on their tour of southwestern Carmel over the past thirty minutes."

"My guess is their police department patrols the southern edges of the city pretty heavily, since it connects to northern Indy," said Rich. "Give them the green light."

Less than a minute later, the widescreen monitor mirrored Gupta's screen, giving them a green-scale night vision view from the drone's nose.

"Everything looks good," said Gupta. "Here we go."

The pavement started to rush by, picking up speed as parking lot lines blurred underneath.

"You're running out of room," said Rich, noting the same rapidly approaching line of trees Devin had just spotted.

"Oh ye of little faith," said Gupta, the camera feed suddenly lurching skyward. "And liftoff. With plenty of room to spare. It's not my first rodeo, folks."

Graves turned in his chair. "What my friend here forgot to tell everyone is that the Albatross UAV's flight can be almost entirely autonomous, including the takeoff you just witnessed."

"Always raining on my parade," said Gupta.

"That's because you're always parading," said Graves. "Shall I spoil the rest?"

"Go ahead," said Gupta. "The cat's out of the bag."

"We've already programmed a series of waypoints that will take the drone over the target from several different angles, giving us a ton of footage to study. We'll manipulate the surveillance cameras, but that's pretty much it. It'll land in the same parking lot by itself if that's still an option," said Graves.

"Several passes will attract too much attention," said Berg. "I think one or two at most. Right?"

Devin wanted to jump in and answer, but he held back and let Graves handle the concern. The FBI's SSG had a division that fielded a variety of drones—fixed wing and shaped like the Albatross along with a wide selection of rotary wing–like quadcopters. They came in handy when surveilling from a distance, especially drones like the Albatross.

"The drone is capable of gliding unpowered. We've programmed it to gain significant altitude well outside of audible detection range from the neighborhood before turning toward the target for a long glide. The citizens of Carmel will hear some buzzing overhead, but not around the golf course. And we've arranged the waypoints, so each altitude climb will occur in a different cardinal direction from the target. Check it out."

The monitor changed to show the planned flight pattern, which resembled a flower with several petals. Exactly what he expected. Graves and Gupta knew what they were doing.

"Drone is climbing and tracking toward the first waypoint," said Gupta.

"This is nerve-racking," said Marnie, putting a hand on Devin's shoulder. "I'm expecting the Barbers to have a pool party in full swing."

He squeezed her hand for a moment before taking it away.

"And we are in glide mode," said Gupta. "Activating surveillance suite."

The monitor's screen split in half, the left side showing the green night vision view from the nose. House lights burned bright, creating the vague outline of an extensive neighborhood. A patchwork of light and dark green in the distance somewhat resembled a golf course, though Devin probably wouldn't be able to guess that if he didn't know what he was looking for. The right side of the screen showed a gray scale infrared image of roughly the same picture on the left, but far less defined. A few dozen "hot spots" appeared close to where the lights had previously burned bright, representing people outside of their homes, backyard grills, hot tubs, and firepits.

"Marking the target house for reference. You'll see a distance to target and the distance to our closest point of approach, which will be directly down one of the fairways," said Gupta, a blue square appearing in the distant left of the gray scale image. "We'll start with IR to see if we can pick up anyone in the yard or immediate vicinity, then switch to night vision for a detailed look."

Nobody said a word as the distance rapidly decreased. When the square started to drift left, he knew without looking at the numbers that the drone was nearing its closest point of approach. On cue, the camera panned left to track the target as it passed. Devin knew what he was looking at before Gupta started to explain. This looked like a once-in-an-operative's-lifetime opportunity.

"I have two hot spots in the backyard. One is definitely the hot tub. Another is the grill," said Gupta. "Wait. Hold on. I have what looks like two people in the hot tub. Switching to night vision."

"You might want to close your eyes," said Devin.

Marnie took her hand off his shoulder. "Seriously?"

When the image shifted back to night vision and zoomed in, Gupta started laughing.

"I think it's safe to assume the kids aren't home," said Marnie. "Unless that's one of their kids."

"Can you zoom in any further," said Berg, "and pull up pictures of Mr. and Mrs. Barber?"

"Are you sure? I'd like to keep my dinner down," said Gupta.

Graves started typing and clicking, replacing the image on the left with the Barbers, while Gupta zoomed in so close that Devin could barely watch. The action had the figures facing the back of the property, both of their faces fully exposed to the drone's camera. If either of them had looked about fifteen degrees above the top of the tree line that separated their yard from the fairway, they might have spotted the drone—but they were clearly too caught up in the moment to notice.

"Looks like the Barbers to me," said Berg. "Definitely William Barber. A little difficult to positively ID Stacy."

"I say we hit them right now," said Rich. "It doesn't matter if that's Mrs. Barber. Actually, I'd prefer if it wasn't. We could use that as leverage."

"Get Alex, Mike, and Rico back here immediately," said Rich. "We'll gear up and head over. Devin and Marnie, you'll drive us to the drop-off point on Crooked Branch Lane, right off One Hundred Sixth Street, and peel off. We'll let you know when we're five minutes out from extraction. You'll pull into the circular driveway right in front of their house for the pickup."

"Whoa. Whoa. Wait a minute," said Devin. "I'm going into that house with you."

"So am I," said Marnie.

"Not a chance. This is a last-second decision to pile into an unknown situation," said Rich. "I need a single team thinking and acting as one. Not a split crew that I have to coach along. If this were tomorrow or later tonight, after we talked through the plan a number of times, I wouldn't hesitate to bring you in with us."

"We're grabbing two middle-age, clearly out-of-shape adults who have been going at it in a hot tub," said Marnie. "We're not abducting a CrossFit couple."

"Either we're in or this is a no go," said Devin.

"What exactly does that mean?" said Rich.

Berg held a hand up. "He's right."

"This time," said Rich. "The two of you better keep up. Emily and Jared. You're driving."

Emily popped up from the foot of the bed and glared at Marnie. "Are you fucking kidding me?"

"I'll drive. Anish can hold down the fort here," said Graves.

"The drone is flying itself," said Gupta. "See? No more gross middle-age couple in the hot tub scene. It's already climbing and turning toward its next waypoint. All I'm doing is keeping an eye on the house and neighborhood for you."

"And the police scanner traffic, and you're shutting down the home security system," said Rich.

"He's got it," said Graves, clapping Gupta on the shoulder.

Rich shook his head but quickly relented. "Fine. Keep the door open so you can watch the antenna array. We don't need someone tripping over it and taking our drone off-line."

"There's like six cars in the whole parking lot, and three of them are ours," said Jared, who had stuck his head in the door. "I don't think we have anything to worry about."

"Just saying," said Rich.

"We deserve to be a part of this."

"Okay," said Rich.

"To make it easier for decision-making purposes moving forward, you can consider the two of us to be one now," said Devin.

Berg grinned and nodded at Marnie. "See. I told you he was solid."

CHAPTER 38

Marnie Young jog-walked next to Karl Berg, the two of them falling well behind the rest of the team, which had already started to vanish into the trees directly behind the Barbers' property. She kept an eye peeled and an ear open for any commotion or movement from the backyards to their immediate right. The tree line separating the homes from the golf course was no more than a few trees and manicured shrubs deep. Designed for basic privacy from golfers, not as concealment. To a more observant and vigilant neighbor, their presence on the golf course would appear to be more than just a few teenagers strolling around after hours.

"Thanks for keeping an old guy company," whispered Berg.

"My pleasure," said Marnie before taking a moment to scan the western sky for the drone.

"I don't think you'll be able to spot it," said Berg. "It'll be coming in from the west. That'll be its least-detectable profile."

He was right. She couldn't pick it out of the navy-blue sky, which would soon go black, when the thin strip of light blue still stretched across the horizon entirely vanished. Berg stopped and cocked his head, which put her on alert. She focused her senses on the sights and sounds around them, detecting nothing unusual.

"They want us to hold up while they move in," said Berg. "The Barbers are lounging on the patio furniture, enjoying a bottle of wine."

"With their clothes on. Hopefully."

"Robes," said Berg, guiding them to the edge of the trees on the border of the Barbers' property, where the team had disappeared a minute ago.

They both crouched low and waited. A single shriek pierced the night, followed by a quick verbal challenge that ended in a muffled voice. It was hard to tell, but she thought she heard a Taser discharge and telltale crackle of electricity. Marnie peered into the neighbor's yard, searching for any sign that the brief scuffle had drawn any attention. Nothing moved on the patio or inside the house. So far. So good. She couldn't say the same about the neighbor on the other side but had to assume someone was keeping an eye on the situation.

A few minutes later, Berg was told the situation was under control and that they could approach. Marnie led them through the trees and bushes to the edge of the grass, then straight across the yard and around the pool. Emily stood at the open patio slider, motioning them inside, where most of the lights had been turned off or dimmed. She shut the slider behind them and pointed toward an open staircase off the kitchen, leading downward.

"Don't forget your masks and gloves," she said.

Marnie took a few steps before turning around. "Do you want me to keep an eye on things up here?"

She felt as though maybe she was responsible for Emily being assigned what amounted to glorified sentry duty.

Emily shook her head. "I appreciate the offer, but our jobs have been assigned for this one. Maybe next time."

"Sorry for throwing a wrench into the works back at the motel," said Marnie.

"No wrench at all," she said.

Marnie nodded and followed Berg toward the staircase, donning her balaclava ski mask and black leather gloves before descending into the basement. The first thing she noticed when she reached the bottom of the stairs was that the Indianapolis sports team–themed finished basement might cover more square footage than her parents' house. She'd never seen a basement like this before in her life. Full granite-topped kitchen and island with several high-backed stools. Expansive mahogany bar with seating for nearly a dozen, plus two separate pub-style booths. Massive movie screening area with three rows of theater seating. Pool table. A half dozen other doors, probably leading to a few spare bedrooms and bathrooms.

She had no idea what a supervising attorney for a state attorney general's office earned, but she suspected Stacy Barber's job at ADT paid for most of this. The second thing she noticed was that the woman duct-taped to the wooden chair next to William Barber was not in fact Mrs. Barber. She looked roughly the same age but was definitely not Stacy. The two had been arranged side by side along the end of the pool table that faced the kitchen.

Berg joined Rich, who stood glaring at them with his arms crossed. Scott and Rico flanked the two closely—not that their captives were going anywhere. Mike and Alex sat at the kitchen island, working on something she couldn't see. They had a laptop and a small plastic case open. That was all she could tell. She stood next to Devin, who had moved closer to Berg but remained separated from the two who would conduct the interrogation.

"Who wants to go first?" asked Rich.

The woman screamed through the duct tape covering her mouth. Rich nodded at Scott, who tore the piece free. She immediately started pleading for her life, which caught Marnie off guard, almost causing her to gasp. Devin gave her a reassuring look, though he appeared anything but sure about the situation. When the woman had settled down, Rich glanced up at Alex, who held up a driver's license and motioned for him to come over.

"See what's going on," Devin said to Marnie.

She followed Rich to the kitchen island, where they formed a huddle around the two operatives. She glanced over her shoulders to see

William Barber and his mistress straining their necks to look at the kitchen. Scott and Rico faced them forward.

"What's up?" asked Rich.

"Read the name on the ID," said Alex.

Rich took it, and Marnie examined it over his shoulder. Illinois driver's license. Karen Jeffries.

"No way," she muttered.

"Way," said Alex, switching to a different tab on the laptop screen.

The Google search string read: *Wife of Harrison Jeffries, Deputy Chief of Staff to the Attorney General in Illinois.*

The top result listed Karen Jeffries. Next was a Wikipedia entry with her name and references to their two children. A LinkedIn profile followed, identifying her as an Illinois state representative. Alex clicked on a Facebook link, which took them to Harrison Jeffries's Facebook page. No further confirmation required. Karen Jeffries, the out-of-state wife of a suspected Russian sleeper agent, was romantically involved with another suspected Russian sleeper. The coincidence raised alarms.

"Interesting," said Marnie.

"Damning is more like it," said Rich. "No reason to tiptoe around these two. They're as thick as thieves. I strongly suspect something. Can you open their phones?"

Mike removed a small plastic kit from the case and opened it, removing what looked like another phone.

"Give me a minute," he said.

"What is that?" asked Marnie.

"It's a scanner with a built-in passcode-analysis application. I just put my device over their screen and hopefully that gives me a high-probability passcode. If not, I'll have to do this old school and dust the screens. The differences can be really subtle, but I should be able to determine the four- or six-digit code based on the amount of oily residue left behind on each number. Might take a few guesses, but it works ninety percent of the time."

"When you open the phones, I want Gupta to run a location track," said Rich. "Then have him do a deep dive into Stacy Barber and Karen Jeffries using the sleeper algorithm Graves has been working on."

"Will do," said Alex.

"What are you thinking?" asked Marnie, already knowing the answer.

"I'm thinking this sleeper situation is more like a family affair with the Barbers and Jeffrieses," said Rich. "Including the children."

His last three words took her breath away for a few moments.

"A third generation?" she said.

"Let's hope not," said Rich. "But something's definitely not adding up."

CHAPTER 39

Devin watched the exchange by the kitchen, wishing he had accompanied Marnie. Something big was brewing. He caught a glimpse of the woman's face on the computer and saw Mike go to work on the phones with what looked like a phone-on-phone scanner. When Marnie returned, he whispered in her ear.

"What's the story?"

"You'll see," she said.

Marnie didn't whisper back, which told him he was in for a show. Rich nodded at Rico, who tore off Barber's strip of duct tape. Barber started protesting immediately, which got him a quick jab to the nose from Rich. Devin didn't like where this was headed, but Rich pulled the punch before it could do any real damage. The hit stunned Barber into silence, a bizarrely malevolent look flashing across the woman's face, just as quickly returning to sobs occasionally interrupted by a mumbled, "Please don't hurt me."

"You can knock off the act, Mrs. Jeffries," said Rich.

Jeffries? As in Harrison Jeffries's wife? He glanced at Marnie, trying not to betray any surprise. She returned the look with a quick nod. Holy mother.

"First question. Where are your kids, William? Are we expecting them home anytime soon?" said Rich. "Your little romp in the hot tub suggests they're either staying overnight with friends or out of town."

"Look. I don't know what's happening here, but I'm guessing my wife put you guys up to this?" said Barber. "Did she tell you who I work for? I don't think you want to mess—"

"The Indiana State Attorney General's Office?" said Rich. "What's next? Is Karen going to threaten me with the power and might of the Illinois AG's office? I don't give a shit who you work for or with. And for the record, your wife didn't put me up to this."

"Was it my husband?" asked Karen. "I'm sure we can work this out. He doesn't want a scandal on his hands any more than any of us do. Please. We'll break this off right now. Never again. I have kids. I don't know what you plan to do, but I want to see them again more than him."

Karen broke into the fake crying again, and Barber took over.

"That's right. It's over. No more," he said. "There's no need to take this any further."

"Karen. I'm having a hard time believing you care about your kids more than Ride 'Em Cowboy Bill over here," said Berg, jumping into the mix. "You didn't look like you were missing them out at the hot tub. What did you do? Leave them with a few frozen pizzas and tell them you'd be back in the morning?"

"They're at summer camp," she said. "Harry and I have been on the outs for years. He's doing his thing this weekend. I'm doing mine."

"What about your kids, William? Did you pass them off to the grandparents?" said Berg. "Maybe get them a hotel suite and a few cases of beer to share with their friends while you defiled the hot tub and probably every other flat surface in the house? Are you gonna drain the hot tub this weekend, or let your kids sit in it with all of your juices swirling around?"

Barber turned a few shades redder. "My kids are at camp, too. My wife is on a girls' weekend trip to Michigan City."

"Really? Are you sure she's not shacked up back in Illinois?" asked Berg. "Be pretty funny, wouldn't it?"

Karen had let her boo-hoo routine slip one too many times at this point to keep it going—and she knew it.

"You guys are sick," she spat. "What do you want from us? Who put you up to this?"

"A daisy chain of events has led us here," said Rich. "Starting with the very painful demise of a few of your comrades."

Neither of them responded to the word *comrades*, which Devin assumed he had used on purpose.

"What are you talking about?" said Barber, trying to stand up and getting slammed back down by Rico. "This has gone far enough!"

Alex got off his stool at the kitchen island, with the laptop, and signaled for Rich to meet him by the bar. This time Devin didn't hang back. None of them did. Alex put the laptop on the bar, and they huddled around it as Alex quietly walked them through what he'd found.

"You're not going to believe this," said Alex. "Location data puts both of them at the Diamond City Marina in Arkansas, about twenty miles southeast of Branson, on Wednesday around four o'clock in the afternoon. They arrived and departed in separate vehicles. The two of them drove about an hour to the Ramada in Mountain Home, Arkansas, where they spent the night. They spent most of Thursday driving here, where they've remained. She hasn't left the house once. Mr. Barber has been to a grocery store, liquor store, and pharmacy."

"Is her car here?" asked Devin.

"We haven't checked the garage for a car with Illinois plates," said Alex. "It appears that they arrived together, but they stopped a few times in and around Indianapolis. They may have stashed her car."

"Radio Emily and have her check," said Rich.

Mike made the call over the radio net.

"So what are we thinking?" asked Berg.

"You tell us," said Rich. "I've been doing too much of the talking."

Berg stifled a laugh. "Looks like you were right about a third generation. I think they dropped their kids—and spouses—off for a few weeks at Comrade Stalin's Great Summer Camp Adventure. Maybe Mr. Jeffries and Mrs. Barber only stay a week, and these two go at it like rabbits until they have to pick them up. I don't know. I can't imagine them taking the whole summer off. Maybe they're running an abbreviated version of the camp these days, and the parents take turns each summer, bonding as traitors for a few weeks. All I know is that this takes the conspiracy to the next level. Helen never identified any second-generation couples, and two were sitting right in front of her. That's not meant as an indictment, Devin. Who the hell would imagine they would risk keeping the chain of treason alive for a third generation, when they had so successfully planted the second generation?"

"At least we know where to start looking," said Devin. "It shouldn't be too difficult to figure this out."

"It's a massive lake system," said Alex, zooming out to reveal the full scope of the problem. "Something like eight or nine hundred miles of shoreline, breaking off into hundreds of coves and lake arms. It winds a good twenty miles east of Diamond City and snakes like a river for about thirty miles to Branson, where it connects to Table Rock Lake. If I had to guess, this is why your mother couldn't find the place. They took off on a boat that could have gone anywhere in this entire lake system."

"Someone around that marina knows what's up," said Devin. "They've been shuttling hundreds of people out to the camp every summer for what—four decades?"

Berg nodded. "Something like that. Assuming they attend from preschool age until they're eighteen, maybe a few refresher summers after high school to make sure the capitalists didn't corrupt them in college."

"Good one," said Marnie.

"I'm glad someone appreciates it," said Berg. "We don't know the size of this third generation, but it was small enough to escape your mother's net. And she was actively looking for the camp."

"Plus, they wouldn't shuttle everyone from the same location," said Rich. "Even during the camp's heyday, they probably had several pickup and drop-off sites. The operation would have blended right into summer on the Ozarks. Those lakes must be packed with vacationers and locals this time of year."

"Okay. So where do we go from here?" asked Devin. "Can we track their spouses' phones?"

"That's not as easy as it sounds," said Berg. "Hit or miss whether we can get that favor, and if the person doing us that favor figures out the connection to these two, the whole thing could backfire spectacularly. As in we go to the top of the FBI's Most Wanted list."

"Wouldn't be the first time," said Rich.

"I'd like to stay off it for a while," said Berg.

"Then what? We sit on these two at the secondary interrogation site until their families return to the marina?" asked Marnie.

"We don't have that kind of time," said Rich. "My guess is the entire network has been put on some kind of alert based on what happened in Baltimore, which probably means a daily check-in of some kind. That way the people running the sleepers can determine if we've started to work our way through the network. That's why we identified Barber and Jeffries as targets. If one didn't work out, we could drive a few hours to the next one and try again before the network went into safe mode."

"What would safe mode look like?" asked Marnie.

"Probably everyone taking vacation or personal time off at once and disappearing," said Devin. "Starve the fire of oxygen until they can determine how to better protect their sleepers."

"While at the same time working on a way to discredit you, me, Marnie, and anyone else they suspect might be involved," said Berg. "We're looking at twenty-four to thirty-six hours, tops, before they confirm something is wrong. Probably not even that long."

"Why am I not seeing a solution?" asked Devin.

"Yeah. Unless these two are willing to—" started Marnie, pausing for a long moment. "Oh. I see."

"You don't see it yet, because you're a good person, Devin," said Rich. "Same with your friend, though she appears a little quicker on the uptake. Might want to keep a close eye on her in the future."

"Shit," said Devin, the cryptic compliment and wry joke suddenly making sense. "I didn't think we'd reach this point that quickly. Or need to reach it at all."

Berg took a deep breath and exhaled before putting a hand on his shoulder.

"This is one of those moments when I need you to trust me. I don't see any other way forward, and we have two people who spent every summer for fifteen years at that camp—right here. We won't get a chance like this again."

"I can't be a part of it, even though I know I'm just as much a part of it as anyone else," said Devin. "Marnie. You're only here because of me. You're not part of this."

She took his hand. "I came to grips with this possibility before we left Baltimore. I'm most definitely part of this, but I won't participate. I know that doesn't absolve me of anything, but that's where I stand."

Rich nodded. "I entirely respect your decisions."

"Me too. For what it's worth. This possibility factored heavily into my decision to bring Rich's crew on board," said Berg, glancing at the operative. "No offense."

"None taken," said Rich. "I'm going to have the two of you walk back the way we came. Keep your radio on, and one of the vehicles will pick you up and shuttle you back to the motel. I don't know how long this is going to take, but I suggest you get some rest. We'll pack up and bolt as soon as we're finished here. Good?"

"Yep," said Devin.

Marnie nodded. He guided them around the other end of the pool table, where they wouldn't have to look at the two people they'd just

261

condemned to an agonizing end. Barber and Jeffries turned their heads to see where they were going, but their guards brutally yanked their heads forward by the hair, beginning the process that Devin hoped would end quickly and mercifully for them.

Devin's radio crackled no more than twenty minutes later, while they knelt in the trees next to the pickup point, waiting on Graves to retrieve the drone from a different church parking lot.

"We're done at the house. Tim. Hold off on the shuttle run," said Rich. "Back to a full team, coordinated extract. No extra passengers. Will advise when we're ready for pickup."

"Copy that," said Graves. "I just packed away the drone. Headed to the primary staging point."

"On my way to the staging point," said Jared.

Devin transmitted. "Everything's quiet on our end."

"We got the location. Mincy Conservation Area just north of the Missouri-Arkansas border," said Rich. "It's still going to be a bit of a nightmare finding the camp. The conservation land is nearly six thousand acres. But I think we got more than enough out of them to figure out where they were dropped off every summer. I'll explain later. We should be at your location in ten minutes."

"Understood. We'll hold down the fort," said Devin, ending the back-and-forth before Rich used the words *clean up*.

"How bad do you think it got in there?" asked Marnie, softly.

"It didn't last long," said Devin. "That's all I can say."

"I guess that's good enough," she said, sitting against the tree next to them.

He joined her on the ground, the two of them leaning into each other—neither of them wanting to say another word about what had just taken place in that basement.

CHAPTER 40

Felix Orlov accessed the dark web site assigned to him for the operation and started to read the update while the team gathered in the RV. He'd received the text message alert less than a minute ago, while stoking the red-hot charcoal at their campsite grill. Oleg had just returned from a shopping run with several thick cuts of preseasoned steak and two shopping bags filled with American picnic foods like potato salad, coleslaw, and chips. A treat to tide them over at this dump of a campground while they impatiently waited for orders. He turned to Oleg, who stood in the kitchen area next to the bags of food.

"We'll have to put the picnic on hold," said Felix. "We need to be at the Allegheny County Airport in less than two hours to hop on a privately chartered jet. We're headed to Branson, Missouri."

"How far away is the airport?" asked Oleg.

"An hour and twenty minutes," said Felix.

"Leaves us enough time to cook the steaks and eat them on the way," said Valerie. "Right?"

"Where the fuck is Branson, Missouri?" asked Oksana, getting a quick laugh out of most of them.

"Branson, Missouri, is in Missouri," said Felix. "And the joke's on all of you, because we have to break down and repack all of the gear into duffel bags for the flight—within the next twenty minutes. I'm leaving us a twenty-minute buffer for traffic. We're leaving the RVs here. I'll make arrangements to extend our reservation at these campsites while you jump through Oksana's ass to get this done."

She winked and cursed at him in Russian.

"You'd like that, wouldn't you?" said Felix before tapping his watch. "Hurry along now. Start with the other RV."

When the team had cleared out, he called Oleg over to the table to take a look at the mission update. He gave him a minute to read through it, so they could compare notes.

"Not what I was expecting," said Oleg. "Why not just ferry us to the site ahead of time, if this is a counterassault mission?"

"That was my first thought, but the target complex is less than a five-minute helicopter flight from the Branson Airport, where we'll be staged. They obviously expect advanced warning of an attack," said Felix.

"Or they suspect the place is already under surveillance from a distance," said Oleg.

"Right. And there's nothing worse than a surprise," said Felix. "They're probably figuring some shock factor into our sudden arrival."

"Anything on who or what we're up against?"

"Oddly, no," said Felix. "But I'm guessing it's an assassination team."

"Easy enough. I'll have them pack the light machine guns and their ammunition in separate bags. One for each helicopter," said Oleg.

"Good idea. And the more I think about it, make sure everyone packs a separate mission bag with their primary weapon, pistol, ammunition, night vision, and plate carrier gear. If privacy turns out to be a concern at the Branson Airport, we'll have to kit up in the helicopters."

"Got it," said Oleg. "No grenades or heavier stuff?"

"Not if we're flying in hot," said Felix. "One unlucky hit and kaboom. Everything that doesn't go in the personal kits should go into sorted bags for easy access if the mission profile changes. I'm told we'll have some friendly support at the hangar to watch over anything we don't take in the helicopters."

"And some friendly ground support at the site? Radio frequencies for contact and coordination?" said Oleg. "What exactly are we defending here? My guess is an oligarch's mansion or one of Pichugin's rich American friends?"

"That was my first guess, but a quick look at the attached maps shows what looks to be some kind of campground or summer retreat," said Felix.

"What? Like a snazzy summer camp where rich people dump their kids?" said Oleg. "I heard the Ozarks are a popular vacation place, but I didn't think people like Pichugin sent their children to the United States."

"To be honest, I don't know what this is," said Felix, opening a few attachments.

One was a schematic representation of the camp's layout and internal roads. Shaped like an X, with four larger buildings and a pool in the center and two square fields a few hundred yards to the north. The four wings of the X appeared to be rows of cabins and longer structures labeled BATHHOUSE. Another contained several photographs of the buildings and cabins. All one-story structures, the cabins built in orderly rows between the trees. The X was simply labeled SITE ZERO.

"Definitely not a camp for rich people," said Oleg. "Unless this is what they're into these days. You can never say, right? I mean, they pay twice as much for tattered clothing."

"Looks abandoned in these pictures," said Felix, still not sure what to make of it.

The next set of pictures gave him an uneasy feeling. A Google Maps satellite image of the same site without any structures, the location only recognizable by the two rectangular clearings shown in the schematic to the north, labeled as ATHLETIC FIELDS. Only the outline of an X meticulously drawn in the center indicating where the camp should be. He searched the image, finding no indication of the camp, or any roads leading to it. A small icon to the east, at the end of a long cover, was labeled DOCK. Only accessible by water and somehow invisible to Google Maps. Definitely not your run-of-the-mill summer camp.

"What the hell is this place?" asked Oleg.

He shook his head. "In the end, it doesn't matter. A job is a job—and Pichugin is paying us well for this one. Brief the team about the gear and get the steaks cooking. It might be a while before we eat again."

"I'm getting a Last Supper vibe," said Oleg.

"Ah. Don't read too much into it," said Felix before doing the exact opposite the moment Oleg stepped out of the RV.

He clicked through the attachments and reread the mission documents at least three more times before concluding that they were in for a very long night. Something was off about this mission. Pichugin hadn't provided any indication of who or what they would be defending. The "why" wasn't important. He didn't care "why," as long as they got paid. But they'd never gone in this blind about the "who" or "what," and that bothered him.

CHAPTER 41

Devin Gray languished under the pontoon boat canopy, the stifling heat and humidity sapping his energy and eroding his enthusiasm for anything but another ice-cold bottled water from their rapidly emptying cooler. He pulled his feet back and out of the sun, his knees now bent at a ninety-degree angle. A few hours from now, the sun's superheated rays would fill the entire boat, adding to the misery—while dangling perilously low on the horizon. Dangerous because they were running out of time.

They'd run headfirst into an entirely overlooked obstacle this morning. With the weekend in full swing, the lake's entire boat-rental inventory had been reserved. Every marina they'd called reported the same thing. All boats had either been checked out yesterday for the weekend or would be picked up today. When they struck out with the last marina, Rich had them hit the list again, this time offering five hundred dollars to bump their name to the top of the cancellation list—cash deliverable within the hour. Five out of the six marinas took him up on the offer, and the team split into three groups to make good on the payment. By midafternoon they had two pontoon boats, but no speedboat, which represented a problem.

Graves and Gupta needed a speedboat to launch the drone, since it had also become clear over the course of the day that their only other launch option would be a deserted stretch of rural road west of the conservation area, which would divert at least one tactical operative from the primary mission. At maximum throttle, the speedboat would serve as a stationary runway, providing the necessary lift for the drone to take to the sky. Retrieving it would be a different story altogether. Graves and Gupta could glide it to a landing on any hard, packed surface and grab it later. Or just ditch it and move on. It would all depend on how the mission unfolded.

As the hours dragged on, the last team gave up on the idea of renting a boat and had started making hard inquiries about paying cash for a few inexpensive speedboats advertised at some of the marina stores. They were in the process of convincing one of the owners to drop everything and trail the boat to the lake, where they'd pay cash on the spot if he could demonstrate that the boat worked.

Marnie was asleep on the other settee. She'd been out for a while now, having tipped her ball cap over her face about an hour and a half ago. Devin got up and put one of the beach blankets they'd purchased this morning over her legs so she didn't wake up with a sunburn. She stirred for a moment and went still. He'd kill for a nap right now, or a swim to cool down, but he didn't want to wake Marnie. Maybe he could quietly slip into the water for a few minutes?

Devin took off his shirt. He made his way to the platform at the back of the boat and had just started down the ladder when a pontoon boat burst into the Woods Hollow at full speed, Rich and his team hooting and hollering the entire way to Devin's anchorage. Marnie bolted upright, looking at him, confused. He quickly climbed back on deck and grabbed the railing to steady himself before the other boat's bow wave hit.

"Hang on!" he said, worried she might topple off the couch.

She grabbed the railing above the cushion as the wave rocked the boat—nowhere near as forcefully as he had imagined. A pontoon boat was, after all, one of the most stable platforms on the water. Marnie yawned and stretched as Rich swung back around and idled his boat alongside.

"Do you think one anchor will hold both boats?" asked Rich.

"I'm not the expert," said Devin, glancing toward Marnie.

"We didn't cover pontoon boat anchoring in the Marine Corps," she said. "But I think we'd be better off swinging around on one anchor than two. And there's no breeze to speak of, so I think one will do it."

Devin reached off the port side to grab the other boat. Marnie leaned over the couch and did the same, the two of them keeping the boats in place while Jared and Emily tied them together. Rich killed his engine and wiped the sweat off his brow. Scott immediately went to work on the pontoon boat's canopy.

"Sorry about the dramatic entry," he said. "Something about boats brings out the kid in me."

"I believe the term you're looking for is *immature jackass*," said Jared. "He was like that the entire trip down. Not kidding. We're carrying several life sentences in weapons and ammunition—and he's weaving around like a drunk."

"He's not driving to the infiltration point," said Emily. "Period."

Rich shrugged. "It was fun while it lasted. Looked like you were going for a swim?"

"I was thinking about it. I'm like fifteen minutes from a reactor core meltdown."

Jared hopped on board, taking shelter under the canopy. "I wouldn't know, since we had a twenty-mile-per-hour wind and lake spray hitting our faces for the past hour."

"These things move faster than I thought," said Devin. "I saw people skiing and tubing behind them."

"Yeah. I had originally envisioned three speedboats, mostly because I don't know a damn thing about lake recreation," said Rich. "But these are actually better overall. More room for gear, and they can navigate shallower water. We still need a speedboat to launch the drone. Gupta isn't confident twenty miles per hour is fast enough. I think it is, but he's not convinced—and the drone surveillance is critical."

"I suppose we could steal one from a marina," said Devin. "How hard could it be to hot-wire one of those things?"

"The thought had crossed my mind. Alex called a few minutes ago and said the deal is almost done. The owner of a Sea Ray is on his way over to a place where they can put the boat in the water to run it. Somewhere not too far south of Diamond City, which isn't too far from here."

"What about Graves and Gupta? It sounds like they'll have to work from one of the boats," said Devin. "We'll have to move one of the pontoon boats to a cove closer to the conservation area. I don't think they'll be able to control the drone from here."

"Berg dropped Graves and Gupta with Alex's team, then secured parking for their vehicle at a motel in Diamond City. No vacancies, but for the same price as a room, you can park in one of the dozen open spaces overnight. They'll run the SUV over, load up the boat, and head our way. We have vehicles all over the lake at this point. Not ideal, but what else could we do?" said Rich. "As far as relocating goes, we won't have to worry about that. They'll use the speedboat. We'll all head out together, and they'll speed ahead to launch it."

"Will they be able to operate the drone from a speedboat?" asked Devin.

"Tim says it'll be fine, and he's a boater. They'll launch the drone, put it in one of those autonomous aerial patterns away from the camp, and find a quiet cove nearby to work their magic."

"What will Karl do while all of this is going on?" asked Devin.

"Good question. I'm thinking he'll hang around closer to Branson and wait for word. There's a La Quinta Inn about a twenty-minute drive from Mincy. Same distance from the OK Marina, if we need to get off the water fast. My thought was that we'd head north after the mission. Berg can grab us at any number of locations along the lake."

"You don't seem too concerned that we lost an entire day hunting down boats," said Marnie. "What's the rest of the plan?"

"We launch the drone, make sure the infiltration point is clear before landing," said Rich. "The drone searches for the camp while we land. Hopefully it finds the camp. Or we're in for a long night."

"That's it?" said Marnie. "I'm not complaining. Just making sure I didn't miss anything."

"Unfortunately, we don't have much more to work with," said Rich. "The place didn't show up on Google Maps satellite imagery."

"What do you mean?" asked Devin. "Is the tree canopy too thick?"

"No. The Google Maps image looks like it was taken after the leaves had fallen. You can see the shadows of the tree trunks on the ground throughout the entire conservation area. It's been scrubbed."

"That's some high-level national security magic," said Devin. "My mother either missed a high-profile sleeper, or we're looking at the possibility of a sleeper in a very unique, but unpublished, national security role."

"Or Barber diverted us from the real camp," said Marnie.

"Always a possibility. All we know is what William Barber told us under considerable duress. One of these hollows, creeks, or whatever you want to call them forks into two. Go right at the fork. There's a dock at the end. The camp is a quarter mile down a trail heading northwest."

"But we're not using that dock," said Devin. "If camp is in session, they'll be watching it somehow. Especially if they've received some kind of alert."

"They have. Gupta found the same text message on both of their phones, received at the same time on Friday morning. Looked like spam, but it came from an SMS short code, which you normally have to opt into to receive. The likelihood of them both getting a skin-care product message for a product that doesn't exist, at the exact same time, is near zero. We'll land on the north shoreline and work our way south to the approximate camp area. There's only one creek that forks into anything along the entire shoreline of the Mincy Conservation Area.

North, south, or west. So we have a pretty solid idea where to look for the camp. A few drone passes should nail down the location."

"Then what?" asked Marnie.

"I'm beginning to feel more than just the heat from the sun here," said Rich.

"Just trying to get a handle on what we're walking into tonight," said Marnie. "And no—I'm not going to wait on the boat. We all need to see the camp for ourselves. The more witnesses the better."

"This is a reconnaissance-only mission," said Rich. "But we're going to push the envelope. I want to get as deep into that camp as possible before turning back. We'll be using rifle-mounted, high-definition, zoomable video cameras to record the operation. They'll be on from start to finish. Anything you point your rifle at will be recorded for further analysis."

"I assume they're night vision capable?" said Devin.

"It's a commercial hunting camera, which works differently than standard military night vision. The advantage of this system is that the camera adjusts for light conditions. A straight-up night vision rig would flare out if you entered a lighted room or caught a flashlight."

"How far do you intend to push the envelope?" asked Devin.

"Depends on what we find, and the level of activity," said Rich. "If possible, I'd like to take a look inside the larger structures, if any exist. Just the presence of the camp, linked to the evidence your mother collected, should be enough to generate some high-level interest. If we can snap pictures of Joseph Stalin plastered all over the walls in some kind of gathering hall, even better. Pictures of camp attendees that can be linked to the profiles Helen generated, or other key people in key technology, industry, or infrastructure positions? Priceless."

"Rules of engagement?" asked Devin.

"We'll go over all of that during the final mission briefing," said Rich. "Anyone up for a swim?"

"After you answer the question," said Devin. "Bottom line ROE."

"This is not an offensive operation. We only fire in self-defense. So, if someone fires at us, we return fire. If someone points a weapon at us, we'll fire first," said Rich. "If we're discovered, and have to beat a hasty retreat, we will consider anyone standing between the team and our boats as an immediate lethal threat. Does that sound about right?"

Marnie nodded. "Sounds uncomplicated—which is more important."

"Exactly," said Rich. "Things tend to get complicated enough on these missions without our help. We strive to simplify where we can."

"Good," said Devin. "Because something tells me tonight is going to be anything but straightforward."

PART V

CHAPTER 42

Timothy Graves slowly increased the Sea Ray 185's speed from fifteen miles per hour to forty, rapidly pulling away from the two pontoon boats. They'd just passed Trucker Hollow Marina to the left, which was marked by a dozen or more bright security lights, marking the start of a straight, three-and-a-half-mile northwest stretch of lake. Red and green running lights spanned the lake ahead, marking boats at varying distances. Most of them were just specks in the darkness, a good mile or two away. His only job right now was to keep them on a steady course for the drone launch—while avoiding any kind of collision that could disable the boat.

He flipped his night vision goggles down over his face and took in the lake through new eyes. The distant lights burned bright white now, momentarily looking closer until the image adjusted. Graves had initially planned to make the run without night vision, but several floating tree stumps had convinced him otherwise. The Sea Ray wasn't exactly a Coast Guard cutter. Hitting one of those trunks at maximum speed would likely rip through the hull and put the boat at the bottom of the lake.

Gupta tapped his shoulder twice, their prearranged signal that he was moments from pressing the button to autonomously launch the drone. Neither of them had attempted a running takeoff before, so they had no idea what to expect when he hit the button. In theory, the propeller blade would start spinning, the sensors would start sensing, and the eighteen-pound drone would instantly reach for the sky—as it did when it achieved takeoff speed during a normal launch. The trick would be letting go at the right time.

They'd conducted a dry run earlier today, the lift generated by a forty-miles-per-hour relative wind making the drone hard to hold on to. He would have preferred executing a full practice launch, but the attention that would have generated was guaranteed to put them on YouTube. Then they'd have to retrieve it. This would be a one-and-done deal. Either it worked or it didn't. Three quick taps landed on his shoulder. The moment of truth. A high-pitched buzz competed with the engine and bow wash.

"Holy shit! Woo-hoo!" yelled Gupta. "It worked!"

He glanced over his shoulder to find Gupta staring almost straight up into the sky, the drone no longer in his raised hands. Graves slowed the boat and searched the sky, catching a glimpse of the drone's sleek, nonreflective shape peeling away to the west. When he'd brought the boat back down to a more manageable cruising speed, he raised the night vision goggles.

"What happened?" asked Graves.

"Fucking took off like a rocket!" said Gupta. "Like it was pissed! If I had tried to hold on to it, I'd be in the drink right now."

"Outstanding. Now we have another trick up our sleeve. We could do the same from a car," said Graves.

"Damn! We're like the drone master DJs," said Gupta. "Add some motorcycle launches to the mix. Maybe a WaveRunner. Have drone, will launch, baby!"

"Okay. That's enough," said Graves. "Voices carry over water."

"We're still like two miles from the southern tip of the conservation area," said Gupta.

"I don't want to take any chances," said Graves. "How does everything look on the laptop?"

Gupta grabbed the open laptop from the rear seat and sat down next to him in the cockpit. He clicked around the dimmed screen for a few seconds before answering.

"She's climbing high on her way to the first waypoint, north of the conservation area. Everything looks good."

The drone's first glide track would take it due south, directly over the primary infiltration site, before turning left to search the dock area referenced by William Barber. If sentries had been posted in that area, they represented a threat to the team's left flank while approaching the camp. Once that surveillance run was completed, the drone would fly east across the river and climb again, positioning itself for a long east-to-west glide over the suspected camp area. Their first glimpse behind the curtain.

CHAPTER 43

The western shoreline, a long darkened mass barely discernible from the night sky, passed down their port side, roughly five hundred feet away. They'd kept to the starboard side of the lake on the trip up, blending in with the scattered traffic on the water. Bull Shoal Lake felt more like a river, long and narrow as it wound through the Ozark Mountains, dipping in and out of Arkansas shortly after they departed the staging area. The hour-long trip had been unremarkable so far, the height of excitement coming from the powerboats that had burned past them at ungodly speeds, presumably headed toward the Branson area—and civilization. Devin still couldn't get over how little existed out here. His earpiece chirped.

"RIFFRAFF. This is OVERWATCH. Primary infiltration site appears clear on IR and visual night vision scan. Dock site shows two heat signatures. Marked as hostile. We'll check them on every pass to make sure they haven't moved."

"This is Rich. Copy your last. River looks clear. We're headed in."

The pontoon boat veered sharply to port and pointed directly at the shoreline. He adjusted his position on the couch to face forward, rifle still lying flat on the cushions behind him, next to a night vision–rigged ballistic helmet. Marnie did the same, settling into place within an arm's reach beyond the aluminum gate that opened to the bow platform. A look behind him at the cockpit revealed Rich's barely illuminated face, his eyes alternating from the muted map screen on the satellite phone in front of him to the rapidly approaching shoreline.

When Devin turned his head, Marnie had already donned her helmet and flipped the night vision goggles down into place over her face. He followed her lead, and they started scanning the brush along the shore. About a hundred feet from the tree-packed shoreline, Jared cut the speed to idle, and they glided quietly across the smooth water. He nudged the engine a few more times, until the front of the pontoon boat gently nestled into a snarl of thick scrub under a canopy of low-hanging branches.

As the boat floated back a few feet, Devin opened the gate and jumped down, landing in thigh-high water. He took the coiled line Marnie had tied to one of the bow cleats and slogged through the brush to reach the nearest tree trunk, where he secured it the best he knew how. Marnie joined him a few moments later, undoing and redoing his work without saying a word. Rich and Jared pushed past them once she was finished and disappeared into the bushes.

"Jared and I are heading about fifty feet inland, due north, to secure the area."

No response was required, unless acknowledgment was a request. This group worked together smoothly, saying very little, which suited him fine. He and Marnie had agreed to stay out of their way, and talk over the radio net only if it were absolutely necessary. The less of a distraction the two of them provided, the better chance they had of getting out of this unscathed.

The second boat arrived a few seconds later. Devin and Marnie grabbed the line on their bow and tied it to a solid tree. With the boats secured, the nine of them fought through the thicker shoreline undergrowth until they reached a more passable forest floor. They knelt in a tight 180-degree perimeter centered on Rich, while Devin and Marnie covered the far-right side.

"Turn your cameras on. Then check your gear one more time while we wait for OVERWATCH to do their thing," said Rich over the net.

There wasn't much to check. Rich wanted them going in light for maximum stealth and maneuverability. His gear consisted of a basic plate carrier with front and back armor inserts, four double-rifle magazine pouches giving him eight spare magazines for his HK416 A5 5.56-millimeter rifle. No knife. No pistol. No first aid kit. Comms worked. Night vision worked. Helmet was tight. He activated the side-mounted camera and mumbled, "Good to go."

Marnie elbowed him, and a quick glance told him he should at least pretend to pat himself down—which he did. She shook her head and rolled her eyes. No words required.

"RIFFRAFF, this is OVERWATCH. East-to-west surveillance run found the camp, which is shaped like an X. In the middle of the X, we spotted five Olive Garden–size buildings and what looks to be an Olympic-size pool, which is empty. I know the restaurant thing is an odd comparison, but that's all I could think of. Olive Garden or Applebee's."

"We get the picture," said Rich.

"Copy. The middle space with the buildings and pool is mostly open, in the shape of a square, with a few big trees in between the buildings. The structures look to be one story. The cabins are arranged in three rows along each branch, extending outward from the center square to form the X shape. You're looking at four branches of cabins. Does that make sense?"

Three rows? How many cabins in each row? The camp sounded significantly larger than what would be necessary to host the seventy-three families his mother had uncovered. Even if the actual number was double.

"Yes. Keep sending," said Rich.

"We spotted a few dozen human heat signatures in the center, at least half of them gathered around two firepits. S'mores with Stalin. We also have a few people walking around the southwest branch of the X. I suspect that's the active housing branch, because we got no hits in the other three branches of cabins."

"How many cabins per row in each branch?" asked Rich, clearly on the same page as Devin.

"It's really hard to tell. The tree canopy is thick, and they built the cabins right among the trees. Before we make a few more passes, I'd estimate twenty. Minimum."

Marnie elbowed him again before whispering, "That's way more than your mother found."

He nodded. "Two hundred and forty at the low end. More than three times the number, if my math is right."

The threat was far more extensive and potentially damaging than they had originally thought. The stakes for this mission had just been raised.

"Did I hear you correctly? Twenty?" asked Rich.

"Minimum. It might be bigger. I'm sending you waypoint coordinates for the tip of the northeast branch of the X. Looks like your best bet will be to start there and determine how you want to approach the center. The active housing area is on the opposite side of the X, so you should be able to get fairly close to the larger structures without running the risk of detection. We'll send updates with every surveillance pass."

"What is your blind time?" asked Rich.

"Six minutes once we pass the camp. Two for the climb and boogie at max speed. Four on the glide back down. I could climb higher and spiral around the camp, but it's a nightmare to use the camera manually that way. It would be hard to provide real-time data if you got jammed up down there. It's your call."

"Let's stick with the steady passes," said Rich. "Got your waypoint. We're moving out."

With that, Rich stood and signaled for the team to form up. He'd briefed them on the formation, which he'd called a modified squad column. Devin got the gist of it. Marnie understood what he meant right away. Every new Marine officer spent their first seven months learning infantry basics before they moved on to their specialty within the Marine Corps, including pilots.

He waited next to her as the first two groups of three moved out, each group spaced about fifteen yards apart. When it was time for them to set off, Mike took the lead, Devin and Marnie spacing out a bit along his flanks. Mike had pulled babysitting duty. Hopefully it would prove to be an easy gig. Devin snapped a stick with his right foot, stopping the entire formation.

"Step slowly and lightly, Devin," whispered Mike over the radio. "We're in no hurry."

Mike was going to earn his money tonight.

CHAPTER 44

Marnie Young moved deliberately, frequently scanning the forest along her right flank and constantly recalculating a few variables. The first was cover. As the team crept closer to the cabins, she became more aware of the threat axis to the southwest, which forced a running evaluation of the best tree to use to block incoming gunfire—in the event of an ambush. The second variable was Devin.

She had no doubt he was invisible when tailing an espionage suspect through the urban jungle of DC, blending seamlessly into Metro station crowds and drawing no suspicion on the streets. But none of those skills seemed to transfer over to sneaking through a pitch-dark forest—even with night vision. The little mental energy Marnie had to spare beyond herself had been focused on the slew of noises Devin made, and whether that might require her to seek cover immediately.

The team clearly felt the same strain. Rich had halted the group at least eight times after Devin stumbled, scraped a tree, ran into a low-hanging branch, or tripped over a root. She was relieved they had almost reached the bottom edge of the northeast cabin wing, even though that meant the start of an infinitely more dangerous phase of the mission. Part of her wanted to suggest that Devin stay at the first set of cabins, to provide rear security. Any excuse to keep him from giving up the team's position as they infiltrated deeper into the camp.

She glanced in his direction, catching him stopped in front of a branch, trying to find it with his hand. Once his hand brushed across it, he ducked and continued forward. At least he was learning. The night vision goggles played havoc with a person's depth perception, particularly at short distances. It took some getting used to. Marnie probably knew this better than anyone here, since she had flown entire missions at night, relying on night vision goggles. With little margin for error when landing in tight spots, she had mastered the complexities of night vision rather quickly. The lives of her crew and the Marines she transported had depended on it.

The forward element of the team reached the first set of three cabins a few minutes later, Rich halting the rest of the group in the forest. They waited while Emily, Alex, and Scott each took positions behind one of the cabins and used binoculars to peer into the camp.

"This is Scott. Overall, we're looking at three fairly even rows of very evenly spaced cabins. I see what looks like a longer cabin in the middle row, about five cabins down. Probably a bathhouse. A straight, ten-foot-wide dirt trail runs from here all the way to the center of the X. I can vaguely see a few of the buildings in the center of the camp from here. The third row of cabins, next to Emily, is connected to the main trail by a dirt path. The cabins look abandoned and neglected, but not completely ignored. I see evidence of weed whacking along the perimeter of the cabins. Alex?"

"Hold on," said Rich. "Can you count the number of cabins in each row?"

"Stand by," said Scott.

Rich turned and signaled for the rear team to move forward. He gathered them in a loose huddle when they arrived.

"Definitely bigger than your mother's numbers suggested," said Rich. "I'm conflicted about how to proceed. Part of me says we go back the way we came and try to pitch this to the FBI using some of Karl's contacts and mine. I have the ear of a US senator that should be able to help. But that approach is like a long, slow-moving train. Once it gets going, it'll be hard to stop, but getting it moving at all is the big trick. And getting it up to speed will give this circus all the time it needs to pull up its tent stakes and flee town. By the time the FBI finally checks this place out, Stalin's traveling sleeper carnival will be long gone."

"What's the faster-moving option?" asked Devin.

"I don't know if there is one," said Rich, "other than document the shit out of this place and try to identify some of the campers."

"We could grab a few," said Jared.

"I don't think that'll strengthen our case with the FBI," said Rich. "I think our best play is to get as close as possible and take photographs of the campers, the buildings—everything. I'm starting to think we might spend more time here than I had originally planned. I'd really like to get into a few of those buildings and steal some of their training material. Take pictures while some of the campers are still awake. Attempt a break-in around two or three in the morning?"

"Whatever it takes," said Devin, everyone else mumbling agreement.

"How long do we have drone coverage?" asked Marnie.

"The drone's enhanced surveillance package puts it at the higher end of the model's takeoff weight range, which taxes the battery," said Rich. "Normally I'd say we had two hours, but the gliding might buy us more time."

Rich activated his radio. "OVERWATCH. How long can you keep the drone up? We're thinking about extending our stay."

"I need to take the drone off station around twelve forty-five to land it safely. If we ditch the drone, and I time its last pass right, you'll have coverage until a little after one."

"The gliding didn't help the battery situation?" said Rich.

"Negative. It came out as a wash. Actually, we may have lost battery time. The altitude hikes eat up power."

"Understood," said Rich, ending the chat with Gupta. "There's your answer. If we stick around for a little breaking and entering, we'll have to do it partially blind, unless everyone up there goes to bed within the next twenty minutes. It's eleven thirty-five right now, and I wouldn't risk cracking open one of those doors until everyone has been down for a good hour or so."

"I think it's worth it," said Devin. "We need to leave here with more than pictures."

"I agree," said Marnie. "If we can do it without waking them up. Don't forget that we're dealing with brainwashed zealots here, and this is sacred ground to them. All bets are off if someone raises the alarm."

"You bring up a really good point. I hadn't thought of it that way," said Rich. "Come to think of it, they probably have some kind of emergency procedure for trespassers that get too close, whether they stumble in here on purpose or unintentionally. I'd be willing to bet there's a history of unexplained disappearances in this county. That said, I still think we should stick around and try."

"WWKD," said Jared.

"Huh?" said Marnie.

"What would Karl do?" said Jared. "When in doubt. WWKD."

"I like it," said Marnie, stifling a laugh. "So. What *would* Karl do?"

"Something a lot more drastic than a late-night break-in," said Rich.

"Like what?" asked Devin.

Don't encourage him, she wanted to say. Marnie had a good idea what Karl would do.

"He'd position most of us in a line at the edge of the camp center, facing the active community branch. Anyone that jumped out of their cabin to investigate our noise would experience a steel-jacketed aneurysm."

"What if they all came out?" asked Devin.

"A massacre," said Marnie, not entirely believing this idea hadn't already crossed Rich's mind.

"We'd be acting in self-defense," said Rich. "And in the interest of the United States."

He had thought of it. Had she just stumbled on some kind of soft coup, unintentionally exposed by Jared's careless joke?

"We're not going that route," said Devin. "I'm not saying we don't set up security when we start poking around the buildings, but we won't be holding the line if we stir up a hornet's nest. We defend ourselves according to the ROE, as we retreat to the boats."

"That's the plan," said Rich.

"It better be," said Marnie.

Rich looked as though he wanted to get the last word in but thought better of it. Her earpiece crackled.

"This is Scott. We've compared notes. The outer rows have thirty to thirty-five cabins. It's impossible to get an exact count from here. The middle is harder to determine because of the bathhouses, but I'd say around twenty-five."

"Anyone good with math?" said Rich.

Devin was ready with an answer. "Three hundred and forty cabins. Assuming each cabin houses one family, which looks to be the case, but needs to be confirmed—we're looking at close to seven hundred second-generation sleepers instead of the one hundred and forty-six she identified. Assuming a twenty-five percent attrition rate, which is roughly what she calculated, we're looking at around six hundred sleepers embedded in US society instead of one hundred and nine."

Rich and Devin were right. They had to do more than take pictures. The stakes were too high.

"What would Karl do?" she said, turning a few heads. "Without killing every man, woman, and child in the camp?"

"That's the trick here," said Rich. "In this business, sometimes you pull a tiger out of the hat instead of a bunny."

"Then we'll have to feel around inside the hat for a while before the big show," said Marnie. "Sit on the place until we're certain we can investigate the buildings without pulling out a tiger."

"WWMD," said Rich.

"Exactly," she said.

What would Marnie do?

CHAPTER 45

Felix Orlov woke from a light nap, the phone on his chest buzzing. He gripped the phone and sat up on the shiny concrete hangar floor, taking a few moments to regain his bearings. When the phone kept buzzing, his stomach sank. Felix assumed he'd just received a text message with a code to access a mission update on the dark web site. He stared at the unfamiliar number for another second, surprised they had called him directly. Pichugin's proxy never arranged direct call protocol.

"Hello?" he said, accepting the call.

"Give the order to start the helicopters. I'll wait."

The voice was modulated to disguise the speaker. Felix yelled at Oleg, who stood in the open pedestrian doorway adjacent to the closed hangar bay door. "Get the helicopters ready for takeoff! Everyone else up and checking their gear."

Oleg bolted out of the hangar, while the rest of the team shook off their naps and got to their feet.

"The order has been given," said Felix.

"The pilots will fly you to the two athletic fields north of SITE ZERO. One helicopter in each field. You'll lead the team to the coordinates I will text to your phone the moment I hang up. The coordinates correspond with a hostile team's boat infiltration point. Friendly forces at SITE ZERO will engage the hostile team and force them to retreat. Our assumption is that they will immediately return to the boats at their original infiltration point, where you will ambush the hostile team."

The high-pitched whine of the helicopters' engines resonated inside the hangar. The blades would reach their full rotor speed in just under a minute.

"We'll pay everyone on your team fifty thousand US dollars per prisoner taken, but there is no penalty for killing the entire team. The hostile force is comprised of nine mercenaries. Nongovernment affiliated. Seven of them to be considered top-tier special operators. The other two have a high level of military firearms proficiency. Do not take any catastrophic risks with your team to capture any of them. You're up against a highly skilled crew. Handle them as your equals."

"Understood. What if they don't retreat from SITE ZERO?" asked Felix.

"I'll be in direct contact with the group at the site. If they can't force a retreat, I'll call you directly and redirect your team."

Oleg reappeared in the doorway and gave him a thumbs-up before assembling the team around the door.

"The helicopters are ready," said Felix.

"Don't let me hold you up." The call disconnected.

He jogged over to the team and repeated their orders, leaving out the part about prisoner bounties. *Handle them as equals* told Felix everything he needed to know about the hostile force. He had to kill all of them quickly and efficiently, or they would extract a heavy price from his team. Fifty thousand dollars was tempting, but not that tempting— to him. He couldn't speak for the rest of the team's financial situations. His life was worth far more than a measly fifty grand, and he wasn't about to put it in the hands of someone who needed a quick money fix to pay off a gambling debt.

Satisfied that everyone understood the parameters of the mission, he turned them loose. They split up into two groups and boarded their assigned helicopters. Felix followed Oksana and Lashev, their sniper, to the leftmost Bell 429 helicopter, where they climbed inside, slid the wide side door into place, and immediately went to work donning their equipment.

The helicopter lifted off a moment later, a feeling of heaviness overtaking him until the helicopter's flight leveled off, headed toward SITE ZERO. The pilot told him it would take no more than four minutes to reach the landing zone, which put them all under a bit of a time crunch to slip into their full combat kit. They worked methodically, starting with their plate carrier vests and moving on to their drop holsters. Rifles attached to one-point carry slings next, followed by helmets and night vision.

"One minute!" yelled the pilot.

He was glad Pichugin had arranged for two helicopters. This particular Bell model was rated for seven passengers, enough to ferry the team to the site, but the cabin felt cramped enough with the three of them unloading and swinging gear around. He couldn't imagine trying to pull this off with the seven operatives in the same space. Not in four minutes. He patted himself down again to make sure he hadn't missed something. All good.

With his personal gear squared away, he went to work on the last duffel bag with Oksana. Together, they wrestled the M249 LMG (light machine gun) out of the bag and onto the rear passenger bench seat. He retrieved one of the seventy-five-round-drum magazines from the bag and inserted it into the magazine well. All a gunner had to do at this point was release the safety and pull the charging handle back. Four additional drums sat in each bag.

"Should we bring one of these along?" asked Oksana. "The firepower might come in handy."

He thought about it for a moment. The light machine gun's high rate of fire would certainly pack a punch, but nobody on the team had much experience on the M249. Nearly all their operational time had been spent behind the gunsights of Russian-made weapons or similar knockoffs, which was most likely why the arsenal in Pennsylvania contained several AK variants. Everyone on the team, except for their sniper, had chosen a compact version of the AK-12 assault rifle.

"How many times have you fired one of these?" asked Felix.

"A few times. It's not the easiest weapon to handle. The rate of fire is extremely high."

He shook his head. The last thing he wanted to do was throw a wrench in the works at the last minute. Especially if their opponents were as skilled as Pichugin's proxy had suggested. If their mission changed and they needed the firepower to dislodge the hostiles from the camp, he could send a team back to grab them.

"Let's stick with what we know," said Felix.

"Thirty seconds!" said the pilot.

Thirty seconds until they hit the ground running—literally. The landing zone and SITE ZERO were nearly equidistant from the ambush site—a race he had no intention of losing if the hostile team retreated faster than Pichugin's planners had anticipated. Second place was an unceremonious death in the Ozark Mountains.

CHAPTER 46

Devin checked the cabin door, surprised to discover that the doorknob turned. They'd moved through twelve sets of cabins while working their way toward the center of camp, finding all of them securely locked. He'd taken a step closer to the door to push it inward when a hand clamped down on his arm. Mike shook his head and motioned for him to stand back, which suddenly struck Devin as a more sensible course of action. Was he really moments from pushing in the only open door they'd found out of the thirty-odd they'd checked? Marnie must have been shaking her head.

Mike crouched and pointed his rifle at the door. "Rich. We found an unlocked door."

"Be right there."

Devin backed up next to Marnie, who knelt in the recently cut weeds several feet behind Mike, her rifle pointed down the long, empty gap between rows that extended all the way to the center of the camp. Unlike the dirt path, several trees grew right up in the middle of the gap, mostly obscuring their view of the buildings. Devin raised his rifle and covered their flank, not that they expected any trouble from the forest.

Rich patted his shoulder as he passed by, quickly joining Mike near the door. The two of them conversed for a moment before Rich very gently turned the knob and opened the door far enough for Mike to take a quick peek inside. He nodded at Rick before disappearing into the cabin, his head poking out a few seconds later.

"It's clear," he said.

Rich turned to Devin and Marnie. "The moment of truth. If this is a two-family cabin, we're defaulting to WWKD."

A two-family cabin meant they were potentially looking at twelve hundred sleepers instead of six hundred. If that turned out to be the case, Devin might have to reconsider his position regarding the building break-in scenario, consequences be damned, whether they pulled the rabbit or the tiger. He got the feeling Marnie would agree.

They followed Rich inside, Devin instantly relieved to see a full bed frame on one side and a bunk bed on the other. A single-family arrangement. Aside from the beds, the dank-smelling cabin contained a nightstand between the beds, wooden chests at the foot of the beds, and a small table and chair set for four near the window. He didn't see any electrical outlets or overhead lights.

"Pretty sparse," whispered Rich.

"That's what I was thinking," said Devin. "Camp Stalin looks more like a gulag than a future training ground for sleepers."

"My guess is that the main buildings are a little more luxurious," said Rich. "The gulags didn't have swimming pools."

"They probably use the pool exclusively for swim training," said Marnie. "This place has a very deprived, utilitarian feel."

"On purpose," said Devin.

"Like a cult," she said. "I wouldn't be surprised if the entire camp looked like this."

"We'll find out later tonight," said Rich. "I'm thinking we work our way up the rows, until we're five or so cabins away from the center, then hunker down until the camp goes night night. Move up to the cabins closest to the center and give it another hour before we send a few people out to scout the buildings."

"Works for me," said Marnie.

"Sounds like a plan," said Devin.

"We won't have drone coverage, but I don't think we'll need it at that point. If the sentries at the dock haven't turned in for the night by the time the drone goes off station, I'll position one of the snipers to cover that approach. We'll probably find a trail leading to the dock from the center of the camp. It doesn't make sense for the campers to trudge through the woods after they're dropped off. Hopefully, they'll go straight to their cabins."

"Getting a good look inside those buildings takes priority," said Marnie. "They probably have fairly extensive files on every kid here. Right? They'd have to in order to monitor the kids' progress, chronicle their loyalty—whatever they do here. That could be the big ticket that wins an FBI raid or at the very least shines a bright light on every family named in the files."

"I like the way you think," said Rich, turning to Devin before leaving the cabin. "She's a keeper."

"Thanks," he said, not sure that was an appropriate response.

Marnie left without saying a word, so he decided not to pursue it. Devin followed and crouched next to her in the gap between cabins, rifles pointed toward the center of camp, as Rich rejoined his team on the dirt path. Mike softly shut the cabin door and paused at the top of the wooden stoop. Marnie scooted behind Devin in a hurry, stopping at the foot of the stairs.

"Did you hear it, too?" she asked.

Mike remained almost perfectly still, his head slowly canting to the side as though he was listening intently for something.

"What did you—"

Then Devin heard it. Just for a few seconds. A distant, deep rhythmic thumping sound that faded in and out. Mike turned to them.

"Take cover behind the cabin," he said before hopping down from the stoop. "There's an airport nearby. Probably the last flight out of—"

Muzzle flashes erupted from the center of camp, bullets snapping overhead and thunking into the cabins—along with the sharp crackle of automatic gunfire. Marnie yanked Devin behind the cabin, moments before gunfire sliced through the space he'd just occupied.

Mike slammed to the ground next to him, a few feet beyond the corner of the cabin. Devin leaned out and grabbed one of his shoulder straps with both hands, hauling him out of the line of fire.

Mike was in bad shape, clutching his throat and cycling his legs wildly. Devin raised his night vision goggles and went in for a closer look, warm blood spraying his face. Mike's hands were soaked, blood pumping through his fingers. Devin triggered his radio.

"Mike's down. Hit in the neck," he said. "It looks really bad."

"Copy that. Emily will be there in a second," said Rich.

"You got this?" asked Marnie, moving to the corner of the cabin.

"Yeah," he said, trying to move Mike's hands to get a better look.

He couldn't budge them. Marnie crouched low and fired a few sustained bursts toward the center of camp. She ducked back as bullets splintered the corner above her head and slapped into the cabin behind them. A dark figure appeared behind the middle cabin, racing in their direction.

"Emily's inbound! Give her some cover fire!" said Devin.

Marnie emptied the rifle magazine as Emily sprinted across the gap. The operative stumbled halfway, losing control of her forward momentum and crashing next to Mike.

"Shit!" Emily said, pounding the ground several times with a fist and groaning.

"You okay?" said Devin.

"I'm fine," she said, immediately going to work on Mike. "Bullet zipped my leg."

If anyone on the team could help him, it would be her. She'd stitched up Devin's shin wound like a practiced surgeon.

"Help me move his hands," she said, straddling Mike.

He planted his knees behind Mike's head, and together they forced his hands apart. Devin kept them pinned against the ground while she assessed the wound. Mike resisted every step of the way, but his strength had clearly diminished since the first time Devin had tried to remove his hands. After a few more seconds of poking and prodding around the profusely bleeding bullet hole, Emily shook her head.

"Mike is gone. There's nothing I can do for him. Bullet went straight through his neck and ripped open one of his carotid arteries." Emily spoke over the net. "Rich. Mike is KIA. He bled out."

"Copy. You're responsible for Devin and Marnie now. I'm sending Jared in your direction. Start laying down suppressing fire so we can give our snipers some breathing room to do their magic. We'll have this under control in no time."

Rich transmitted over the radio. "OVERWATCH, this is RIFFRAFF. We've been engaged by automatic fire originating near the center of camp. Mike is KIA. Need a SITREP."

"Copy. I'll have a SITREP for you in a few seconds."

Another long burst of bullets kicked up dirt in the gap and tore into the cabin behind them, leaving Devin with the distinct impression that Rich's pep talk with Emily was more wishful thinking than reality. The drumbeat of nearby helicopter rotors reinforced that feeling.

CHAPTER 47

Graves watched in horror as the team's situation shifted within a matter of seconds. Several automatic weapons had opened fire on the team, all located near the center of the camp. The hostile muzzle flashes did not correspond with human heat signatures, suggesting that they were firing from inside the cabins or well-concealed positions he had been unable to identify with the drone's sensors.

The dozen or so people gathered around the firepits had rushed into action, sprinting to the nearest building, where they disappeared for a few moments—before reappearing with rifles. And now they had two helicopters landing in the fields north of the camp. The team's arrival had obviously been detected, most likely at the shoreline infiltration point, given what he was seeing at the landing fields.

"I'm taking positive control of the drone," said Gupta. "We only have another minute on this glide path. They're going to need uninterrupted coverage."

"Yep," said Graves, taking a few moments to assess the scene before contacting the team. "RIFFRAFF, this is OVERWATCH. We're taking active control of the drone to pass you continuous information. SITREP follows. A dozen or more armed hostiles are headed toward the concealed gun positions near the center of the camp. From what I can see, they're bringing rifles to the fight. I also have some activity inside the southwest wing of the camp. Small groups forming. No weapons present. How copy?"

"Copy all. Are you seeing helicopters nearby?"

Gunfire on Rich's end of the radio call made it hard to decipher what he had said, but Graves caught the gist of it.

"Affirmative. Two Bell 400-series helicopters landed in the rectangular clearings north of the camp. One in each clearing. Seven hostiles in total exited the helicopters. They're headed east, away from RIFFRAFF, at a rapid pace. My guess is they're going to set up an ambush along your exfiltration route."

"Any more good news?"

"The team dropped off by the helicopters looked like serious types. Helmets. Night vision. Body armor. Rifles with suppressors. Moving like professionals. I do not recommend returning to the boats."

"Copy. We're still weighing our options here. Looks like we might be swimming out. Keep the information flowing."

"We can meet you somewhere along the eastern shoreline. We'll squeeze everyone on board. I'm sending Berg to the marina just south of the conservation area. The boat pickup is looking more and more like the only way out of there."

"We're not out of the fight yet. But I concur. Out."

A quick look at the IR camera view suggested otherwise. They couldn't possibly advance toward the center of the camp without sustaining more casualties, and making a run for the boats would prove catastrophic. He tapped Anish's elbow.

"Prepare an autonomous drone pattern over the camp," said Graves. "My guess is we'll be on a full-speed run to pick them up within minutes."

CHAPTER 48

Marnie sighted in on a muzzle flash through the 4X ACOG scope and pressed her trigger twice, the suppressed rifle biting into her shoulder. Like the other nonsnipers on the team, her rifle scope was not compatible with night vision goggles, so she'd switched from NVGs to the naked eye, which limited her to targeting muzzle flashes or the occasional silhouette. The gunfire at the receiving end of her bullets stopped, but it was impossible to tell if she'd hit the shooter or momentarily discouraged them.

Either outcome accomplished her goal, which was to reduce the level of incoming gunfire to a point where the team's snipers could focus more on shooting and less on hiding behind cover. The two snipers had higher magnification and thermal scopes, which made targeting unfair against opponents at night. The more time they could spend behind those scopes, the better chance the team had of getting out of this intact.

Return fire from the camp continued to snap past the corner of the cabin at different heights off the ground, many of them passing well over her head. She got the impression that the hostile gunfire wasn't well aimed. More of a quantity-over-quality situation—though equally deadly if you got caught out in the open at the wrong moment. They'd managed to advance only one set of cabins since the shooting started, the team miraculously suffering nothing more than a few grazing hits like Emily's. Only sheer luck had prevented another casualty, a reality not lost on Rich. He halted them to reassess the situation.

She fired another series of shots toward a different muzzle blast, pulling back from the corner as a long string of bullets stitched through the gap and slapped into the thick wood cabins around her. Devin remained exposed on the other side of the gap, firing several two-shot bursts until his magazine ran dry—seemingly oblivious to the string of bullets that splintered the wood right below his rifle barrel.

He glanced in her direction and shook his head before reloading. She peeked around the corner with the rifle and rapidly pressed her trigger, emptying the few rounds left in her magazine. Emily lay behind the wooden stoop several feet in front of Marnie, her body pressed against the bottom of the cabin, only her rifle and part of her head exposed. Emily fired relentlessly, seemingly changing magazines every third time Marnie leaned out to shoot.

"Do you need ammo?" asked Marnie.

Emily had turned to reply when a bullet ricocheted off her helmet, driving her head down. She rolled tight against the cabin and checked her night vision, which looked to be intact. Emily looked up at her.

"I'm down to three mags!"

Marnie patted the magazine pouches attached to her plate carrier, finding that she'd expended only two of her eight spares. She removed two and tossed them next to Emily, who snatched one and reloaded her rifle before stuffing the other in an empty pouch on her vest. She gave Marnie a quick thumbs-up and went back to firing. Marnie reloaded and got ready to stick her head and rifle out again.

"This isn't going anywhere!" yelled Devin.

"I know!"

"Rich is assessing the situation," yelled Emily.

How long did it take to assess the fact that the mission was scrubbed? If they didn't start making their way to the eastern shoreline very soon, they ran the risk of getting squeezed by the mercenary team dropped off by the helicopters. Devin leaned out to fire and was driven back by a torrent of gunfire. Enough was enough. She triggered her radio.

"Rich. This is Marnie. We need to start moving east before we get pinched. We're not breaking through to the camp."

"Jared and Melendez are starting to make a difference. If we can hold on here for another minute, I think we'll have a shot at breaking through and mopping up this rabble," said Rich.

"I'm more concerned with the hostile team dropped off by the helicopters," said Marnie.

"If we break through to the center," said Rich, "the hostile team will be forced to respond. We can run a counter-ambush."

"We got pictures of the camp. Video evidence of a heavily armed force. The whole enchilada isn't an option anymore," she said. "We need to get out of here now."

"We'll still have to deal with the mercenary team," said Rich. "If they figure out that we've slipped away, they'll hunt us down with the helicopters. Our extremely overcrowded boat won't last very long on the lake. And the Suburban will stick out like a sore thumb from the air on thermal imaging."

"Maybe we just cross the lake and melt into the forest on the other side," said Marnie.

"We'd just be delaying the inevitable," said Rich. "Maybe we could evade the helicopters on foot. It all depends on the helicopters' surveillance capability."

"Marnie?" said Devin over the net. "Can you fly one of those helicopters?"

Holy shit. With everything going on, they had overlooked the obvious. She could fly them out of here.

"Yes. I can definitely fly one of those helicopters. No doubt about it."

Rich cut into the conversation immediately.

"OVERWATCH, this is RIFFRAFF. Do we have a clear path to the helicopters?"

"*This is OVERWATCH. The path is clear. The nearest hostiles are at the center of camp roughly five hundred feet away. If you head directly to the nearest helicopter, you'll continue to open that distance. With the thick tree cover, you'll get there fine. The mercenary team is set up about a hundred feet in front of the boats, close to a thousand yards away. Even if they hauled ass, they couldn't beat you there. You're about three hundred and fifty yards from the easternmost clearing. I'll send you a waypoint. Designating the helicopter team RIFFRAFF ONE. Cover team is RIFFRAFF TWO.*"

"Copy. No security on the helicopters?" asked Rich.

"*No security. I'm seeing a single pilot in each cockpit, buckled up and waiting to take off. Could be someone hiding in back. The helicopters are shut down, so keep that in mind.*"

"It'll take about a minute to spool up the rotors," said Marnie.

"That'll be a long minute," said Devin.

"Not a problem," said Rich. "We'll post security at the edge of the clearing until the helo is ready for takeoff. The trick will be keeping the armed campers from bum-rushing the helicopter. If they see us bolt north, they'll put two and two together pretty fast. We can't afford a running gun battle. It'll slow us down enough for the mercenaries to possibly beat us to the helicopter or arrive at the same time. Or the helicopter will take off once everyone figures out what we're up to."

"Rich. This is Jared. Rico and I can stay here and keep firing. Give you guys a head start before they figure out what's happening. We'll melt away when the jig is up and rendezvous with the speedboat."

"That could work," said Rich.

"This is Emily. They'll know something's wrong the moment we drop down to two guns. I'll stay behind, too. I can move from one side of the middle cabin to the other, firing long bursts. We should probably leave four behind to buy as much time as possible. The whole point of this is to steal one of those helicopters, right? You could shoot the shit out of the other helicopter and eliminate any risk to the boat extraction."

"Scott. You've been volunteered," said Rich.

"Sounds good."

"Good thing I insisted on bringing a helicopter pilot along," said Rich.

"Yeah. Good thing you didn't try to convince Devin and me to stay behind every step of the way."

"Your next drink is on me," said Rich.

"The next *three* are on you," said Marnie.

"Fair enough," said Rich. "We should probably shift some ammunition around before we take off. Everyone flying out of here with Marnie, cough up some magazines."

She took three of her remaining five rifle magazines and tossed them one by one next to Emily, who glanced back when one of them bounced and hit her leg. A quick turn of the head and nod acknowledged the transfer, the shooter's trigger finger never letting up. Devin tossed her one magazine, which skipped across her back and hit the side of the cabin. She grabbed it without looking and reloaded, barely skipping a beat.

"Devin. Stand by to cross the gap," Marnie said. "Emily and I will cover you."

"Ready," said Devin.

She centered her scope's illuminated crosshairs on a muzzle flash and took some slack off the trigger.

"Now," she said, her rifle barking along with Emily's until Devin slammed into the side of the cabin next to her.

He put a hand on her shoulder and panted from the sprint.

"You can thank me later," said Devin.

"For what?"

"I bet you never thought you'd fly a helicopter again until a few minutes ago," said Devin.

She chuckled. Devin always had a knack for telling the truth, no matter how ridiculous the circumstances. Marnie just hoped she could pull this off so they could laugh about it later.

CHAPTER 49

Devin waited behind the cabin, keeping his eye on Rich, who had ventured about fifteen yards into the forest. A fierce gun battle raged behind Devin, the four members of the team who'd volunteered to stay behind increasing the volume of fire to draw attention away from their escape.

"Devin. You're up. Leapfrog about ten yards past me," said Rich.

"Don't fuck this up," he muttered to himself and stepped into the forest.

He scurried toward Rich, his feet hitting a few roots on the way. Branches weren't a problem anymore—he'd learned to gauge the distances to closer objects better—and it really didn't matter if he snapped a few twigs. Nobody would hear it over the gunfire. He scooted past Rich and settled in behind a thick tree trunk—just glad not to have fallen on his face.

"Nice job," said Rich. "I don't detect any reaction to our movement so far. Marnie and Alex, same drill. Head past Devin and take cover. If your movement goes unnoticed, we'll link up at your position and move out from there at a faster pace."

"Heading out now," said Alex.

Devin watched the two of them duck and weave through the trees, moving at a fast clip. They passed in front of him and halted behind a dense stand of brush about twenty yards away, rifles pointed toward the center of camp. He caught some movement in his peripheral vision. Rich was heading his way, moving significantly faster than before. Rich tapped his shoulder on the way by, and Devin followed in his footsteps, the two of them reaching Marnie and Alex without Devin stumbling or running into anything. He felt as though he was getting the hang of this.

"OVERWATCH, this is RIFFRAFF ONE. Any sign we've been detected?" said Rich.

"Negative. I don't see any unusual movement."

Rich removed a satellite phone from a pouch on his vest and checked the digital navigation screen, which he'd programmed with the waypoint passed to him by Graves. He compared the screen to his wrist compass, aiming the two in the presumed direction of the helicopter, before turning to address the group.

"We have about three hundred yards to go. I say we jog the rest of the way. Space ourselves about twenty feet apart."

"This may sound like a dumb question, but what do we do if we start taking fire?" asked Devin.

"Not a dumb question. Given the range and density of the forest, I say skip the return-fire part and just haul ass. It'll take one hell of a shot to hit a running target at this range through all of these trees. The farther we run, the harder it will be for them," said Rich. "Alex and I will take the lead. We'll have to deal with the pilot when we reach the clearing. Marnie. Can you still fly the helicopter if we pop a few holes in the windshield?"

"Yeah. Just keep your shots as high as possible to avoid hitting the instruments," she said. "I'd say no more than two shots, tightly spaced to avoid compromising the windshield's integrity. I can fly it with busted glass, but I'd have to fly a lot slower."

"Easy enough. If we fuck it up too badly, we can try and grab the other helicopter," said Rich. "Let's get moving."

They took off in a column—Rich followed shortly by Alex. Devin tapped Marnie's shoulder.

"You're next," he said.

She nodded and chased after them. Devin waited until she looked to be about the right distance away and followed her path through the trees. He didn't get far before a bullet cracked overhead, followed by another—both of them striking trees somewhere past him.

"Taking fire," said Devin over the radio net.

"Haul ass and follow me," said Rich.

The surrounding forest came alive with zips and thunks as imprecise gunfire raked their formation, ricocheting off tree trunks and snapping branches. The gunfire intensified for several seconds—pushing Rich's "it'll take a hell of a shot" theory to the limit with a few near misses—before it tapered off to a few scattered bullets.

"Everyone still with us?" asked Rich.

"All good," said Marnie.

"Bringing up the rear," said Devin, glancing over his left shoulder in the direction of the few remaining muzzle flashes. "We must be out of range."

"RIFFRAFF ONE, this is OVERWATCH. You have about a dozen hostiles from the center of the camp headed in your direction. They're moving fast, but as long as you keep up your pace, they won't be a problem."

"Understood. Have the mercenaries moved?" asked Rich.

"Negative. And the helicopter rotors remain stationary. Looking good so far."

Devin focused his attention on Marnie, who had gained some distance on him while he was looking over his shoulder. His only job right now was to keep her in sight so he didn't get lost, and to not fall down. A simple set of tasks if you weren't running for your life through an unfamiliar forest—with no depth perception.

CHAPTER 50

Felix Orlov listened intently to the distant gunfire, detecting a shift beyond the significant drop in intensity. Or maybe his judgment had been impaired by his impatience. This whole thing was taking entirely too long. It was obvious that the team he'd been sent to ambush had hunkered down among the cabins, content to exchange fire with the group that had been assigned to scare them into a hasty retreat.

If the target team was as good as Pichugin's proxy alleged, they would be able to assess what stood in their way, quickly determining the odds of pushing through—and what it would cost them. This team had clearly made the decision to slug it out at the camp, which meant there would be no ambush. Not here, at least.

More gunfire, this time definitely coming from a slightly different direction. He hit his radio button.

"Oleg. Is the direction of the gunfire moving, or am I imagining things?" asked Felix.

"It's shifting to the right," replied Oleg.

"Sounds like a one-sided battle," said Lashev, the team's sniper. "I don't hear any more suppressed shots."

Something was off. He removed his satellite phone and hit redial on the number that had called him at the hangar. After several ring tones, he ended the call. Ridiculous. Why wasn't anyone passing him information?

"Moving fast, too," added Lashev.

Felix scanned the forest ahead of them with a handheld infrared scope, finding nothing. He pointed it in the new direction of gunfire, still coming up empty. The action was too far away to detect with a portable thermal imaging device. He checked the Garmin Foretrex strapped to his wrist to get an idea of the direction of the gunfire. Almost due west, when it should be coming from the southwest. *Shit.*

"They're headed for the helicopters," he said over the radio net. "One of them must be a pilot."

"Why would they bring a pilot on a direct-action mission?" asked Oksana.

"I don't know, but why the fuck else would they be headed for the helicopters?" said Felix. "Valerie. Oksana. We're headed to the helicopters. All-out sprint."

"Our orders haven't changed," said Oksana.

"Our orders are to kill that team," said Felix. "And that's what I intend to do. Oleg. If they show up along the planned ambush route for some bizarre reason, take down as many as you can and radio me immediately. We'll flank the survivors."

"Understood," said Oleg, not sounding too enthusiastic about the decision.

Felix pressed a few buttons on his wrist-mounted GPS unit to select the waypoint he'd inputted when they first landed—and took off at a full sprint. At this point, he'd be lucky if they arrived in time to stop the team from stealing one of the helicopters, but he had to try. As he ducked under branches and dodged trees, another thought hit him like a hammer. The machine guns.

It didn't matter if they could fly the helicopters out or not. If that team took possession of the M249s, or even just one of them, they could flip the odds definitively in their favor. He hoped he hadn't waited too long to prevent a disaster.

CHAPTER 51

The helicopter engine started somewhere ahead of them and slowly began to power up. Devin still had no idea how far they had to go to reach the clearing. He'd caught up with Marnie after she tripped and tumbled to the forest floor—quickly getting her back on her feet and moving again. By the time they'd resumed sprinting, presumably in the right direction, Alex and Rich had vanished into the sea of green ahead of them.

"We don't have much time," said Marnie, picking up what felt like an impossible pace.

Two suppressed shots echoed off the trees, giving him no indication of a direction. He barreled through the forest a few steps behind her, thinking they couldn't possibly miss a one-hundred-yard-wide clearing. Or could they? His earpiece crackled.

"Where the hell are you two?" asked Rich.

"We should be there any—" he started, the two of them breaking through a jumble of bushes into the clearing.

The helicopter stood in the center of what looked like a mowed field, its rotors slowly picking up speed. Alex stood next to the helicopter, pointing his rifle inside.

"There you are," said Rich, waving to them from the eastern edge of the clearing before vanishing into the forest.

"Cabin is clear," said Alex. "I found an M249—ready to rock and roll. Do you want it on the tree line?"

"Negative. We'll be wheels up in forty seconds or less. I don't see anything moving out here," said Rich.

"Copy. On my way over," said Alex, already scrambling across the field toward Rich.

"Marnie. Do whatever you need to do to get us out of here," said Rich. "Remember. There's another helicopter in the clearing west of here, maybe fifty yards away. My guess is they're pretty desperate to stop us, so watch your three o'clock on the way out."

"Got it."

The two side-by-side bullet holes in the windshield came into focus when they passed under the rotor blade arc. Marnie reached the helicopter first, immediately opening the pilot-side door and going to work on the dead pilot's seat harness. She'd pulled him free of the helicopter just as Devin hopped into the cabin. Marnie poked her head between the front seats, nodding at the machine gun.

"Do you know how to work that?" she asked.

"I've held one, but never fired one," said Devin, lifting the machine gun off the bench seat to examine it. "But I can't imagine it's that complicated."

"It's not. Press the trigger for a second or two at most. It has a very high rate of fire. Very hard to control if you don't brace it against something. And don't forget about the safety. It's a button right about where your thumb rests. You have to push it from the other side with your index finger to take it off safe. And make sure to fire very short bursts."

"Shouldn't you be worried about taking off?" asked Devin, taking a seat with the machine gun pointed toward the forest.

"The Bell 429 kind of flies itself," said Marnie.

"I'm willing to bet it doesn't," said Devin.

His radio squawked. "Marnie. How long until takeoff? We have company coming in from the east."

She plopped down in the pilot's seat. "Rotor speed is still building, but it's starting to level off. Fifteen to twenty seconds max."

312

"Copy. We're on our way back. It's going to be a close call," said Rich. "Devin. I need you on that 249. The moment we jump on board, start hosing down the tree line where we pop out. You should be able to see us—right about now."

Devin looked up and caught the two of them emerging from the forest and sprinting toward the helicopter. *Jesus. Here we go.* He quickly located the safety button on the right side of the trigger grip and pressed it. Rich and Alex piled into the helicopter moments later, nearly knocking him over.

"Hit the tree line!" said Rich, slapping him on the shoulder. "Marnie. Get us the fuck out of here!"

Devin braced the M249 against the doorframe and aimed at the point where they had emerged, pressing the trigger briefly. The machine gun pounded his shoulder, rattling off a short burst. Marnie hadn't been kidding. The gun was a beast. He pressed the trigger again, holding it for a full second. The machine gun wasn't as hard to control now that he knew what to expect. Devin repeated the process six more times before the magazine drum emptied—methodically shifting his aim along a twenty-yard stretch of tree line. The helicopter lurched skyward as he fired the last burst.

CHAPTER 52

Felix Orlov knew they were running out of time when he heard the two suppressed gunshots. His only hope of preventing a catastrophic mission failure lay in reaching the landing zone and surprising the hostile force before they could either take off or put the machine gun to use against the group that had chased them to the helicopters. The race would be extremely close. The helicopter sounded as though it was ready for takeoff.

He weaved around trees, ducked under branches, and brute-forced his way through the brush, single-mindedly focused on catching a glimpse of the helicopter through the thick forest. Once Felix spotted the helicopter, he would halt the team and unleash a storm of gunfire. Two full magazines before moving forward to assess the situation. The rotor pitch suddenly deepened, meaning one thing. Someone on the team knew how to fly a helicopter!

He was about to give the order to fire blindly ahead of them when his satellite phone buzzed.

About fucking time!

He slowed to remove the phone from his vest, the other two operatives burning past him.

"Hold up!" he yelled before stopping to accept the phone call.

Automatic gunfire ripped through the trees, a single short burst at first, passing well overhead. He darted to the right and dived behind a thick tree trunk, barely escaping the longer bursts that followed—which struck at waist height. When the shooting stopped for a few seconds, he peeked around the tree with his rifle and fired on full automatic until the magazine ran dry. None of his bullets hit their mark. A stiff gust of dusty air washed through the foliage, indicating that the helicopter had already taken off.

Felix searched the ground next to him for the satellite phone. He'd dropped it when he slammed into the tree. His hand bumped into it next to his foot. He snatched it up and put it to his ear. "This is Felix!"

"It doesn't sound like you're at the ambush site."

"They got away," said Felix.

"Not for long. We managed to get a few of our friendlies on the second helicopter. Head back to the ambush site and wait for instructions."

The call disconnected, and he threw the phone to the ground.

"Valerie. Oksana. What's your status?" he said over the net.

No response—and he had no intention of breaking cover to check on them visually. He was still well in range of the M249 LMG. A few seconds later, he risked a look, seeing one of them on the ground, arms and legs splayed in a manner that strongly suggested they wouldn't be getting back up. Ever.

Screw it. Felix launched to his feet and sprinted for the tree next to Oksana, making it halfway before tripping on a pair of legs hidden by the brush. He landed face-to-face with Valerie, the young operative's lifeless eyes competing for Felix's attention with the small bullet hole an inch to the side of the man's nose.

Two KIA in the blink of an eye. He'd known this would be a shit show the moment he saw the mission packet—but you didn't turn down work when Yuri Pichugin offered it. Once you started working for his organization, you were either on his payroll or you were dead.

CHAPTER 53

Timothy Graves eased the Sea Ray into a wide starboard turn, with the full intention of opening the throttle once they had cleared the cove. RIFFRAFF TWO was on the move, estimated to arrive at the eastern shoreline in roughly ten minutes. Plenty of time for Graves to get the boat in position for a quick extraction.

"Stop the boat!" screamed Anish, near scaring him out of his skin.

He yanked the throttle back, putting the engine into idle, before shifting into reverse and bringing the boat to a quick stop. They lurched forward from the sudden deceleration, Gupta uttering a few choice words as he straightened himself out in the seat.

"What's happening?" said Graves, leaning across the seat to get a better view of the laptop screen.

"The second helo took off with armed passengers from the camp," said Gupta. "I'm going to crash the drone into the helicopter."

"What?" said Graves.

"No time to explain," said Gupta, taking positive control of the drone. "Warn the team."

"Marnie, this is OVERWATCH. The second helicopter took on armed passengers. Gupta is going to take it out with the drone."

"Say again?"

"We're going to ram the second helicopter with the drone," said Graves. "Bank hard left."

The laptop's screen switched from the navigation map to the drone's night vision–enhanced nose view. Two helicopters rose from the forest a few hundred yards away, the closest one turning left as soon as it had cleared the treetops. The first helicopter zipped out of view, the drone passing it at eighty miles per hour. Gupta centered the nose-view reticle on the starboard-side windshield of the pursuing helicopter and kept it locked in place until the screen went blank.

"I guess that worked?" said Gupta.

"You just slammed a twenty-pound drone traveling at eighty miles per hour into a windshield designed to deflect a bird," said Graves. "I suspect it worked."

A bright orange fireball rose above the northwest horizon, reflecting off the glassy-smooth lake.

"There's your proof. Hang on," said Graves, giving Gupta a few moments before pushing the throttle forward.

A deep boom echoed across the lake several seconds later as they raced down the middle of the lake toward RIFFRAFF TWO's primary extraction point.

CHAPTER 54

An ear-crunching detonation rattled the helicopter, Marnie's view through the night vision goggles flaring bright white and blinding her at the worst possible time for a helicopter pilot—in the middle of a hard turn at treetop level. She flipped the goggles up, instantly determining why her night vision had unexpectedly whited out.

A fireball rose skyward from the trees to their left, rapidly dissipating in the starry night sky. She maneuvered the helicopter out of the turn and picked up some altitude to give herself a little more space above the trees. When the fuel explosion burned out, the forest instantly darkened, once again rendering her blind. She swung her goggles back into place over her face and readjusted to the green-scale view.

"Thanks for the assist, OVERWATCH," said Marnie. "Scratch one hostile helicopter."

"For the record, that was all Gupta. I'm just kicking back driving a boat."

"Hat tip to Anish," said Marnie.

"What happened to the whole drinks-are-on-me thing?"

"You don't even drink, Anish," said Rich.

"I know. Just want to feel like part of the team."

"You are part of—" started Rich.

"Drinks are on me, Anish," she said before glancing over her shoulder. "Did we lose anyone?"

She was only half kidding. Marnie had given them a few seconds of warning before banking hard left, but a sudden, unannounced turn like that could throw someone out of the helicopter, if the maneuver caught them off guard and off balance.

"I still count three of us," said Rich. "Good try, though."

"Don't tempt me," said Marnie.

Her night vision goggles flared again, and she knocked them away from her face. "Dammit!"

"Jesus. Look at that," said Devin.

Marnie peered through her door's window, catching a glimpse of a broken, burning helicopter fuselage through the dense tree cover. The ground around the helicopter flickered from hundreds of little fires created by the explosions.

"I guess that solves our second helicopter problem," said Rich.

"Bummer. I was looking forward to machine-gunning it out of the sky. Mike would have approved of that," said Alex.

"He would have, but I have something else in mind," said Rich. "Marnie. I need you to fly us over the center of camp."

"Shouldn't we get the hell out of here?" she asked. "We're almost over the lake to the north of the conservation area."

"We need to do more than just take pictures and give them a helicopter to clean up," said Rich.

"If this is about avenging Mike, forget it," said Marnie. "We've pushed our luck far enough tonight. They might have a heavy-caliber machine gun set up on one of those roofs."

"Drone surveillance didn't show anything like that," said Rich. "Trust me on this, Marnie. We need to draw some serious attention to this place. Get people asking questions."

"They heard that explosion all the way in Branson," said Marnie. "Not to mention the gun battle that probably woke everyone for miles."

"It won't be enough," said Rich. "The maps might say Mincy Conservation Area, but I guarantee you the camp is on a large tract of private property. Probably a few thousand acres. Shooting up your own land isn't a crime. The explosion might draw some attention; my guess is that the crash will be covered with netting by the morning. We're left with some compelling video that we could have created in a studio."

Marnie put the helicopter into a gentle right turn. "What's the plan?"

"I'd like to burn their buildings down. Leave something the authorities can see in the morning," said Rich. "At the very least, I'd like to put Camp Stalin out of business."

She laughed. "May as well add arsonist to my rapidly expanding résumé. You guys don't happen to be hiring, do you?"

"No. But I'm pretty sure I speak for everyone when I say that we'd make room for a combat-decorated Marine helicopter pilot. Same offer applies to any former FBI SSG investigative specialists."

"Is that your first job offer?" asked Devin.

"Nice. As a matter of fact, it is," she said. "Have to sleep on it, though. Hey. We're about fifteen seconds out from the camp center. I can slow us down if you're not ready."

She heard the M249 charging bolt slide home.

"They're ready," said Devin.

Marnie took a longer look behind her, disturbed by what she saw. Alex had scooted to the edge of the bench seat next to the portside door, machine gun in his lap and three additional drum magazines on the seat next to him. Rich sat on the opposite side of the bench seat, having opened the starboard-side door at some point in all the excitement. He held a cylindrical grenade in both hands. Devin sat directly behind her. For all she knew, he had a stick of dynamite and a lighter in his hand. Rich had a way of coaxing bad behavior out of everyone.

"Rich, is that a white phosphorus grenade?" said Marnie.

"Maybe," he said. "And maybe I have three more in my drop pouch."

Her pilot instincts flashed red. Pyrotechnic devices ranked right up there with explosives on a pilot's "fuck no" list.

320

"Rich. If you drop that in the helicopter, I will bank this thing ninety degrees and empty you and your grenades right over the side," said Marnie.

"I would expect nothing less," said Rich. "Pick four buildings. Your choice. We'll be out of here in thirty seconds."

She slowed down for the approach, the buildings in the camp's center suddenly appearing in the square-shaped opening. Five one-story structures, all flat roofed. The rooftop adjacent to the northeast branch of cabins, where the team had been ambushed, held three armed figures. She turned the helicopter so its port side faced the rooftop and let the helicopter drift slowly in the building's direction.

"Three targets on the nearest rooftop," said Marnie.

Alex didn't respond. The M249 buzzed for a few seconds, and all three shooters dropped to the roof in contorted positions. Marnie made no adjustments to the helicopter's flight, sliding directly over the building for a few seconds. She put them in a hover, glancing downward at the chin window below her feet.

"Perfect alignment," said Rich. "Grenade away."

Marnie spun the helicopter in place until the rest of the compound came into view. A bullet thunked inside, somewhere near the cockpit. She slid left over the adjacent building.

"Grenade away! Next!" said Rich.

Several bullets peppered the fuselage, one puncturing the copilot's door window and putting a hole in the top of the cockpit. Her night vision flared from the first grenade but didn't white out for more than a fraction of a second. The grenade had exploded fifty feet below on the other side of the helicopter, scattering white-hot chunks across the rooftop.

"I have no targets," said Alex. "We're facing the wrong way."

"I'm aware of that," she said, flying forward for a few seconds before going into a hover again.

She spun the helicopter 180 degrees, pointing Alex and Devin in the direction of the incoming ground fire. A torrent of gunfire erupted from the cabin the moment she stopped the spin. The second grenade detonated, momentarily blinding her. She popped her night vision goggles, determining that she had enough light from the fires below to pull this off with the naked eye.

"Give me about twenty feet directly to the right," said Rich.

"Tell me when," said Marnie, putting the helicopter into a slow drift in the direction Rich had requested.

"Grenade out!" he said. "One more! Let's go for the big one on the western side."

Devin yelled as a string of bullets hit the pilot's side of the helicopter. The door window next to her shattered, a sharp pain creasing her forearm. Alex's machine gun responded with burst after burst. The third grenade exploded, illuminating the trees around them.

"Devin?" she said, getting no answer.

She looked over her shoulder in time to see Rich sidearm his last grenade out the starboard-side door. *Fuck this. We're out of here.* She pulled up on the collective lever and took them higher, until they'd risen about three hundred feet above the buildings, where she pushed the cyclic forward. The helicopter angled down several degrees and sped away from the camp.

"Is Devin okay?" she asked.

"I'm fine. Just got a little preoccupied there for a moment," said Devin. "Nice flying, by the way."

"Thank you. It's been a little while."

"Just like riding a bike," said Rich. "But about a thousand times more complicated."

"Something like that," she said.

The treetops below lit up for a moment, the last grenade hopefully spreading its flammable contents over the roof of the biggest building in the camp.

"Did you land it on the roof?" she asked, peeking over her shoulder.

Rich pulled his head back inside the helicopter. "Looks like it. Can I ask you for one more favor?"

"What?"

"I'd like to have Alex disable our pontoon boats," he said. "I don't want any of those fuckers getting a free ride out of there tonight."

"We certainly can't allow that," said Marnie.

She lowered her night vision goggles over her face before putting them into a wide left turn and taking them back over the northeastern tip of the Mincy Conservation Area.

CHAPTER 55

Devin somehow fell asleep on the short trip down the lake to Diamond City. He woke to Rich shaking his arm, the helicopter rapidly descending.

"Rise and shine. We're almost at the motel," he said.

He squinted and looked around, noticing that the M249 was gone. "Where did the machine gun go?"

"We dumped it in the lake about a minute back," said Rich. "I can't say for sure, but I'm guessing the serial number on that weapon can be traced to a batch of M249 Squad Automatic Weapons that either never made it to their final destination or were reported stolen from a US military armory. We do not want to get caught with a stolen military firearm. Particularly a machine gun."

"And the rest of this gear is clean?" asked Devin.

Rich shrugged. "We could explain the rest of this away, if we had to. I'd rather not, since it would tie us up for a while."

"You mean we'd be sitting in jail while a team of expensive lawyers worked on getting us releases so we could flee the country and have to travel on forged IDs for the rest of our lives."

"Something like that," said Rich.

Alex laughed, which was a welcome shift away from the dark mood that had enveloped him since Mike's death. The two of them had obviously been close. Devin had overheard Scott talking with Emily about how they had been plank owners in the original program—whatever that meant. The story behind Rich's team was still unclear.

"Alex. I'm very sorry about Mike," said Devin, not sure if he had stepped over the line.

"We've all lived far longer than we should have," said Alex.

"That's for sure," said Rich.

"We're almost there," said Marnie over the radio. "I'm going to set us down toward the southern end of the campground. I don't want to get us caught up in any power lines. Looks like a short jog to the motel."

"Works for me," replied Rich before turning to Alex. "It's kind of late to ask this, but do you have the keys to the SUV?"

Alex lifted a set of keys by his index finger. "They were in Mike's pocket. I thought about them right before we headed for the helicopter."

"I'm glad one of us was thinking," said Rich.

An old-fashioned white streetlight rose slowly in the distance as the helicopter gently bounced on its wheels before settling into the landing. The high-pitched whine of the turboshaft engines shifted to a slightly lower tone as Marnie shut down the helicopter. Rich pointed toward the streetlight.

"Let's head to the road and take a right instead of trying to cut through someone's backyard," said Rich. "I don't want to get shot and killed by a local after running Stalin's gauntlet back at the camp. The whole town is probably on alert from the combination of the explosion and a helicopter suddenly landing. This is tinfoil-hat country."

"Hard to argue with not getting shot," said Devin, and they set off for the road.

A short jog later, they arrived safely at the motel parking lot, where they immediately removed their tactical gear and stowed it in the back of the SUV, along with their rifles. Rich handed one of the rifles to Devin, along with a few spare magazines.

"Keep this out of sight, but accessible if I need it."

"Still not out of the woods, so to speak?" said Marnie.

"I hate to break this to you, but we just stepped deeper in the woods with tonight's stunt," said Rich, shutting the rear liftgate. "*Out of the woods* means busting up this sleeper conspiracy."

"Wonderful," she said.

Devin opened the door to the back seat for Marnie, who hopped in and took the rifle. As soon as Devin shut the door behind him, Alex tore out of the parking lot, throwing him against the seat. He'd noticed that Rich's people weren't big on wasting time, even under the most mundane circumstances. Every second counted with these people, which was probably one of dozens of reasons why they were still alive. Most of them, anyway.

"We still need to pick up the third vehicle at Highway Marina," said Rich, checking his satellite phone. "Berg will meet us there so we can balance out the vehicles. He's still waiting for the speedboat. Should be there any minute."

"Then what?" asked Devin.

"Then we get off these rural roads onto some kind of interstate highway. Get as far from here as possible by sunrise. The Ozarks will be crawling with law enforcement sooner than later," said Rich.

"At some point I'm going to need some sleep," said Devin.

"Why? You slept on the helicopter," said Rich.

"Really?" said Marnie.

"He was out like a light once the shooting stopped."

"I apologize if that's a faux pas when your best friend is flying the helicopter. Something about the rhythm of the rotors or something just pulled me under," said Devin.

"It's actually pretty normal," she said. "We'd take off with a platoon of Marines, headed for a hot LZ, and half of them would be out within the first five minutes—like they were in the back seat of a car on a road trip. Then again, they were always exhausted when we were flying them around."

"That's me right now," said Devin. "Five minutes from passing out again."

"We're all right there with you," said Rich. "We'll pick a decent-size city we can reach by dawn and find a motel with a few sets of adjoining rooms. Rest up and go through what we collected on video. Scan the news out of Branson. Figure out our next move. Based on what we saw at the camp, we'll have to up our game somehow. Convince some people at a much higher level to take a serious look at what we've assembled. We're looking at somewhere around six hundred sleepers, most in positions we might not be able to figure out—until they've done their damage."

"I don't see how we're going to crack this," said Devin.

"Your mother did," said Rich. "She put you and Karl Berg together for a reason. If anyone can figure out a way to pull this off, it'll be him. Karl's cracked a few major conspiracies before."

"True America?"

Rich didn't answer right away, which confirmed what Devin had suspected. Either Karl or Rich had had a hand in whatever had happened to True America. Possibly both of them.

"What did Karl tell you about True America?"

"He said it was a story for another time," said Devin.

"Well. I'll let him decide when that time arrives," said Rich.

Devin let it go for now. He was too tired to pursue a dead-end conversation. Marnie put her head on his shoulder and held his hand, the two of them drifting asleep in the company of two shadowy mercenaries they'd barely known for forty-eight hours. Not coincidentally the same amount of time he'd been awake. Devin didn't resist the sandman. He had a feeling Rich's idea of rest would amount to an hour-long nap while they waited for him to wake up. He'd have to take whatever sleep he could get, whenever he could take it.

CHAPTER 56

Felix Orlov crawled up the muddy shore and shrugged off his rucksack, exhausted from the long swim. He rolled onto his back and rested in the fetid sludge, staring at the clear night sky. The fire raging across the lake flickered at the bottom of his field of vision. After he'd caught his breath, he turned his head to see who else had washed up on shore with him. One lay in the muck about forty feet away, where the lake broke off into a cove. He couldn't tell if they were facedown or on their back. Another clambered out of the water between them and dropped flat. Ksenia, judging by the longer hair. Just two?

He propped himself up on his elbows to scan the lake. The third slogged through the water about fifty feet out, kicking and splashing hard enough to suggest panic. That had to be Lashev. The sniper had spent more time trying to convince them to somehow paddle one of the half-sunken pontoon boats across the lake rather than fessing up that he could barely swim. None of them had wanted to abandon most of their gear and swim several hundred yards to an unfamiliar shore, but the M249 machine gun Felix had chosen to leave in the helicopter had made the decision for them.

And staying on the other side of the lake, trusting their fate to whoever called that camp home, wasn't a viable option. Not after the small war that had been waged out there for close to fifteen minutes, not to mention the helicopter explosion that had probably rattled windows and set off car alarms for miles. The police would be all over this place soon, the several-story-high bonfire rising above the treetops serving as their beacon. The team was better off on their own, which meant a long swim.

Felix got up on wobbly legs and reentered the water, wading half-way to his struggling colleague, before he could no longer feel the bottom of the lake. He sidestroked the rest of the way and made the mistake of approaching Lashev directly. Like all terrified swimmers in a near-drowning situation, his teammate instinctively grabbed on to Felix the moment he arrived, intent on dragging him to the bottom, too. He pounded Lashev's face a few times, stunning him long enough to implement a forced-rescue hold—and start swimming.

He dragged Lashev to waist-high water and let go. The operative thrashed for a few seconds before realizing he could stand. He imme-diately waded to shore and sat next to Ksenia. Oleg got up from his spot near the break in the shoreline and plopped down beside Lashev.

"No rest for the wicked," said Felix, trudging out of the water. "We need to steal a boat or a car and get the hell out of here. I'm leaning toward one of the covered docks we spotted inside the cove. Less chance of getting shot trespassing. Most Americans are more heavily armed than the police."

"I saw tire tracks near the cove entrance," said Oleg. "Looks like they lead in the direction of the docks."

"Can't they just drive our Jeeps over from the airport?" asked Ksenia.

"The people watching over our gear and Jeeps back at the hangar have been diverted to evacuate the camp burning across the lake," said Felix. "They moved everything away from the hangar, because the heli-copters will eventually be traced back to the airport—but that's all I know. They'll contact us when they can spare the personnel to reunite us with our vehicles. Until then, I want to get as far from here as possible."

Felix grabbed his backpack and tossed it in front of the group. He'd volunteered to carry the fifteen- to twenty-pound bag because he was a strong swimmer—and didn't think anyone else would make it across with the equivalent of an anchor strapped to their back. Boots, socks, pistols, and ammunition. The essentials. He'd sealed his satellite phone and wallet in a waterproof bag and stuffed it in one of his cargo pockets.

They'd thrown everything else—the rifles, body armor, helmets, and night vision gear—into the water, as far off the shoreline on the other side of the lake as possible. Why give investigators a sense of their true numbers? Whoever combed through the property would eventually find Oksana and Valerie, unless the camp's residents cleaned up their bodies. He'd provided their general location to Pichugin's contact after the helicopter exploded. Let them deal with it.

"Five minutes. Don't forget to drain your pistols and work the action a few times. Hold your magazines upside down until they stop dripping. We might not be done using them tonight."

PART VI

CHAPTER 57

Devin opened his eyes to a dark, unfamiliar room. It took a few seconds to figure out exactly where he'd woken up and why. They'd driven through the night to Nashville, passing through the city and checking into the most nondescript motel he'd ever seen—basically, a two-story rectangle with evenly spaced doors and windows. About as inconspicuous as he could imagine, which was almost as big a selling point as the Cracker Barrel restaurant next door.

They settled into three sets of adjoining rooms, clearly a big coup for the mostly unoccupied motel, since an "exception" was made regarding the usual check-in time. Everyone got their own bed to rest, Rich insisting the team needed to take a time-out before going any further. All Devin really remembered after that was ordering three times the amount of Cracker Barrel he could possibly eat and putting himself into a food coma.

He glanced over at the other bed, finding the blankets rumpled but empty. A quick look at the open, dark bathroom doorway told him Marnie had slipped out at some point to join the team. They'd probably taken a few hours off and gone back to work. How long had he been out? The light peeking through the shade told him he hadn't slept into the night. His watch said he'd given it his best effort: 6:48 p.m. He'd been out for more than ten hours. Rich and Karl probably had the next operation planned by now.

Devin rolled off the cheap mattress and reached for the ceiling to give his stiff body a quick stretch. He noticed a fresh pair of jeans, a few

T-shirts, socks, and underwear on the dresser. Someone had been busy. He grabbed the jeans and checked the inside of the waist, finding them a few sizes too large—but not big enough to slide off. The shirt was a large, which would hang off him but otherwise work just fine for now.

He took everything into the bathroom and changed out of the swampy outfit he'd been wearing, before indulging in a quick shower to wash away the grime of last evening's mission. Feeling deceptively refreshed, he tucked his wallet and satellite phone into his pockets and stepped into the crusty boots next to his bed. The sort-of-human feeling the shower and new clothes had loaned him took a hit when his feet sank into the damp boots. More than just damp. He stood up, and they squished—not that he was complaining.

He swiped the old-school metal key from his nightstand and headed out to find the team. His search didn't last long. A pizza-delivery car idled in the parking lot below, where a teenager was unloading about a dozen pizza boxes between Scott and Alex.

The past week didn't feel real. From setting off to follow his mother's clues to the apartment to the forty-eight-hour whirlwind tour of violence across three states, none of it seemed possible. But here he was—watching a mercenary who had easily killed a half dozen or more people over the past three nights dig into his pocket to pay a pizza-delivery kid. An entirely unremarkable transaction to an outside observer. It made him wonder how many times he'd witnessed something this extraordinary before without even knowing it. Devin met them a few rooms down.

"Welcome back to the land of the living," said Scott.

"You didn't have to let me sleep that long," said Devin, opening the door for them.

"Marnie said you were snoring like a sawmill," said Alex, pausing in the doorway. "You didn't miss much. Most of us crashed well into the afternoon. Except for Rich and Karl. I have no idea how those two are still upright and talking in complete sentences."

"Seriously," said Devin, following him into the crowded room and closing the door.

Everyone was dressed in jeans and plain gray T-shirts. The only way it could look more comical was if all the T-shirts had the same pattern.

"There he is," said Berg, standing in the doorway between the adjoining rooms. "Did they tell you that the Russians surrendered while you were asleep? It's all over."

"Pizza coming through," said Alex, making his way past Berg into the other room.

Rich appeared in the doorway. "Pizza, soda, water, and beer. One-beer limit."

"Seriously?" said Gupta, seated next to Graves at the foot of one of the beds. "I think I can be trusted—"

"You don't drink, knucklehead," said Graves.

"It's the principle that matters," said Gupta.

"Can I have his beer?" asked Marnie.

"Yes. And Devin is welcome to mine," said Rich.

"That still leaves two. It's a twelve-pack," said Gupta.

"There's no rule requiring that they be consumed," said Graves. "Do I have to share a room with him? I'm retired. Doesn't that get me my own room?"

"Nobody pulling security tonight goes past the limit. We have no idea what kind of law enforcement or government tracking muscle they're capable of harnessing through the people we haven't identified in the network," said Rich. "We may have to shoot our way out of here in an hour."

"I'll pass on the second," said Marnie, who sat cross-legged with her back against the dresser. "Consider me part of the watch rotation."

"Count me in, too," said Devin.

Marnie motioned for him to join her.

"Good. I'll put the two of you on the four to sunrise, since you slept most of the day," said Rich as he crossed the room. "Grab some slices and fuel up. Karl has a few things to go over with the team."

Devin dropped next to Marnie as the room emptied.

"I'm not really hungry," she said. "But I'll take that beer."

He started to get up, his leg muscles screaming from last night's operation.

"Sorry," she said. "I can get it."

"Don't even think about it," said Devin. "Drinks are on me, even if I'm not buying."

Rich leaned through the doorway with two cans of Budweiser. "Heads up. Pure Americana coming through."

Devin slid back down to the threadbare carpet as the beers floated through the air. Marnie snatched them both out of the air, her hands at least two feet apart when she grabbed them. She handed one off to Devin faster than a blackjack dealer spitting out cards.

"Nice trick," said Rich.

"Hand-eye coordination," said Marnie. "It's a helicopter pilot quirk."

Devin popped his can, followed by Marnie. "So . . . we actually have a next move?"

Rich scooted into the room with a Coke and sat on the bed in front of them, a cryptic smile on his face.

"Karl's been busy. He spent part of yesterday and all of today researching a lead that sounds promising. Something that could crack the wider sleeper list open. There's that and the big news that came later this afternoon while examining the gun-camera footage. Nice shooting to both of you, by the way. Saw some likely hits when we were slugging it out at the cabins. Impossible to say one hundred percent at night with those cameras, but I'd score them as confirmed."

"This is bizarre," said Marnie, taking a long sip of her beer.

"Yeah. There's absolutely nothing normal about this," said Devin. "Anyway. What's the big news?"

"Scott's team took out the sentries from the boat dock, on their way east to link up with Graves and Gupta. The two never knew what hit them, and the team certainly didn't know who they hit—until we reviewed Emily's gun-camera footage. She put a light on them while they were down, to give us a better shot at identifying them," said Rich. "Berg recognized one of them immediately. Senator Robert Filmore's wife, Emma. The other KIA was their son, Thomas."

"This is going to be front-page news," said Marnie.

"It's definitely going to test the sleeper network's spin doctors."

"How the hell did my mother miss them?" asked Devin.

"I thought the same thing, but Gupta and Graves did some digging, and neither of their family backgrounds would have raised alarms. It has to be some kind of digital historical-archive manipulation. I'm thinking they only do this for high-profile sleepers."

"This kind of calls into question everything," said Marnie. "If we can't identify them even when we're looking right at them. And if we can't trust Helen's vetting process, how can we trust anyone that fits the age profile?"

"We can't," said Rich. "Right now, we have to assume the worst. Our circle of trust just shrank considerably."

"The Russians will have to assume that we discovered their identities," said Devin. "What if they go to work digitally altering all of the family histories? Make it impossible to root out the rest."

"That's why we have to approach this from multiple angles," said Rich. "Senator Filmore represents an opportunity. We just don't know what it is yet. We're waiting to see how the Russians handle it. For all we know, they'll arrange some kind of accident that eliminates the entire Filmore family. It wouldn't surprise me. He represents a loose end."

"That's gruesome," said Marnie.

"But not out of the realm of possibilities," said Devin. "Nothing is out of the realm at this point. Not with the Russians. They'll do anything to protect their sleeper network. Speaking of protecting networks—I need to check on my dad and sister."

"I'll put you in direct touch with them when we finish up here," said Rich. "I spoke with the contact who arranged their protection, and everything is going well. Your sister wasn't exactly pleased with the work interruption, but I'm told she's making the adjustment. Same with your father. I trust the group watching over them. They'll keep your family safe for as long as this takes."

"Do we have any idea how long that might be?" asked Devin. "I understand this isn't exactly a timeline-driven operation, but what's your gut feeling?"

"It's impossible to say," said Rich. "Graves and Gupta are putting together a video of the drone footage, gun-camera evidence, and proof-of-death stills. We could upload that to the internet and promote it as evidence of some kind of cult that committed a mass homicide-suicide at the camp. Draw conspiracy crazies from all over the country to the Ozarks to see for themselves and to bug the shit out of Senator Filmore. Put some pressure on the system. Force an error, maybe. I don't know. It's a work in progress. We could go your route and expose and disrupt the current network. Get the whole country working on finding the sleepers. Whatever they're up to, they seem to be picking up speed."

"That could give them the cover they need to continue operating right in the open, until it's too late. If everyone is a potential sleeper agent, the whole thing devolves into a perverse, hyper-McCarthyism tornado," said Devin.

Rich shrugged. "Karl is reaching out to some trusted allies to try and get them on board. One of them could get the CIA involved. The other might get us to the source."

"In Russia?" asked Devin.

"Most likely," said Rich. "Based on what Karl discovered."

"What did he discover?" said Marnie.

"I did some research into who owns the land used for the camp," said Berg, suddenly looming in the doorway.

Marnie flinched, nearly dropping her beer.

"Jesus. You scared me," she said.

"A little jumpy, are we?" said Berg. "Welcome to the club. It never goes away if you do this kind of work long enough."

"I don't feel edgy," said Rich.

"You don't count, and I mean that in the friendliest possible way," said Berg, getting a laugh out of all of them. "Anyway. The Dreery family bought the land encompassing the Mincy Conservation Area in the early eighteen hundreds. I think. The history is unclear. What we do know is that they leased much of the land to the Missouri Conservation Department in the nineteen thirties, withholding a few large parcels for their own use, to include the fifteen hundred or so acres now encompassing the camp. That parcel was sold to a corporation named Firebird Development, owned by the Belsky family, in 1971.

"Long story short, the original Belskys emigrated to the US from Russia in the late eighteen hundreds and accumulated a tidy fortune by American standards. Today's Belskys renounced their US citizenship in 2001, after selling the company to Concordia Management and Consulting for an undisclosed sum, and emerged as well-connected oligarchs on the Moscow scene. Concordia Management and Consulting is owned by mega-oligarch Yuri Pichugin, one of Vladimir Putin's closest confidants. Pichugin rose to prominence between 2001 and 2003, after running a very successful Saint Petersburg catering company. He reportedly met Putin, who is a Saint Petersburg native, through catered events."

"He must have served a mean pierogi," said Devin, the joke falling flat.

"Piroshki, maybe," said Berg. "Every eastern European country has a version of pierogi."

"Sounds the same," said Rich.

"Not even close. It's a sweet or savory stuffed bun, panfried right before serving. To die for," said Berg. "But I doubt that's how Pichugin rose so quickly into the highest stratosphere of Russian power and wealth. I think the Belsky family originally bought the land, on behalf of the Soviets, for the original summer camp. Maybe they were secret Communists. Maybe they got paid. Who knows?"

"They sound like opportunists," said Devin.

"Communists. Opportunists. All the same in the end," said Berg. "Whatever the deal is—the Belskys turn the land over to the GRU, or whoever is running the sleeper network, and everything runs smoothly. The second generation is indoctrinated and trained at the camp before being launched into the world. Then things go dormant for a while, waiting for the third generation. Somewhere along the line, the Belskys figure out a way to cash out of this valuable possession."

"Opportunism at its finest," said Rich.

"It has to be Pichugin. I just don't know how he got his mitts on the program. That's the missing link here. How did the sleeper program come into his possession? Unless the Russian Federation outsourced it to him, and he's just a proxy. My gut tells me it's the other way around."

"Why don't we just go after Pichugin?" asked Devin.

Rich took over from there.

"First. His entire network of businesses is located in Russia or former Soviet satellite countries. We've operated in Russia before, but not in a while—and it's far easier said than done. Second. The guy owns the largest private military contracting agency in the world. He supplies entire mercenary paramilitary units to the highest bidders around the world. Putin allegedly uses Pichugin's forces when he's looking for plausible deniability about Russia's involvement in a conflict, like the eastern Ukraine front, Crimean Peninsula, or Syria. We'd need a small army of our own to go after him."

"They all have their weaknesses," said Berg. "We've hit harder targets than Pichugin."

"Only as a last resort," said Rich.

"Fair enough," said Berg.

"How did you piece together the link between Belsky's company and Pichugin's?"

"A hunch," said Berg. "Firebird Development was kind of a dead end. An anonymous Delaware corporation, with its listing agent registered as another anonymous Delaware corporation. Classic hide-the-owner shell game. With Russia on my mind, I ran a search through the US Department of the Treasury's Office of Foreign Assets Control public database to see if Firebird Development was on their sanctions list. Stab in the dark."

"Bingo?" said Devin.

"Big time," said Berg. "Firebird Development popped up on Yuri Pichugin's asset list. Pichugin had been sanctioned through the Magnitsky Act in early 2013, which bans him from entering the United States and freezes all of his US-based assets, including Firebird Development. I found Andrei and Viktor Belsky listed in the sanction filing as the previous owners. Apparently, the US Treasury Department cut through the corporate shell game and surfaced their names. A quick Google search confirmed that the Belskys had indeed moved up in the world."

"This is a head-scratcher," said Devin. "I mean . . . how do we use that information? Try to get the Treasury Department interested?"

"We don't have anything to offer them. They did their job. Firebird Development's assets, if any still exist, are frozen in accordance with the Magnitsky Act ruling," said Berg.

"It didn't look like they'd skipped a beat, other than reduced attendance," said Devin.

"Kids these days. Addicted to their phones and social media," said Rich. "In the seventies and eighties you still had a shot at brainwashing people."

"I'd laugh if it weren't so true," said Berg. "I'm going to reach out to someone in Russia who might be able to help. It's a long shot, but I'm convinced it's an opportunity to unravel the entire sleeper network. Sergei Kozlov, the GRU general who passed information to your mother in Saint Petersburg, knew more than three names. He likely had access to the entire roster. That's what I suspect he was going to offer the CIA—but he never got past the second meeting. Kozlov may not have been the only senior-level officer at the GRU with access to that information. I'm hoping my contact can point us in the right direction—so we can arrange a chat with one of those officers."

"That sounds like something my team could pull off," said Rich. "With a little inside help. We don't have any assets in Russia right now."

"I might be able to help with that, but it'll be a long shot," said Berg. "We have to approach this from as many angles as possible. Your mother got the sense that the sleeper network was building up to something. That it had accelerated its pace. That's what convinced her to kidnap Wilson. I get the same sense that we're up against a deadline. Maybe not an endgame, but something pivotal."

"And we may have accelerated their timeline with our actions over the past few days," said Devin.

"Correct," said Berg. "Every time we hit them without delivering a crippling or mortal blow, they make an adjustment, though they may not have much flexibility with a major deadline. It's something to consider when we're planning how to proceed."

"If we're looking for more angles of attack, I think we should approach MINERVA—whether I'm still employed or not," said Devin. "Given Jolene Rudd's connection to the DEVTEK honey-trap ploy, I think it's fair to assume that MINERVA has not been compromised.

Not by anyone involved in the planning or execution of MINERVA's operation."

"What would be in it for MINERVA?" asked Rich. "Aside from doing their patriotic duty to the United States."

Devin couldn't tell if Rich was being sarcastic.

"I see two ways to draw them in. The first would be to give them the opportunity to best serve their client. MINERVA is all about client satisfaction. With our information, they could inform DEVTEK that the risks to the company extend well beyond industrial espionage—to possible product sabotage and ruin. I could see them setting up another sting and integrating us into that operation. The other approach is to pay them as a client to boost our surveillance and counterespionage capability," said Devin.

"Or offer them the DEVTEK information as payment for their services," said Marnie.

"Right. Or both," said Devin. "Karl. You mentioned some kind of financial backing behind this team? Would it be enough to pay them on top of handing them the DEVTEK lead?"

"That's another angle altogether," said Rich.

"One we can't rule out," said Berg.

"First we have to vet the hell out of MINERVA," said Rich. "I'm not even clear how we'd go about that. My guess is that their employee roster is a well-kept secret."

"That's why I think paying them makes more sense, if that's feasible. As clients, we could insist on a custom vetting process. Maybe even dangle the DEVTEK information over their heads. Make the information contingent on vetting," said Devin.

"That's going to put you in an uncomfortable position," said Rich. "Going this route will most likely terminate your employment with them."

"What choice do I have?" asked Devin. "It's a long shot, but like Rich said, the more angles we explore, the better."

"Hard to argue with that," said Berg, shrugging. "I just wish we had something up our sleeves that wasn't such a long shot."

"One of them has to work," said Rich.

"Not necessarily," said Berg. "But it is what it is."

"How long will it take to hear back from your contacts?" asked Devin.

"The bigger question is, How long will it take them to make a difference?" said Berg.

"That's assuming they agree to help," said Rich.

"Fair point. This will put them in awkward positions at best. Dangerous at worst," said Berg. "It could take a few weeks. Until things start shaping up, we'll need to lie low. A small group of us should head back to Helen's apartment in Baltimore and keep digging through the files. We're bound to find an opportunity we missed on the first few passes through the information. We barely scratched the surface, to be honest."

"I'll scatter the rest of the team nearby," said Rich. "We can move fast if we find anything in the files, or one of your contacts comes through."

"We'll need to invest in some basic disguises," said Berg. "Nothing dramatic, but enough to throw off facial-recognition software. There's no telling what the Russians can access through their sleeper network. The DC area has a lot of public-facing cameras."

"Noted," said Rich. "We'll put together some basics before we set off for Baltimore."

"When will we take off?" said Devin.

"After I get a good night's sleep," said Berg. "We'll head straight to your mother's apartment and wait for one or more of our long shots to pay off."

Marnie raised her beer. "To long shots."

"To not getting shot," said Rich.

"Cheers to both," said Berg, raising his can. "Though if I had to choose between the two, I'm going with not getting shot."

Was it possible to have it both ways if they took the fight against the Russians to the next level? Devin clinked all their cans, a heavy sense of dread hanging over the toast. He couldn't shake the distinct feeling that they wouldn't all be alive for the next one.

CHAPTER 58

Yuri Pichugin took General Kuznetzov's call on a secure line in the state-of-the-art, surveillance-proof room deep inside his Lake Ladoga mansion complex. Modeled after the sensitive compartmented information facility concept used by major world intelligence agencies, Pichugin had consulted with the world's top information security consultants to ensure it met or exceeded industry standards.

In truth, it was more for show than anything else. A luxuriously appointed, soundproofed, and electromagnetically sealed space that he mostly used to impress new clients and reassure long-standing allies. He could arrange to have the secure phone line run to either of his offices inside the mansion, and not risk acoustic or digital eavesdropping.

"It's late," said Pichugin. "More bad news, I assume?"

"More of the same, unfortunately," said the general. "I have the final casualty count. We lost twenty-six of the parents and fifteen of the children. Plus eight of the ten GRU sleepers brought in for the cabin side of the ambush. Farrington's sharpshooters took a hefty toll."

"Have we confirmed it was Farrington?"

"No. But this has his team's fingerprints all over it," said the general. "From Baltimore to the torture job on the two morons in Indianapolis—and now this mess. Given Berg's involvement, it has to be Farrington."

"And they brought the helicopter pilot along, obviously."

"Nobody anticipated that. Sanderson and Farrington have never operated in the field with outsiders," said the general.

He supposed it could have been worse, though he wasn't sure how. The camp had been operating at its new full capacity when it was attacked. Thirty-nine sets of siblings representing the third generation, along with one of their parents, had been on site. Not only did this represent a sizable blow to the currently active network, but it also potentially endangered the network by further exposing it to Devin Gray and Karl Berg, who would undoubtedly be combing the news and law enforcement bulletins for missing person reports or deadly accidents involving teens and adults, or, in some cases, child and parent. You couldn't just hide the fact that someone was missing in the United States.

"Where are the survivors?"

"The team that had been watching over Orlov's gear at the airport scrambled to arrange transportation out of there. Everyone has been evacuated to a friendly site just off the lake, about a mile south of the Missouri-Arkansas border. That includes the bodies. We're going to keep them there until things settle down, then start smuggling people out in small groups. They managed to retrieve all of the files from the buildings before the fires got out of control, so that's one less thing to worry about."

"Big consolation," said Pichugin, sensing that Kuznetzov was building up to something.

"There's one thing that's going to be a significant problem," said the general.

"Just one? What is it?"

"Senator Filmore's wife and son were killed during the attack. They were found along the trail between the boat landing and the camp. Both of them shot twice in the chest."

That was how it could be worse. They'd just lost one of the highest-placed sleepers in the entire network.

"We have to assume that Farrington's people have identified them. They probably documented the entire raid with video cameras.

They'll go after the senator at some point, if only to fuck with us," said Pichugin. "Has Senator Filmore been notified?"

"None of the families have been notified," said the general. "And strict communications protocols have been activated at the evacuation site."

"I see," said Pichugin. "Hold off on any notifications, and under no circumstances are any of the sleepers to make contact with anyone. I need to think about how we're going to deal with this, particularly the senator's situation."

"Understood," said the general. "May I make a suggestion?"

"Of course."

"I think we need to strongly consider eliminating Senator Filmore and his daughter," said the general. "Put all of their bodies on a private jet and crash it."

"Was the daughter at the camp?" asked Pichugin.

"Yes. She survived."

He didn't see any way to salvage the situation with Senator Filmore at this point. If Farrington's people started circulating pictures of the wife and son, the media and federal law enforcement would start asking questions that nobody could adequately answer. They needed to get ahead of that. A tidy plane crash with all four of them on board would snuff out the fire generated by the pictures.

"Make it happen. Quickly," said Pichugin. "And have Alexei prepare a list of the entire network. I want the sleepers broken down into three categories: critical, essential, and nonessential to FIREBIRD. Then break each of those categories down into public sector or private sector. Any operative that can be easily identified represents a risk to FIREBIRD and an opportunity for Farrington and Berg. I expect them to sharpen their sleeper-hunting skills in the upcoming days. The fewer liabilities we have out there—the better."

"As in permanently retire?" said the general.

"I mean recall them. Give them twenty-four hours to get on a plane and leave the United States behind," said Pichugin. "Why? What did you think I meant?"

"I was just making sure," said the general.

"Don't get me wrong, Grigory," said Pichugin. "If we activate a recall of noncritical sleepers, anyone that doesn't comply with the order will experience the other type of recall."

"Understood," said the general.

"I'll need to speak with the big man regarding a recall. He may not want to dismantle that much of FIREBIRD yet," said Pichugin.

"Will you be coming to Moscow, then?" asked the general.

"No. He's in Saint Petersburg. I'll arrange a meeting this afternoon," said Pichugin. "And Grigory? A few more things."

"Yes?"

"First. Have we made any progress toward finding Gray, Berg, or any of their suspected associates?" asked Pichugin.

"Kazakhstan filed a Red Notice for Karl Berg and Richard Farrington yesterday. Russia will file one today, citing the same charges related to their alleged involvement in terrorist attacks against state facilities. Both of them are actually suspected to have been involved with the attack on the Vector Institute in Novosibirsk and the downing of two Russian helicopters in Kazakhstan," said the general.

"They like blowing up helicopters," grumbled Pichugin.

"Apparently so. The Red Notices will give our people in US law enforcement an excuse to put some more robust surveillance and detection measures into action. We're still looking at a few days before that gets rolling. We can expand the list of names to other known associates of General Terrence Sanderson—Farrington's mentor—and Farrington himself. Once we get a bunch of names in there, our people inside US law enforcement can start looking at Devin Gray and Marnie Young."

"Very well," said Pichugin. "And what about DEVTEK? Are we making any progress on that front? Without a back door to their infrastructure-security software, we'll have to do things the hard way—which represents a significant delay. Not to mention the risk."

"We're working on it. As you can imagine, a company that provides state-of-the-art cybersecurity solutions isn't easy to hack," said the general. "We're exploring more direct options, but their guard is up after the honey-trap debacle. Kind of ironic that Gray may have been involved in the DEVTEK operation."

"More like annoying," said Pichugin. "Keep a close eye on MINERVA. If Gray makes the same connection, he could complicate our efforts to breach DEVTEK."

"We're doing what we can to monitor MINERVA without alerting them to our presence. Not the easiest task, given their specialty," said the general. "Was there anything else?"

"Yes. Give Felix Orlov whatever he needs to make sure the job gets done next time," said Pichugin.

"It wasn't his fault."

"I know it wasn't his fault," said Pichugin, on the verge of screaming at Kuznetzov for underutilizing Orlov. "Which is why I don't want him restrained in any way. We're licking our wounds this time. Next time we'll be mopping our blood off the floor. We can't afford another setback. Not this close to the finish line. The final dominoes should fall within the next few weeks, driving a permanent wedge between the Americans and their European allies—reopening doors long shut to Russia."

CHAPTER 59

Alexei Kaparov sat alone on a concrete bench a few blocks from his apartment, the dingy gray of Soviet-era block-style high-rises peeking through the trees. Old men crowded around chessboards on the stone tables lining one side of the park's wide brick promenade, pigeons navigating their feet to peck at the lunch crumbs as they fell.

Kaparov had never taken to chess. He'd taken to vodka instead during his spare time, which had been scarce before he'd retired from the FSB a few years ago. Now, he had all the time in the world on his hands, and there was only so much time he could spend drinking—a challenge he rose to every day. Maybe he should take up smoking again to fill the void.

He took a short pull from the stainless-steel flask he had brought on his daily walk and relished in the comfortably warm glow that followed. His buzz was cut short by the phone in his pocket. Kaparov debated whether to check the phone or take another swig of vodka. He didn't get many calls these days, so he set the flask on the bench next to him and pulled the phone from his pocket, noticing that he'd received a text message a minute earlier that had somehow gone unnoticed.

The message came from a different number, containing a code word established long ago by an old friend. Kaparov was coming up on the second anniversary of his retirement, a benchmark the two of them had agreed would be the earliest they could finally meet in person as allies and not adversaries. He answered the call.

"Karl. So good of you to call," said Kaparov. "I'm very much looking forward to next year's trip, though it's difficult to determine if this all-inclusive idea of yours is legitimate or some kind of scam to get you out of paying full price. I saw something on Tripadvisor about top-shelf liquors not being served, so—"

"Alexei. Sorry to interrupt, but I'm afraid this is a business call, and a very serious one at that," said Karl Berg.

"You know what I'm doing right now?" asked Kaparov.

"Drinking vodka."

"Besides that."

"I haven't a clue," said Berg.

"I'm sitting on a park bench watching people older than me play chess," said Kaparov. "Thinking about learning chess. Because I'm bored out of my fucking mind after retiring. I'm retired, Karl, which means I'm no longer in a position to help you."

"I think you might be able to help," said Berg. "What do you know about Yuri Pichugin? Specifically, his ties to the GRU."

"Please tell me you haven't somehow made enemies with Yuri Pichugin," said Kaparov. "He's one of the wealthiest and connected oligarchs in Russia. Connected right to the top, if you know what I mean."

"I do. I've stumbled across something that might be connected to him," said Berg. "It's definitely connected to Viktor Belsky. Does that name sound familiar?"

"I know the name, but not much more than that," said Kaparov. "Midlevel oligarch with decent connections. Returned to Russia from the US in the mid–two thousands, if my memory serves me correctly."

"It serves you well. Viktor Belsky and his father sold a company based in the United States to Yuri Pichugin around that time," said Berg.

"Must have been a very successful company," said Kaparov.

"That's the thing," said Berg. "The Belskys had money, but not that kind of money, and the company they sold to Pichugin didn't appear

352

to have any assets beyond a sizable chunk of land in the middle of the United States. Valuable, but not that valuable."

"Karl. Maybe my brain is a little mushy these days," said Kaparov. "But what are we talking about here?"

"The bottom line is that I believe Yuri Pichugin is bankrolling a Soviet-era GRU-run sleeper network in the United States through this company and is pulling the strings on behalf of your beloved leaders."

"And you have evidence of this?"

"We're piecing it together, but the network is real. I've seen it first-hand. The network's training camp was located on the land the Belskys sold to Pichugin. I've seen that, too," said Karl. "The problem is that we're unable to identify close to eighty percent of the network. We're talking upwards of six hundred sleepers."

"Six hundred! Come on. That's a ludicrous number," said Kaparov. "But assuming it was true, they'd all be in their seventies by now."

"I'm talking about their children," said Berg.

"Second generation?" said Kaparov. "That's the stuff of legends."

"Not anymore," said Berg. "They've penetrated everything here. One of them is a senator. And they're working on a third generation."

"Maybe this would be a better conversation to have in person," said Kaparov.

"I would gladly discuss this with you in person, in private, but Russia and Kazakhstan have just put me on Interpol's Red Notice list. We've stirred up a bit of a hornet's nest over here."

"We?"

"Some of the same off-the-books associates I've used before in the course of our dealings," said Berg.

"I still don't see what I can do to help," said Kaparov.

"Without going into too much detail, the decades-long process of discovering this network started with a GRU general who threw himself under a tram in Saint Petersburg in 2003, immediately after passing some very specific information about the network to one of our officers," said Berg. "The general was one of a handful of Soviet-era hard-liners still active in the GRU at the time, which is why we were surprised he wanted to defect to the United States. We were in the process of verifying what he had to offer when everything went sideways. He couldn't have been the only GRU general with knowledge of this program. If we can identify another, perhaps we could take the next step toward unearthing the rest of the network."

"Two thousand three was a very unlucky year for GRU generals and high-ranking officers," said Berg. "A few dozen committed suicide, died in car accidents, or drowned in puddles near their dachas. Everyone in the GRU feared some kind of purge, but nobody could figure out if they were next. The only discernible pattern was that there was no pattern. Nobody could figure out where they worked within the GRU. People started calling it the Lost Directorate; then word came down from the top to stop talking about it—and that was it. Reinforced by firings and a few more suspicious deaths."

"The Lost Directorate. Sounds like they were running something off the books," said Berg.

"Nothing was *off the books* in the Soviet Union. We documented and accounted for everything, and we still do. It's in our DNA," said Kaparov.

"Then what I'm asking you to do is lean on some of your Soviet-era comrades in arms to see if any of the possible members of this Lost Directorate survived the purge," said Berg.

"Then you'll send people here to have a friendly chat with them?"

"Something like that."

"Let me see what I can dig up without getting myself killed," said Kaparov. "This reminds me of something. Have you ever heard the term Khrushchev's Ghost?"

"I've obviously heard of Khrushchev, but I'm unfamiliar with his ghost."

"It's a term that floated around in the late sixties, in the aftermath of Khrushchev's reign. Rumors about a group of hard-liners unhappy with the direction Brezhnev was taking the country. Just whispers here and there about Khrushchev's Ghost watching over the country. Nothing ever came of it. I only brought it up because it somehow rings the same."

"It does, and it sounds creepy as hell, if you ask me," said Berg.

"I thought you'd like it," said Kaparov. "A word of warning, my friend. If this sleeper network is as extensive as you've suggested and has any connection to Khrushchev's Ghost, or any Cold War–era hard-liner faction, it will be positioned to inflict maximum damage on the United States. Meaning—it represents the ultimate under-the-table leverage. Whoever controls it will not go gently into the night. Be very careful with this one."

"That's the plan," said Berg.

"And if Pichugin's pulling the strings," said Kaparov, "keep a close eye on Ukraine. Rumor has it that nearly three-quarters of the separatist ground forces massed near the Donbass region are mercenaries. Battalion-size units in some cases. This represents a significant increase over last year. Something is brewing over there."

"Sounds like the Wegner Group?"

"Nobody will confirm it," said Kaparov. "But who else could it be? The Wegner Group has been Pichugin's private army for close to a decade."

"More like Putin's private army," said Berg.

"Once again, nobody will confirm either connection. At least nobody that wants to live to a ripe old age," said Kaparov.

"Thank you for helping out with this, Alexei. As always, watch your back," said Berg. "And I owe you again. For the record, all-inclusive is the way to go when you're drinking from nine in the morning into the late hours of the night on a Caribbean vacation. And it's not like you're drinking the high-end stuff anyway."

"Ha! I just don't want you to think my services come cheap!"

"I'm well aware they don't," said Berg.

"I'll call as soon as I know something," said Kaparov. "Or be on the next flight out of Moscow, headed to the Caribbean, if I somehow kick the same hornet's nest here."

He ended the call convinced that Karl Berg would be the end of him and determined to soak every ruble possible out of him when they finally met up. If he survived the latest mess Karl had stepped in.

ACKNOWLEDGMENTS

To start, a big thank-you to my family for supporting this book during the pandemic. *Deep Sleep* is the second manuscript I produced in "lockdown," and I'm not going to lie: it took every bit of focus I could muster. Everyone here at home played a significant role in keeping me on my deadline.

To Kosia, my better half, for locking me in the office when necessary and banning me from social media when my attention strayed. More importantly, for taking the conspiracy I created for this story to the next level. The wider geopolitical scope and deeper penetration of the conspiracy were a direct result of a series of brainstorming sessions conducted months before I put words on the pages.

As always, to the editorial team at Thomas & Mercer for enthusiastically giving *Deep Sleep* the green light and throwing their full support behind it. And to Megha for believing in this project!

To Kevin, who put the final developmental touches on the story. Four books together, and I don't bother to argue with him anymore. I know he's right. I can't wait to get the next book into your hands.

To the Mountainside crew for listening to the earliest iteration of the *Deep Sleep* concept and passing along invaluable feedback. I had no idea at the time that the vague idea I presented over drinks would be my next series, but the notes I took stuck with me long after our visit.

To my advance reader team. I've enjoyed sharing sneak peeks, cover reveals, and advance copies with you. Thank you for getting the word out!

Finally, to the readers. I know I say this every time, but without you, none of this would be possible.

ABOUT THE AUTHOR

Steven Konkoly is a *Wall Street Journal* and *USA Today* bestselling author, a graduate of the US Naval Academy, and a veteran of several regular and elite US Navy and Marine Corps units. He has brought his in-depth military experience to bear in his fiction, which includes *The Rescue*, *The Raid*, *The Mountain*, and *Skystorm* in the Ryan Decker series; the speculative postapocalyptic thrillers *The Jakarta Pandemic* and *The Perseid Collapse*; the Fractured State series; the Black Flagged series; and the Zulu Virus Chronicles. Konkoly lives in central Indiana with his family. For more information, visit www.stevenkonkoly.com.